A MODEL OF DISCRETION

Tessa backed away. The man was in earnest. There was no use trying to reason with a madman, handsome and brilliant artist though he might be, and she made a dash for the door. He caught her in one stride and spun her into his arms. How strong he was. His eyes were wild feral things flashing in the candlelight, devouring her.

He began fumbling with the neck of her frock. "How do you get shot of this deuced thing?"

"I'm no Penzance roundheels!" she cried, swatting his hand away. He winced when the blow grazed the scar near his wrist, but her anger was such that she could not raise an ounce of compassion. "Oh yes, I've heard all about the harlots you Cornish have out this way," she went on. "They put Whitechapel unfortunates to shame. It was one of those trollops that left here naked in your coach just now, wasn't it? Well, I am no such creature. I've been trying to tell you there's been a mistake. Let me go, sir! You will *not* get me into that bed!"

DAWN THOMPSON

The Bride of Time

LOVE SPELL NEW YORK CITY

LOVE SPELL®

August 2008

Published by

Dorchester Publishing Co., Inc.
200 Madison Avenue
New York, NY 10016

ISBN 10: 0-505-52728-6
ISBN 13: 978-0-505-52728-8

The name "Love Spell" and its logo are trademarks of Dorchester Publishing Co., Inc.

Printed in the United States of America.

10 9 8 7 6 5 4 3 2 1

Visit us on the web at www.dorchesterpub.com.

The Bride of Time

Chapter One

London, 1903

It was happening again. She was running over the patch-work hills through the mist, her heart hammering in her breast. He was gaining on her, his heavy footfalls vibrating on the spongy heath through the soles of her morocco leather slippers. She couldn't see his face, though his hot breath puffing against the back of her neck covered her with gooseflesh. Raw fright forced her to surge ahead, until a clump of bracken snagged the hem of her bombazine frock. It scarcely caused a hitch in her stride. She hoisted the skirt up and kept running—running for her life!

Tessa LaPrelle sat bolt upright in bed, her breast heaving as if she'd run her heart out. He was getting closer. She'd never felt his breath dampening the tendrils on the back of her neck before. Terror gripped her heart like an icy fist. Who was he? What did it all mean?

She glanced about her dingy chamber, half-expecting the phantom of her nightmare to materialize out of the shadows. Mercifully, he did not. She gripped the counterpane tight to her breast in both fists, as if to keep her thudding heart from bursting through her skin. After a time, her heart slowed and she took a ragged breath. It was over again . . . at least for now.

Tessa swung her bare feet to the cold wood floor and padded to the window. It was not yet first light. The moon had long since vacated the sky in that ultimate darkness before dawn. She wiped the damp window-pane and her hand came away smudged with lamp soot and dust. No one bothered to clean the maid's chambers, and when the day was done, the servants were too tuckered to address them on their own time. Once a month the lots were drawn, and the girl who lost was designated and obliged to address the servants' quarters' sleeping cells with mop and broom, but the chambers never got more than a slapdash wave of the duster. Her employer, Jasper Poole, optician extraordinaire—so said the shingle on his little office in Cornhill Street—was a hard taskmaster in every other regard. He couldn't care less about the servants' rooms.

It was a hard life, but what else was an orphaned girl to do, unless she was to beg in the streets or become a Whitechapel lightskirt? At least signing on as a scullery maid in a respectable house was honest work for honest wages, even if it was no more than drudgery for a pittance.

It was Tuesday; her day. As long as she returned to the Poole's home on the fringes of Cheapside by dark, she could do as she pleased. That meant going back to the little gallery just south of Threadneedle Street, where it all began. Was that only a sennight ago? It seemed an eternity.

Tessa had found the little gallery quite by accident on one of her Tuesday jaunts. She'd been on her way back home when it began to rain. Caught without an umbrella, she'd ducked inside the gallery to wait out the storm and had become so enthralled with what she'd found that she nearly got locked in at closing time. As it was, she was late and missed curfew, which earned her a public chastisement before the other servants at supper that evening.

Tessa moved away from the window. There was still some time before her outing. She was too wide awake, thanks to the nightmare, to go back to bed. Mrs. Atkins, the housekeeper, and Cook would be up and about in the kitchen. Chores started early at Poole House. Deciding to go down for a cup of tea, she washed with the cold water in her pitcher and dressed in her Sunday-best indigo bombazine frock with the little Brussels lace collar. She ordered her thick chestnut hair—her best feature, so everyone told her—with the aid of three tortoiseshell hairpins, her only possessions of any value, and examined her reflection in a shard of broken mirror glass she'd propped on her dressing chest.

The nightmare was still with her, and her hands shook as she pinned her coin purse inside her bodice, something she always did when going abroad in Cheapside. Cutpurses still existed, the new century hadn't changed that, and they would, she had no doubt, until the end of time. Well, they would not get their greedy hands upon her hard-earned wages. She was far too clever for that—especially as she carried her savings with her wherever she went; she did not trust any hiding place in her rooms. Her toilette complete, she straightened her posture and went below.

Bessie Harper, the kitchen maid, was already scrubbing the kitchen floor on her hands and knees with strong lye soap and a well-worn brush when Tessa entered. Bessie gave her a scathing look, raking her from head to toe in her unofficial togs. The maid was doing Tessa's chores, since it was Tessa's day off—and none too happily, Tessa thought, judging from the girl's clenched posture and staccato jabs of the brush.

"Well," Bessie said, "If it ain't Miss High and Mighty

Gallery-goer in the flesh. Up early enough on your day off, I see, 'my lady.' A bleedin' shame ya can't manage it the rest o' the week now, ain't it?"

Tessa didn't reply. The kettle was simmering on the back of the Majestic coal stove, and she made herself a cup of tea and took a seat at the old scarred wooden table in the center of the room. She would not let Bessie drive her from the kitchen. Her day was her own.

Bessie slapped the scrub brush back down on the floor, flinging suds that came close to spattering Tessa's slippers. Tessa pulled her feet back beneath her chair, out of harm's way, and took a sip from her cup. She *wouldn't* let them chase her. This was common enough behavior in such houses. The lowest servant always took abuse from the rest, and there was nothing lower in the pecking order than a scullery maid. She would not let them ruin her day.

"So," Bessie taunted, "are ya goin' back to that fancy gallery, then?"

"A little culture might be beneficial to you, also," Tessa said sweetly. "You might try it on your day off, Bessie."

Cook flashed a gap-tooth grin and Bessie bristled. "Well, ya won't be goin' nowhere till the missus finds her pearl brooch what's gone missin'."

"What brooch?"

"I dunno," said Bessie. "I ain't seen it. She come in here all out straight an hour ago. 'Nobody leaves this 'ouse till my brooch is found!' she says. She's checkin' the chambers right now. So, Miss High and Mighty Gallery-goer, ya ain't goin' nowhere till this coil is unwound."

"Do you mean to say she believes one of *us* took it?" Tessa asked, incredulous.

"Well, it didn't walk off by itself, did it?" Bessie shot back. Wisps of brown hair had escaped her mobcap, and she brushed them back from her eyes.

"That cannot include me," Tessa said. "I have no access above stairs."

"Makes 'erself out better'n us, don't she, Cook?" Bessie taunted. "Puttin' on airs. We all has 'access' if we wants it. Them upstairs can't watch us every minute, can they? That ain't goin' ta save ya."

"I hardly need saving, Bessie. I've nothing to hide."

"So she says, la di da, with her voice so refined," Bessie said through a snigger to Cook, who was larding a pheasant at the other end of the table, and getting more lard on her pendulous bosom than the poor flaccid bird. "Ain't she a regular funnyosity, though, voice like a lady, goin' about in threadbare togs? That pearl brooch would look right nice on that raggedy old bombazine frock, now, wouldn't it?"

Tessa shouldn't rise to the occasion, but she would not stand being accused. "Are you suggesting that *I* took the brooch, Bessie?" she asked coolly. "If you are, you'd best have proof. And I speak as I do because I had someone to teach me, who cared enough to hope it would help me better myself."

That had been one strike against Tessa the minute she entered Poole House. Thanks to the upbringing she'd had with her aunt before the woman died and she'd been forced into a life of servitude, she'd learned at least to talk like a lady. It hadn't helped her in her current circumstances, and she said no more. Hopefully, the missing brooch would be found, and she would be on her way to gaze once more upon the painting that had captured her eye so severely, and the formidable, darkly brooding self-portrait of its creator, one Giles Longworth, among other of his works on display. It was titled "The Bride of Time," a large—almost life-size—canvas of a naked woman, scantily draped in what appeared to be a bridal veil that looked no denser than spider silk and hid none of her charms. She was lounging upon an opulent couch, gazing reverently toward a gilded hour-glass in her hands. Through an open window behind the woman, rolling patchwork hills had been painted draped in fog, with the crenellations of a manor house of great proportions, reputed to be the artist's Cornwall estate, poking through the distant mist.

There was nothing remarkable about the painting. It was typical of the artwork of the era. Tessa wouldn't have given the canvas a second thought if several patrons hadn't gasped and called attention to the fact that the girl in the painting resembled her. One had gone so far as to ask if she might have posed for the artist!

Scandalous!

This was 1903. That painting was done at the turn of the century, around a hundred years ago, at the social and economic beginning of the decadent Regency period. Those times, and the people who lived then, had long since fascinated Tessa. The world had changed so much in a mere hundred years, but not enough to blur the edges between the classes. Boundaries still existed that could not be breached. C. D. Gibson may have created an image of the new woman for a new century with his famed Gibson Girls, but some things would never change. Scullery maids still wore bombazine and thread-bare faille for Sunday best, and mobcaps beneath their unadorned bonnets.

Tessa finished her tea and helped herself to a cheese biscuit besides, but she refused to continue the conversation. When Mrs. Atkins floated into the kitchen sometime later, her countenance no less scathing than the others, Tessa excused herself and went back to her chamber to fetch her cloak and bonnet. She would stop to feed the pigeons in the little gated park in the square, and by time she reached the gallery it would be open. She could relax there. She could escape, pretend she lived in that grand abbey in the painting. She could pretend she had posed for the portrait of that bride from a different time. It was a pleasant fiction that lifted her out of the doldrums of her everyday existence, even though she wasn't convinced of the likeness. Oh, the woman in the painting had her coloring, her long chestnut hair and eyes more violet than blue, but that woman was beautiful. Tessa had always considered herself plain.

Besides, it wasn't the woman in the painting that drew her back to the little gallery time and time again. It was the view through that little painted window of the rolling patchwork hills and the manor house half-hidden in the mist. There was something familiar about those hills. She would stare and stare, praying for the mist to lift so she could have a better view, wishing she could walk those hills; if she could only escape to that wild Cornish wilderness of misty moors in a time gone by.

Last Tuesday, standing before that canvas, she'd almost mesmerized herself into believing she was able to feel the thick, sweet grass under her feet. She could almost smell the heather-laced wind drifting past her nostrils from the splotch of violet the artist had suggested peeking through the mist. How far would her imagination take her today? Far enough to escape her meager existence—far enough to reach those double doors on that sprawling manor?

As she climbed the back stairs to her little cell, the image of the artist who had created the painting ghosted across her memory. It almost made her misstep on the narrow winding stairs. Giles Longworth looked a man to be reckoned with, with his eyes as black as sin, his mahogany hair that appeared to have been combed by the infamous Cornish wind worn rather long, waving about his earlobes, and his broad shoulders straining the fabric of his poet's shirt. The curator had described him as a mysterious fellow. But then, he would have to be in order to conceive the work of art that had so taken her over, for it had done just that. She'd thought of little else since she first clapped eyes upon "The Bride of Time."

The curator had said some accused Longworth of sorcery, that dark, evil things were attributed to him, not the least of which was the murder of several local women, as well as Longworth's wife and her lover, and that he'd kept his nephew locked away in the Abbey. Some even said Longworth was a werewolf, because of the way the women were savaged, with their throats torn out. But the Cornish folk were at best a superstitious lot, and none of this was ever proven, of course. However, as with most colorful tales, they grew over the years and only gained notoriety after Longworth's mysterious disappearance following the completion of "The Bride of Time."

Tessa never mentioned Giles Longworth to the others at Poole House. He was her secret. She would not share him with the vicious, jealous cats she'd found a home amongst. She was becoming more and more sorry she'd mentioned the little gallery and the painting at all. At four and twenty, she was still naïve enough to imagine she could win over folk like Bessie, Cook and Mrs. Atkins. It would be her undoing one day; she was certain of it.

Having reached her chamber to find her door ajar, Tessa slowed her pace. Reaching with one finger, she eased the door open wider and peered inside. "Is someone there?" she asked, coming face-to-face with Mrs. Poole and Gibbons the butler rummaging through her dressing chest. She opened the door wider still. "I beg your pardon?" she said. "Those things are mine!"

"Are they, then?" Mrs. Poole asked loftily. "Then perhaps you might like to explain how you've come by this?" She held out her hand, palm upward, exhibiting a pearl brooch.

The woman reminded Tessa of a hooded cobra. Her reptilian eyes were glaring down her nose accusingly, her piled-high, Gibson-style coiffure trembling as she bristled, emphasizing her overlong neck. Could the woman actually imagine that she, Tessa LaPrelle, had stolen the brooch, or that she was dunce enough to have left it in an unlocked drawer if she had? Stupid with astonishment, Tessa stared.

"See that?" Mrs. Poole said to the butler. "Not a blink of remorse! That is the thanks I get for hiring a French girl!"

"I beg your pardon, ma'am," Tessa said, her back ramrod-rigid. "I am as English as you are. My father's father was half-French, and even he was born here. I am not ashamed of my French ancestry, since I take from it what little culture my English ancestors have denied me." It was bold talk, of course, but that didn't matter. Her situation was lost no matter what; that was obvious. "Speak to me as you will, but I will not allow you to malign my name."

"Well!" Mrs. Poole erupted. "I never did! Here you stand, caught out red-handed with my brooch, and you dare to speak to me in that manner?"

"I did not take your brooch, ma'am. I do not presume to know how it got in that drawer, but I did not put it there. Never once in all the months I've been here in your employ have I gone beyond the green baize door!"

"This is the thanks I get for giving you this fine room to yourself!" Mrs. Poole railed. *Fine room?* The window glass was cracked, as were the chamber pot, pitcher and basin, and the mattress was nothing but a bag of straw. *Fine room indeed!* "I should have put you in with Lizzie and Bessie, and made you sleep two to a bed, but no, I let you have this here, and this is how I am repaid—with thievery!"

"I beg your pardon, ma'am, but perhaps you should have done. You did me no favors putting me here. I have been punished by the others below stairs since the day I came for being 'privileged.'" She gestured toward the brooch in the woman's outstretched hand. "If you want to sort that out, you might inquire of them as to which one put it there to be rid of me!"

"I've heard enough of this," Mrs. Poole said, thrusting Tessa's cloak and bonnet at her. "Take her below to the wine cellar and lock her in, Gibbons. Then fetch the bobbies from the Yard. Let the magistrates sort her out. I wash my hands of her."

The butler had hold of Tessa's arm before she could blink. Steering her out into the hallway, he led her farther down the darkened stairwell toward the lower regions where the wine was kept. Tessa's mind was racing. This couldn't be happening, but it was. She was innocent, but there was no way to prove it. She couldn't let them lock her away.

She waited until they'd reached the level of the rear servants' entrance to Poole House, then shoved the aging butler just hard enough to make him lose his grip while steadying himself against the wall. Racing out into the fog, she ran from the house, down the walk, through the gate in the ornamental spiked-iron fence that surrounded the stately town house, and burst out onto the avenue, leaving the servants' entrance door flung wide behind her.

It was the wrong thing to do, of course. Running would only seal her fate. But convinced that there was no justice to be had for someone like her, Tessa didn't credit that. With Mrs. Poole's shrill voice and Gibbons's rasping bark echoing in her ears, Tessa ran blind in the fog that hadn't burned off with the dawn in the direction of Threadneedle Street, and the little gallery.

There didn't seem to be any in pursuit, and after a time she slowed her pace. She still had her cloak, but her bonnet had been lost when she fled. No matter. The cloak was hooded, and she slipped it around her. Mornings were cool in London on the cusp of September, especially in the fog. The sodden damp could penetrate the finest of mantles, and hers was hardly that.

Her heart was hammering in her breast as she passed the little tea room just around the corner from the gallery. Tatum's Gallery. Had she mentioned the name to the others? She couldn't remember. If she had, they would surely know where to find her. What was she even doing here? She should be making her way out of the city while the fog still abetted her escape. London fogs were unpredictable. They could linger for days, or lift in a heartbeat. But no, she had to reach the gallery— the only scrap of safe ground in her entire world. Her only sanctuary, where she could forget for just a little while once each week on Tuesday, not who she was, but who she wasn't.

The curator had just unlocked the doors when she reached the gallery. Motor cars and horse-drawn carriages clogged the street already, barely visible behind the milling fog. From somewhere nearby, a bobby's whistle sounded. He couldn't be looking for her—not yet. It was too soon. Nevertheless, she ducked inside the gallery and went straight to the alcove designated for "The Bride of Time"—but it was gone! So was Longworth's eerie self-portrait, and his other works as well. Different paintings hung there now. It was as if Giles Longworth's works had never been.

Tessa rushed at the curator. "Where are the paintings that used to hang here?" she begged the astonished man.

"W-why, they've been sold, miss," he stammered.

Tessa's hand fell away from the man's arm. "When?" she asked. "Who bought them?"

The poor man looked as if he'd seen a ghost. Twice he opened his mouth as if to speak, and shut it again. It was clear he wasn't often set upon by young ladies.

"Please, sir," Tessa persisted. "Was it a local buyer?"

"Actually . . . no," the man said. "It was a young couple from Yorkshire. I did not make the sale personally, my business partner did. Look here, are you all right, miss? You've gone white as the fog of a sudden."

"I'm quite well, thank you," Tessa lied. It wouldn't do to call attention to herself now, when any minute bobbies might swarm over the place, seeking her.

Other patrons began trickling in, and Tessa moved off to browse the various collections. There was a station nearby, where she could take a horse-drawn bus out of the city proper. Deciding on that, she approached the door, only to pull back when a swarm of bobbies poured into the gallery. Patrons and curate alike gathered around them. Should she as well? Probably, but she was not so brave. Guilt was written all over her face, which was odd, because she was innocent. Nevertheless, she didn't need a mirror to tell her she'd gone crimson. Her ears were on fire from the hot blood that had rushed to her head when the bobbies stormed in. If only she hadn't lost her bonnet.

Reeling into a convenient alcove, she hugged the shadows, hoping for a rear exit. All such establishments had them. They opened into narrow alleyways and mews in that quarter. Now to find it.

"Service class, about so high?" the curator was saying, illustrating her height to the officers. He craned his neck toward the gathering. "Why, a young woman answering that description was here just a moment ago . . ."

All at once the little gallery was swarming with police and curious patrons. Escape through the main door was impossible. A crowd had already begun to form outside. All over a silly pearl brooch that had been recovered. She'd made the right decision in running after all. These people were relentless.

Tessa's eyes snapped in all directions, and finally came to rest upon the rear door. It was too far. The loo was closer, and she reeled inside and locked the door behind her. There was no other exit, only a small stained-glass window above the commode. She climbed up and lifted the latch, acutely aware of the sound of muffled voices leaking through the scarred paneling.

"She couldn't have gone that way," the curator said. "See? The bolt is intact. She must have slipped out the front."

There wasn't a moment to lose. The alley was vacant, and she shimmied through the little window and jumped to the cobblestones below. The shock to her knees as she landed on the hard, uneven stones pulled her up short for a moment. Then, racing through the fog, she rounded the corner and slowed her pace. There was no choice. Her right leg had taken the brunt of the shock and she favored it, limping, leaning upon the slimy, fog-drenched façades of several buildings before she was able to walk without making herself conspicuous.

Behind, the sound of bobbies' whistles amplified by the fog grew distant. That they were still in pursuit amazed her. But why wouldn't they be? Anxious to make an example of her, they would certainly press charges. The fact that she'd run had sealed her fate with the law. There was no way for her to prove her innocence now. She had to get out of the city; but how? It was too risky.

She pressed on, scarcely able to make out the shapes of buildings lining the road. The tall, square silhouette of a church bell tower loomed up before her. She'd passed several like it since she left the gallery. She was tempted to seek sanctuary inside just for a little while. The sky showed signs of brightening. She was about to lose the protection of the fog.

Then, all at once, the sun abandoned trying to poke through and slipped behind a cloud. The sky grew darker and darker. The fog grew denser . . . and deeper. She couldn't see the church now. She could barely see where she was going. Somehow, she'd gotten onto a narrow lane that was softer underfoot, and kinder than cobblestones to the knee she'd jammed jumping from the gallery loo window. This road wasn't all that well traveled. Tufts of grass marched down the middle, and the edges encroached upon the gravel from both sides. Could she have gotten out of the city so soon? It wasn't likely. If only she could see through the thick, milling fog.

A wind seemed to rise out of nowhere. It blew the hood back off her head and plucked out the tendrils that always wreathed her face in damp weather, but it wasn't strong enough to chase the fog. All at once a mournful howl broke the silence, echoing from somewhere close by. The heart-stopping sound raised the short hairs at the back of Tessa's neck, and she quickened her step despite the limp. She hadn't gone far, when the sound of what she took to be a horse-drawn bus approaching broke the silence that had fallen over the lane, and she moved off to the shoulder, overgrown with bracken and gorse, for fear of being run down. Shielding her eyes, she strained the milling vapors for some sign of the vehicle, for it was coming on at a rapid pace, but it was several moments before she saw the haloed glow of the carriage lamps. It wasn't a bus at all. It was an old coach lumbering along the path.

The driver reined in at sight of her. "Halloo!" he

called. "Would you be the new governess for Longhollow Abbey, then?"

"Longhollow Abbey?" Tessa breathed.

The coachman set the brake and climbed down. Flinging the coach door open, he set the steps. "Well, get in then," he said. "You was supposed ta wait at the coaching inn for me ta fetch ya. Didn't nobody tell ya it ain't safe ta walk these moors after dark?"

As if on cue, the plaintive howl pierced the quiet again, setting Tessa in motion. It was closer now, and she scarcely limped while scrambling into the carriage. It didn't matter where it was going; the coach was carrying her away from the city and away from whatever was making that god-awful sound. But Longhollow Abbey . . . He'd said Longhollow Abbey, and it wasn't after dark. It couldn't even be noon yet! Was the man in his cups?

"Where are your bags?" the man said. She couldn't get a really good look due to the fog, but he appeared to be a portly man past middle age, with a pleasant countenance.

"Bags?" she murmured. "I . . . have none, sir."

He shrugged. "A mite peculiar," he said, "but no matter, 'tis less for me to lug."

"Driver, wait!" she cried as the coachman climbed back up into the box. "I believe there's been a mistake, I'm not—"

"No mistake," the man called, meanwhile snapping his whip. "Unless that howlin' creature gets ya. The master would skin me alive if that was ta happen. Hold on to the strap in there! The road gets rough ahead."

The horse bolted forward then, and Tessa was knocked about as the coach sped off along the lane. She seized the hand strap and braced herself against the squabs. The tufted leather had a pleasant odor about it: tangy salt air and sweet-smelling tobacco. It was comforting somehow, and would have relaxed her if the ride wasn't such a harrowing one.

Tessa strained her eyes, trying to catch a glimpse of the terrain through the isinglass window as the coach tooled on. At first all she saw was the ghost-gray fog. Then a sudden wind swept it away and the land zipping past the window came into view. Rolling patchwork hills silvered in the moonlight stretched as far as the eye could see. Tessa gasped as recognition struck. Crippling chills walking down her spine clenched her posture on the seat, and she gripped the hand strap until it bit into the tender flesh of her palm. For one desperate moment, she tried to call up some such landscape from her past that made this scene seem so familiar. And then she knew. It was the misty rolling patchwork hills of her nightmare, and she was speeding headlong into them.

Chapter Two

Tessa sank back against the squabs, trying to remember if the nightmares had begun before or after she'd seen Giles Longworth's infamous painting. For the hills in "The Bride of Time," the hills in the dreadful dreams, and these stretching before her now were the very same. But she could not remember. At first she thought it must all be a dream, but no, it was really happening! Then she thought her imagination had run wild; and why wouldn't it, living so long in her unhappy condition, and now becoming a fugitive besides? Yes, that had to be it, she decided, until the manor house came into view, picked out ahead by the moonlight on a little rise above the moor. Longhollow Abbey in all its sprawling, castle-like splendor silhouetted against the night sky . . . waiting for her. All things considered, it didn't matter how or why.

The coach rumbled to a stop in the circular Welsh bluestone drive, and the coachman climbed down and set the steps. Tessa's conscience demanded she make one last attempt before exiting the coach, and she held back.

"Sir, wait," she said.

"The name's Able, miss," he said. "Me and m'boy Andy keep the stables for the master."

Tessa nodded. "Able," she began again, "I really think there's been some mistake. I'm not who you think I am, I . . ." Her voice trailed off as a rumpus began, capturing their attention. The door of the Abbey flew open, and a half-naked woman came running into the drive clutching some anonymous garment to her bare breasts, her long chestnut hair streaming behind her. Her shrill cries fractured the stillness. A man was chasing her. Darkly handsome, he was fully dressed, from his Byronic poet's shirt and buckskin breeches stretched over his well-turned thighs, to the brown-top turned-down boots defining the long muscular legs propelling him over the drive.

"Better get down outta there, missy," Able said, taking hold of Tessa's elbow. "Better do it quick!"

Tessa scrambled down just in time, as the woman almost knocked her over while leaping into the coach. At close examination, Tessa saw that the person wasn't just half-naked; the woman didn't have a stitch on underneath the garment she was clutching. The moon showed the round globes of her bare bottom clearly.

"You've been well paid for services rendered," the man seethed, having reached the coach. "And poor services you've given for that king's ransom, I'll be bound. Give back what you've stolen, you thieving slag, or I'll have the guards from the Watch in to sort you out!"

"Go ahead, and won't I have a mouthful ta tell 'em, ya drunken whoremaster!" the woman retorted.

The man flashed wild eyes as dark as sin toward the coachman, who had started to climb back into the box. "Able, do not set whip to that beast until I have back what is mine!" he warned.

"No, sir!" the coachman said, plopping down on the seat above as if such a scene was a matter of course.

"You're off your head, ya bloody lunatic!" the woman shrilled, latching the coach door as the man took hold of it. She attempted to roll the window closed, but his quick hand stopped it. "Leggo o' that!" she cried.

"The snuff box!" the man said, extending his free hand, palm upward, long fingers working anxiously.

Tessa took note of the dark hairs curling on the back of the man's hand. There was a ragged scar on the back of it, close to the wrist, that looked fairly recent. He hadn't seemed to notice her at all, yet he was close enough to touch, close enough for her to feel his body heat and smell his musky scent wafting toward her from the sweat glistening on his skin. He smelled pleasantly familiar, of cheroot smoke and brandy drunk recently, and something more: fresh oil paint, linseed oil, and gum spirits. She breathed him in deeply and gasped. That was it! He smelled of the *gallery*.

"Here's your damn snuff box!" the trollop snapped, lobbing it at him. It bounced off his broad shoulder and hit the ground. "It ain't decent anyway, what's carved on it."

The man stooped to retrieve it, and Tessa gasped again. It was a rather large piece which appeared to be solid silver, with a naked couple engaged in the sex act embossed in bold relief on the cover. After examining it, he polished the piece on his shirtsleeve and thrust it into his pocket.

"Quite so," he said. "But it would have brought a pretty pence, decent or no, at the Truro market, now wouldn't it? Lucky for you it hasn't been scratched or dented. Then you would have really felt my wrath. It was a gift from the Prince Regent himself." He caught Abel's eye. "Take her back to the brothel," he charged.

Abel raised his whip and Tessa stiffened. Was he just going to leave her there with this drunken madman? A strangled sound left her throat at the prospect, and the man's eyes flashed toward her.

"Who the devil are you?" he demanded, scrutinizing her. How he towered. How black his eyes were, dilated in the darkness, how they shone in the nimbus of lemon-colored light haloing the carriage lamp. Trust her to come fresh from one theft into the midst of another, was all she could think under that fierce gaze, and another sound leaked from her. What on earth could she tell him?

He didn't wait for an answer. "You intercepted Andy, I take it?" he said to the coachman. "It's just as well. He hasn't the knack for procuring."

"Well, no, sir, not exactly," Able said. "She's—"

"Silence! Be still!" the man thundered. Seizing Tessa's arm, he spun her to and fro, taking her measure. "Hmm," he said. "I suppose she'll do."

"But Mr. Longworth, sir—"

The sharp-voiced creature in the coach interrupted the flustered driver. "If ya know what's good for ya, you'll climb right back inta this coach with me and come away, missy!" the woman barked. "He's a bloody Bedlamite, he is, and worse, a drunken rakehell! Ya better get in! You'll come to no good at Longhollow Abbey, ya mark my words!"

Muttering a string of blue expletives, Giles Longworth strode to the front of the coach and gave the right nervous leader a slap on the rump, setting the vehicle in motion.

"But, sir!" the coachman cried, scrambling to grab hold of the ribbons still wrapped around the brake as the horses plunged forward. " 'Tisn't what ya think. She ain't—!"

"Yes, yes," Longworth called. "Just get the trollop gone before I change my mind and have the guards in anyway. I'll see to this one."

Able said more, but his words were wasted, drowned out by the lightskirt's obscene parting remarks shouted over the racket of the horses prancing over the gravel drive.

Longworth turned to Tessa. Oh, it *was!* She'd known that long before Able called him by name. He was much handsomer than his portrait suggested, and much more frightening.

"Where the devil did Andy find you?" he asked, circling her as he spoke. "Not in that brothel on the moor, by the look of you."

"I . . . he . . ." she stammered. She had no idea what to say, what he would believe. She didn't know what *she* believed. And where had the pain in her knee gone? It was as if it had never been socked at all. It was passing bizarre. Somehow one moment it was early morning in London, the next it was the dead of night in Cornwall—at least a two-day journey in such an antiquated carriage. After the scene she'd just witnessed, how could she tell him the truth: that she was fleeing the London police who suspected her of theft?

"And what manner of frock is that?" he went on, seeming not to expect an answer, much to Tessa's relief. Whether that was just a quirk of the man's nature or by-product of the brandy he'd drunk, she was grateful for it. "It is so . . . form-fitting, and your ankles show. Have you grown out of it or what? It does look somewhat threadbare."

Tessa glowered at the hulking brute. She wanted to say that, after what she'd just seen, he was in no position to criticize exposed ankles. Discretion, however, checked her tongue.

"This costume is the height of fashion where I come from," she got out. "And it hardly signifies. I'm afraid there's been a mistake. You see—"

"That there has," Longworth interrupted, taking hold

of her arm. "And it just left in that coach you arrived in. Well? Come along. Half the night's been wasted. Let's see how well you do while I'm still in the mood, eh?"

They had nearly reached the entrance to the Abbey when the heart-stopping howl Tessa had heard earlier came again. Longworth stopped in his tracks, glancing first at the moon, then toward the patchwork hills at the edge of the open moor. It was a brief hesitation. When he turned back, his countenance had changed. There was suddenly a haunted, almost feral look about him. In the light of the imperfect moon beaming down, Tessa watched his fine lips form a thin bloodless line, and his dark eyes recede into the deep shadows beneath the ledge of his beetled brow. His jaw muscles had begun to twitch. Whatever moved him then had sobered him, and from the look of things, Tessa decided she liked the drunken, savage Longworth better than the image he presented to her now.

"Come," he said, leading her inside.

There wasn't a servant to be seen as Longworth rushed her up four flights of carpeted stairs to a rooftop solarium, its domed glass ceiling a window to the star-studded vault of the night.

A huge easel and an opulent chaise lounge stood on the far side of the room, alongside a table heaped with artist's materials. A rumpled bed dominated the shadowy space on the opposite wall, which called to mind the naked doxy who had just fled the Abbey. Adrenaline surged through Tessa's body as it struck her that she was evidently that creature's replacement.

Her protests unheeded, Longworth strolled around her again, his boot heels echoing on the bare floor. When he plucked the three tortoiseshell pins from her hair, Tessa cried out, reaching for them.

"How dare you! Give me those!" she demanded.

Holding her at bay with one massive hand on her

shoulder, he thrust the pins into his pocket. Her long chestnut hair had fallen down her back, teasing her buttocks. Whatever next? Tessa didn't dare imagine. She swung at him with both hands balled into fists, but his arm was too long for her to make contact.

"Stop that!" he growled through clenched teeth. How strong and white they were, especially his canines, catching glints from the nearby candles. "You'll get them back when we're finished. Stop that infernal jigging about! One might think you'd never done this before. Stop it, I say! And get out of that rig."

"I beg your pardon?"

"That ridiculous rag you're wearing. Take it off."

Tessa gasped. "I will not!" she breathed.

"Am I to be forever doomed to frustration at the hands of bird-witted females?" he snapped, speaking to whom Tessa couldn't imagine; certainly not to her. More likely some demon dredged up from the dregs of alcoholic derangement. "Ah! Of course!" he blurted, as if a light had gone on in his fogged brain. Producing several crumpled notes from the pocket of his buckskins, he slapped them on a nearby drum table with flourish. "Do forgive me," he said. "There then, now get out of that costume and let us get down to it, eh?"

"I will not disrobe before you, sir," Tessa assured him. "You are quite mad, I—"

"Very possibly," Longworth interrupted. "And I will stay so 'til we get on with this. You've been paid, now take off that frock, or I'll do it for you."

Tessa backed away. The man was in earnest. There was no use trying to reason with a madman, and she made a dash for the door. He caught her in one stride and spun her into his arms. How strong he was. His eyes were wild feral things flashing in the candlelight, devouring her. When he began probing her collar front and back, she screamed.

"Let me go at once or I'll bring this house down!" she shrilled.

"Not before I get my blunt's worth!" he said, fumbling with the neck of her frock. "How do you get shot of this deuced thing?"

"I'm no Penzance roundheels!" she cried, swatting his hand away. He winced when the blow grazed the scar near his wrist, but her anger was such that she could not raise an ounce of compassion. "Oh yes, I've heard all about the harlots you Cornish have out this way," she went on. "They put Whitechapel unfortunates to shame. It was one of those trollops that left here naked in your coach just now, wasn't it? Well, I am no such creature. I've been trying to tell you there's been a mistake. Let me go! You will *not* get me into that bed, sir!"

He froze as if she'd struck him, his gaze a study in confusion. His hand fell away from her Brussels lace collar. He'd managed to free four of the tiny buttons that had challenged his thick fingers, exposing the notch at the base of her throat.

"Bed," he murmured. "You think . . . ?" Seizing her arm, he propelled her toward the easel and spun her around to face the canvas. Tessa swayed in his arms. With the strange happenings of late, she'd all but forgotten. Here was "The Bride of Time" in the early stages of completion. "That slag wasn't here for bed sport; she was my model," he told her. "Didn't Andy explain?"

"I have been trying to tell you. Your coachman even tried to tell you. I never saw your 'Andy' person—"

"Who are you then?" Longworth asked, raking his dark hair back from a sweaty brow. "What were you doing in my coach?" She almost felt sorry for him then . . . almost, but not quite. He was still a brute and a madman, and she was still at his mercy.

"M-my name is Tessa LaPrelle," she said, ordering her frock. "I . . . I've come about . . . about the governess position." What else could she say? What other excuse could she give him? She should run, and keep on running. But where would she run to? She wasn't even in her own time. How could that have happened? How could she get back to London in her own day and age? Did she even want to, what with a charge of theft hanging over her head? But how could she stay here with *him*, with this wild-eyed drunken madman? There was a connection, there had to be. She was here, wasn't she? For all that the situation was passing strange, and considering her mundane existence in her own time, she was brave enough to want to find out why the fates had cast her adrift in a blink of time's eye.

Longworth let her go, muttering a string of expletives. "I do beg your pardon," he said, sketching an awkward bow. "You should have said something!"

"I tried," Tessa pronounced, fastening the buttons on her bodice.

Longworth straightened up, fussing with his shirt-sleeves. He seemed to be trying to cover the scar on the back of his wrist with the lace ruffled cuff. "I know it's no excuse, of course," he said, "but I'm half-castaway, or I never would have given you such a clumsy welcome to Longhollow Abbey. Brandy has an odd effect upon me, I'm afraid. I assure you that in normal circumstances I am a gentleman."

"*Clumsy?*" Tessa blurted. "That does not even approach the description of my 'welcome,' sir. Tell me: do you imbibe often, then?"

"Only when needs must, dear lady."

Tessa extended her hand. "My hairpins, please," she said icily.

He lurched as if she'd struck him, reached into his

pocket and produced the pins. "Frightfully sorry," he said. "You must think me a jackanapes."

"Mmmm," Tessa said, taking hold of her long, thick hair.

Longworth's hand shot out and stopped just short of making contact. "Oh, please don't," he said. "It's perfect as it is."

"It's highly inappropriate as it is, sir," Tessa snapped, coiling her hair into a Gibson crown—no small feat without a mirror, but she had never had the privilege of a lady's maid, and she was adept at dressing her hair herself.

He cocked his head in a curious attitude. "Another 'height of fashion' where you come from?" he asked her.

"You might say that, yes."

He studied her thoughtfully. "It's been a long time since I've visited Town," he observed, half to himself. "Too long, if things have changed this much in my absence. The coiffure is . . . quite becoming. I cannot say as much for the frock, though." He was looking at her with the eyes of an artist now, and Tessa wasn't quite sure if that was a good sign or a bad one.

"Yes, well, that hardly signifies," she said, giving the frock a punishing twist. "Has the position been filled?"

For a moment he brightened, his eyes flashing toward the unfinished canvas on the easel.

"The governess position," she put in, for it was clear he had quite something else in mind.

"Ah, yes," he said, his posture deflating. He clouded suddenly, and seemed distracted. The moon had shifted in the sky. It had broken through the clouds, and was clearly visible now through the glass ceiling. It threw a shaft of silvery light between them, and he jumped back as if it were a lightning bolt.

"Well, it either is or it isn't," Tessa snapped.

He was standing so close she could feel his body heat again, and smell his scent. The most peculiar expression had darkened his face despite the moonlight streaming down. It was almost as if he was struggling with those inner demons she'd detected in him. Was it the alcohol? Tessa wasn't accustomed to being in the company of drunken men. He wasn't falling-down drunk; that would have been safe enough. He was under the influence, but not enough to render him harmless, just enough to make him dangerous, judging from his behavior thus far. This fine display gave rise to new opinions about the temperance movement, but she wouldn't mention that. He was having enough difficulty becoming accustomed to twentieth-century hairstyles and women's attire.

"The position is still open," he said at last, "but . . ."

"But what, sir?"

Again he hesitated. "Nothing. I'm just amazed that you will still consider taking a position at Longhollow Abbey."

"Well, I won't be governing *you*, now will I?"

He winced. "Touché," he said. "I deserved that. When could you begin?"

"I should like to begin at once, if that's convenient," Tessa said, amazed at her command of the situation, though she had a gut-wrenching feeling that this was all terribly wrong.

His demeanor softened suddenly, and he strolled to the canvas, running his thumb along the edge. It came away stained with green paint, the color of the patchwork hills. He rubbed it away with his index finger. "In addition," he drawled, "might you possibly consider—"

"Certainly not!" she cried, eyeing the naked woman outlined on the canvas.

He raised both hands in a gesture of defeat. "I had to

ask," he said. "You can see the resemblance yourself, and that *hair* . . ."

Tessa marched toward the door. Her position had to be made unequivocally clear at the outset.

"All right," Longworth said, intercepting her. "If you should change your mind, you have only to say so. It would mean a substantial increase in your salary, of course, should you decide to model for me in your spare time." He didn't give her time to respond. "My ward, Monty, will be your charge. He is nine. I shan't deceive you, he's a difficult child. We'll settle you in and you'll meet him tomorrow. Did you have bags in the coach?"

"N-no, Mr. Longworth. I left in rather a hurry, just as I will leave here if you persist about that painting."

"No matter," he said, ignoring the last. "Dorcas, my housekeeper, will outfit you with some of my wife's old things. You cannot go about in that costume. It isn't suitable."

Tessa nodded. "If your wife wouldn't mind, until I can purchase suitable costumes locally."

"She won't mind," he said, through what could only be described as a sneer, Tessa decided, having been startled by it. His eyes had taken on a fiendish glare. "She's dead, you see," he went on drolly. "Folks hereabouts say I killed her."

Chapter Three

"You can sleep in this," the housekeeper said, laying a folded nightdress on the chiffonier. I'll bring up a few frocks for your inspection first thing in the mornin'."

"Thank you, Dorcas," Tessa said. "You are most kind." The woman had settled her in what had been termed the Viridian Suite, the governess's apartments, chosen for its close proximity to those of her charge. The walls were papered in pastoral scenes in shades of green, reminding Tessa of French toile; a guest suite no doubt, definitely a woman's apartments on the third floor, with an adjoining sitting room and dressing room. The sight took Tessa's breath away. She had never slept in a room so grand.

"They used ta hold huntin' parties at Longhollow Abbey in the old days," Dorcas said, as if answering Tessa's thoughts. "These rooms up here haven't been in use since the master's father was alive."

"It's . . . beautiful," Tessa murmured, gazing about at the frescoed ceiling, draped sleigh bed and white French lacquered furniture. "I have never seen the like."

"The Holland covers spared a lot o' the furniture, and we put on fresh bedding, but these rooms want a good goin' over. I'll see ta that in the mornin', too, while you're with Master Monty. We're short-staffed here since the mistress . . . died. There's the maids Lettie and Lottie—sisters, don't ya know—Rigby, the butler, Evers, the footman, Foster, the master's valet, Cook, and Effie in the scullery, and meself. Oh, and there's Able and Andy in the stables, but they keep to the loft out there in their own quarters."

"That is a short staff for such a house as this."

Dorcas shrugged. "We make do," she said. "We don't stand on ceremony here at Longhollow Abbey, not like the gentry does in Town. If a job needs doin', a body'll cross the line and do it if needs must, just so's it gets done. Will ya be sendin' for your things, then?"

Tessa hesitated. "No," she said. "The master doesn't approve of my attire. I shall purchase new costumes here locally."

"Oh, pshaw!" Dorcas grumbled. "What would he know? None o' his females wears any clothes at all!"

Tessa suppressed a smile. "I'm sure I'll find something suitable in Truro on my day off," she said.

"Well, I'll have ta send one o' the maids with ya when ya go," Dorcas said. "It just ain't safe, a woman on her own travelin' about, and you'll have old Able, too. This ain't like London Town out here. There's all sorts o' mischief afoot."

Tessa wanted to say there was mischief afoot aplenty in London Town as well, but she held her peace. "That can wait for a bit," she said. "Tell me a little about my charge. My employment here depends upon how we get on together, Master Monty and I."

Dorcas clouded. She began fidgeting with her pinafore, her stubby little fingers working over the top-stitched hem. She was a rotund, red-cheeked woman of middle age, with a pleasant though toil-worn counte-nance and what seemed like a good heart—the exact op-posite of the servants Tessa had left behind at Poole

House. It was a tremendous relief. At least that part of her prayer had been answered.

"Well, I ain't goin' ta lie to ya," the woman began. "He's a handful, is Master Monty. Montclair Albert Montague III, though none o' us ever calls him by any name but Monty, unless the master's got him on the carpet. The master' sister's child, he is. Well, not really. The boy's no blood kin to the Longworths. Montague was married afore, and young Monty was his son. When she died—the master's sister; Ursula was her name—young Monty become the master's ward. Miss Ursula—she'll always be Miss Ursula ta me; I didn't much care for that husband o' hers—well, she was increasing when she died. 'Twas a dreadful accident that killed mother and child. Montague fell fighting Napoleon."

"And the master took the lad in?"

"They *was* in, him and Miss Ursula—a bit o' a scandal there, but it ain't my place ta tell it. When Miss Ursula died, little Monty became the master's charge."

"What happened to his last governess?"

"She run off—all of them did," Dorcas admitted. "We try to do our best for the boy, but like I said, we're short-staffed out here."

"The boy can't be all that bad," Tessa scoffed.

"Oh no? Just wait," Dorcas said. "And it ain't just the boy, 'tis the master, too. He don't get on well with people."

Tessa could appreciate that. She wouldn't probe the woman. She'd been brought here for some reason. She needed to find out what that reason was.

"Listen ta me goin' on," Dorcas said. "I don't want ta scare ya off. Pay me no mind. I'm always speakin' outa turn. We're all glad you've come. Cook's fixin' a tray for ya. Ya must be starved. Eat then get some sleep. You'll need ta be well rested for dealin' with young master tomorrow."

"Oh no, tell Cook not to trouble," Tessa said. "I'm really too tired to eat. That bed looks so inviting, I think I'll just go straight to sleep."

"It's no trouble, miss, but if you're sure . . ."

"I'm sure. You've been most kind."

Dorcas turned the bed down and started toward the door. She turned back when she reached it. "Oh, and there's just one more thing, miss," she said awkwardly. "Be sure ta lock your door."

Tessa didn't need to be told to do that. It was the first thing on her agenda, but still she asked, "Why?" The short hairs on the back of her neck were standing on end at the woman's odd expression.

Dorcas shrugged. "It's just somethin' we do here at the Abbey, is all," she said. "The master'll tell ya the same. Just . . . lock it."

Giles Longworth dragged himself up the bifurcated staircase that divided the house into two wings and trudged to his master suite apartments. The fog in his brain was lifting. He was sobering, heaven forbid. There was more brandy in his bedchamber, and he headed straight for it only to be intercepted by Foster, his valet, an antiquated curmudgeon whom his father had bequeathed to him when he turned sixteen. Giles had thanked Divine Providence every day since for that bequest . . . except when, like now, he was half-foxed, and the valet had custody of the brandy decanter.

"Give it here, damn you, Foster," Giles growled. "I'm not in the mood to spar with you. I've just made a damned fool of myself, and I need to soften the edges."

"Don't you think it would be best to sober up in order to do that, sir?" Foster said.

"I don't think at all when I'm under the influence,"

Giles responded, working his hand impatiently. "That's the point, old boy, now hand it over."

The valet ignored him. "How is it you've embarrassed yourself this time, then?" he asked. "No doubt there's a female involved."

Giles raked his fingers through his hair impatiently. "I confused the new governess with the model I sent for to replace the thieving little slag I just put off the place is all. Tell me that is not worthy of a swig of that rotgut you're holding captive there."

"You wouldn't have embarrassed yourself but for the brandy in the first place," the valet returned.

A sage, was Foster: always right and always at him. The valet had taken Giles's father's directive seriously when he'd instructed the man to keep his son on the straight and narrow. Truth be told, Giles loved Foster for it, but not in circumstances like these.

"That is not the only bottle of brandy in this house, Foster," he reminded the valet.

"No, 'tisn't," Foster agreed. "But 'tis the closest, and you look too tuckered to go fetch another. Besides, I've got something better. I've fixed you a nice hot bath. Why don't you have that, and then if you still want this . . ." He brandished the decanter.

The man was a sadist, though a hot bath did sound inviting. Giles stank of painting medium and sweat. "All right, you win, Foster," he conceded, "but I will have that when I've done, you can bet your blunt upon it."

He followed the valet into his dressing room, stripped off his clothes, and climbed into the tin tub set before the fire. The nights weren't particularly cold yet, but the dampness was another matter: something they contended with all year round, and a good hot fire was the only thing that chased it. This one was fueled by apple wood, from a tree that had been uprooted during the last gale, and the whole suite smelled delightfully like a cider mill.

"Tell me, how have we come by her, the new governess?" Foster asked, dumping a bucket of cold water over Giles's head.

"Lud, man! You did that a-purpose!" Giles bellowed, slapping the water in the tub with his fist.

"It slipped, sir," Foster said stoically.

"Mmmm . . . You're full of happy little accidents of late, aren't you? Never mind. Where were we? Oh yes! I told Dorcas to advertise; she must have done. The gel arrived tonight. Truth to be told, I think I wished her here. How does that old Mother Goose rhyme go: '*If wishes were horses, beggars would ride* . . .'? Well, I was begging any ears in the cosmos that would hear me to send another governess for the little bastard, and why wouldn't I, after he drove the last one off, and the one before that? I need to get shot of him for a bit. I'm at the end of my tether with Master Monty, Foster."

"Don't we all know it," the valet said.

Foster wasn't aware of the whole of it, of the danger; neither were the others. No doubt they all suspected something untoward was going on with the boy, but Giles had never made the situation plain, primarily because it was so bizarre they wouldn't have believed him if he had. They would have been certain it was a brandy-induced hallucination. They were all safe enough. None of them courted the child's company. And Foster was perceptive enough to be wary on general principle. He would have to tell the valet soon, though. The situation was worsening, and the moon would be full again in two days. Miss Tessa LaPrelle was in no danger, or so he had convinced himself. Giles would arrange her hours with the boy to make certain of that.

". . . and she just turned up out of the blue?" Foster was asking.

Giles nodded. "Literally. I thought she was the model I'd sent Andy to fetch. And why wouldn't I? She's perfect for it; exactly my vision for 'The Bride of Time.'"

"And she refused to model for you," Foster said, answering his own question.

"That's putting it mildly," Giles said through a guttural chuckle. There was no humor in it.

"You didn't disgrace yourself, did you, sir?" Foster asked warily. "Though they've just made her acquaintance, everybody below stairs has taken a liking to the lass. She presents a personable appearance, if a bit of an odd dresser, and she speaks like a lady."

"Good God, man, you make it sound as if I tried to ravish the gel. No, I did not disgrace myself . . . at least not in the way you imply . . . I don't think . . . I don't know; damn it, man. Suffice it to say she didn't run screaming from the house. That should recommend me to civility somewhat, I should imagine."

The valet hummed, dumping another pail of water—warmer, this time—over Giles's head. Giles cast him a scathing glance, shaking himself like a dog.

"Don't look at me," Foster intoned. "You've gotten off lucky. It should have been cold again to get all the suds out. Stop squirming or I'll have to do it again."

"Well, hurry up with it, man, I want to address something while it's still fresh in my mind."

"You can climb out whenever you will, sir," Foster said. "It's no skin off my nose if you want to go about sticky with soap and green paint in your hair."

Giles said no more. It wasn't any use when the valet took that tack. It was better just to let him have his way. Besides, the bathwater was soothing his frayed nerves. He remained submerged until the water began to turn cold before climbing out into the thick bath towel Foster held at the ready.

"We need to talk, Foster," he said, rubbing himself

briskly. "I'll want to speak with you tomorrow about the situation here; after breakfast in the study will be as good a time as any. I'll settle Miss LaPrelle in with Master Monty first. We won't want to be disturbed."

"Why don't you just speak your piece now?" Foster suggested. "There's no one to disturb us here, sir."

Giles shook his head. "No, old boy, not now," he said. "I'm too weary to do the subject matter justice."

"As you wish, sir. I'll fetch your dressing gown and turn down your bed then."

"No," Giles said. "Fetch me fresh togs instead, and leave the brandy. I want to go up to the studio for a while."

"But you've just gotten shot of the paint and all!"

"Doesn't matter; I need to work while I still can."

"You mean to paint without a model, sir?"

"I mean to do what I can from memory while Miss LaPrelle's image is fresh in my mind, since she chooses not to pose for me. She has the most exquisite hair. . . ."

The nursery was situated on the third floor even beyond her rooms at the far end of the east wing, with the boy's sleeping chamber adjoining. It appeared to Tessa that the master of Longhollow Abbey had ranged the boy as far from the rest in residence as was humanly possible. *It must be dreadfully inconvenient caring for the boy at such a distance in an understaffed house,* she thought, trying to keep up with Longworth's long-legged stride.

Longworth didn't knock, but barged into the nursery as if he meant to catch the boy out doing something scandalous, and scowled unattractively when he found the opposite to be true. Monty was seated at a low child's table, drawing on a slate tablet with a piece of worn chalk.

"Get up, you little gudgeon, and receive Miss LaPrelle, your new governess, like a gentleman," Longworth said, hauling the boy to his feet by the arm. "Miss

LaPrelle, my ward, Montclair Albert Montague, III, my late sister's stepchild."

"I'm glad to make your acquaintance, Miss LaPrelle," the boy said, extending his hand. He was a handsome child, all eyes, it seemed; they were large and darker than his uncle's, dominating his small, pale face.

Tessa took the boy's limp fingers in hers. They were clammy and cold. The disdain between surrogate uncle and child was jarring at best. Taken aback by the display, Tessa was compelled to speak up.

"Do not bully the boy," she said, as jovially as she could manage, though her meaning was clear. "Let him get to know me at his own rate." Tessa had no experience with children whatsoever, but she knew striking out on the right foot at the outset might preserve her situation there, though she couldn't for the life of her figure out why she would want to after what she'd seen of Longhollow Abbey's enigmatic master thus far.

"Oh, that is quite all right," the boy put in. "I'm quite accustomed to uncle's foul tempers." Did Longworth wince? "He's cross because I bit him, you see."

"Enough, Monty!" Longworth said, his tone unequivocal. He jerked the ruffled shirtsleeve down over the scar Tessa had noticed the night before. So that's how it happened! This was not going to be easy. What possible circumstances could have caused the child to bite his uncle? And such a savage bite! It was ragged and deep. She would never have taken it for a human bite, much less that of a small child.

"Might I have a word with you alone, Mr. Longworth?" she asked sweetly.

He started toward the door, and Tessa turned back to the boy. "I shall return presently, Master Monty," she said, "and then we shall get to know one another."

Once outside, Tessa bristled. "What sort of display was that?" she demanded. "Evidently, you are just as much of a brute sober as you are in your cups, sir! He is only a child. No wonder your former governesses ran off. It wasn't because of Master Monty, either, I'll wager."

Longworth flung his arm toward the staircase. "There's the door!" he seethed. "Just follow the stairs. You may join them with my blessing, madam, whenever you please. There is much here of which you are in ignorance, so I would hold my peace if I were you until you have all the facts before you pass judgment upon me."

"Whatever the circumstances, sir, there is no reason to revenge yourself upon that poor child. He seems a lovely, well-mannered boy. I've only been in his company a few brief moments, and I must say, I'm concerned."

Longworth loosed a humorless laugh. "Before the sennight's out, you will be coming to me with your 'concerns' regarding my ward, Miss LaPrelle, but I guarantee you they will be of quite a different nature. But we waste time. Far be it from me to keep you from your duties." He swept his arm wide toward the boy's chamber and sketched a dramatic bow. "Do carry on. I wish you well. Good morning!"

Spinning on his heel, Longworth stormed off toward the landing, his long-legged stomps shaking the corridor underfoot. Tessa stared after him for a hesitant moment before re-entering the nursery. What had she gotten herself into? There were mysteries afoot here, mysteries she was almost too afraid to solve, and yet, like a moth to the flame, she was drawn to do just that. If the Fates had put her here, they had to have a reason, and she was determined to discover what that reason was. She decided then and there that it would begin with Master Monty; and she shut the door and flashed him her most winsome smile.

"So, Master Monty," she began. "What is your favorite subject?"

"Uncle," the boy said flatly.

Tessa laughed. "No, silly, your favorite academic subject . . . what did your former governesses plan for your lessons?"

"Oh, that," the boy said, pouting. He shrugged. "They didn't do lessons overmuch. They weren't here long enough."

Tessa frowned. "How is it that your uncle hasn't sent you off to school? You're old enough."

Again the boy shrugged. "You will have to ask Uncle," he said.

"You could be with other boys your own age at school. Wouldn't you like that?" Her thought was to separate uncle from child, for they seemed a volatile mix.

"Don't you want to stay and be my governess?" the boy asked.

The look of him then sent a cold chill down Tessa's spine. Of a sudden, there was almost a fiendish glare older than his years in the child's innocent eyes. "W-well, of course I do, Master Monty. I was just thinking—"

"You were thinking I would be safer," the boy interrupted her, his lips curving in a smug smile.

"I was thinking, young man, that you might benefit from the company of other children your own age. Are there no other children for you to play with hereabouts?"

Monty shook his head. "You aren't going to start changing things about, are you?" he said.

"Of course not," Tessa assured him. No, this wasn't going to be easy. It wasn't going to be easy at all. A dark shadow had fallen across the child's riveting eyes that her answer hadn't dispelled. It set a rush of fresh chills loose upon her spine.

"Good!" said the boy. "Because I wouldn't like that."

Why had he made it seem like a threat, or at the very least an ultimatum? Tessa's blood ran cold, but still she was determined. "Well!" she said buoyantly. "Since your lessons are sorely lacking, wipe off that slate and let us see how skilled you are at sums. There's a good boy."

"Don't you like my drawing?"

"Of course I do," Tessa assured him. "It's a fine tree you've drawn, but sums would be more practical at the moment . . . since you haven't had much practice."

"Uncle draws," the child observed, wiping the slate clean.

"Yes," Tessa said.

"Do you like his paintings?"

"I haven't seen enough of his work to judge," Tessa replied.

"He's better than me."

"Yes, well, you're very young, Master Monty. I'm sure when you're his age—"

"He doesn't like me to draw," Monty cut in.

Tessa studied the boy for a long moment. "Master Monty," she began hesitantly. "You didn't really bite your uncle, did you?"

"I did," the boy said with pride.

"Why would you do such a thing?"

"Because he made me angry," the boy said flatly. "Take care that *you* do not make me angry, too."

Chapter Four

Giles sprinted down the stairs and stalked to the study, his boot heels clacking an angry rhythm on the parquetry. Who the devil *was* this exasperating female? He'd wished for, *prayed* for . . . the perfect Bride of Time, and what did he get? Tessa LaPrelle! No milk-and-water-miss, she. She was what he'd envisioned for the painting of his heart and soul, the painting that would establish him as an artist to be reckoned with, and in less than twenty-four hours she had dashed his hopes and touched his heart, and turned his life upside down.

Never in his thirty-eight stormy miserable years had he ever painted without a model, set down an image from memory as exactly as he had done last night. And it was good! He had almost captured her likeness. That hair! That glorious hair, as soft as silk. His fingers had grazed it when he snatched the tortoiseshell pins from the intricacy of that strange coiffure. What he wouldn't give to fondle that hair, to run his fingers through the magnificent length. What a treat for the eyes and the senses, when all the women from Land's End to London were shearing their tresses—in some cases shorter than their male counterparts. He could still smell its fragrance. What flower was it that haunted him? He wracked his brain trying to place it, but he couldn't. It would come to him when he least expected it. That was happening a lot lately. He was too preoccupied, too distracted by the nightmare of his shocking existence to concentrate upon the everyday wonders of the world that everyone else took for granted, like the simple pleasure of smelling flowers.

Having reached the study, Giles rang for Foster and sank into the chair behind his desk, his head in his hands. He hadn't gotten much sleep, between painting and the disquieting feeling that had come over him because Tessa LaPrelle was sleeping under his roof in grave peril from all factors. What had he done?

He lurched as if he'd been shot when Foster's knock broke the silence. "Come!" he said. The valet crossed the threshold and closed the door behind him in response to Giles's nod. "Take a seat, Foster," Giles said. "You'll want something underneath you for this."

"Thank you, sir, but I prefer to stand," Foster replied.

Giles slapped his hands down upon the desktop and laced his fingers together. They were still smeared with paint. It gave him something to focus upon while he said his piece, though his eyes strayed to the jagged scar on the back of his left hand and wrist, angry-looking still, though it had healed since he was wounded a month ago. He couldn't look the valet in the eyes.

"Foster, needs must there are . . . things that you should be made aware of, and should have been for some time now."

"Yes, sir."

"They concern some of the . . . situations that have been arising at Longhollow Abbey since the death of my wife."

"Yes, sir."

Giles cleared his voice. "I didn't kill her, Foster."

"I know, sir."

"You answer quickly. Is that because you believe me, or you want to get past it?"

" 'Twas an animal that killed her, sir," said Foster. "Everyone knows that."

"I am blamed for it nonetheless, because she cuckolded me with that rakehell Osborne. I didn't kill him, either, though they say that of me, too, don't they, Foster?"

"Yes, sir."

How was he to tell the valet? How was he to reveal to the poor man something so bizarre he scarcely believed it himself, without sending him off coattails flying after a half-century of faithful service? On the other hand, how could he not? There was no contest. Giles had no choice. Foster had to be told, and he had to be told now—before the moon was full again tomorrow night. But telling would surely make him a prime candidate for St. Mary's of Bethlehem Hospital in London, the infamous Bedlam. He would just have to risk it.

"That they were found dead together bloody near damned me, and may yet," Giles said.

"You think they will re-open the investigation, sir?" the valet spoke up.

"It isn't over, Foster. The nightmare has only just begun."

"I do not take your meaning, sir? They are dead. How can it not be over?"

"There is still Master Monty."

The valet's expression hardened, causing shadows to mar his wrinkled face. "If I may be so bold—" he began, causing laughter to erupt from Giles's throat.

"When has propriety ever stopped you, Foster?" Giles asked bitterly.

The valet cleared his voice. "Why do you keep the boy here?" he asked. "I should think you'd have packed him off to school long ago, since you find his company so disagreeable."

"I cannot," Giles said flatly. Rising from the chair, he began to pace the length of the Aubusson carpet.

"But why, sir?" Foster persisted. "To my thinking—"

"This is why," Giles said, thrusting out his wounded wrist. "The little savage bit me last month just before the moon waxed full. When it did . . . I changed, Foster. The morning after, I woke naked on the moor. I'd been drinking rather heavily. At first, I thought the brandy was to blame, but there was blood on me and it wasn't mine. Shortly after that, there were reports of some wild animal attacking the livestock in the parish—"

"Those *werewolf* rumors?" Foster interrupted. "You can't possibly believe that gammon, sir, much less imagine that you—"

"I'm not imagining anything, Foster." He brandished his wrist. "Am I imagining this? I am telling you that little demon bit me, and when the moon waxed full . . . something happened to me and I savaged some sheep."

Foster's ramrod-rigid posture collapsed, and he sank into the wing chair Giles had offered him earlier. His complexion was ghost-gray. "If such a thing were true, that would mean that Master Monty is a . . . a . . ."

"Exactly," Giles said. "Which is why I haven't packed him off to school. If he is a lycanthrope, or *thinks* he is, I shouldn't want to be responsible for setting him loose in a boy's boarding school."

"So you let him run lose *here?* Have you gone mad?"

"He's hardly running loose," Giles returned. "Besides, Miss LaPrelle is with him."

Foster vaulted out of the chair with the agility of a man half his age. "You've left her alone with the boy?" he cried.

"Take ease, old man. If the legend is true, and such

things are possible, she will be safe enough during the day and at night as well, except when the moon is full. That won't occur until tomorrow night, which is why we're having this conversation now. I need to be certain my suspicions are correct before I can take action concerning the boy. I have something in mind, but I will need your help."

"You have never gotten on with that boy from the day your poor sister, God rest her, showed up on the doorstep with the lad in tow."

"Ursula was a fool to have gotten mixed up with Montague," Giles reflected. "Master Monty was his from a previous . . . association. I'm sorry to say it wasn't a marriage. The chit ran off and left the boy for Montague to raise, some dark-eyed Gypsy wench he'd shacked up with. The little blighter favors her, no doubt; Montague was fair. Then when Montigue died doing his bit, fighting for King and country, the boy's care fell to Ursula. The bairn in Ursula's belly when she arrived here *was* Montague's, however. Master Monty was jealous of it. Ursula was afraid of the boy, if you can imagine that. We spoke at length on it. I pooh-poohed it at first, of course. I'm sorry now that I wasn't more sympathetic. You know how she died. I will never believe it was a suicide. *Never.*"

"You can't seriously believe—"

"I don't know what to believe. That's why I need your help, Foster. The boy's been knocking about on his own much of the time. Nobody wishes to court his company. We're all to blame for that. But, by God, it ends here and now. I don't want to frighten the others, but supervision is imperative until we sort this out."

"You mean that task is mine, I gather?"

"Until tomorrow night, if you're game."

"If what you suspect is true, God help us, that could

mean Master Monty might also be responsible for the deaths of the mistress and that . . . Osborne person!"

"All of which should prove to you that I did not kill them, Foster. They were murdered long before I was bitten, and no man could have savaged them the way they were found."

"But . . . he's only a lad. How could he have?"

"That is precisely what I mean to find out."

Foster paused before speaking. "How exactly do you mean to enlist my help?" he asked at last.

That wasn't a good sign. In all his years with the valet, Giles had never known him to hesitate, or place conditions upon a directive as he did now. That meant there was room for doubt. The poor man probably did think him off his head. Maybe he was. It was passing bizarre, yet too coincidental to be dismissed lightly.

"Does that mean you will help?" Giles prompted.

"I am still concerned about Miss LaPrelle," the valet hedged. "Whatever possessed you to take her on here in the midst of all this? That was most irresponsible, especially considering your . . . suspicions. Why? Forgive me, sir, but I need to know what you could possibly have been thinking."

"Why?" Giles said absently. "I do not know if I can answer you. You know how important 'The Bride of Time' is to us. We need the blunt, and the Prince Regent is interested. His patronage could make my name a household word. His interests flag, however, and I'm anxious to finish the painting before that occurs. I've had his favor ever since I painted that miniature of Maria Fitzherbert for his pocket watchcase. You remember, he paid me handsomely, and gave me the snuff box that doxy tried to steal last night as a bonus."

"Vulgar piece," Foster observed.

"Quite, but a bonus all the same, and that commission led to another possible sale if I can finish 'The

Bride' in a timely fashion. Working on it takes my mind off the situation, and the brandy . . . I don't even like the stuff, but it blunts the edges. You know the run of bad luck I've been having with models. . . ."

"Yes, but I fail to see how all this answers my question about Miss LaPrelle, sir."

"You will, if you let me finish," Giles said, somewhat less than patiently. "I've been praying for someone like her to inspire me to finish the work. When she arrived, in my drunken haze, I thought I'd had an answer to my prayers. She is perfect for 'The Bride.' She *is* The Bride; so much so that I had to have her at any cost, even though she'd come about the governess position. I do not expect you to understand it. I don't understand it myself, but there it is. There's something about her . . . something fresh and new. I wanted that. I *needed* that, in more ways than one."

"For the painting," Foster said, answering his own question, albeit skeptically.

Giles's eyebrow lifted. "What else?"

"It isn't up to me to say, sir. You must search yourself for the answer to that."

"Hah! Nothing has ever stopped you before, old boy."

"Suffice it to say . . . I wouldn't want the lass to come to harm because of selfish motives, sir."

Giles gave it thought. "I suppose it is selfish of me to some degree," he admitted finally. "After the sordid business with Elena, I expect the company of a decent woman under this roof would not go amiss. I've had my fill of tragedy. If this nightmare turns out to be real, I will not become a slave to it. I will have a life—a decent life."

"Which brings us back to exactly what you expect of me now, sir."

Giles nodded. "I want you to keep an eye upon Master

Monty from a discreet distance until just before dusk tomorrow, when the moon rises. I mean to lock him in. Then, I shall give you my chatelaine, and I want you to lock me in the solarium, and no matter what occurs— no matter what you hear, or what I command or beg for, or what Master Monty demands—you mustn't unlock either door. When dawn breaks, you will come for me first, and we will unlock Master Monty's chamber together."

"How will that prove anything?"

"I know the state I was in when I woke naked on that moor smeared with blood. Believe me, if either of us has changed, you will know."

"And what will I do with the knowledge, sir, if it is as you fear? What will *you* do—kill the child, kill yourself? Do not expect it of me."

"For now, let us just do this test," Giles said. "We will deal with what's to be done with whatever we're facing after we learn what it is."

"You've been going through a bad patch, sir," Foster said. "It's understandable that you would be a little . . . irrational."

"A bad patch, Foster?" Giles blurted. "My pregnant sister, so full of hope for the future, dies, her death deemed a suicide, leaving me with a savage little ward to raise, who isn't even blood kin. My wife and her lover are found ravaged with their throats torn out on the moor, and I am suspected. We are bloody near rolled up, dependent upon the patronage of the Prince Regent, until the *on-dits* that have driven all my local patrons away reach his ears in London, and I cannot find a model for the work that has captured his interest. Oh and, here is the best bit. Just when I think I have her, the perfect Bride of Time, she refuses and I am forced to try to do the work from memory. Irrational? Believe me, old friend, you have not begun to see 'irrational,' but unless I miss my guess, and I dearly hope I do, you will see it in full force tomorrow night. You can bet your blunt upon it!"

Chapter Five

Tessa didn't see Giles Longworth again that day. She took her meals in the servants' hall, while her charge ate alone in his rooms, which she thought rather odd, since most children Monty's age in such a house were trained early in dining room etiquette as a matter of course. Nevertheless, she was relieved over it. The tension between the child and his surrogate uncle was palpable. Dorcas assured her that this was the normal protocol for meals at Longhollow Abbey, since the master rarely ate in the dining parlor. The housekeeper complained that he rarely ate at all of late, and what food he did take was had in his solarium studio. It seemed an odd business, but then nothing seemed normal since she'd arrived, including how she'd arrived. She still hadn't come to terms with that.

Preparing the boy for bed fell to the maid, Lottie. After Tessa finished her evening meal, she decided to look in on the child before she retired. She found him standing before the window in his nightshirt, gazing at the almost-full moon. He should have been in bed, and she was about to say so when he spun on his bare heels and faced her. The look in his eyes backed her up a pace. It wasn't the look of a child at all. It was the look of a demon eons old, the eyes dark staring things beneath the ledge of his brow. His lips were fixed in a sneer. It was a fleeting expression that quickly changed back to the cherubic countenance he'd presented thus far, but it was so profound it riddled Tessa with crippling chills from her scalp to her toes.

"Well, Master Monty," she said, regaining her lost composure and her footing as well. "You should be abed, shouldn't you?"

"I've been waiting for you," the boy said sweetly.

"How odd, since I didn't know I was coming."

"I knew you would come. You want to make a good impression upon Uncle. It won't do you any good, you know, but you're curious. The others were as well." He yawned and stretched. How innocent he looked now, in his fine lawn nightshift, his little pink toes peeking out from beneath the hem, his hair all mussed. "They were sorry after, just as you will be, miss."

"And how is that, Master Monty?" Tessa persisted, determined to draw the child out. He was either play-acting, or possessed of a devious, obstreperous nature. She meant to find out which.

"You just will," the boy responded. Padding to the window, he turned his back on her and again gave his full and fierce attention to the moon. "Just like all the others."

"Is that supposed to frighten me?" she asked, with what she hoped was a lighthearted laugh. "I think you rather like to play that game, but you will find that I do not frighten easily."

The boy shrugged and loosed a high-pitched giggle, but made no response. The sound alone was enough to raise her hackles without any spoken word he might have uttered.

"I was given to understand that once Lottie readied you for bed and tucked you in at night, you were to remain in it till morning, unless you have need of the chamber pot. Am I mistaken? Being new, you see, I do need to have the way of things clear in my mind."

The boy nodded, Tessa assumed, in reply to her question. She wasn't about to probe him.

"Yes, well . . . that being the case, suppose I tuck you in again, since Lottie has retired for the day."

"I'm not tired yet," the boy intoned.

"Still, rules are rules, and we have to do what needs must." She took a step nearer, reaching to take hold of him. "If you aren't tired, I could read you a bedtime story. Would you like that?"

As her hand connected with his shoulder, the child spun and lowered his open mouth—canines gleaming—over her wrist. It hovered there, nearly touching her skin, and Tessa quickly pulled her hand back out of harm's way.

"Here!" she cried. "What is the meaning of this?"

"Do not touch my person," the boy growled. "No one touches my person except the maid who dresses and bathes me. Uncle found that out. He wears the scar to prove it."

"H-has your uncle ever harmed you, Master Monty?" Tessa murmured. Why else would the boy act this way? Her heart sank. She had become attracted to Giles Longworth before they ever met, and the image of the man Possibility posed was deeply troubling.

"No," the boy said, somewhat alleviating her fears. "And he shan't, because he shan't get close enough. Neither shall you."

"I meant you no harm. For pity's sake, young man, it's way past your bedtime. I only meant to walk you to bed and tuck you in. You had no call to attack me."

"I didn't attack you. I simply let you know what to expect should you touch me again."

"I will overlook it this time," Tessa said, in her most authoritative voice. "But if you ever threaten my person again, I will have no choice but to report it to your uncle. Now get into that bed before I change my mind and tell him forthwith." The line had to be drawn here and now if she was to have any sort of control over the child. Longworth might not keep her on if she couldn't manage him. "Well? I am waiting," she said to the boy's back.

Monty spun around, his arms folded across his chest. "Make me!" he said, a maddening half-smile spreading across his face.

"Oh, I see," Tessa said. "So you can bite me like you did your uncle? A very clever demonstration, young man, but I think not. You will find that I am not like your past governesses. You aren't going to drive me out like you did the others, so you may as well give over trying. I would have liked this to be a pleasant relationship. I am sorry if that cannot be. I am still willing, but we can have it either way. That will be up to you. What will it be?"

The child spun back toward the window in a gesture of dismissal. "You are not the boss of me," he said. "I will get into bed when I am tired."

"No, I am not your boss," Tessa said. "But I know who is."

Without another word, she stalked out of the chamber and shut the door behind her.

Tessa hadn't reached the third-floor landing when she caught sight of Foster making his descent from the upper regions. "Foster!" she cried, halting him on the step.

"Yes, miss?" he replied, waiting.

"Where might I find the master at this hour?" she asked.

"Well, he would be in his studio now, miss, but he really does not wish to be disturbed when he's working."

"I'm afraid that cannot be helped, Foster," she said, turning back toward the attic stairs.

"Is there anything I can do?" the valet called after her. "You really shouldn't—"

"Thank you, no," Tessa called out.

Foster sprinted after her with the agility of a man half his age. "At least let me light the candle sconces," he said. "The master doesn't require them lit, as he carries a candle branch to and fro, so the upper region is dark. You could do yourself a mischief."

Tessa scurried on ahead of the valet. The last thing she wanted was a witness to what she was about to say to Giles Longworth. "That's all right, Foster," she called over her shoulder. "You needn't trouble. I remember the way."

The attic region was dark, but enough light filtered up the stairs from the landing below and kept her from misstepping. A sliver of light coming from under the solarium doorsill was all she needed to guide her the rest of the way, and she didn't slow her pace until she'd reached it and pounded boldly on the door, startled by the sound her tiny fist made on the ancient wood.

Almost at once, the vibration of heavy footfalls moved the floorboards beneath her feet, and the door came open in Longworth's hand. Tessa swayed at the sight of him. His eyes, dark and riveting, stared down at her with a strange mix of apprehension and excitement. It was almost a disoriented look, as if he didn't believe what he was seeing. His brandy-laced scent drifted toward her, infused with the musk of his maleness. It floated over her, overriding the musty smell of dust and disuse that hovered about the upper regions of the house, and did strange things to her equilibrium, causing her hand to steady her against the doorjamb.

His fine lawn shirt was open nearly to the waist, giving a glimpse of the muscular chest beneath, and the arrow-straight line of dark hair disappearing beneath the waistband of his breeches. He was a feast for Tessa's eyes beyond anything suggested by his portrait in the little London gallery. He was flesh and blood and feral magnetism, a living breathing danger to her heart and senses that took her breath away until his deep, sultry voice interrupted the magic that held her spellbound.

"Well, well," he said. "Have you changed your mind, then?"

It was a moment before Tessa took his meaning, and she bristled. "No, I have not!" she snapped at him—a little too severely, she feared, but lines had to be drawn in all quarters at Longhollow Abbey, and this seemed to be the night to draw them all the way around. "I am sorry to disturb you, but a . . . situation has arisen with Master Monty that requires your attention."

"And what might that be? I thought I made it clear that you were to be in complete charge of my ward."

Tessa hesitated, praying he wouldn't think her too incompetent to supervise her charge and dismiss her. That the boy was turning out to be a bit more than she could handle didn't enter into the equation; she didn't want to leave Longhollow Abbey.

"Y-yes, you did," she stammered. "But this is something that I am sure I do not have the authority to . . . correct."

He pulled the door open wider, his expression dark. His handsome lips were forming that bloodless crimped line she'd seen when first they'd met in the Welsh bluestone drive, and his jaw muscle had begun to twitch.

He stood aside. "Won't you come in?"

Tessa hesitated. Glancing past him, she saw that he had been working, but she couldn't see the front of the canvas. The easel had been moved since the night before. It no longer faced the lounge. "I . . . I think not," she said. "What I have to tell you can be said right here, sir."

"Then out with it!" he said. "As you can see, I am busy."

"After supper, I looked in on Master Monty," she began. "It was long past his bedtime, and I attempted to see him to bed. He was argumentative, even threatening, which I thought reasonable enough, since he's been on his own for so long and suddenly tethered to a governess again. I ignored his behavior and offered to read him a bedtime story. When I reached to turn him toward the bed, he . . . attacked me, or almost did. He swooped down as if he was about to bite my hand . . . like he did yours, he pointed out. It was a test staged to frighten me, and it did, though I tried not to show it."

Giles flung his paintbrush down and seized her forearms, examining them frantically. His touch was like a lightning strike. His warm fingers denting her bare flesh struck a chord deep at the epicenter of her sex, flooding her loins with hot sensation that undermined her balance.

"Don't!" she cried, trying to pull away, but his grip was firm.

"Where—show me *where*," he demanded. "Did he break the skin?"

"No," she cried. "Stop! You're hurting me! He swooped down and hovered over my wrist with his teeth bared, as if he was going to take a bite out of it, then as much as said if I ever touched him again, he would bite me the way he bit you. This is something I do not have the authority to address. That's why I've come to you."

He pulled her over the threshold and let her go. "By God, this will not be borne!" he seethed. "Stay here until I return."

When he tried to move past her, she seized his arm, freezing him in his tracks. His taut biceps rippled beneath her fingers through the thin shirtsleeve. His eyes, gleaming like onyx chips, flashed toward her hand from the shadows beneath the ledge of his brow, then met her gaze relentlessly. The heady scent of brandy drifted toward her. He'd been drinking, but he wasn't in his cups. To the contrary, he was as sober as she was. The look, the feral scent, the very intensity of the man paralyzed her senses and numbed her tongue, but only for a moment.

"No!" she cried. "Not like this! Not in a rage. He's only a boy. He's crossed the line. He needs to know his limits. Do not make a martyr of that child. Can't you see that's what he wants, to cause a rift between us three? If you go storming into that chamber now in a blind rage, I will never be able to control the child. He will hate me for it!"

"I see," said the master of Longhollow, his nostrils flared, his breathing deep and audible. He looked for all the world like a fire-breathing dragon—so much so, Tessa half-expected flames to shoot out of his nose and smoke to pour out of his ears. "Well, if you possess the sage wisdom to handle the situation, why the devil did you come after me?"

"I only meant—"

"I know what you meant," he interrupted. "I am not a fiend, Miss LaPrelle. I do not go about brutalizing children. But Master Monty is no ordinary child, and he is not the only inmate in this madhouse crossing lines. I am still master of Longhollow Abbey. Now I will thank you to stand aside, and stay put while I deal with this!"

Her hand fell away from his arm then. He hesitated, blinked, and streaked through the door, almost knocking down Foster, who had no doubt been listening in the corridor. From the doorway, Tessa watched the pair of them disappear in the shadowy recesses of the landing.

She teetered on the threshold. She didn't have to enter the chamber—really enter it. She could just wait where she was. What was she thinking? There was no harm in entering his sanctum sanctorum in his absence; the danger lay in his presence. She knew that now if she hadn't before. Something vital passed between them with physical contact, something that flagged every kind of danger. It drew her like a magnet.

Stepping across the threshold and into the room, Tessa strolled to the window. Only one candle branch was lit on the table where Longworth's artist's materials were spread out in a jumble of pots and jars, brushes, trowels, and rags. The moon, dodging scudding clouds, threw a beam at her feet, alive with dust motes. She followed it with her eyes and turned to find that it illuminated the painting. She gasped. "The Bride of Time"! He had been working on the face since she first viewed the canvas. He'd given the woman *her* face. From memory? The likeness was good but not perfect, just as it had been at the gallery, where others remarked upon it but she hadn't been convinced. She saw now what they'd seen—enough of a likeness to pass—but now she noticed more. She gasped again. The hair! He had only seen it flowing loose briefly, and yet he'd captured it exactly, from the color to the way it waved about her face, complete with the tendrils that always crept out no matter how diligently she tried to tame them. He hadn't touched the body.

Hot blood surged to her temples. All at once she saw herself back at the little gallery, gazing at the canvas before her now, wishing she could feel the grass of the patchwork hills beneath her feet and smell the heather. How could any of this be possible? How had she even come here? It was a mystery she almost feared to solve.

That he had only just begun to work on the body intrigued her, since it was completed when she'd seen it at the gallery. She had arrived at Longhollow Abbey before its completion. Did that mean she would remain until it was finished, or something else? There was no way to tell. She was pondering that when Giles Longworth burst through the door.

"The little blighter isn't in his rooms," he said. "Come, I'll see you to your chamber. Foster and I will ferret him out and see he's well-versed in crossing lines."

Tessa didn't reply. They were halfway to the landing before she broke the awkward silence. "What do you mean to do to the boy?"

He stopped mid-step. "Miss LaPrelle," he said. "You were right to come to me. Now you must let me deal with the problem. Monty is a . . . difficult child. There are . . . situations of which you are unaware."

"Well, since he is to be my charge, don't you think you ought to make me aware?" she interrupted him.

Longworth stared. A strange parade of emotions flashed across his face. At first he looked contemplative; then the look softened, though that quickly changed to something dark and brooding. He was a complex individual and, she feared, a volatile one. He was livid with rage that seemed excessive, and though she longed to draw him out, she was wise enough to know this was not the time.

"Of course," he said, "but not tonight."

They continued down the stairs, and Tessa didn't speak again until they reached her rooms. "You haven't answered my question," she said. "What do you mean to do to that boy?"

He scowled at her. "Zeus, what a look!" he replied. "Nothing unlawful, I assure you. He will be found and confined to his rooms. You are certain he didn't really bite you?"

"I'm certain."

"No skin was broken?"

Tessa bristled. "No, none. Now, look here—"

"Very well, then," he interrupted her. "You will report to me before you resume your duties in the morning. Now, I must ask that you lock yourself in your suite and stay put. Good night, Miss LaPrelle."

Chapter Six

He was aroused—*aroused!* How the devil could he be hard against the seam in these dire circumstances? Nonetheless he was, gazing down into Tessa's limpid eyes, which sparkled in the soft glimmer issuing from the candle sconces. His arm still tingled from the touch of her hand. He'd felt its warmth through the fine lawn fabric. He could feel it still. He balled his hands into white-knuckled fists at his sides to keep from reaching out and taking her in his arms, from ravishing those dewy lips with his own. What would they feel like? What would they taste like, those soft-looking, sweet, pouty lips shaped like Cupid's bow?

It wasn't the brandy. He'd sobered as if he hadn't touched a drop the minute she said the child tried to bite her. Foster was right. He'd put her in harm's way—not only from the child, but from himself. Tomorrow night the moon would be full. He could already feel the pull of it, the strange unrest it brought to bear upon every cell in his body as the moon waxed closer and closer to fullness, the bestial restlessness that mounted until the blackout. Then he would no longer be in control until the dawn. The last time it had been thus for four nights altogether: one coming on, like now; two full-blown nightmarish nights while the moon was at its fullest; and one more as it began to wane. Then the madness subsided until the moon waxed full again. Would it always be the same? He had no way of knowing. That was the worst of it. Lycanthropy was myth, not fact; at least that is what he'd always believed until now.

Tessa was safe enough from that for the moment, but not from his other urges. It had been too long since he'd had the pleasure of soft, willing flesh in his arms, and a warm, eager body to welcome his release. But he kept his distance. He might be a savage when the moon was full, but elsewise he'd always prided himself on being a gentleman. Besides, it was too soon. Make a move now and he would spoil any chance he might have if he waited. It was some time since he'd had to play these silly mating games. All that seemed so ridiculous now. And, of course, it was clear she did not return his favor in kind.

"In you get," he said. "Lock the doors, and stay inside no matter what you hear or think you hear." She seemed reluctant, and he muttered an exasperated string of expletives under his breath. "No harm will come to the boy, you have my word," he said. He brandished his wrist. "Hah! *I'm* the savaged one; or had you forgotten? Keep in mind that you could have very well been next."

"You have a vile temper, Mr. Longworth," Tessa said frostily. "I saw it in action when I arrived on your estate. Directed toward the doxy, it was shocking enough. I would entreat you to curb it before meting out your brand of justice—nay, *retribution*—upon the boy. And, I would hope that you do not go so far as to make my position here impossible afterward. I wish I'd never called the matter to your attention."

"Well, you did, and there it is. Now kindly step inside and lock the door, and leave us to do what needs be done."

Despite all his noble resolve, Giles couldn't keep his roaming hand from reaching out and pressing against the small of her back as he guided her over the threshold. The warmth of her rushed through the thin gray muslin. Her scent ghosted past his nostrils. Why couldn't he identify that flower? Had that stifled moan just come from his own throat?

His hand jerked back as if he'd touched live coals, and he cleared his voice. "Remember," he said, "I will call you to me in the morning before you resume your duties with the boy."

Tessa nodded, and he waited until he heard the rasp of the bolt being thrown before sprinting off toward the staircase.

He'd just started down the stairs when Foster met him coming up from the first-floor landing. The valet wore a haggard look. Giles didn't need to ask him if he'd found the boy; failure was written all over Foster's face. Clinging to hope, Giles asked nonetheless.

"No luck, I take it," he said.

The valet wagged his head, leaning on the banister. "I've searched his usual hiding places on the first floor and below stairs, but he isn't in any of them. I've alerted the others."

"You didn't tell them—?"

"No, no, of course not!" the valet assured him. "We wouldn't have a servant on the place if I did. Trust me to have some semblance of intelligence. Besides, I scarce believe it myself!"

"Yes, well, you overheard I'm sure, so I shan't go into it again. We have to find the boy and see he doesn't escape again. The little blighter is dangerous. Considering what he's done to me, no one in residence is exempt from danger, and meanwhile, Miss LaPrelle thinks I am a beast who brutalizes children. God only knows what lies he's told her."

"Begging your pardon, sir, but don't you think you need to make her aware now?"

"Once I know exactly what we're facing, yes," Giles said.

The valet clicked his tongue and wagged his head. "You're afraid she'll leave the Abbey," he said.

"Let us just say I would not like her to do so for no reason, and we'll leave it at that, shall we?"

"If you're forming a *tendre* for the gel, I'd imagine keeping her safe from harm would be your first priority, sir."

Giles heaved a sigh and raked his hair back roughly. Foster meant well, but this was not the time for moralizing. "Not now, Foster." He slapped his forehead. "Zeus! I forgot to lock the studio. I wouldn't put it past the little bastard to savage 'The Bride of Time'! Go 'round to the stables and ask Able and Andy to search the grounds . . . just in case. I'll join you directly."

Turning back the way he'd come, Giles scaled the staircase toward the upper regions, taking the steps two at a stride.

Tessa listened at the door until Giles's footfalls grew distant along the corridor. She would stay put, indeed. She was not about to go prowling about the darkened halls of Longhollow Abbey in search of an obstreperous child. Giles Longworth could have that pleasure. If she had any sense, she'd leave the Abbey straightaway. It was plain Longworth did not share her attraction; she was merely a convenience to keep the boy out of his way. Yes, she should leave. She should run and keep on running, but she couldn't. The fates had brought her here. There must be a reason.

Wracking her brain, she tried to pinpoint the exact moment she'd crossed over from her time to his. She'd been running eastward, trying to get out of the city, and she'd traveled some distance when the cobblestones underfoot softened to a dirt lane tufted with grass down the center. Tall clumps of grass, bracken and gorse hemmed it. Could she have stumbled upon a lay line in the fog? Folks claimed there were such corridors cross-hatching the land between London and the Cornish coast. It was said that they threaded through the region, linking churches named St. Michael's like beads on a string. It was also said that the churches were built on the invisible lines deliberately, and named for the Warrior Angel of God to ward off the supernatural phenomena associated with lay lines, not the least of which was that they were avenues leading back and forth in time. Tessa had never credited anything but the existence of lay lines themselves as more than superstition . . . until now.

She had passed several churches on the way. Were any of them St. Michael's? Tessa couldn't remember. All she recalled was their spires and square bell towers shrouded in the fog. Lay lines? Everyone knew they existed, but to credit them with such as this! Could the superstitions be true? What other explanation could there be? There was no use to puzzle over it. She was here and that was that. The whys and wherefores were the mystery of the Fates.

Tessa took a nightdress from the chiffonier, lifted the candle branch and went into the dressing room. Since she wasn't privileged to have the services of a lady's maid, Dorcas had selected frocks that were easily donned and didn't require a corset that laced in back. She was grateful for that, wriggling out of the gown, and equally grateful that the nightdress of butter-soft lawn slipped over her head just as easily. It was very finely made, hand-stitched, and sheer. Tessa had never seen anything so delicate, much less felt the like against her skin. She'd known nothing but homespun, and on occasion muslin.

Sitting at the vanity, she took the three tortoiseshell hairpins from her Gibson coiffure and set them on the vanity top in a neat row. A shake of her head and the long curtain of mahogany hair the pins had tethered fell about her shoulders in a cascade of silken waves to her buttocks. There was a brush on the vanity with silver *repoussé* roses on the back and handle, and she took it up and began brushing her hair. There was a matching comb, and a pink glass hair receiver also; she laughed at the latter. She had no need of hairpieces to feed into it at the end of the day through the little hole in the silver lid. Her hair was voluminous enough without such.

She pulled the length of it in front over her shoulder, and began brushing from the scalp to the ends; long, rhythmic strokes. How soothing it was with such a fine brush. A soft moan escaped her, and she shut her eyes, basking in the sheer pleasure of the task. When they fluttered open again, she froze in place, her shuddering stare riveted to the mirror, where another image glared back at her.

Tessa vaulted to her feet. "Master Monty!" she breathed. "What are you doing here?" She snatched her wrapper, which was draped over the chair, and shrugged it on. "Do you know what time it is, young man? The whole house is in an uproar looking for you."

"You told Uncle," the boy said.

"I had no choice," Tessa returned. "You gave me none."

"You are not afraid of me," the boy said, marveling.

"No, Master Monty, I am not."

"You should be, you know, and you will be. Uncle is."

"Your uncle does not impress me as someone who frightens easily, Master Monty." The boy giggled, and the sound ran her through like a javelin. She added steadily, "You haven't told me what you are doing here. These are my rooms. You do not belong here."

The boy shrugged. It seemed his favorite mannerism. "None of the rooms are 'your rooms,'" the boy snapped. "Now you know that!" Giggling again, he darted past Tessa, flipping the vanity chair over in her path, and ran through the rooms to the sitting room door, where he threw open the bolt and burst out into the corridor.

Slowed for righting the toppled chair, Tessa entered the hallway in time to see the boy skip over the landing, fly down the stairs and disappear in the shadows of the second-floor east wing corridor below. In close pursuit, she rushed down the stairs . . . and ran right into the arms of Giles Longworth, approaching from the opposite direction. The impact of her soft flesh against his hard-muscled body caught the breath in her throat. Her breasts flattened against his chest became hard, traitorous things, her nipples tightened to turgid buds pressed up against him through the thin gown and wrapper. His posture clenched upon contact. His hands were holding her to lend support, for they had impacted with force enough to knock the breath from her body; at least that's what it seemed at first. Why didn't he let her go? She was steady enough now.

Reluctantly, she met his gaze and gasped in spite of herself. It was like facing a dog whose tail was wagging while its teeth were bared. His embrace was warm and inviting, arousing feelings hitherto unknown to her— frightening, delicious feelings deep inside that pulsed through her like liquid fire—but that look in his eyes was deadly, smoldering with rage. She didn't know which to believe, much less trust, and a strangled sound escaped her throat as he shook her gently.

"What are you doing down here like that?" he snapped. "I thought I told you to stay put!"

"And what, be savaged in my own rooms?" she defended, wrenching free of his grip. "I *was* 'put,' sir!

That little devil was in my apartments. I might have caught him if I hadn't collided with you just now."

"Did he harm you?" he pleaded.

"No! He's a *child*, Mr. Longworth," Tessa reminded him. "A disgruntled child. You make him out a fiend. He's hardly that."

Longworth's eyes flashed about the darkened corridor. "Which way did he go?" he demanded.

"That way," Tessa said, pointing toward the east wing chambers. "He threw a chair in my path or he never would have gotten out of my rooms."

Just then, Foster came shuffling along the corridor, out of breath. "Able is searching the grounds," he panted. "If the boy is out there, he'll find him."

"He was in Miss LaPrelle's rooms," Giles said. "Didn't you search them first?"

"Why, no, sir, I thought you—"

"Never mind now," Giles interrupted. "The damage is done." He gestured toward the shadowy east wing. "He went that way. I'll fetch him. You wait by the landing. He cannot escape us from there without passing the stairs. Be ready, and be quick . . . but be careful, Foster." He turned to Tessa, his gaze sliding the length of her. Only then did she realize how transparent her nightrail was. It was only a brief glance, but his hooded eyes stripped her naked, and she tugged the wrapper close in a vain attempt to hide what he'd already seen. He cleared his voice. "Go back up to your rooms at once and let us handle this," he said gruffly. "This time, stay there."

For one fleeting moment, their gazes locked, onyx jousting with blue-violet; then, spinning on his heel, Longworth stalked off into the east wing shadows.

Chapter Seven

Seizing a lit candle branch from the hall table, Giles stormed through the east wing chambers like a man possessed. How could he have neglected to search Tessa's chamber first? Capital! Now he was calling her *Tessa* in his thoughts. There was no hope for it. He was smitten. How had that happened? He'd always been in total control of his emotions and his urges. Now, but for the crisis, he'd have made a complete fool of himself.

Having left the entire east wing in sixes and sevens in search of the child with no results, Giles doubled back and met Foster at the landing.

"No sign of him, sir," the valet reported.

Giles nodded. "I've searched every chamber in the east wing on this floor as best I could with one smoking candle branch in the dead of night. The clever little bugger is down there somewhere. He couldn't have gotten past you."

"Would you want me to have a look, sir?" the valet said. "He might have relaxed his guard a bit now that you've abandoned the search, and I have a lighter step."

"No need," Giles said, jiggling his chatelaine. "I've locked every room. He isn't going anywhere." He started to climb the stairs. "I can play his game as well as he can, especially since he's made me what he is. Stay here until I come back down," he charged.

"Yes, sir. What are you going to do?"

"I'm going to check on Miss LaPrelle and lock Master Monty's chamber door."

"What good will locking the boy's door do if he's not in his chamber?"

"If he does manage to escape whatever rooms he's hiding in, he won't get into his own until I have him first. Look sharp. He will be feeling the pull of the moon."

"How do you know that, sir?"

"Because *I* am!" Giles growled, thumping his chest with his fist.

It was true. The minute the moon rose, he'd felt the pull: gnawing, bestial cravings. It was as if his heart was beating to a different rhythm, as though a feral beast was living in his body. This he could control while the moon was waxing full, but when it rose again, that beast would take over doing what savagery he shuddered to wonder. So would it be with Master Monty. He had to be found before the moon rose full again.

Giles listened outside Tessa's door for a long moment. The shuffling within suggested that she was pacing. He hesitated, then rapped lightly on the azure-paned door adorned with plasterwork. The sound of her light footfalls pattering toward the door gave him a rush of relief.

"Who is it?" she asked.

"It is I, Giles Longworth," he replied. "No! Do not unlock the door," he cautioned at the rasp of the key in the lock. He waited while it scraped shut again. "I am come only to see that you are all right."

"I am," she said. "Have you found him?"

Giles hesitated. Tell her no, and she'd likely insist upon joining the search. Tell her yes, and if the boy did get loose and attempt to accost her again, he would never forgive himself were she to come to harm.

"Damn!" he muttered under his breath. "Yes . . . and no," he said, wincing at the half-truth. "We know where he is and he is confined there for the time being. Foster and I will ferret him out in the morning. You are quite safe so long as you remain in your locked apartments."

"Aren't you being a bit excessive, Mr. Longworth?" Tessa queried.

Even with the door between, her sweet voice had aroused him. All he could think of was how beautiful she was, with her satiny chestnut hair falling to her buttocks and her exquisite body barely concealed beneath the transparent nightrail. These urges, too, were part of the madness; he was certain of it. She was safe enough now, but what of tomorrow night, when the moon made a monster of him again?

"Miss LaPrelle," he said. "Needs must that you leave things of which you know nothing to those who do. Trust me to know what is 'excessive' where Master Monty is concerned, and please respect my wishes. They are imposed only to be certain you suffer no more unpleasantness."

"Don't you think it time you enlighten me, sir?"

"Yes," he quickly said, "and I will do so after you break your fast in the morning as we arranged. I shall await you in my study then. Meanwhile, I must insist that you remain in your apartments with the doors locked until Dorcas brings the water for your toilette."

"But—"

"Good night, Miss LaPrelle."

Uncomfortable wearing the traitorous Elena Longworth's castoff gowns, Tessa begged a plain black bombazine frock from the maids. The style was different from the frock she'd arrived in, reminding her of some of the portraits she'd seen at Poole House, but the drab, somber fabric hadn't changed in over a hundred years. Feeling much more comfortable attired thus, Tessa kept her appointment with Giles Longworth after breakfast in his book-lined study, which smelled of lemon polish and the musty odor peculiar to old book bindings.

He wore a haggard look, as if he hadn't slept. His hair was mussed, though attractively. The ghost of dark stubble darkened his face, and he was wearing the same shirt and buckskins he'd worn when she'd last seen him the night before. He vaulted to his feet from his chair behind the desk when she entered. For a moment, he stared.

"What the devil are you doing in one of the maid's costumes?" he demanded, his anger evident. How those black stares spoiled his handsome face. "Didn't I provide you with appropriate attire?"

"You did, sir," Tessa returned. "I do not feel comfortable in them. I am not accustomed to dressing in such finery."

"Well, I will not have you going about dressed like a scullion. It will not do."

"I do not intend to do so on a regular basis," Tessa said calmly to his bluster. "As soon as it can be arranged, I mean to go into Truro to select my own costumes."

Longworth heaved an exasperated sigh and motioned her to take a seat in the wing chair at the edge of the carpet. "Sit you down," he said. "I owe you an explanation. I will do my best to provide it, or at least as much as I know of it, though you aren't likely to believe. Please sit. I shan't begin until you do."

Tessa sank into the chair. She almost laughed. After the bizarre way she'd gotten to Longhollow Abbey, she was almost ready to believe anything. She felt a moment of fiendish pleasure wondering if she should give him a dose of his own medicine and see if he'd believe *her* secret. She sincerely doubted it, since she scarcely believed it herself.

"Is the boy found?" she asked instead.

"If you mean, is he safe and sound in his chamber, the answer is no, he is not. If you mean, do we know where he is, yes, we do, and he will be seen to, you have my word."

"That makes no sense," Tessa snapped. "None of this makes any sense."

"I am hoping to remedy that, if you will let me."

"I am waiting," Tessa said. Her frosty tone was her only defense. If she let herself, it would be easy to become captivated by the dashing man behind the desk.

"Master Monty is not a blood relation to me, and he is not a normal child. My sister married Montclair Albert Montague II, a captain in Wellington's army, who came into this family with baggage, so to speak, in the person of Master Monty. The child's mother was a wild Gypsy girl. They were married by Gypsy rite, and no other. After the child was born, the girl abandoned Montague and the child. She later died of typhus. Several years passed before my sister Ursula met Montague, and they married."

"And your sister raised the child as her own?"

He nodded. "Yes, until she . . . died," he said. "When Montague was called to active duty, Ursula and the boy came here, where we could look after her during her confinement while her husband was marching to the colors. She was pregnant, you see, with Montague's child. She died before it was born."

"How awful!"

"Yes, it was."

"How . . . did she die?"

"She fell from the balustrade on the terrace outside her bedchamber, the turret chamber next to Master Monty's on the third floor. The authorities deemed it a suicide, but I know it wasn't. She was full of hope for the future and joy over the expected birth, especially since Montague's death in battle. The night before she died, we talked at length about the coming birth, and about Master Monty. She was afraid of him."

"If not suicide . . . what, then? Surely you don't suspect foul play?"

"I do, Miss LaPrelle. I believe Master Monty to be responsible for Ursula's death."

"But that's preposterous! He's only a child! Why would he? How could he have?"

"Master Monty was jealous of the child Ursula was carrying. He became harder and harder to control. They fought constantly. Monty was always at Ursula, and the night before she died, the child bit her just as he bit me and nearly bit you."

"What has that to do with anything?" Tessa asked.

"I don't *know* that it does, but I know the boy's bite to be . . . infectious. I do not know another way to put it. That is why I was so concerned that you might have been bitten. It seems to worsen when the moon is full, and it's close to that now—tonight, to be exact."

"But how could the child have become infected?"

"Master Monty's mother was a full-blooded Gypsy. All sorts of strange occurrences are attributed to the Roma hereabouts. Tales have spread about shapeshifters and the undead. There have been cries of *revenant*, of the dead rising from their graves. Crooked headstones are all it takes to unleash all manner of superstitious twaddle. Cornish folk are a superstitious lot to begin with. It doesn't take much to give such suspicions substance with words."

"Surely you do not believe in such ridiculous superstitions?" Tessa asked, incredulous.

"No, but evidently Master Monty does. The mind is a very complex and enigmatic part of the human anatomy,

Miss LaPrelle; it can make the impossible possible for those who believe. And we all know how the full moon affects those shut up in madhouses."

"How long has this been going on?" Tessa murmured.

"Since Ursula died last spring."

"There is more that you aren't telling," Tessa knew.

"There is," Giles agreed, "but nothing you're ready to hear or I'm ready to put forth without proof. Suffice it to say that danger exists, and until we know exactly what we're facing, we must err on the side of caution."

"And . . . if your suspicions are correct, what do you plan to do with the child? You can hardly keep him here if he's a danger to all in residence."

"There are institutions, Miss LaPrelle, but it's much too early to speculate on that."

"You would shut him up in an asylum—a nine-year-old child?" Tessa was shocked.

"Certainly not!" Giles defended. "There are private sanatoriums for individuals suffering from such delusional ailments. He will be well cared for if such is necessary, and cured if it is possible. But for now, needs must that I ask you to be careful in this house no matter how preposterous you find the situation. I will, of course, keep you apprised. In the meanwhile, your duties as Master Monty's governess will be curtailed." He hesitated, clearing his voice. "If you would like to fill your idle hours and increase your income while this is sorted out, you could . . . assist me in my studio . . ."

Tessa vaulted to her feet. "I told you *no*, Mr. Longworth," she said icily. "I will not pose for that scandalous painting!"

Giles got to his feet and threw his hands up in a gesture to stay her. "Please hear me out," he said. "I do not expect you to disrobe and pose in the nude, Miss LaPrelle," he explained. "You've made your views on that quite plain. And it isn't a 'scandalous painting.' It is a work of art. Celebrated artists through the ages have painted nudes, or at the very least sketched them. It is essential in order to get the anatomy correct. All right, I know I am no Michelangelo, but unless I am allowed to pursue my craft in the manner of the masters, my talent, such as it is, will never be recognized."

Tessa was thinking the Masters never drove naked lightskirts from their doors drunk in the dead of night, at least none she'd ever heard of, though there was no denying artists were a scandalous lot. "I take a different view," she said instead.

"And I need someone to hold the hourglass," he went on, as if he hadn't heard. "I can hardly paint what isn't there, now can I?"

"Oh, I don't know," she sallied. "It seems you've done a fine job of it already."

"You saw that, then," he replied, answering his own question.

"Don't pretend you didn't want me to see it, Mr. Longworth. Do not insult my intelligence."

"Of course I wanted you to see it," he snapped. "How else were you to know I meant you no harm? I worked on your hair, and your face, though I don't have the latter quite right; that's why I've suggested that you model for me. You are perfect for The Bride."

"Where did you get that ridiculous title?" Tessa hedged.

"I can neither take the credit nor the blame for that," Giles said through a chuckle. "You will have to admonish Prinny, I'm afraid. For all that he is decadent and powerful, the Prince Regent is a very lonely man. He masks his loneliness with flamboyance, but deep down he longs for a love he cannot know. Marriage for love, marriage for necessity, marriage for the Crown—one the people would accept—the Devil take the desires of his heart. 'Somewhere in time there is a bride for me,' he once said to me, 'a bride for good and all,' and the title was born."

"I don't quite understand," Tessa said. "The man has everything he could ever hope to want."

"Ahhh, yes, everything but what he *really* wants," Giles corrected. "It was to be his fantasy, a woman waiting somewhere in time just for him—George, the man, not George the would-be king, under the dictates of the Crown and everything it brought to bear upon him— hence the symbolism of the hourglass. She couldn't have the face of anyone he knew, neither wife nor any of his mistresses, of course, that would cause all manner of *on-dits* to circulate 'round Town. It was dangerous enough doing the likeness for his watchcase."

"Who posed for that?" Tessa asked.

"The woman herself, under the most secretive circumstances, and it was a miniature, easily concealed in an object he alone has custody of, an object no other was privileged to touch. A canvas of the dimensions of my current project would cause a scandal. So! His secret love had to be an image created from his imagination. He designed her—someone he could gaze upon and fantasize about in lonely moments—the composite of wife, mistresses, and lovers—the best of all worlds— rolled into one; his dream bride. It is my job to paint her, and I added Longhollow Abbey in the background to further deter suspicion. He didn't even dare commission such a painting officially, else it get out, though we have a verbal agreement—if the bride is right, of course. You *are* The Bride of Time, Prinny's fantasy in the flesh."

Tessa hesitated. It sounded more sad than scandalous the way he'd put it, but still, from the look in his eyes, she was certain it wouldn't take long for one thing to lead to another. This man had a volatile nature. Something almost bestial lived beneath his skin, something that would be hard for her to control if it ever got loose, considering her curiosity, and yes, her undeniable attraction to the man formed long before she set foot inside his mysterious manor in the patchwork hills of Cornwall.

"All right," he said on a sigh. "You needn't give me your answer now. All I ask is that you think upon it. All proprieties will be met and strictly enforced."

What that meant exactly in an understaffed household, where doors were bolted against a nine-year-old child, Tessa had no idea. He seemed sincere, but still, the half-naked image of the doxy fleeing the Abbey with Longworth on her heels wouldn't leave her.

"Only my hair and face?" she said at last.

It was as if dawn had broken over his gloomy countenance. This was a side of Giles Longworth Tessa had never seen. It brought a lump to her throat.

"And your hands," he added excitedly, "holding the hourglass. Miss LaPrelle, I know I've made a bad first impression, but I assure you I am a gentleman . . . when I'm not dealing with thieves who take advantage of my generosity and good nature. I will never ask you to do anything that will make you uncomfortable."

The mention of thieves struck a sour chord inside her, reminding her of what she'd left behind. Considering his abhorrence of thieves, what would he think of her if he knew he harbored a suspected thief under his very roof? That thought kept pricking at her like a stubborn splinter, but other thoughts now beat those nagging worries back.

"And . . . who will you have pose for the body?" she queried. Whatever possessed her to say that? It just seemed to come rolling off her tongue of its own volition; she bit it for spite. Hot blood pumping through her veins rushed to her temples. She could only imagine the color of her cheeks; they were on fire.

"I will hire someone for that," he replied with a dismissive wave of his hand.

Why did that stab her with a crippling pang of jealousy? Did her posture really clench? She hoped not, but she feared so. It scarcely signified. He seemed so bowled over by her response, she doubted he'd noticed.

"Does that mean you will?" he asked.

That soft, warm expression hadn't left him; the unguarded, boyish look that charmed her so had banished the hard, brooding countenance she remembered from the self-portrait in the little London gallery.

He had strolled nearer, so near she could feel his body heat. When had that happened? How tall he was, standing over her. How dark his eyes were gazing down. They were lit with an inner fire that sent shivers racing along her spine. His scent, all musk and maleness, drifted toward her. It wasn't laced with brandy now. She breathed him in deeply. What a delight he was for the senses, crackling with virility, with feral volatility at cross purposes with the innocence and boyish charm.

She took a faltering step back. "If that is all you require," she said hesitantly. "It might be arranged. At least I would be earning my keep—"

"I cannot thank you enough!" he said, taking another step toward her. Backing up another pace brought her flush against the wing chair she'd vacated. When he reached out to steady her, the world tilted on its axis. His hands were warm, their moistness penetrating the bombazine fabric of her sleeve. Her heart leapt, and he slid the hand down until it had captured hers and lifted it to his lips. "I promise you, you shan't regret it," he murmured.

That those lips lingered longer than necessary on the back of her hand didn't matter. She didn't pull her hand away—couldn't—*wouldn't* pull it away, even though her mind and traitorous body demanded separation.

When he finally released her trembling fingers, she broke eye contact and sidestepped his closeness. "O-only during the d-daylight hours," she stammered.

"Of course," he agreed. "I'll work with the body model in the evenings, when light is not as critical as it is while painting facial features and the shadow play that gives dimension to hair. We shall commence after nuncheon. The successful completion of this project is crucial to the economic upkeep of Longhollow Abbey. Oh, we are hardly rolled up here, you understand, just swimming a bit at low tide because of the unfortunate affairs that have cost me my local clientele. The Prince Regent's patronage for future commissions would set things to rights. I shall send Able after a body model straightaway. You needn't have worried in that regard. You wouldn't have been quite right for that in any case. Prinny prefers his women . . . a little more voluptuous. So, you see? There it is: an amiable solution all around. I cannot thank you enough, Miss LaPrelle." He turned her toward the door. The pressure of his splayed palm against the small of her back seared her like a firebrand. Did he have to move it like that—like a caress? Lud! It *was* a caress.

"Until after nuncheon," she intoned, escaping through the study door the minute he lifted the latch.

Chapter Eight

Giles made a visible trip to the stables after his interview with Tessa, just in case she might be observing him from the window in her suite, which faced that direction. That was a stroke of genius. He had no intention of hiring a body model, especially not now, with the full moon looming and Master Monty still not confined to his chamber for the test. Not to mention his own reaction to the full moon when it rose tonight.

No. The pretext was believable, at least believable enough to prompt a reaction from Miss Tessa LaPrelle, which was his intent. The look on her face when he criticized her exquisite body nearly cost him the ruse. It was all he could do to suppress a laugh. She was absolutely livid at the comment. How she could possibly believe her image wouldn't give rise to a eunuch's manhood was beyond him. Women! He'd gotten the answer he'd been seeking. The adorable little hypocrite wouldn't dream of posing naked for him, yet she'd turned pea-green with envy at the thought of another doing so. That gave him hope that at least the attraction was mutual. It fed fuel to his own fantasy that somewhere in his own imperfect time, he'd found a woman without guile who

might even be tempted to love him for who he was—
sans the wolf that lurked just beneath the surface, ready
to devour his newfound hope with one ravenous chomp.
For that brief space of stolen time, like an oasis in the
midst of a parching desert, it was a pleasant fiction.

Giles only half-expected Tessa to come to the solarium after nuncheon, and he was visibly surprised when
she did just that. It was an awkward moment when he
turned to find her standing on the threshold. The gentle rap of her knuckles on the seasoned wood of the
open doorframe spun him toward her.

He strode at once to her side and, taking her elbow,
led her into the room. He'd repositioned the easel facing the lounge and gestured toward the canvas. "I would
like you to recline on the chaise thus," he said, pointing
to the model's position with the handle of the paintbrush he'd been using when she entered, ". . . with your
hands just so."

He handed her the hourglass and motioned her toward
the lounge. Once she had reclined there, he gestured toward her hair. "May I?" he asked, waiting. Handing her
the hourglass was a stroke of genius. He would give anything to feel that wonderful hair again, to let its soft, fragrant silkiness spill down over his hands. She would have
to give the glass back to him, if she were to take the hair
down herself. Since his fingers were at the ready, poised
over the tortoiseshell hairpins, he hoped she would allow him. For a moment she hesitated, then nodded per-
mission, and he withdrew the pins. "Thank you," he
said, slipping the hairpins into the pocket of his buckskins. "I just need to arrange it as I have it begun on the
canvas. It won't take but a minute."

Giles suppressed the breathless moan that lived in his
throat as her hair slid through his fingers. How he
longed to scoop up handfuls of that luxurious hair, press

it to his nose, and inhale the sweet scent of wildflowers drifting toward him from it until it filled his senses. He wished he'd tossed back a couple gulps of brandy earlier. That might have blunted the edges of desire that gripped him now. Something else was gripping him as well, the pull of the un-risen moon. If it was so strong before dark, what would it be when the sun set and the full moon rose over the patchwork hills, over the Abbey? When would he lose consciousness? When would the nightmare begin? He had no way of knowing, for he had no memory of any of that from the last time the moon rose full in the indigo vault above and drove him naked onto the moor. He couldn't think about that now. Moonrise was still a few hours off, and he was facing The Bride of Time in all her radiant glory. Tessa LaPrelle had bewitched him. She had cast a glamour over him, arriving in the dead of night out of nowhere with naught but the clothes on her back; a lady of mystery. It suddenly occurred to him that she knew all about him, but he knew virtually nothing about her.

Having lingered over her hair as long as he dared, Giles captured her hands and positioned them in the proper attitude holding the hourglass. "Perfect," he said, backing away for a panoramic view. "Place your left hand under the glass . . . That's it; now caress it with your right, but let the sand show . . . There! That's it. Hold that if you will. Tell me when you tire, and you can rest. I shouldn't want to wear you out on your first day."

Tessa didn't answer, and he frowned. There was a wide-eyed look of apprehension on her face, reminding him of a roe deer he'd caught in his sites, staring down the barrel of his musket last season. He frowned. He'd hoped he'd put her at ease; that was why he'd left the solarium door open. Evidently he'd failed. The look on that face was pure fright. It simply wouldn't do.

"We must do something about that startled expression," he said. "I cannot paint that. Perhaps a little pleasant conversation, while I work. It occurred to me earlier that you have my tale entire, whilst I know next to naught about you. Where do you come from . . . where is your home?"

Again she hesitated. *Zeus!* Perhaps drawing her out wasn't a good idea after all. She'd suddenly lost what color she had, her posture had clenched, and the frightened doe look in those magnificent eyes had intensified tenfold.

"London," she said.

Giles stopped painting mid-stroke. "Oh, yes. Still, my advertisement for a governess reached *London?*" he said, incredulous. "I don't recall sending word—"

"You didn't," she interrupted him. "I . . . I'm here in Cornwall on holiday. I heard of the position . . . from one of the locals."

Giles resumed painting. "Were you employed as a governess in Town? Things happened so quickly, I didn't even ask to see references. Not that it matters any longer."

"I . . . I lived with my aunt until she passed," Tessa said.

"Why Cornwall . . . so far from Town?"

"I wanted to get away from Town for a bit before going into service. I always wanted to see Cornwall. I fell in love with a painting I saw once of the Cornish moors . . . in a little gallery near Threadneedle Street. I wanted to see it for myself."

"No suitors . . . no beaux?"

"No," she said.

That was a relief. Giles had feared she might be spoken for. She seemed a bit more relaxed, but there was still something in those limpid eyes that trembled with fear. His artist's eye was infallible when seeking out the complexities of his subjects. That talent gave his portraits much greater depth. He was seeing something now that puzzled him. The girl was an enigma. It was almost as if she'd built a wall around herself, like the stacked stone walls hemming the lanes that sidled through the hills. She was a challenge, and he'd always met a challenge head-on.

"Are you tiring?" he asked. "You look a bit... strained."

"Not really."

He glanced toward the glass roof. "We won't have much more light," he observed. "Twilight comes early in Cornwall this time of the year. If you are willing, I would like to take advantage of it."

Tessa nodded. "That would be fine," she murmured.

"Good! We always count ourselves fortunate when we have the sun. It so often rains hereabouts, or the dampness conjures belching fogs that have us lighting lamps and candles by mid-afternoon. Sometimes, what the old folk call *flaws*—fearsome gales—set in and linger for days on end, bringing horizontal rain and flesh-tearing winds that would flay the hairs right off your head. During those cyclones, the candles are lit night and day, and the hearths as well, winter and summer. Artificial light is quite different when one is painting. The values are all wrong."

"Then it must be difficult when you continue on into the night," Tessa said.

"Oh, it is," Giles assured her. "But when the muse beckons, one must heed the call."

"Have you found a body model yet?" she queried.

Taken aback, Giles stared. He'd forgotten about that, and almost laughed at the look of her then. The apples of her cheeks had suddenly taken on color. It was clear that curiosity had gotten the better of her. She bit her lip, and color rushed there.

"That's it!" he cried. "Wet your lips. I want to place the highlights."

She was hesitant at first. Her lips parted once, twice, but still she hesitated.

"Like this," he said, tracing the shape of his own lips with the tip of his tongue.

After a moment, Tessa licked her lips as he had done, and a soft sound escaped his throat watching the pink tip of her tongue glide over the Cupid's bow. Something shifted in his loins. The vision of her reclining there, her long chestnut mane rippling over her shoulders, her dewy lips still parted, had aroused him from across the room. What would those lips feel like beneath his own? He could almost taste their honey sweetness. Would that tongue, those lips, betray him as Elena's had done? Dared he chance finding out? Could he suffer betrayal again?

Never had a woman—any woman, lady or whore, for he'd known his share of both—affected him the way this mysterious female did. Was she angel or witch? It didn't matter. He was captivated. His manhood was tight against the seam of his buckskins, his heart hammering in his breast. Cold sweat trickled down his spine, riding gooseflesh that had raised the fine hairs from the nape of his neck to the small of his back. His loins were on fire.

"I'm sorry," he said. "What did you ask me just now?"

Tessa gasped. All at once her focus shifted and her eyes flashed. From her position, she had seen what he could not from his vantage at the easel, until his head snapped toward the doorway and Master Monty standing barefoot in his soiled and wrinkled nightshirt.

Muttering a string of oaths, Giles slapped the palette down on the table, scattering paint and brushes, and made a lunge for the boy. But Monty darted straight for Tessa, who had vaulted to her feet, and threw his arms around her waist, clinging fast with pinching fingers.

"I . . . I'm sorry. I've been bad, miss," the boy hiccupped, tears streaming down his face. "I got locked in a room . . . It was dark, and . . . and . . ."

Tessa was just about to embrace the boy when Giles wrenched him away from her none too gently and propelled him toward the door, his white-knuckled fist wound tightly in the back of Monty's nightshirt, out of the way of the boy's deadly teeth.

"Mr. Longworth, please. He's only a child!" Tessa shrilled.

Exasperated, Giles flashed her a look that backed her up a pace. "That is all we'll do today, Miss LaPrelle," he said, steering the boy through the door. "The light is soon gone in any case. You are dismissed."

"You're a clever little bastard, aren't you, Master Monty?" Giles seethed, hauling the boy along the corridor toward a narrow staircase at the far end of the hall. "Trying to seduce the new governess, eh? You won't send this one screaming from the Abbey. She's onto you. You've met your match, finally."

"I . . . I don't know what you mean," the boy whined. "Where are you taking me?"

"Where you can cause no harm until morning,"

"I'm hungry," the child wailed.

"You will be fed."

"I'm cold!"

"My hand will warm your bottom if you do not stop that infernal whining!" Giles warned him.

"It will be dark soon," the child reminded him. Cold chills of a different breed riddled Giles's spine with gooseflesh now, at the sound of that rasping adult voice coming from his nine-year-old ward. He needed no reminders. The sun was going down. Soon the moon would rise. The

full moon. There was much to do before then, and not a
moment to lose.

They were nearly halfway up the back staircase when
Foster came running at a pace Giles would not have believed unless he'd seen it himself.

"You've found him!" the valet cried, sagging against
the wall. "He broke the lock on the tapestry suite bedchamber door. You will not believe the devastation in
those rooms, sir!"

"Never mind," Giles replied. "I'm taking him to the
old tower room. Go down and fetch a tray of food for
our little savage here, and bring bed linens for the cot up
there. No candles. The moon will give off enough light
for his shenanigans."

The words were scarcely out when Foster was set in
motion. Giles would see that the child's creature com-
forts were met. The boy would have a full belly and
clean bedding, but no candles to set the Abbey afire.
The tower chamber was used for storage, and much of
what was stored there was flammable. The boy could
scream the house down and he wouldn't be heard from
there, and if his suspicions were correct and young
Monty was a lycanthrope or fancied he was, he could
not escape and threaten the rest in residence. The tower
room door could be barred from the outside.

Foster soon returned with the food and bedding. The
child made no protest when they locked him inside, but
dosed them with his maddening half-smile until they'd
shut the door, slid the bolt, and dropped the heavy
wooden bar in place.

"Are you certain he cannot get out of there?" Foster
asked, as they made their way back down to the second
floor.

"No, he cannot. That bar is six inches thick. I only
wish there was a way to observe him inside once the
moon rises."

"Not I," said Foster. "And as to the rest, you haven't seen the tapestry suite, sir."

They had nearly reached those rooms, and the valet swept his arm wide. "Be my guest," he said, standing aside to let Giles enter.

Giles burst through the door, taking note of the broken latch. The sitting room looked as if a Cornish flaw had ripped through and kept on churning until it had destroyed the bedchamber and dressing room as well. The rugs were rumpled in a heap on the floor. Everything breakable was broken, from serviceable pitcher and basin to priceless antiques. Drawers had been emptied, draperies half torn down, candle stands and fire screens toppled, and the bed curtains had been consigned to the dead hearth.

"Zeus afire!" Giles seethed, surveying the devastation.

"I shall have the maids put this to rights straightaway, sir."

"No, you will not!" Giles said. "After our little test, I will fetch Master Monty, and *he* will set this to rights. I shall stand over him until he does. Is that clear?"

"Y-yes, sir."

Giles raked his hair back roughly. "After nearly biting Tes—Miss LaPrelle, the little demon burst into the studio before and threw his arms around her—tried to seduce her into believing *he* was the injured party here, the poor, innocent, abused waif, with *this*"—he gestured—"in his wake! And she bought it—went all maternal up there!" He stared at the staved-in lock on the door. Not far from it lay the tool that had won the child his freedom: one of the pokers from the hearth. Squatting down, he snatched the iron and examined it and the shattered French porcelain figurine beside it. As he did, something stabbed him in the thigh, and he vaulted to his feet. Plunging his hand into his pocket, he produced the cause: one of Tessa's hairpins.

Giles threw the poker down and darted into the hall. "*She* needs to see this," he snarled. "By God, she will!"

"Sir, may I remind you, the light is failing!" Foster called after him.

"I know, I can see!" Giles snapped. "Meet me in the studio in half an hour!"

Chapter Nine

Tessa had locked her chamber door and opted for a tray in her room. She had no desire to be abroad in the house with a madman on the loose. That is what she assessed Giles Longworth to be after the scene she'd just witnessed in his studio. Her new employer was a multi-faceted individual, there was no question. She'd seen him range from drunken lunatic, to gentleman, to soft-eyed little boy and back to madness again, this time without the inducement of alcohol.

For a moment in the studio when she saw his softer side, she'd hoped that, in her inexperience with the complexities of human nature, she might have exaggerated his other moods, hoped that there *was* hope. But there was none. Drunk or sober, the man was as volatile as blasting powder, as mercurial as the weather and as dangerous as any monster she could conjure from her imagination. She'd certainly never seen the like of Giles Longworth.

She flushed, recalling how he'd tried to draw her out with personal questions. It was only fair, she supposed, since he'd unburdened himself to her, and would have been acceptable if she hadn't had to stretch the truth to answer him. It was later that her poise really became challenged, when he'd caught the pose he was looking for. His whole face lit up as if the sun burst over his head. His childlike awe had melted her. She was so captivated by him in that guise she neglected to press the question of the body model. But that was Master Monty's fault more than hers. For it was then that Monty appeared, and the boyish Giles Longworth died before her very eyes, usurped by the madman.

And then there was something else, something in his glazed eyes that flagged danger. It was as if he stripped her naked, for he was devouring her then. She hadn't imagined it. Her heart leapt as she recalled that look, recalled how his eyelids slid half-closed, hooding the dilated pupils beneath. Those dark, heavy-lashed eyes were pure seduction.

When the knock came at the door, she nearly jumped out of her skin. It wasn't a light rap but more closely resembled cannon fire, and she rushed to answer, but hesitated, her ear against the door, until the knock came again, vibrating the wood and extracting a stifled cry from her parched throat.

"W-who is it . . . ?" she stammered, knowing full well who it was.

"It is I, Longworth!" came the gruff reply. "Open the door!"

Instead, she backed away.

"Miss LaPrelle, open the door!" he repeated. "I have your hairpins. . . ."

Tessa's hand flew to her hair. She'd totally forgotten the tortoiseshell pins, her only possession of value. A squeak escaped her as she rushed to the door and unlocked it. That squeak became a full-blown gasp at sight of Giles Longworth looming over her, brandishing the pins in the gloom of twilight that clung about the corridor, a dark scowl deepening the shadows collecting about his deep-set eyes. The muscles were ticking along his broad jaw, and his handsome lips had formed that hard, crimped line again, just as they had done when first they'd met. His scent ghosted past her nostrils, musky and male, but there wasn't a trace of brandy now.

When she reached for the hairpins, his free hand clamped around her wrist, and he pulled her over the threshold. "Come with me, I want to show you something," he charged through clenched teeth, meanwhile rushing her toward the landing.

Tessa dug in her heels. "Give me my hairpins and let me go!" she cried. "I do believe you are mad, sir!"

"Very nearly, and it's about to get worse. Let go of that newel post! I'm not going to harm you. I want to show you something—something you need to see."

Tessa let go of the post and let him lead her down to the second floor. It was strange. She had no true fear of him, though he projected a bestial aura that was not just his outward appearance, which could only be described as disheveled. No, it went far deeper than that. It was in his pulse, in his very breath puffing through those flared nostrils that brought a fire-breathing dragon to mind. Still, she humored him, watching the nuances of expression as his face showed checked rage and courted shadows from the candles in their sconces which they passed.

When they neared an open door on the south side of the east wing hall, Giles took up a candle branch from the hall table and lit Tessa's way inside. She gasped, and gasped again.

"Oh, this is nothing," he said, leading her into the bedroom. "The bed curtains stuffed in the hearth were a nice touch, don't you think? And that broken piss pot there was not empty when it broke upon the rug. No, no, we aren't finished. There's more . . ."

He led her into the dressing room, where the cheval glass stood wounded with hundreds of spiderweb cracks radiating from a central dent, the andiron that had caused the damage at her feet. Tessa turned away from her distorted reflection in the broken mirror only to collide with an upturned hip bath. Giles shot his free hand out to steady her, but she quickly righted herself and moved past him back into the bedroom.

"What happened here?" she murmured, her eyes snapping in all directions toward one desecration after another.

"Master Monty 'happened' here, Miss LaPrelle," Giles said. "And then the little blighter broke in on us and threw his arms around you, playing the poor abused innocent!"

"Good God, you make it seem like a lover's embrace," she retorted in disgust.

Giles slapped the candle branch down on the chiffonier and faced her, arms akimbo. "It was nothing less than a seduction," he said hotly. "He was playing upon your sympathies, winning you over to his side, getting close enough to sink those vicious fangs of his into you. But you are right. It wasn't a lover's embrace. *This* is a lover's embrace . . ."

Seizing her in strong arms, he wrenched her against the bruising bulk of the arousal challenging the seam of his buckskins. Burying one hand in her hair, he took her lips with a hungry mouth, his warm tongue gliding between her teeth, tasting her deeply, while his other hand roamed the length of her spine, followed her curves and came to rest upon the swell of her breast, his thumb grazing her hardened nipple through the crisp bombazine fabric. For a moment, Tessa was too stunned to react, though her traitorous lips responded to his sultry kiss. It wasn't until his hand cupped her breast and fondled her nipple, igniting her loins with drenching fire, that she reared back and struck him a shattering blow with the flat of her hand against his startled face.

"How dare you, sir!" she shrilled. "Stand out of my way!"

Giles stared down at her, his eyes misted from the blow, and wiped the corner of his mouth. "Forgive me," he said, sketching a stiff bow. "I did not mean for that to happen. I mean . . . it wasn't why I brought you here. I wanted you to see exactly what you're dealing with in Master Monty for yourself. Now that you have, I trust you will be more careful in your dealings with the boy. No ordinary nine-year-old could have inflicted this devastation. Good God, woman, look around you. He has destroyed every beautiful thing in these apartments out of sheer viciousness. There was no need. He wanted out. The poker freed him. He broke the lock with it. That was all that was wanted to free him." He gestured toward the entire circumstance. "All this was naught but fiendish vindictiveness."

Tessa marched past him into the sitting room without a word. Heaving a sigh, Giles took up the candle branch again and followed her.

"Miss LaPrelle," he said softly. She turned toward him from the threshold. "I give you my word as a gentleman . . . what happened here just now will not occur again. I am a cad and a jackanapes, and any other foul name you wish to confer upon me, and I have no excuse except that your beauty overwhelmed me. But I swear to you, it will not happen again."

"No. Indeed it will not, Mr. Longworth," Tessa got out, her voice atremble, "because if you ever put your hands upon my person again—in any manner, sir—I will set the authorities on you!"

"Understood."

"What have you done with that child?" she demanded. "Have you killed him, then?"

Giles popped a humorless laugh through a smile that did not reach his eyes. "He is confined to an upper room, where there are no priceless antiques for him to destroy. He has a full tray of food and a clean night-shirt, and will meditate upon his misdeeds this day. It is more than he deserves. And to answer your next question: no, I did not lay a hand on the boy. His punishment will be cleaning these rooms until one might eat off the floor, and at that he's getting off cheap."

Tessa stared long and hard at Giles. He hadn't moved until now. When he started toward her, she was set to run. "Keep your distance, sir!" she warned.

Giles's posture collapsed. "Here," he said, extending the candle branch toward her. "I only meant to give you this. I do not need candles to light my way in this house, but you are unfamiliar with the Abbey. It's growing dark. I wouldn't want you to do yourself a mischief. It would be wise to return to your rooms and stay in them until morning."

"Might I remind you, I *was* in them, sir, content to stay there, until you dragged me out."

His fingers grazed hers as Tessa took the candles, igniting that inner fire again. Radiant thrills spread through her whole body, like the ripples a pebble makes breaking the surface of a stream. Unprepared, she nearly lost her grip upon the candle branch.

"Is it too heavy for you?" he asked, his hand at the ready to assist.

"Hardly!" she snapped at him. "I didn't have a good grip, but I do have one now, I assure you. Good night, Mr. Longworth."

Giles roughly walked his fingers through his mussed hair. Darkness pressed up against the mullioned panes in the absence of the candles. The moon had not yet risen, but the pull was already unbearable. Her parting words had reached his ears as if through an echo chamber. He'd sent her off just in time.

He jammed his hands into his pockets and groaned as his fingers closed around Tessa's tortoiseshell hairpins. In the heat of the argument, he'd forgotten all about returning them. It was too late now. There wasn't a moment to lose. Besides, the pins would give him another excuse to approach her in the morning. With that decided, he staggered through the open door, made his way to the landing, and started to climb.

What had ever possessed him to seize her like that? He couldn't have made a more serious blunder. It was way too early for such intimacy. He was fortunate that she didn't run screaming from the house. Tessa LaPrelle was no doxy. She had all the bearing of a lady regardless of her class, and he'd treated her like a common bird of paradise. Perhaps it was the pull of the full moon and the all-consuming urge to ravage that came with it which caused him to give in to lust. She had responded, however. He'd felt her breath catch and her heart quicken. He'd felt her melt against him as he tasted her honey sweetness. He'd felt the feeble pressure of her warm hand over his heart, a cursory rebuff, for those fingers had fisted in his shirt front, drawing him closer as their throaty moans mingled. It was shortly after that she'd struck him. Was it in anger at him for taking such liberties, or anger at herself for allowing them? There was no time to analyze it now. The moon was rising. He didn't need to see it to be certain. He could *feel* it.

Foster was waiting for him in the solarium. He had removed the easel and cleared the table of most of the artist materials. A tray of food rested there now, mutton cutlets, mayonnaise of chicken, and a bit of leftover larded pheasant, with some sauced vegetables too disguised to identify.

"I was just about to come after you, sir. The moon is

rising," the valet said. He gestured toward the vacant spot where the easel had rested. "I took the liberty," he explained.

"What's this?" Giles asked, nonplussed.

"The painting," said the valet. "I . . . I know how important it is to you. I've put it in the suite next door . . . to keep it safe from harm. If you are correct—I say *if*, because I cannot bring myself to believe it—we do not know how the transformation will affect you in confinement. I feared it might come to harm here, sir."

"What would I do without you, Foster?" Giles said fondly. "I never would have thought of it. I've too much on my mind, old friend. Thank you."

"Is there anything else, sir?"

"No," Giles said. "I want you to go back to the servants' quarters and stay there. Lock the green baize door, and do not open it no matter what you hear."

"Oh, I won't hear anything once I lock you in up here, sir. No one will. You are too far removed from the rest way up here in the attic, as is Master Monty."

"You are assuming that the hasp will hold on that door," Giles said. "There is no bar on it, like there is on the attic storage room where Master Monty is confined. You are assuming the iron hasp and padlock will hold whatever beast is in me, Foster. I can only pray you are right."

Tessa slammed the door to her apartments and locked it. Her heart was pounding. Her body, still on fire from Longworth's embrace, had betrayed her. She had responded. She had clung to him like one of his Penzance roundheels! She felt her cheeks; they were scorching hot. That could be excused away as anger, but still, she must look a fright.

Streaking through the sitting room and bedroom, she flopped down on the vanity chair and observed her face.

It was worse than she'd imagined. Her cheeks were hopelessly blotched with crimson patches. Her eyes were swollen, and tear tracks marred her face. When had she cried? Tears of anger shed returning to her room? It must have been. She was too upset to remember.

Reaching with both hands, she threaded them through her hair. Her hair! Her pins! Where were her hairpins? What with the heat of the dustup, he'd forgotten to give them to her, and she'd forgotten to ask for them. She could hardly go about with her hair bouncing against her buttocks. She had to have the hairpins back—now, before he lost them. She had no other means of dressing her hair, and she couldn't appear in the servant's hall to break her fast come morning with her hair flowing loose like a schoolgirl's. More than likely Longworth had returned to his studio. She would catch him before he retired—but not like this, not with tear tracks and great crimson splotches spoiling her face. She wouldn't give him the satisfaction of knowing he'd made her cry.

Tessa poured some of the water Dorcas had left for her evening toilette from the pitcher on the dry sink into the basin beneath, and splashed it on her face. It took several applications to fade the redness, but her puffy eyelids remained. There was nothing for it. Hopefully, if she stayed within the shadows he wouldn't notice. She would not enter the studio, after all. This business would be conducted from the hallway. With that decided she took up the candle branch, unlocked the door, and hurried toward the landing.

She had just started up the third-floor staircase when she heard what sounded like howling funneling down the attic stairwell. It couldn't be. There were no animals in the Abbey.

"Mr. Longworth?" she called hesitantly.

The sound came again, only now it more closely

resembled a growl, then a definite feral whine and what sounded like wood splintering. It was a blood-chilling racket that backed Tessa down the attic stairs, the hem of her black bombazine frock sweeping the newel post.

Blowing out the candles, she set the silver branch down on the third-floor hall table and flattened herself against the wall in a shadowy alcove, scarcely breathing. There wasn't time for her to reach her suite without being seen. After a moment, a deafening cracking noise ruptured the eerie silence that had fallen. Then the guttural growls began again, and she glimpsed the bulk of a large, dark shadow streaking down the attic stairs, over the landing to disappear in the lower regions of the Abbey. Her heart fairly stopped when the dreadful howl came again, and then the sound of breaking glass.

Tessa stood rooted to the spot until the snarling, whining, howling sounds grew distant before venturing out of the alcove. Had some wild beast gotten into the house? And where was Giles Longworth? Why hadn't he answered her? Forcing one foot in front of the other, she snatched the candle branch from the table, to use as a weapon if needs must, and inched her way toward the staircase, fearful of finding him savaged in his solarium studio.

The door was hanging half off its hinges, hasp and padlock still attached. Why had it been locked from the outside? Is this where Master Monty had been confined? Was that him she'd heard howling like an animal? Was it the boy she'd seen streaking down the stairs? How could a mere child have done such as this? She almost rescinded that thought the minute it crossed her mind. After seeing the devastation in the chamber below, she was almost ready to believe anything of the rage-bitten child. *But this!*

"M-Mr. Longworth . . . ?" she called again, approaching the gaping studio door. Still no answer came, and she stepped over the threshold and gasped at the sight that met her eyes.

Toppled furniture was scattered about the room. The Aubusson carpet was rolled back in a heap, peppered with food and the tray it had rested on, broken china, some of the paint and brushes she'd seen there earlier, and what looked like Longworth's clothes strewn about. The easel was gone. Tessa was relieved at that. By the look of the rest of the room, the canvas would likely have been destroyed.

Moonlight was streaming in through the glass ceiling, and Tessa made her way to the window. How clear the sky was, and studded with stars. There wasn't a cloud in sight. The full moon had lit the patchwork hills as bright as day. She gazed down longingly, remembering how in love with those hills and moors she had been gazing at Longworth's painting in the little gallery. How she'd longed to feel the grass of those little hills and valleys beneath her feet. She was in the midst of them now, but there was no euphoria, only darkness and fear. What had become of her beautiful fantasy?

All at once, motion caught her eye. Something was streaking across the courtyard. It looked like an animal, a huge dog, or a *wolf*. How could that be? There were no wolves in England. Tessa blinked to clear her vision, certain she'd imagined it, but no. The animal was large and shaggy and black, its fur silvered in the moonlight. At the edge of the thicket that hemmed the lawn, the animal stopped, one foreleg suspended, threw back its head, and let loose a howl that all but curdled her blood before it disappeared in the darkness.

A chill traversed Tessa's spine as she stood for a long moment staring after the animal, hoping for another glimpse, trying to make sense of what she'd just seen. After her discussion about the boy with Longworth, had her imagination conjured a werewolf out there? Had she just seen Master Monty running away from the second devastation he'd left in his wake that day? Glancing about, she had to admit the condition of the solarium was almost identical to the child's handiwork which Longworth had shown her below earlier.

Shuddering again, she turned and tripped over Longworth's boots and breeches among the debris. Something fell out of the pocket of the buckskins. A shaft of moonlight illuminated the object: one of Tessa's tortoiseshell hairpins. Her breath caught as she bent to retrieve it, remembering why she'd come up to the studio in the first place.

Foraging through the pocket it had fallen from, she unearthed the other two pins. She hesitated. If she took them back, he would know she'd been here—seen this. But did that really matter? They were hers, weren't they? She had to decide. He could return at any moment and find her going through his pockets. He might think her a thief, and she knew well his view of thieves.

Deciding, she dropped the buckskins as if they were live coals and, clutching the precious hairpins, scurried back to her chamber and locked the door.

Chapter Ten

Giles climbed back inside by way of the oriel window he'd crashed through when he left the Abbey, just as the streamers of first light brightened the horizon. There was blood on his shoulder and thigh where he'd cut them on the broken glass coming and going, and upon his face, from whatever he'd savaged in wolf form. Praying it was an animal, he streaked naked through the deserted halls to his chamber, where he washed and made himself presentable before climbing up to the studio to see what his transformation had wrought. Foster had reached the solarium before him, and was already addressing the mess he'd found there.

"Leave that," Giles said. "We need to check on the boy."

"Yes, sir," Foster said. "I haven't heard a peep out of him up there."

"Eh . . . about the oriel window downstairs . . ."

"It's already being seen to," Foster said. "Able is going to board it up until we can replace the glass."

"On top of things as usual, Foster, thank you, but we still have two more nights to get through. Have Able clear the glass away, and leave it until the moon begins to wane."

"Yes, sir. Did you hurt yourself, sir?"

"A few scratches; they'll mend."

"I'll draw your bath after breakfast, sir. Those 'scratches' will need proper tending if they are to heal. If I know you, they're a lot more serious than you make out. I've seen the window and the blood upon it. You risk infection."

One of his wounds was deep, on the inside of his thigh, where one of the shards pierced him climbing back in. Foster was right, of course, but there wasn't time. All too soon the day would be gone, and the nightmare would begin again. Much had to be done before that, far too much to indulge in the luxury of a bath.

"That will just have to wait. The Gypsies are camped out on the south moor again. I want to consult with them about the boy."

"How do you know they've come back, sir?"

"I saw them last night. I don't remember much, but I do remember that."

"You went all the way to the south moor, sir?" the valet asked, incredulous.

Giles nodded. "You'd be surprised how far a fleet-footed wolf can run."

Giles said no more as they made their way to the storage chamber. To his relief, the door was still on its hinges, and the bar was still in place. Monty was evidently better at this than he was, but then the boy had had a bit more practice.

Giles lifted the bar and unlocked the door. Much of the furniture, trunks and crates stored inside were piled so high they blocked some of the windows, and it took a moment for his eyes to become accustomed to the darkness. A fractured shaft of daylight streaming in through the uppermost window, which was clear of stored items, showed them Monty sleeping soundly on his cot; not a hair was out of place. The food they'd left him had been eaten, the dishes neatly stacked on their tray. The room was just as they'd left it, no evidence of disarray. Giles and the valet stared at each other, nonplussed. Below, the child yawned and stretched like a cherub.

"All right, Master Monty," Giles said, throwing back the quilt. He turned to Foster. "Take him below and have Lottie tend him. Stay with him. Once he's dressed and has eaten, take him to the tapestry suite and stay with him while he repairs the damage he's done."

The boy's Gypsy eyes flashed, and a scowl replaced the smug half-smile.

"Oh yes, Master Monty," Giles said. "You will undo what you have done to the tapestry suite. You will remain there until every last fragment of broken porcelain has been swept up, and every stick of furniture put back where it belongs, if it takes a sennight, so you'd best eat a hearty breakfast, young man. You've got your chore set out for you." A nod to Foster saw them in motion, and Giles went back to the solarium to begin his own restoration.

He decided to leave the easel and the painting where Foster had put them until all danger of them coming to harm was past. Thoughts of the painting darkened his spirits suddenly. Had he ruined all chances of ever having Tessa model again? Had he finally found the perfect model for the project, the perfect woman all the way around, only to muck it up by behaving like a rake? Could he charm his way back into her good graces? More pointedly, did he have the right to pursue her, considering the curse the strange Gypsy child had conferred upon him?

Thinking these thoughts, he almost didn't see Dorcas approaching him from the servant's quarters when he stepped off the first-floor landing.

"Sir, I was just comin' ta find ya," she said, sketching a curtsy. "Miss LaPrelle has expressed a wish to go in search of suitable togs, since her duties with Master Monty have been postponed, so ta speak."

Relief flooded Giles from head to toe. At least she wasn't going to run screaming from the house. He might have his second chance at that. He would be more careful this time.

"You may tell her that would be quite acceptable, Dorcas," he said.

"I'll have ta have Able take her," Dorcas said. "I was goin' ta go with her when she went, but what with the house in sixes and sevens this mornin', I can't dare leave it all to the maids ta set ta rights."

"That will be fine, Dorcas," Giles said. "I shall be out of the house for a while this afternoon myself. I was just on my way to inform Able to ready Valiant for me after nuncheon. I won't be needing him after that, so you can employ him here as needs must; Andy as well."

"Very good, sir," Dorcas said, but he called her back when she turned to go.

"No, wait!" he said. "I've a better idea. My errand takes me to the south moor. 'Tisn't Truro, but the shops in Bodmin should suffice for her needs. I'll have Able ready the small chaise instead and I'll drive. That way, he can remain here . . . just in case you have need of him. Tell Miss LaPrelle to meet me in the drive after nuncheon. Oh, and Dorcas, if the 'sixes and sevens' you are referring to have anything to do with the tapestry suite, you are not to trouble. Master Monty will clean up the mess he's made. You aren't to aid him in any way. Foster will see to it. Is that clear?"

"Y-yes, sir," Dorcas said. Sketching another curtsy, she waddled off.

Giles went on his way. Stepping out in the sunshine, he could scarcely believe the horror of the night before. Passing the gaping oriel window, he sighed. Had he really turned into a wolf and crashed headlong through that window? The nagging pain on the inside of his thigh responded to that. Crashing through the oriel window was the last thing he remembered until sighting the Gypsy camp.

Able was shoeing a horse when he entered the stables. The man froze in position when Giles entered. "Forgive me if I don't let go," the stabler said. "It's took me half-an-hour to get his leg between my knees . . ."

"Carry on, Able," Giles said. "When you're done there, I'd like you to ready the two-seater chaise. I've an errand to run after nuncheon, and I'd like to take Miss LaPrelle with me to fetch her togs from Bodmin, since it's close by."

"That old chaise?" Able asked, frozen in place. "Why don't ya let me drive ya 'round in the brougham?"

"Because I need you here, Able," Giles said. "Master Monty's acting up again. I've left him in Foster's care, but if he can't handle the boy, I'd like to know there's someone about who can put the fear of God into him."

"You've got Rigby and Evers," the stabler reminded him.

"Rigby will have no truck with the boy, and Evers is little more than a boy himself. I need you here in my absence from now on . . . until the matter is settled."

"As you say, sir," Able replied, wagging his head as he drove another nail into the horse's hoof. "She's in pretty fair shape—the chaise, that is. I've oiled the leather straps her chassis is hung on regular. But that don't mean nothin' in all the damp hereabouts. The calash hood is creased in spots, though I've oiled that, too. I wouldn't take her at a gallop, sir. I wouldn't take her at all, come ta that, but if you take her slow, she'll get ya ta Bodmin and back."

"Good! Bring it 'round to the drive in an hour, and,

Able, if you have to have dealings with Master Monty, keep clear of his teeth. He's a biter."

Tessa sat ramrod-rigid beside Giles in the chaise, trying to keep a respectable distance from him, but that was impossible in the small two-seater. No matter how she strained to distance herself from him, her thigh still leaned against his. He'd noticed that she had her hairpins back. The minute she'd stepped into the drive, his eyes were riveted to her coiffure. He either didn't want to discuss it, or didn't realize she must have gone into the solarium to get them. She certainly wasn't going to bring the matter up. Instead, she tried to enjoy the beautiful patchwork hills they drove through, and they were approaching the south moor before Giles broke the silence she was trying to preserve.

"I'm glad you agreed to grant me this outing," he said. "My business in the south shan't take long. Afterward, I'll drive you into Bodmin to make your selections."

"What exactly is your business in the south?" Tessa asked, certain he'd contrived the whole outing just to force her company.

"It's regarding your charge, actually," he said. "Which is another reason I thought you should accompany me."

"Master Monty?"

He nodded. "He is half-Gypsy, after all, and Gypsies have camped down here on the south moor. They do so every year. I consulted the old healer among them before they decamped last spring when this nightmare began. I was hoping they could shed some light upon the boy's malady. She said if things . . . worsened, to come again. It is real, Miss LaPrelle, and I must confess I do not know how to deal with it, short of shutting him up in a sanatorium somewhere. I'm hoping they can give me an alternative."

"You really believe he is a . . . a werewolf, don't you?"

"I *know* he is, but I also know you won't believe me unless you see for yourself firsthand. I'm hoping this little jaunt today will at the very least give you pause for thought."

"I've always been possessed of an open mind, Mr. Longworth, but—"

"Since we are to be working closely together, mightn't we dispense with some of the formalities? We are hardly *haute ton* here. Could you see your way clear to calling me 'Giles'? As things are, by time you get 'Mr. Longworth' out, you could have come to serious harm."

Tessa thought on it. It was a shameless ploy to promote familiarity, but he did have a point. *Mr. Longworth* was a mouthful to say in an emergency. Still, she made him wait a long time before replying.

"As you wish," she finally said.

"Ah, good!" he cried. "And may I call you 'Tessa'?"

"Yes, but that doesn't mean—"

"Oh, I know," he interrupted. "It's just a convenience . . . and a precaution."

As her employer, he had the right to call her however he pleased. Still, she knew what was behind the intimacy, and deep down, despite his scandalous behavior last night, she wanted it. She'd wanted it since the little gallery off Threadneedle Street. That he evidently wanted it, too, was more than she could have hoped for. But still she was wary. It was too soon, and his behavior was too mercurial to be trusted; she was in awe of it.

Mercifully, he said no more until they reached the Gypsy camp and reined the horse in alongside a low bracken hedge. Climbing out of the chaise, he reached to lift her down beside him, but she declined.

"No," she said. "I shall wait with the carriage."

Seizing her about the waist, he lifted her down without ceremony, wrenching a cry from her throat. "No," he said. "You need to hear this more than I do. Please . . . indulge me, Tessa. It could well mean your life."

He could have told her to jump into the sea from the Cornish cliffs, speaking her name in that sultry, deep-throated burr, and she would have jumped gladly. It riveted her to the very soul and made her giddy enough to accept his arm in support as they approached the Gypsy campfire. An old woman seated there gave a nod and swept her arm wide, inviting them to sit upon logs set about in lieu of chairs.

"Steady on, Tessa," Giles whispered. "I know these. They camp here on my land every fall and winter. They've come early this year. That means the winter will be a hard one, with many flaws, and maybe even snow, which occurs in Cornwall only every twenty years of so, give or take a year. Moraiva is a Roma princess. She is very wise."

Others milling about the camp kept their distance. They almost seemed afraid to Tessa. Not so Moraiva, whose hard-eyed smile was trained upon her. In spite of all misgivings, Tessa took a seat and offered a token smile. It wouldn't do to disrespect a Gypsy; with all that had befallen her, the last thing Tessa wanted was to court a Gypsy curse.

"You are come early this year," Giles said to the woman.

Moraiva nodded, stirring the fire with a long thin branch. "Soon the snow flies everywhere else," she said. "A winter like no other. We are come in hopes Cornwall will be spared, for there will be heavy snows and bitter winds to drive them in places that have never seen the like."

"We can take that forecast as gospel, Tessa," Giles said, though he never took his eyes from the old Gypsy's wrinkled face. "You are welcome, as always," he told the

Gypsy. "And I am glad you've come early. There is a matter that wants your expertise . . . if you will give it."

The woman nodded. "You speak of the child," she said. "Naught has changed?"

"No," he responded, "except that it's gotten worse since it began last spring."

The woman cast a long hard look in Tessa's direction, which made her more than a little uncomfortable. "This is your lady?" she asked Giles.

"I am the boy's governess." Tessa spoke up before he could reply.

"Which is why I wanted her to hear much of this conversation," Giles concluded.

The Gypsy *hmm*ed, giving the fire a stir that sent sparks shooting into the air. "You will need to be especially careful in the handling of the child, miss."

"He flaunts his . . . situation, Moraiva," Giles said. "He pretended to bite her—"

"But he did not?" the Gypsy interrupted, her eyes frightening to view, so frightening that Tessa gasped.

"No, he did not, and Tessa here is not convinced of the problem."

The woman smiled a smile that did not reach her eyes, and held out her hand to Tessa, palm upward. "Give me your hand," she said.

Tessa hesitated, then finally did as the woman bade her.

Moraiva squinted toward Tessa's palm for some time before her raisin-like eyes flashed up with a look that drove Tessa's eyes away. "How have you come here?" she asked.

"I . . . I came from London . . . seeking employment," Tessa said. *Lud! Could she tell? Did she know somehow she'd traveled through time? Would she tell Giles?* Cold chills crippled her while imagining it. If she was revealed, he would surely demand an explanation, and she had no idea what she would tell him.

The woman stared long and hard at her, seeming to digest her answer. "When you return to London, you must stay in the good and perfect time that has lent you to us here."

Even Giles was nonplussed at that, but Tessa knew exactly what the woman was trying to say. She was not safe here in his time, but she wasn't safe there in her own time, either. Nodding, she lowered her eyes demurely.

"You know the child's background," Giles said to the Gypsy. "I believe he caused my sister's death, Moraiva, and ironically I have become his guardian! I thought of sending him to boarding school, but I couldn't inflict that upon the innocents there. I thought of a sanatorium, but I cannot bring myself to—"

"You are a good man, Giles Longworth," the Gypsy said. "But sometimes . . . we cannot be good if we would do right. You are not alone. There are many like the boy among the Roma—those who were cursed before birth, those who have been infected through the parent host, or by way of an outside force through no fault of their own . . . and those who are pure evil. I see hope in your eyes, but there is none. There is no cure for a lycanthrope—a *werewolf*. I will come tomorrow, when much of the danger is past, but enough remains for me to see where he falls in the spectrum. Meanwhile, there are . . . precautions."

"Any help you can give, Moraiva," Giles pleaded.

The woman nodded. "He will need to be confined the night before the moon is full, when it is at its fullest, and the night after," she said. "All danger will not be past until the shape of the waning is visible. During this time, arm yourself with silver. It will repel the beast . . . and it will also kill the beast if it comes in contact with a vital organ, whether it be a pistol ball, a silver sword, or a silver candlestick or other bludgeoning instrument. That is the only way to kill a werewolf."

"That is not an option," Giles said. "He is a child."

"No, not for the child, but there will be . . . others," the Gypsy warned. Holding her finger up, she got to her feet stiffly. "One moment," she said, shuffling off to the nearest wagon.

"Where is she going?" Tessa wondered.

"Into her wagon," Giles replied. "We must wait. I've learned to indulge her."

"I think you are all quite mad!" Tessa said.

"If only it were all that simple," Giles murmured. "Well, at least now you know others believe in lycanthropy besides myself, and the child."

"That does not make it so."

"I cannot believe, after what you saw in the tapestry suite, that you could possibly doubt."

"What I saw in the tapestry suite, sir, were the ravages of a disgruntled child in dire need of attention and affection entombed in a house where there is neither. What could you expect? You locked him away for the night. What sort of damage did he do after he continued his rampage in your studio?" Giles stiffened as if he'd been struck, and Tessa bit her lip. She hadn't meant to bring that up.

"You went back to the studio?" Giles queried warily.

Tessa nodded, touching her Gibson coiffure. "You neglected to give me back my hairpins," she said. "I could hardly disgrace myself by breaking my fast with the others in the servants' hall with my hair undressed."

"Ah!" he said, as if a light had just gone on in his brain. "I thought I was losing my mind altogether. I couldn't remember returning them to you, and then when I saw you with your hair done up . . . well, I'm glad you have them back. Much to do over three tortoiseshell hairpins, I dare say."

Anger pumped hot blood to Tessa's cheeks and temples. The man was insufferable! So why was his closeness such torture? Why was her heart beating so erratically, why was his musky male scent paralyzing her senses to all other aromas, and why was she longing to feel the fire of those hungry, sensuous lips upon her own again?

"These three hairpins are the sum total of my valuables, sir," she snapped at him. "They are the only means I have of making myself presentable. And I am tenacious enough of my possessions to brave your sanctum sanctorum to have them back, since you chose to hold them hostage."

"I forgot to give them back to you," Giles defended. "I hardly held them hostage."

"Well, as you say, I have them back. I must have arrived right after Master Monty revenged himself up there, because I saw him fleeing afterward . . . at least I believe I saw him. I saw . . . something running down the stairs, and then heard glass breaking. The oriel window, I presume?"

"Whether you choose to believe it or not, there is a serious problem with Master Monty," Giles said. Why wouldn't he meet her eyes? "That is why I've brought you with me today. Whether he is or he isn't, the boy believes himself to be a werewolf. That belief alone could put you to the hazard. I want you to realize the dangers this position entails before we go further."

Tessa hesitated, remembering the animal she'd seen streaking over the grounds in the moonlight. Could it have been coincidence, or could it be possible for one who believed himself to be a werewolf to actually take on the characteristics of one? She shook her head in denial. Preposterous!

"What?" Giles asked.

"N-nothing," she responded. She wouldn't tell him she'd seen that creature in the moonlight. "Look . . . she's coming back," she said of the Gypsy, who shuffled toward them, something shiny in her hands.

"Wear this," she said, handing Tessa a silver chain. A round amulet hung from it in the shape of an inverted circled star. "The silver pentacle," the Gypsy explained. "It is the sign of the wolf."

"It is heathen!" Tessa cried, shunning the offering.

"And what is the wolf?" Moraiva responded. "Young woman, that amulet will repel the beast that rises when the moon is full. It will protect you."

"If she is uncomfortable wearing the necklace, we shan't force it upon her," Giles said.

The Gypsy cast him a meaningful glower. Tessa only wished she could read the message in it, for it silenced Giles Longworth as if he'd been stricken dumb.

"I would speak with you privately," Moraiva said to him.

Tessa rose from the log. "I'll wait with the chaise," she suggested, turning to go.

Moraiva held her back with a wrinkled hand on her arm. "Wear the necklace," she said, crimping Tessa's fingers around it. "If you do not believe in the pentacle, it cannot harm you to wear it. The wolf believes. It holds a power greater than his, and he will fear it. Thus it will protect you. Do not be foolish. Take it! Your God will not think less of you for arming yourself against His enemies."

Tessa nodded, mesmerized by the glow in the old woman's raisin-like eyes, and took the necklace. There was something almost desperate in the old Gypsy's gaze that riveted her with chills, watching the woman turn back to Giles beside the campfire.

Giles kept a close eye upon Tessa, who made her way to the chaise. She had taken the necklace, but would she wear it?

Moraiva *hmm*ed. "You have been bitten," she said. "Let me see."

Giles hesitated. Tessa hadn't seemed to connect his bite to the situation thus far. Not that it would matter in view of her obvious disbelief, but still, he turned away when he presented his hand for the Gypsy to view.

Moraiva *hmm*ed again. "The bite is deep and scarcely healed. When did it occur?"

"Last month."

"When the moon was full?"

Giles nodded.

"Then it was *you* I saw on these moors last night," Moraiva said. "I feared as much. I saw you in the wolf. I saw your spirit in it."

"Tell me I harmed none of yours," Giles pleaded.

"No, none," the Gypsy assured him. "You looked me in the eyes and ran off. I was positive, when you reacted to the pentacle I gave your lady just now. If you were untouched, you would have insisted that she wear it, but you did not, did you? Instead, you tried to dissuade her. Why? Because you long to hold her in your arms, and when the moon rises, it will repel you. You realize, Giles Longworth, that your lady is in as much danger from you as she is from the child, if not more, because whether she knows it yet or not, she longs for your love, and she will let you near enough to corrupt her. She must wear the pentacle."

"And what of me, Moraiva . . . is there no hope for me?"

"You know there is no cure."

"There has to be *something*. There has to be."

"Shhhh, lower your voice. You have captured her attention." The Gypsy seemed to go into a trance then, swaying to some unheard rhythm, her eyes half-shuttered. "If whomever you savage survives your bite they will become as you are—a werewolf, just as you have become one from the bite of the child. It need not be deep. It wants only for the skin to be broken and blood to flow to pass on the curse.

"She is safe with you all month until the moon waxes full and wanes again as I have described. Three days at the least each month she will be in mortal danger from you. You must separate yourself from her before the moon rises—before the moon madness takes you, for madness kills what it loves, and you will hunt her because she is your soul mate, young son."

"How do you know that?" Giles asked, placing a coin in her palm.

The old Gypsy gave a patronizing smile. "I know much," she said. "And I have seen more with these old eyes than you will see in a lifetime. Go! She grows restless, and time is short if you will have her back to the Abbey before nightfall. And there is one more thing. Beware! Your offspring may be tainted just as you are. There is no way to predict these things. The condition varies with each subject. You have only to look to your ward for the truth of what I speak. If you do naught else, persuade her to wear the pentacle. Her life may well depend upon it."

Chapter Eleven

Tessa was dying to ask Giles what the Gypsy had said to him. He'd been silent since he climbed back into the chaise. It was none of her business, she told herself, but it really was. She was certain of it. Still, she held her peace. There was a look about him then that wouldn't bear probing, as dark as a thunderhead, as volatile as a lightning strike. His was the face in the portrait now, brooding and tormented; the face that had somehow drawn her to this place.

The shops on Fore Street provided Tessa with the selections she wanted. Giles insisted upon advancing her stipend for her purchases. Tessa dug in her heels at that prospect until she saw the difference in the currency of the time. There was no question that she had to give in. She would have caused a brouhaha if she had presented turn-of-the-century money instead of 1811 blunt in the shops of Bodmin, even though it would have bought her twice as much.

Since she had no lady's maid, she chose frocks without back lacing. These were high-waisted, made of fine muslin—serviceable stuff in shades of gray, befitting her situation—with tucked and pleated inserts to fill in the low décolleté fashions of the day, which she doubted she would ever become accustomed to no matter how she tried. But that was a mild shock compared to what she suffered learning that bloomers were unheard of in 1811 England, while stockings were mandatory!

The sun was beginning to descend by the time she'd made her selections, which included a Sunday-best frock of robin's-egg-blue muslin, an indigo pelerine with a matching bonnet, and a winter pelisse of gunmetal gray with *soutache* braid trim.

Giles was becoming increasingly agitated. He insisted she exchange the drab bombazine she was wearing for one of her new gray frocks, then after a brief respite at a local inn, they started back toward the moor and Longhollow Abbey beyond.

The day had been unseasonably warm, and as the sun slid lower, a thick ground-creeping mist began to carpet the moor, slowing progress, for the horse was reluctant to trot over ground it could not see, though Giles drove the animal relentlessly. Tessa seized his arm as they struck a rut. The muscles beneath her fingers were rock-hard, their corded strength like steel bands through the chocolate-brown superfine sleeve of his frock coat. His thigh pressed up against her was no less rigid, and the heat and constant pressure of it leaning against her in the little chaise sent shock waves of drenching fire coursing through her body—waves that had nothing to do with the fright she felt as the chaise bounced along over the narrow invisible path through the heath. The combined emotions were so overwhelming she feared she'd swoon.

"You'd best hang on," he said, quickening the horse's pace. "Needs must that we reach the Abbey by sundown, and the evening fog will bring it sooner."

"Because of the child?" Tessa asked him. "What use if you kill us both in the attempt?"

"I've traveled these hills and moors since I was a

child," Giles assured her. "I know every inch of these paths. This one is difficult, I'll own, but it is the quickest way back to the Abbey, a shortcut through the hills."

"The horse doesn't seem to share your confidence," Tessa observed, gripping the side of the calash hood.

Giles snapped his whip over the animal's head. "He will feed off mine," he replied.

Tessa wished she could feed off his confidence as well, but she was terrified. Tooling over the patchwork hills through the gathering mist at a gallop, with twilight approaching, was an eerie experience at best. What upset her more was his obsession over reaching the Abbey before dark. Whatever she believed, he believed them to be in real danger from werewolves.

"Please," she pleaded. "I beg you, slow the pace. Whatever did that Gypsy tell you to set you off like this? You know as well as I do that they are a superstitious lot. You cannot take them so seriously."

He didn't reply. The light was failing and the mist thickening. Eerily, there wasn't a cloud in the sky. Tessa had heard tales of the strange Cornish mists that seemed to pick and choose the dips and valleys they visited as if they had a will of their own. She'd heard how they would settle stubbornly in one valley and miss the next one right alongside altogether. This was one of those strange phenomena happening now, for off in the distance, the land was clearly visible. The carriage groaned like a living being as Giles drove the horse mercilessly, and the chassis had begun to bounce and sway on its frame, the leather strap suspension clearly taxed to its limit.

When the chaise struck a rut neither of them could see, the leather snapped on the passenger side, and the listing chassis plunged ground-ward, digging a trench in the spongy heath, pitching Tessa out into a thick clump of bracken and wild rosemary that hemmed in the path, half-hidden in the mist. Tessa's scream in concert with the horse's frantic whinnies, and Giles's shouts of command, filled the misty twilight with a racket that sent meadowlarks and lapwings soaring skyward from their safe havens in clouds of flapping, squawking frenzy. Dazed, Tessa tried to right herself, but the awkward position she found herself in prevented her. Giles was beside her in seconds, gathering her into his arms.

"Are you all right?" he pleaded. "You took a nasty spill, Tessa."

She nodded against his shoulder. "I . . . I think so," she murmured.

He crushed her closer still. "This is all my fault," he said. "Able warned me not to take the chaise at a gallop. It hasn't been used in a while, and the leather straps that hold the chassis in place have all dried out, despite a regular soaping and oiling. I'm afraid the Cornish damp wreaks havoc upon anything disuse will corrupt."

"Can it be mended?"

"Able will have to be the judge of that," Giles said. "Not in time to see us home, however. Damn and blast! I shall have to unhitch the horse and we shall have to ride the rest of the way."

He ran his hand along her shoulder, along her arm and legs. "Are you sure nothing is broken?" he asked.

"Reasonably sure," she said. "Nothing hurts overmuch. I expect the only thing wounded is my pride." That was a certainty. With her frock hiked up in an indecent aspect—one, she noted, he made no move to correct—and the rest of her attire in dishabille, she had never been so embarrassed. Especially since his dark, hooded eyes were ravishing her through their sweeping lashes, and his lips parted, drawing nearer.

She could excuse her boldness as being a product of her dazed state, but it wasn't. She wanted him to kiss her, wanted to feel the smooth, constant pressure of those skilled lips opening hers beneath. When it happened, she leaned into the kiss, moaning as his tongue slid into her mouth, tasting her deeply.

When did he lie down beside her in the pine-scented brush? When did he fold her so close to his dynamic body? He was aroused, the thick bulk of his erection leaning heavily against her naked thigh through his soft buckskin breeches. But for her stockings, Tessa was naked to the waist, her bulky bloomers not having fit beneath the slender style of the frock meant to be worn without underpinnings. She stiffened as his hand reached beneath her skirt and came to rest upon the V of soft hair curling between her thighs.

Stabbing waves of silken fire surged through her to the very core as his fingers probed deeper, and she uttered a stifled cry. "Shhh," he crooned. "I think you have bewitched me, Tessa."

Unbuttoning his breeches, he lifted his sex free and drove her hand against his naked hardness. It leapt at her touch, and her breath caught in her throat as he crimped her traitorous fingers around his hot, veined shaft.

Tessa had never been touched intimately before, and she had never seen, much less fondled, a man's organ. The closest she'd come to such as that was viewing what the masters had made of it in their paintings and sculptures, but *this!* This was gargantuan by comparison to the artists' renderings. It was warm and alive, as hard as marble, yet as soft as hot silk to the touch.

"I will not ask anything of you that you would not freely give," he murmured in her ear.

"Giles, please . . ." Tessa murmured. Her heart was saying one thing and her head another.

"I know it's too soon, Tessa," he whispered in her ear. "But . . . I fear if I wait to make love to you it will be too late . . ."

"W-why?" she breathed. "Too late for what?"

"I do not know," he said, between light kisses upon her face, her throat, and décolleté, for he had spread her bodice open, baring her breasts to the mist swirling around them like ghostly spectators. "You came to me out of the night like an answer to a prayer. From the first moment I clapped eyes upon you . . . I knew it would come to this. I have this gnawing fear that, like the wraith you appeared, you will disappear. It is almost as if you are a figment of my imagination . . . that you aren't really . . . real, like Prinny's Bride of Time is something his imagination conjured. And yet, here you are . . . the perfect bride . . . alive and warm in my arms . . ."

Now would be the perfect time to tell him why he felt that fear. Now would be the moment to confide that somehow she had folded a pleat in time to come to him. Was that not just as preposterous as his imagining his ward to be a werewolf? But she couldn't bring herself to speak it, not when his hands were roaming over her body, not while his lips were tugging at her nipples and his sex was growing harder and more urgent under her caress. Instead, she buried her free hand in his hair and held his head against her breast.

Suddenly, the light was gone, and darkness fell around them. Overhead the stars played hide-and-seek among fleeting clouds. Giles's heartbeat began to quicken. Tessa could feel it hammering against her. His grip became stronger, his arms crushing her against him, his lips smothering, so anxious his teeth pierced her lower lip, and she tasted the salty, metallic flavor of blood. An unstoppable frenzy seemed to take him, and the moan in his throat more closely resembled a snarl.

Tessa gripped his shoulders, searching deep in his eyes. They seemed to glow with an inner fire in the ghostly, undulating darkness. "Giles, the light," she cried. "It's grown dark. You wanted to be back at the Abbey by now!"

For a moment, he stared as if he'd just awakened from a trance. Shaking himself like a dog, he staggered to his feet, raking his hair back roughly as if he meant to keep his brain from bursting through his skull, and reeled off in the direction of the broken chaise.

Tessa scrambled to her feet and ordered her frock. She had stopped him just short of consummation, and her loins ached for him to fill her, ached for his life to live inside her. Her throbbing sex, drenched in the fire of unstoppable passion, was moist and swollen with un-climaxed desire. Across the way, Giles struggled to free the horse from the chaise. He was like a man possessed, grappling with the animal's bridle, his free hand fisted in the horse's mane.

"Where is the pentacle?" he thundered, gravel-voiced.

"I-in my pocket," she cried.

"Put it on," he charged as the horse reared, pawing the misty air, its terrified shrieks amplified by the fog. "Do it now, Tessa!"

Gripped with icy chills from head to toe, Tessa groped the slit in the side of her frock and withdrew the little pocket suspended on its ribbon. Foraging inside, she produced the pentacle. Her hands were trembling so, she dropped it while trying to work the clasp and fell to her knees, groping the ground beneath the mist.

Overhead, the scudding clouds passed over the moon. It shone down eerily, and in its light, Tessa caught a glimmer from the silver amulet hanging from one of the bracken clumps. Snatching it, she fastened it about her neck and started toward Giles, still struggling with the horse. It almost seemed as if the animal was trying to trample him. It seemed terrified.

"No! Stay where you are!" Giles thundered.

Tessa froze in her tracks. Giles had gotten the horse

unhitched, but he couldn't control it. It seemed to have gone wild, rearing back on its hind legs and bucking, menacing Giles with its high-flying forefeet churning the mist. Though she wasn't a skilled rider, Tessa had been around horses all her life and she had never seen the like. She was just about to call out a warning, when she screamed instead as the horse wheeled about, struck Giles with its rump and drove him to the ground, then galloped off crazily into the mist.

Tessa started to run to him, but his thunderous voice stopped her in her tracks. "No!" he shouted. "Don't come!" On his feet now, he began tearing at his clothing like a man possessed. "Run, Tessa! Follow the path the way we were traveling over the hills . . . You're almost there . . ."

"Giles . . . you're scaring me now! What is it?"

"Just do as I say! In the name of God, Tessa, don't look back—run!"

The desperate tone of his voice set her in motion. It was happening again. She was running over the patchwork hills through the mist, her heart hammering in her breast. He was gaining on her, his heavy footfalls vibrating on the spongy heath through the soles of her morocco leather slippers. She couldn't see his face, though his hot breath puffing against the back of her neck riveted her with gooseflesh. Raw fright forced her to surge ahead, until a clump of bracken snagged the hem of her bombazine frock. It scarcely caused a hitch in her stride. She hoisted up her skirt and kept running—running for her life.

It was her nightmare! But this time, the nightmare was real, and she knew who was chasing her; but it wasn't Giles, it was a huge snarling wolf snapping at her heels, and she called upon every ounce of her strength to stay one step ahead of it as it closed in upon her.

All at once the steeple of a little church poked through

the misty darkness ahead, and she streaked into the deep
shadows that clung about the little graveyard alongside
it. On she ran until her legs failed her and she fell in a
heap of black bombazine by the side of the road. The
last thing she saw before consciousness failed her was a
horse-drawn bus tooling along the lane, of the type she
was seeking when she fled London. Neither Giles, nor
the chaise, nor the wolf were anywhere in sight.

Chapter Twelve

"Don't touch her! She could be contagious . . . or in her cups," someone shrilled—a woman, Tessa thought, coming around. She was so dreadfully dizzy she could scarcely see the press of unfamiliar bodies as individuals gaped at her. They appeared more like a connected wreath surrounding her, a dark presence looming over her, where she lay dazed in the lane.

"Where could she have come from in that scandalous rig?" another wondered. "I've never seen the like, 'ave you, Mable?"

"Only in the picture galleries," said the other. "They wore such frocks a hundred years ago. The fashion come from old Boney's wife in France. The women back then wore next ta no tops on their dresses at all and no bloomers underneath 'em."

"All right, you lot, back in the bus!" a man's gruff voice charged. He leaned over Tessa, a portly man in bus driver's livery, her woolen shawl in his hand. "This yours, miss?" he queried. "I found it a few yards off over yonder."

Tessa nodded, and he helped her to a sitting position, wrapping it around her. "Comin' from a costume fete, was ya?" he asked. "This is the season for 'em."

Tessa didn't answer. Why was she so groggy? How long had she lain there by the roadside like this? It wasn't night any longer; it was daylight. And the horse-drawn bus! There were no such things in Giles Longworth's time. Had she crossed back over into her own? Her heart leapt in fear that she had. What had become of Giles . . . of the wolf?

The wolf!

Tessa felt the blood drain from her face. Giles wasn't anxious to reach the Abbey before dark because of Master Monty at all. He'd wanted to reach the Abbey in daylight because of *himself,* because of what he might become. Giles had been bitten. It was he, not the child, who posed the danger to her on that moor beneath the full moon. Why hadn't she realized it before? She was so concerned that the Gypsy would betray her secret, she'd forgotten about his. He didn't want her to see him turn into the beast that she saw streaking through the courtyard. Could he have been the one who did the damage in the studio? Was it in fact Giles who crashed through the oriel window, not Master Monty at all? Could they *both* be werewolves? Was that why he was so insistent that she put the amulet on at the last, why he'd begun to tear off his clothing?

The amulet!

Tessa groped her throat for the silver chain that held the pentacle the old Gypsy had given her. Yes, it was there. It was cold to the touch, and then seemed to burn her fingers. She tucked it inside her bodice.

"She's a doxy what's strayed from Whitechapel, is what she is," one of the women said, climbing back on the horse-drawn bus. "The lightskirts don't care what scandalous togs they get themselves up in."

"Here now, none o' that!" the bus driver said. Then to Tessa, "Where was ya goin', then?"

"I . . . I am no doxy," Tessa defended. "I . . . I was

looking for the bus station, and I lost my way in the fog.
I stumbled over a rock avoiding a carriage. I . . . I must
have struck my head upon it . . ."

"Where are ya goin'?"

"Where am I now?" Tessa probed.

"Ya don't know where ya are?" the bus driver marveled. "That bump on the head addled your wits, I
shouldn't wonder, and give ya a fine cut on your lip inta
the bargain, I see."

"I told you I lost my way."

"Well, you're a far cry from London, if that's where
you're comin' from in that fancy getup. Ladies hereabouts don't get decked out so peculiar." He leaned
closer. "Beggin' your pardon, but that's what's set them
peahens off, ya know."

London was the last place Tessa wanted to go. She'd
traveled in time, but to what time? Would the police
still be looking for her? No, she couldn't chance it with
nowhere to go. She had to return to Cornwall, to Longhollow Abbey.

"No, I'm not going to London," she spoke up. "Cornwall . . . Longhollow Abbey on Bodmin Moor . . ."

The bus driver gave a start. His demeanor sent shivers down her spine. "Well, you're in luck," he said.
"You're on Dartmoor. I'll have ya ta Bodmin Moor
quick enough if you've got the fare. But why would ya
want ta go to the old Abbey?"

"That, sir, is my affair," Tessa said, getting to her feet
with his help. Opening her pocket, she paid the man and
moved toward the bus.

The driver glanced down at the coins in his hand.
"Oy, what's this ya give me?" he asked.

Tessa felt the blood drain away from her scalp. Fumbling with her pocket, she fished out a twentieth-century
coin and offered it. "I'll have that back, if you please," she
said. "I collect old coins . . . and that one is quite rare."

"I should say so," the driver said, returning it. "About a hundred years old, this." He took the new one, bit down upon it, then shoved it in his pocket. "That's better then," he said with a nod. "Don't want no funny money, no matter how rare 'tis. It ain't no use ta me."

"Don't let her on!" an old woman passenger called out. "We're at the crossroads! When I was a girl they buried the *revenant*—evil souls who would rise after death to corrupt the living—at crossroads to confuse them when they got up outta their graves. Where did she come from way out here? By the look of her, she's confused, all right. Leave 'er, I say!"

The bus driver shook his head. "Well, *I* say she comes. Ya can't leave a body out here all alone with dark comin' quick in these parts this time o' year. Where's your Christian charity?" Then to Tessa, as he helped her into the lower level of the bus, "In ya get, miss."

Tessa hesitated, a sea of faces spread with scowls of righteous indignation trained upon her. Could they actually believe she was a ghoul risen from the crossroads? She shuddered.

"Go on then," the driver urged. "Pay no attention to the old magpies. There's naught ta fear. It's safe as houses . . ."

Tessa had no choice. Taking her seat, she pulled her shawl close about her, and gave the scenery her full and fierce attention through the little window as the driver cracked his whip and set the horses in motion.

She didn't have to turn to know all eyes were still upon her. Once they left Dartmoor, the roads widened into new coaching routes wide enough to accommodate both horse-drawn and motor vehicles. It seemed strange to Tessa, having come so recently from a vintage Regency two-seater horse-drawn chaise. But that too had seemed odd to her when she'd first climbed into it after living in Town and using modern transportation.

She was going mad. She had to be. How was it possible to travel back and forth through time? But she had. What would she find at Longhollow Abbey now? The cheeky bus driver had cast her such a strange look when she'd given it as her destination. If only she knew what year it was. If only she were bold enough to ask. They would surely pack her off to Bedlam if she did. Sane people were generally credited with knowing the current year.

They crossed over into Cornwall at dusk. The driver made several stops along the route, including one to take on fresh horses, before continuing on to Bodmin Moor. The terrain there hadn't changed overmuch. Her beloved rolling patchwork hills seemed just the same, and the moors little vales of heath and desolation, breathtaking in their wild beauty beneath the risen moon. They reached the Abbey before Tessa realized it, and the driver pulled the bus to a halt and opened the door.

"You're sure you want to stay way out here alone this time of night, miss?" he asked, helping her down. "There's a proper inn a mile south as the crow flies."

"Quite sure," Tessa said.

"Have it your way," the driver replied. "Ain't any o' my business who you're meetin' way out here, but if ya change your mind, I'll be passin' back this way again in half-an-hour."

Tessa nodded, and the driver climbed back into the box and cracked his whip, setting the bus in motion. Only then did she turn toward the blackened silhouette of Longhollow Abbey, steeped in deep darkness and whitewashed in fog.

All at once the fog drifted, presenting a clearer view. At the sight of the house now looming before her, Tessa gasped and stumbled to a halt. No wonder the bus driver was reluctant to leave her there. Before her, all that remained was the blackened shell of what had once been Giles Longworth's grand mansion. Fire had reduced it to a burned-out shadow of its former self, standing wounded in the misty moonlight.

The wolf ran back and forth over the heath, its plaintive whines giving way to heart-stopping howls as it bounded through the fog. The man trapped inside the beast was desperate, but he scarcely knew why. That was the way of the wolf when it took over. Precious little would be remembered from the time it took possession of its host until it spat him out again, cold and naked on the heath to wonder what or whom he had savaged while the wolf was in control.

Giles never remembered more than fragments of the events that occurred after he shape-shifted into the werewolf. The moon was on the wane. Tomorrow night its altered shape would be visible, and the phenomenon would not occur again until next month, when the moon waxed full again. At least that was how it had been before. All this was new to him. These were things he knew when sanity returned, when he was in his human body again. Now he was the wolf, running mad over heath soggy with the morning dew, waiting for the dawn to free him from the nightmare.

Some inner instinct, some invisible cord that tied him to his humanity led him south through the misty darkness to the Gypsy camp. Moraiva was seated beside the campfire almost as if waiting for him, a folded lap robe beside her.

Slinking closer, the wolf threw back its head and loosed a howl into the darkness before dawn. The moon had passed from view, and clouds had begun to outnumber the stars. The wolf fell on its side, letting out its high-pitched whine. Transforming back into human form was agonizing at best. Pain overwhelming both man and beast wrenched another howl from the wolf. It stiffened, convulsed, and in a moment of flesh, muscle and bone expansion, surged into the writhing shape of Giles Longworth, its human host.

Moraiva got to her feet stiffly, the lap robe in hand, and went to Giles, gazing down at him where he lay beside the fire. She threw the robe over him and took her seat upon the log again.

"She is . . . gone," Giles moaned. "I've run the moors until I can run no more. Over and over I have followed the course she took. She disappeared before my very eyes!"

"You remember that then?" the Gypsy asked. "Curious. You all recall . . . differently. It is the way of the wolf."

"Do not count me among their number," Giles spat out through clenched teeth. "I did not ask for this!"

"Neither did they, your lycanthrope brethren," she replied. "You are cursed—all of you. You are no better or worse than the creature that cursed you, for all your innocence. So many souls . . . lost . . . so many among my tribe alone. My heart breaks for you. You are a good man . . . a fine figure of a man. If I were thirty summers younger . . ." She waved her hand in dismissal of the thought. "Your clothes are in the wagon," she said, crooking her finger toward the turquoise-and-yellow-painted vehicle nearest the fire. "I took the liberty."

Giles scrambled to his feet and staggered toward it, clutching the lap robe about his nakedness. He was exhausted, wanting that bath Foster had offered him what seemed a lifetime ago, and fearful of what might have happened at the Abbey in his absence. But what had him on the brink of madness was Tessa's disappearance. Praying that Moraiva would be able to shed some light upon that, he rejoined her beside the fire as the first rays of a fish-gray dawn broke over the horizon.

"I have to find her," he said, taking the tin cup of strong, black coffee in Moraiva's outstretched hand. "I was right behind her . . . and she vanished before my eyes."

"Were you man or wolf?"

"I . . . I don't remember, Moraiva. I was trying to unhitch the horse from the chaise after the leather suspension straps gave way and pitched Tessa into the bracken. I could feel the change coming on. The horse was in a frenzy. He never behaved like that before—"

"He feared the wolf in you. Such is not uncommon. Horses and dogs will act that way, sensing the wolf."

"I remember tearing at my clothes, then begging her to run. But I ran after her . . . I couldn't help myself. Then she just . . . disappeared. All the while I searched, I was certain I'd find her dead, and that I had killed her. Where could she be, Moraiva?"

"She has gone back where she came from," the Gypsy said, "back to her own time."

Giles froze, the coffee cup suspended in his hand. "What do you mean?" he murmured.

"She is not of your hour, Giles Longworth. She is from the future. She traveled here through time and space by way of the time corridors that link the churches."

"That is preposterous!"

"Yes, but true."

"How do you know this?"

They Gypsy hesitated. "I saw it in her palm," she said. "But that is not all. I know because I have done it."

"You have traveled through time," Giles said in disbelief.

The old Gypsy smiled, though no trace reached her eyes, and nodded. "Did you not notice something . . . different about her?" she asked.

Giles raked his hair back from a sweaty brow. His mind reeled back to the night he'd found her in his carriage in the drive. He remembered her strange frock and hairstyle, and that she'd arrived in the dead of night with no luggage. But . . . how?

The old Gypsy nodded at his expression. "You know it to be true, don't you?" she asked.

The sky was lightening, and others were milling about the camp. Giles would not have them hear this conversation. Being a superstitious lot, they would break camp and flee; he was fortunate that they hadn't seen him transform from wolf to man earlier. He needed the old Gypsy now. She may well be the only link he had to Tessa. He had to have her back, and if there was any hope that Moraiva could help him do that, he had to avail himself without risking the suspicion of the others.

Moraiva had promised to come to Longhollow Abbey. He helped her hitch up an old dilapidated wagon, and together they set out across the moor just as an eerie pink haze swallowed the fish-gray dawn, looking more like blood as the sun rose higher.

"A storm will come," the Gypsy said, nodding toward the horizon. "When the dawn turns to blood, before it breaks again there will be a flaw. It is Nature's warning."

She was hedging. This Giles would not allow. "You *knew*," he said. "Why didn't you tell me?"

The old Gypsy shrugged. "I saw fear in her eyes," she said. "She did not want you to know, at least not that way. Besides, would you have believed me?"

Giles gave it thought. "Probably not," he conceded. "I do not even know if I believe you now. But the fact remains that she disappeared in front of my very eyes, and she is nowhere to be found. I need to have her back, Moraiva. She is the only model to assist me with the painting I'm creating that has sparked the Prince Regent's interest. I *need* her!"

Moraiva erupted in a toothless laugh. "You need her, Giles Longworth, but not to model for you. You need that pretty packet of flesh to warm your bed."

"I can get that from any harlot at the Thistle and Thorn Inn," Giles countered.

The old Gypsy's smug smile contradicted him.

"Ahhh," Giles growled. "Have it your way, just tell me how to go where she has gone."

"The guardians of the corridors are Otherworldly beings," she said. "They let in whom they please and when. It is not a highway to be traveled by the masses, Giles Longworth. It is a privilege granted by those unseen powers to whomever they will."

"Is there no way to bribe them, then, your 'keepers of the corridors'? All men have a price."

"Not these," she said. "For they are not men but spirits, and they let pass whom they will."

"How?" Giles pronounced. "Tell me how, and I will act on my own."

"There are invisible passageways . . . subterranean highways, if you will, called spirit roads, corridors, and gateways that exist beneath the surface of the Earth—one of the great mysteries of the universe. It is along these corridors that the spirits of the dead traverse, and the fey and all manner of Otherworldly creatures roam. The phenomena are called lay lines. All scholars know of them, but none know how to navigate them like we Gypsies do."

"But if you cannot see them . . . ."

"The ancients of the Orient built their temples and holy sites upon these lines that crosshatch the earth. Here in England, they seem to be threaded through a string of churches. I find them where St. Michael's churches are built."

"If such is true, both Tessa and I were traveling one

of these corridors. How is it that she was accepted and I was shunned? I was right behind her!"

The Gypsy shrugged. "I told you, they do not open to everyone. That you were rejected could well be your condition, or her favor, in that they sought to protect her from you in pursuit. I do not know. They may reject you today and accept you tomorrow. There is no way of telling for certain, and you will drive yourself mad if you try to solve that mystery."

"And you have done this?"

She nodded proudly. "Sometimes, when weather is too brutal here in winter, or in the spring, when flaws ravage this coast, and in times of persecution, we Gypsies cross over until all is safe again. Sometimes we go forward in time, and sometimes we go into the past. Have you never wondered where we go when we leave these moors you so graciously allow us to winter upon?"

Truthfully, Giles had not, but he wouldn't confess that. This was far too important to risk vexing her. "But . . . do the people where you go not find you . . . peculiar?"

"How? Gypsies have existed upon the earth since time out of mind. Our attire does not change overmuch from century to century. How are we peculiar?"

Swaying along with the rickety old wagon, they had nearly reached the Abbey. Behind, the blood-red morning sky had given birth to the sun. Giles found it hard to believe that from such a glorious sunrise a storm would come of such devastating proportions as Molavia described, but a cold wind had already risen. Was it a harbinger of an innocent storm, or an ill omen? Giles didn't dwell upon those thoughts. Somehow, he had to find Tessa. That was all that mattered at the moment.

The wagon wheels had scarcely stopped rolling in the drive when Avery the butler burst through the door.

"Oh, sir!" he cried. "We thought you a goner! When the horse came back without you or the chaise, we feared the worst! I am so relieved to see you safe and sound, sir!"

Giles was so addled it had never occurred to him that the staff would be worried. What had Tessa done to him? He must be bewitched. With everything that was happening, all he could think of was the petal softness of her lips beneath his own, the honey sweetness of her on his tongue as he tasted her deeply; he could taste her still. He could almost feel her nipples puckering between his lips as he laved the tawny buds until they hardened against his tongue. Recalling the soft touch of her gentle hand upon his aroused sex brought it to life again, and he groaned. He had to have her back, no matter the cost.

"Where is Foster?" he asked the butler.

"Why, he and Able are out searching for all of you," said Avery, clearly taken aback.

"All of us?" Giles queried.

"Yes, sir," said the butler, "you and Miss LaPrelle, and Master Monty."

"What of Master Monty? Speak up, man!"

"H-he ran off right after dark last night, sir," Avery said warily. "We couldn't hold him, sir. There was nothing we could do."

"Was anyone . . . hurt? The child has taken to biting. Was anyone . . . bitten?"

"No, sir, but the boy tripped poor Foster up and gave him a nasty spill."

Like an ocean wave crashes to the strand and then ebbs away, so did hot blood surge to Giles's temples and recede, draining strength and color with it. Had the boy found Moraiva's corridor as well? He had to find Tessa now, before it was too late.

"Moraiva, will you stay?" he asked the Gypsy. "I mean to join the search for Master Monty so that you can examine him."

"I will stay," she said, "but you will not find the child . . . until he wants to be found."

Chapter Thirteen

Tessa trudged over the moor in the darkness. The closer she came to Longhollow Abbey, the more borne down she became. She would not find Giles here now. It was not his time. But was it hers? She couldn't be certain of anything, except that somewhere in time, Longhollow Abbey had suffered a great devastation. The once-proud mansion was but a ghost of its former self, the intricate construction of the chimney system now overgrown and rooted to the ground by creeping tendrils of woodbine and ivy.

If only she'd inquired of the year. All she could surmise from the situation, from the attire of the passengers on the horse-drawn bus, of their speech, their colloquialisms, was that she'd crossed back close to her time. In any event, she wasn't about to chance going back to London.

From above, the moon shone down and lit her way as she approached the Abbey. It wasn't full now; it was in its second quarter. That was a relief. At least she wouldn't have to worry about werewolves for the moment. All she wanted was to feel Giles's arms around her again, those strong, muscular arms holding her, clasping her fast to his dynamic body. She could still feel his hands roaming over her. She could still feel his warm, eager lips possessing hers.

Approaching the drive, she realized that in his own time he could be treading the same ground. They could both be occupying the same space, only a century apart. It boggled the mind. Somewhere, his warm volatile body lived and breathed and wanted her. He was here— *right here*—and she could neither hear nor see him. His living, breathing flesh was treading the same patchwork hills her feet now trod, yet she couldn't reach out and touch him. But she could feel him. Somehow, his presence was palpable despite the time that separated them. He was here, in the mist, in the night, in the very air she breathed. His scent wafted across her memory, his sultry, musky maleness. It was all around her, ghosting through her, driving her mad.

There was no door, no grand staircase to enter, and no Great Hall to welcome her. No evidence of rooms had survived, only most of the chimney structure. Tessa couldn't help but marvel at how well the house had been constructed to have withstood such devastation with anything left standing. She wondered when it had happened, and how? Was it an accident, or was it deliberate? Why did Master Monty come to mind with that question? One thing was certain. "The Bride of Time" had been finished and somehow found its way to the little gallery off Threadneedle Street before the fire. If only she knew what had happened to Giles.

Cold chills walked up and down her spine at that thought. She dared not think on it. The curator at the gallery simply said he'd disappeared. No mention was made of his death. The very word brought tears to her eyes. She could not bear the thought of his dying, though of course he had; but she prayed he had not died in that blaze. The wounded house was breeding morbid thoughts. She would not have it! She would find him.

She had to find him! They had nearly been intimate together. If the moon hadn't risen . . . No! She would not
dwell upon that, either. Somehow, they would overcome
the curse if it were true. She still doubted, but only because she could not bear the truth. It was too terrible.

She picked her way through the ground-creeping vines
among the brickwork columns in the moonlight. Everything was in ruins, black with petrified char. Whenever
the disaster had happened, it wasn't recent. She was just
about to turn away, when a voice from behind booming
through the quiet spun her around and froze her to the
spot. Tessa gasped. She was looking down the double
barrels of a shotgun in the hands of an angry-looking
man past middle age. A nimbus of gray hair fanned out
about his face, and his eyes, like black onyx beads peeking out from beneath wrinkled eyelids, twinkled in the
eerie moonlight.

"Hold it right there, missy," he said, cocking the
weapon. The sound ran Tessa through. "And who
might you be, eh? And what are ya doin' up in here?
Don't come no closer! It don't matter ta me if a tres-
passer's wearin' trousers or skirts."

"Put that ridiculous gun down!" Tessa charged. "I'm
doing no harm. What possible damage could I do to
this?" She gestured toward the entire circumstance. "You
scared me half to death!"

"Aye, and well ya should be scared, and will be when
the place starts fallin' in on ya." He gestured toward her
swollen lip. "Looks like you've already done yourself a
mischief. Who are ya, and what are ya doin' in here?"

"My name is Tessa LaPrelle, and I . . . I knew someone who was employed here once. Who might you be,
sir?"

"Ezra Jones, the caretaker," the man said. "The
Longworth Trust pays me good money ta keep folks
like you out. And if you knew somebody who worked

here, that would have been long before my time, missy—and yours. You'll have to do better than that. Now, who are ya and what do ya want here?"

"I have already told you, Mr. Jones. I didn't say I knew the party personally. It happened to be a distant relative of mine. Her name was LaPrelle, too. Look here, I've done no harm. You have no right to treat me like a common criminal. This is no way to treat a lady!"

"Izzat so?" he countered. "Well, you don't look like no lady ta me, all got up in them whore's duds, Miss LaPell, or whatever your real name is. Now git, before I set the guards on ya!"

" It's *LaPrelle*, and how dare you, sir!"

"Don't make me shoot this thing. I don't hold with shootin' women, no matter their profession, but you was told to git, so move!"

"Very well. I'm going, but could you at least tell me what happened here?"

"Why? What's it to ya?"

"I told you . . . one of my ancestors used to be employed here as governess to a young boy."

"Hah! 'Twas a young boy what set the place afire," Jones said. "Some say there was a curse on the little blighter, that his guardian used ta lock him up when the moon was full. Balderdash, if ya ask me. He was a bad hat, old Longworth. All them artist fellas are a peculiar lot, drinkin' and carousing about with the bawds."

"If a trust is paying you to watch over the place, why has it never been restored?"

"It's a curiosity, is why, more valuable like it is. Folks come out here just to gawk and hear about the scandal. Folks don't care how they throw their money away these days. The place is up for sale, has been for years. Let the new owners do the repair work, that's what the solicitors say, meanwhile it's takin' in a fair bit o' change from the tourists that come up here to poke about and hear the scandalous tale. Folks do love a scandal. It pays me wages; the rest goes to the Crown."

"Well, that being the case, I don't see how you can object to me being here."

"First off, you haven't paid. Second, we don't give tours in the dead o' night, only on weekends, and third, nobody gets to come up in here. We don't put nobody to the hazard."

"And you live here?"

"No, I don't live here. The stables wasn't burnt. Ain't no horses now, but the loft apartment is where I live. It's right comfortable, and close enough to chase off any intruders like yourself. Seems ta me I asked you to git!"

Tessa ignored him. "If I pay, will you tell the tale to me?" she asked him. Slipping the pocket from the side of her frock, she shook it, rattling the coins inside. He hesitated, and Tessa picked out two coins, being careful to choose the right currency, and handed them over. "There," she said. "That should be more than enough. Tell your tale. My bus comes by soon, and I shall have to be below by the lane to flag it down."

"You're a cheeky little snippety-snap, ain't ya?" he said, jingling the coins in his palm. "All right, but then ya git!"

"Agreed."

"I told ya it was before my time," he began. "Almost a hundred years ago, it was, when the scandal broke. Everybody said old Longworth was mad as a brush, shut up in this house, with what he said was his models comin' and goin' at all hours, but they was whores, and him carin' for a little boy and all right under the same roof. No wonder the scamp run off." He shook his head in disapproval.

"Who ran off?" Tessa cut in.

"The boy up and run off one night. Rumors spread that old Longworth done for the lad, till the boy come back and done this." He swept his arm wide. "The guards from the Watch they had back then was onto Longworth, and one o' them got killed. They blamed that on old Longworth, too. He got what was comin' to him when this here went up in flames. There was a young woman hired on ta tend the boy, come ta think of it. Don't know her name—"

"And was she here when all this occurred?" Tessa interrupted him.

"That she was," Jones said. "Shameless hussy! She took ta posin' for Longworth, who was workin' on a scandalous painting. 'Twas called 'The Bride of Time,' some fancy o' the Prince Regent, George IV . . ."

"What happened to her—Longworth's model?" Tessa asked, almost afraid of the answer.

"I'm gettin' ta that," Jones replied testily. "If ya want ta hear the tale, ya have ta stop interruptin' me. You're mixin' me up."

"Sorry. It's just that she was my ancestor, you see, and I'm anxious to know."

"Mmmm, I can believe that—on both counts," Jones said, taking her measure disrespectfully. It was clear he assumed her to be a doxy. That hardly mattered. He could think anything he liked, as long as he told his tale.

"Do continue, sir," she prodded.

"Ummm, where was I now? Oh yes! Old Longworth finished his painting—shameful thing, the woman in it nekked and all. 'Twas supposed ta be art, but I'd call it somethin' else from what folks say—"

"Yes, well you shouldn't make judgments upon things you haven't seen firsthand," Tessa interrupted.

"There ya go, interruptin' again!" Jones admonished her, looking daggers down the gun barrel. "Anyhow, 'twas delivered ta the Prince Regent, and he must have approved, because after the tragedy, the Prince set up a trust for Longworth. Then, all o' Longworth's paintings sold to the highest bidder. Everybody wanted ta own something done by the artist who'd painted old Prinny's Bride o' Time, and Longworth became a success overnight, he did. 'Twas what they call a 'posthumous' success—that means he was dead by time he got famous. I dunno what happened to that scandalous painting afterward."

Tessa wanted to tell him she knew what happened to it. Somehow it had found its way to a little gallery off Threadneedle Street in London, and had probably been donated years ago. But that didn't matter. There was a question she had to ask. Though she needed to know, she was afraid to ask it, and she let him natter on about nothing in particular and everything in general until she'd mustered the courage to put it into words.

"What happened to Longworth?" she murmured. "H-how did he die?"

Again the caretaker waved his arm. "Here, in this," he said. "Burnt ta death in 'is bed with 'is doxy. All three o' 'em died in the blaze, so goes the tale. The servants done what they could to put the fire out, but not a soul would come to the rescue. 'Let it burn!' was the hue and cry when she went up like a tinderbox. A flaw come on, a real screamer with winds strong enough ta lift the hair clean off your head, so they say, and it spread the blaze long before the rain come ta put it out. Their ashes was scattered far and wide, 'cause no trace of any of 'em was ever found, not that folks was lookin' all that hard for 'em, mind ya."

"Are you saying no one lifted a finger to help put the fire out?" Tessa cried. "Why, that's barbarous!"

"No, and why would they?" he responded. "Rumors spread that they was *werewolves*—the boy and all. People 'round these parts are a superstitious lot, missy. They believe in faeries and knocker gnomes in the tin mines, and giants and devils from hell ta this day! This be

Cornwall, not your fancy London Town, though the towners eat this gammon up when they come for a tour of old Longhollow Abbey."

"But to just let them all perish . . ." It was more than Tessa could take in. Her breath was coming short, and her heart was pounding in her breast. White pinpoints of blinding light starred her vision. She could bear no more. There was nothing for her here, nothing but death and desolation. She had to get away. She had to get back to the Abbey when it was whole and grand and alive, and Giles Longworth was flesh and bone, not dust blown to the four winds in a Cornish flaw.

"What's the matter with ya?" Jones asked, squinting toward her. "You've gone all funny of a sudden—whiter than fog. Don't ya go giddy on me here! You've got ta git now. I told ya your tale, and then some, so you can just be on your way."

"Yes," Tessa said, stumbling past him over vines that seemed to grope her feet and ankles like living things. "I shall do that. Thank you for the 'tour,' Mr. Jones. I shall trouble you no further."

He said more as she fled the debris, but she couldn't make out what he was saying. It was as if his voice was coming at her through an echo chamber, the delay between each word bleeding into the next. She wasn't herself until she burst out of the ruins into the starry night, taking deep, shuddering breaths of the stiff Cornish wind that had risen sharply since she entered the remains of the Abbey. The lane seemed so far away now. It was nearly time for the bus to pass by again. She had to be there waiting when it did. Only one thing was certain: she had to find Giles now, before it was too late.

At least now she knew more of what she was facing, though it left her so desolate she could scarcely put one foot in front of the other. Reaching the lane, she climbed over a stile by the roadside and sank down upon it to wait for the bus. Her knees were so wobbly she couldn't have gone another step.

Her mind was racing, trying to digest all Ezra Jones had told her. Giles had finished the painting before the fire, but she knew that because she'd seen it. That it had found a home in the little gallery wasn't surprising. Many paintings owned by royals were loaned or donated to museums, or sold outright when new monarchs took the throne. Sons of nobles deep in debt often sold such artifacts to keep from going into Dun territory. Some things never changed. Someone very rich must have bought it from the little gallery on Threadneedle Street. What had the curator said . . . a couple from Yorkshire had purchased it?

No matter. More relevant was the fire, the fire that took Giles Longworth's life . . . and hers. Unless . . . perhaps he had another woman in his bed at the time, which wouldn't surprise her, considering the outlandish behavior of the man thus far. Why did that jealous thought flush her cheeks with hot blood? Jealousy. There was no other name for it. She drove the images back, but no matter which way her mind turned then, Giles Longworth's virile image in bed with another woman bit her sore.

Then there was the part about the child running away, and the authorities believing Giles had murdered the boy, that theory to be refuted when the child returned and set the fire that destroyed them all. That hadn't happened yet, nor had the painting been finished. There was still time—to do what exactly, Tessa had no idea. She had to get back to Giles's time, and she craned her neck, looking down the lane into deep darkness, praying it would give birth to the bus lanterns.

But it wasn't the bus that came rattling along the narrow, windswept lane, with a single lantern swaying from a metal crook. It was a rickety old wagon. A woman was driving it, an old Gypsy woman. Tessa shielded her eyes from the wind and squinted toward the image emerging from the darkness. Vaulting to her feet, she gasped. It was Moraiva, the old Gypsy on the moor who had read her palm. But how could this be?

The Gypsy pulled the wagon to a halt. "Get in," she charged.

"Y-you're the Gypsy from the moor. You read my palm. How can you be here?"

Moraiva smiled her curious smile that did not reach her eyes. "The same way that you have come here, daughter," she said. "What? You think you are the only one that knows the secret of the time corridors? We Gypsies have crossed over since time out of mind. Get in! Time matters gravely. This you do not know, but Moraiva knows. Climb up, daughter."

Tessa scrambled into the wagon. "Giles . . . is he—"

"He fares well but for worry over you," the Gypsy said.

"Does he know?"

"About the lay lines? Yes, daughter."

"And that I . . . ?"

"He knows."

Tessa wasn't thrilled about that, but she was relieved that the old Gypsy had spared her the telling of it. One thing still bothered her, however. "And he chose not to come for me?" she queried. It did not bode well.

"He could not come after you. The corridors are closed to him presently."

"For how long?" Tessa asked.

"Who knows these things?" the Gypsy replied with a shrug. "The gate keepers decide who may enter the corridors and who may not. There is naught to be done about it."

Moraiva was turning the cart around in the narrow lane, heading back in the opposite direction, and Tessa grabbed her arm. "No!" she cried. "I must go back the way I've come . . . to the place where the bus that brought me here found me by the side of the road."

Again the Gypsy smiled her patronizing smile. "The lines run north to south and east to west. Where had that bus just come from that picked you up?"

"L-London, I believe," Tessa said.

"Do you wish to go there, then?"

"*No*, of course not! I want to go back . . . I want to go to Giles!"

"Then keep still and pay attention. One day you will need to remember this lesson, daughter; much will depend upon it. Where were you coming from when you entered the corridor that brought you here?"

"I . . . I was running from Giles. He told me to run, and I ran. I . . . we were taking a shortcut across the moor to the Abbey after leaving you, when the suspension straps on the chaise broke and the horse ran off."

"I know it," said the Gypsy. "If you would return to the place you've come from, you must access the same corridor, for what runs one way also runs the other— and no other. Access a different corridor, and you could come out anywhere in time. You never should have gotten on that bus. When you did, you left the corridor you'd come through. You changed direction. You should have turned 'round and re-traced your steps the way you'd come. It would have brought you back."

"Even though I'd already crossed over?" Tessa asked.

The Gypsy nodded. "You would have simply faded into the mist."

"And you came how . . . ?"

"The way you did," the Gypsy told her. "But I know how to navigate the passages. We go back now to the place where you left Longworth, where we leave this corridor and access the other, then over the open moor to the Abbey, the way you would have gone if the chaise had not broken." She nodded toward the wound on Tessa's lip. "You were injured?" she probed. "That is dried blood I see there."

Tessa hesitated, touching her mouth gingerly, for it was still tender. Her mind reeled back to the moment she'd been flung from the chaise, then to Giles's embrace, and she froze, reliving Giles's teeth piercing her lip in the heat of passion.

She had been *bitten*.

Riveting chills visited her spine. Did that mean . . . ? No! She couldn't even think it. But the look in Moraiva's eyes all but made her blood curdle. After a moment, the old Gypsy looked away and gave the lane ahead her full and fierce attention.

It was some time before Moraiva broke the awful silence between them. "See there," she said, pointing toward the blackened shape of Longhollow Abbey silhouetted against the star-studded sky. "We are home, but you will not find the master in the house, not for a while yet."

"Why not?" Tessa asked.

"He has joined the search."

"What search?" Tessa queried.

"The boy has gone missing," Moraiva said, and said no more.

Chapter Fourteen

Moraiva was right. Giles was not in residence when Tessa arrived at Longhollow Abbey. The Gypsy left her on the threshold and drove off to join the others in the search for Master Monty. The end had been put in motion with the child's disappearance, and Tessa's heart sank. She knew it would happen, but she'd had no idea it would be so soon.

There was nothing to be done but ride out the firestorm that loomed over the mansion, and Tessa dragged herself inside to be met by a full complement of anxious servants beside themselves over her absence. Everyone thought she had joined in the search also. It was best to let them continue to think it. The truth would not help them, even if through some miracle they did believe it.

Pleading exhaustion, she asked that the French-enameled bathtub be filled in her dressing room. Once Rigby, the butler, and Evers, the footman, lent their strength to the chore, she dismissed them. She sought no help from the maids. She was accustomed to bathing on her own. She had never had the privilege of a lady's maid, being a maid herself, and she promptly sprinkled rosewater and lavender oil into the steaming tub, shed her soiled and torn frock and hose, and climbed into the silky water.

The tub was lined with a fine linen sheet, and she leaned her head back against it and shut her eyes, inhaling the hot, steamy water. It was heaven. The servants at Poole House were only allowed one tub bath a month. The rest of the time they were restricted to what Mrs. Poole called whore's baths. These were slapdash affairs executed with pitcher and basin, and with water that was tepid at best but for the most part cold, and in winter, frozen, at least the top layer, which would have to be broken to gain access to the icy water beneath.

Tessa reached for the cake of soap resting in a shell-shaped dish on a little table beside the tub. She raised the cake to her nose and inhaled deeply. Lavender. And it was soft-milled, making rich lather the minute it touched the water. She moaned in approval. At Poole house, the soap was either carbolic or lye, except during the holidays, when the servants were treated to leftover slivers of pine tar soap donated from above stairs.

There was a sea sponge on the table, and she soaked it in the water and began squeezing handfuls of fragrant lather over her skin, over her throat, her breasts, over her long, slender legs, and over her belly. The sponge slipped lower, between her thighs, bringing her sex to life, reminding her of Giles, of his anxious fingers probing her there. A soft moan escaped her, rekindling his volatile embrace, reliving the passionate lips that wounded hers. She wouldn't think about that now, not while the fragrant steam was rising around her. Not while her loins were on fire. Not while every nerve in her body throbbed a steady rhythm, and that secret place, that forbidden mystery deep inside at her very core palpated to the rhythm of the memory of his hard-muscled flesh in her arms.

Leaning her head back against the damp sheet, Tessa

closed her eyes again. The water was still hot around her, cradling her, the fluffy lather gliding over her wet skin. The sponge fell from her hand and floated to the side of the tub. She was totally relaxed, her arms floating at her sides. Across the way a fire in the hearth crackled pleasantly, lulling her to sleep, as she lay cradled in the gently lapping womb of lavender and rosewater caressing every recess, every pore, every orifice and crevice of her body.

She didn't wake until the third pin was lifted from her hair and it fell loose about her. All at once, Tessa gave a lurch and seized the sides of the tub, attempting to sit upright. Water sloshed over onto the floor as strong hands held her back, and a familiar voice crooned softly.

"Shhhhh," Giles said, dropping to his knees, his hands gentle but firm upon her shoulders. "I left the search and came back the moment Moraiva said you'd returned. Lie back and relax, Tessa."

At first she thought she was dreaming, that he was a figment of her imagination brought on by reliving his embrace on the moor, but then he took up the sponge and soaped it, moving it over her shoulders in slow concentric circles. This was no apparition. He was real! She should slap his hand away. Every instinct in her begged that she put him from her—demand he leave her; but the firelight was gleaming in his eyes, dilated black in the shadow-steeped chamber. It picked out auburn glints in the mussed mahogany hair curling about his earlobes, and defined the angles and planes of his bronzed face. It played wickedly about the sensuous shape of his lips, and deepened the thumbprint cleft in his strong chin.

It was no use. She wanted him. She had always wanted him, from the first moment she'd set eyes upon his self-portrait in the little gallery. He was wearing a similar shirt to the one in the painting, though the sleeves were rolled back to the biceps, exposing the hard rippling muscles clenching as he continued to soap her. The shirt gaped open in front, giving her a glimpse of dark hair pointing arrow-straight to disappear beneath the waistband of his breeches.

The sponge had reached her breasts, and she writhed in the water as it scraped her nipples, overflowing with suds. The water was like silk, his touch as light as air. Though his fingers trembled as they grazed the hard, tawny buds, he played them like a skilled musician plays his instrument, with reverence and adoration. Just under the surface of his skin, Tessa could feel the pent-up passion, the harnessed volatility she'd seen in him that first night in the drive and more recently on the moor. It was bewitching and frightening all at once, and it took her breath away.

"Tell me," he murmured, lifting her leg to soap it. "What is it like at the turn of the twentieth century?"

Tessa gave a start. It was a sobering question, though her body was on fire for him, and she hardly knew which emotion to embrace. "Moraiva told you," she said.

He nodded. Returning her leg to the water, he lifted the other and began soaping it as well. "Why did you not tell me, Tessa?"

"Would you have believed me?"

He hesitated. "After what has happened to me, I might have," he said. "At any rate, I do now. Like so many Doubting Thomases in the world, I saw you disappear with my own eyes, and Moraiva has brought you back to me. There is naught to fear, the moon has waned."

"I'm not afraid of you, Giles. I'm afraid of myself, of loving where there is no hope."

"You haven't answered my question," he said. "What

is it like in your time? What did you do there? Where did you live? Who reigns? There is so much I want to know . . . so many questions . . ."

Tessa took a deep breath. It was so hard trying to concentrate upon trivia while his skilled hands were soaping every inch of her body. "I come from the year 1903," she began. "Your Prinny finally took the throne in 1820, followed by William IV in 1830, then Queen Victoria in 1837, and in my time, Edward VII, who took the throne in 1901."

"Amazing," Giles said distractedly. His eyes had become glazed, hooded with desire, his breath audible as he stroked her.

"I come from London," Tessa went on. "That was the truth. I . . . I was a scullery maid in the home of a noted optician."

"Did you tell me the truth? Have you no family, no beaux, no . . . husband back in London?"

"No, none," Tessa told him. "I am quite alone."

"How did you come here?"

Tessa hesitated. "I would rather not say," she murmured.

"Why? I want no secrets between us. How could it possibly be graver than mine?"

"I . . . I'm afraid you won't believe me, and I have no way to prove myself . . ."

Giles laughed. "My beautiful little fool," he said. "Here I kneel, so hard against the seam that I fear my breeches will burst, so bewitched by your charms that all I can think of—all I can dream of—is you. Do you really think anything you could tell me would change that?"

"I don't want to take the chance," she murmured.

Giles swooped down and took her lips in a smothering kiss that stole her breath away. He deepened the kiss, and she melted against him, a soft moan escaping as his fingers stroked her wet breast slickened with lather, fondling the hard, dark nipple. Tessa winced as he bore down on her wounded lip, and he pulled back, wiping blood from his mouth, and tilted her head up to the firelight.

"What's this?" he asked her, washing the blood from her lip. "Did you do this when you fell from the chaise?"

Tessa hesitated, looking long and hard into his worried eyes. He didn't remember biting her, and she dared not tell him now, not *now*. Maybe it was nothing. It wasn't deep. Maybe it wasn't serious enough to pass on the infection; oh, how she prayed.

"Yes," she said. "When I fell from the chaise." It wasn't really a lie. That was when it did occur, after all. She had just omitted the particulars. But if he continued to look at her so intensely, he would know there was something wrong. She was not skilled at deception, and she pulled him close in her arms to avoid that analytical artist's stare, wetting the front of his shirt with the embrace. "It's nothing," she murmured in his ear. "Nothing at all."

After a moment, he leaned her back against the sheet-draped tub again and gazed into her eyes. "I want to make love to you," he said, his voice husky with desire. "I have wanted to do this from the moment I first clapped eyes upon you in the drive."

Tessa didn't answer. There was no need. Reaching, her hand dripping warm, fragrant water, she laced her fingers through his shaggy hair. How handsome he was with those dark mahogany waves combed by the Cornish wind. They fell just so, across his brow in a rakish attitude even after she brushed them back, and curled randomly about his earlobes. Yes, his was a handsome face, but ruggedly handsome, all angles and planes; oddly, she thought, the kind of face an artist would love to paint. He had done well at that, but he hadn't done himself justice. He had captured the volatile Giles, not the sultry, passionate Giles gazing at her now. He had captured the wolf.

"I have no right to ask you to trust me when I can't even trust myself in this damnable mess," he said. "I know I was too bold on the moor, though I cannot remember how bold. That was not me, not the real me. It was the wolf inside me, Tessa. It's evil . . . and insidious, and afterward I cannot remember much of what occurs when the wolf takes over, only snippets. I'm almost grateful for that, because I don't believe I could live with it . . ."

"Giles—"

"No, you must let me finish," he said. "Whatever I did . . . if I frightened you, took liberties I wasn't allowed . . . I want you to know the real me would rather throw himself from the battlements than cause you harm. It is safe now that the moon has waned, but when it waxes full again, for a day before, during, and a day or two after, you will not be safe with me after dark . . . after moonrise. Then you must lock yourself out of harm's way. This is not a request. This is what must be, Tessa. In this one thing alone, you must not oppose me."

Tessa wanted to tell him that it might already be too late. The hellish thing was, she wouldn't be certain until the moon waxed full again. A whole month! How would she ever bear it? Instead, she nodded acquiescence and fisted her hand in his damp hair, bringing his head down until their lips touched.

It was a gentle kiss, sensuous and deep, concentrated upon her un-bruised upper lip, that wrenched a soft moan from them both as their tongues entwined. Giles was almost as wet as she was. His poet's shirt was soaked, plastered to his hard-muscled chest, the full rolled-back sleeves trailing suds. When his hand slipped beneath the water and settled upon the V of soft curls between her thighs, Tessa's breath caught in her throat.

Slowly at first, with the lightest touch, he began to stroke her, probing beneath the curls to the virgin skin beneath. Tessa leaned into the probing fingers that spread shock waves of drenching fire through her loins. The delicious sensation radiated outward over her belly and thighs, like ripples in a quiet pond when a skimming stone breaks the surface of still water.

Giles looked her in the eyes and murmured, "Tessa . . . are you sure?"

"I'm sure," she replied.

Giles took her lips in another smoldering kiss as his fingers deftly stroked her sex faster, deeper, causing sensations to rush at her very core until she arched her spine against the friction causing the ecstasy, then groaned as release washed over her like waves of liquid fire. It was then, while she was in the throes of deep orgasmic contractions, that his fingers slipped inside her, first one and then another, gliding on the silk of her inner wetness.

Tessa scarcely felt the pain as he made her his. She clung to him as he lifted her out of the water. Setting her on her feet, he wrapped her in the soft towels from the chiffonier, scooped her up in his arms, and carried her into the bedroom. The featherbed and counterpane were cool against her damp skin as she burrowed between them.

"No, don't," Giles said, yanking off his top boots. "I want to look at you."

Tessa lay still, watching while he stripped off his wet shirt and buckskins and padded to the bed. He was aroused, and the sight of him took her breath away. He was perfectly formed and strongly made, from his broad shoulders and narrow waist, to those well turned corded thighs. Tessa's fingers itched to touch him. It was scandalous to feel this way. It had to be. But the minute he climbed in beside her, she reached to stroke his strong back, following the curve of his spine to the narrow waist and firm buttocks.

His hands roaming over her body brought her to the brink of ecstasy again. His fiery kiss, blazing a searing trail from the base of her throat to the hardened buds of her nipples, seemed to set her very soul ablaze. She was malleable in his hands, and everywhere he touched, every line and curve of her body palpated with an inner fire as if her very bones were melting.

"I have no right to take you," he said, his voice husky and deep. "What can I possibly offer you as I am?"

"Your love," Tessa murmured. "Your love."

Giles crushed her close, his strong arms molding her body to his. Easing himself between her legs, he guided those around his waist, lifting the rounds of her buttocks as he penetrated her in one long, tantalizing thrust that molded her to him, like a sword in its scabbard. Tessa moved to the rhythm of his thrusts, taking him deeper as he plunged and swayed and undulated inside her. All the while, his hooded gaze was riveted to her face, his dark eyes catching glints from the fire. Tessa couldn't keep her hands from riding up and down his spine, from gripping his buttocks as he filled her.

All at once he rolled over, taking her with him. On his back now, she straddled him, her long hair teasing his thighs as she moved to his pistoning thrusts. His eyes still devoured her. She could almost see the wolf in them, ravenous, hungering; but there was no fear. She was driven to love him as he was never loved before, her innocence notwithstanding. And she met his gaze as he cupped her breasts, crushing her tender hardened nipples against the thick, roughened cushion of his palms until she feared she would faint for the firestorm of sensation.

Giles pulled her forward until his lips closed around one turgid nipple, laving it with his tongue. The tug resonated at Tessa's very core, triggering a release that all but drained her sense. He gripped her waist and took her deeper still, riding her wetness, raising her up and down, his rapid thrusts hammering into her, until he groaned and held her down upon his hard shaft as his climax pumped him dry.

Tessa felt the pulse of him, the very beat of his life force palpating inside her as his seed filled her. Her hands splayed out over his taut, heaving chest, felt the pounding beat of his heart. It shuddered against her soft skin so violently she feared it would burst from his chest. His breath coming short, he rolled her on her side and gathered her to him greedily, like a starving beggar at a banquet, his eyes—those dark, mysterious, feral eyes— ravishing her still.

"You are mine," he murmured huskily. "You are. I saw it in your eyes . . . and I have no right to you, no business taking you. Whatever alchemy is afoot here . . . whatever twist of fickle fate has brought you to me has damned us both, but if you ever were to leave me—"

Her fingers on his lips silenced him. That mouth was scorching to the touch, as if a raging fever boiled his blood. "I fell in love with you before I ever came here," she said. "Fate, as you say, did the rest. I still do not completely understand it, though I lived it, and am still living it. All I know is that somehow this—*we*—were meant to be . . ."

"You never told me how you did come here. Will you tell me now? Do you trust me enough to share it with me, since it compels us both?"

Tessa hesitated. She was still afraid to tell him, but now she knew she had to, for he was right: whatever alchemy indeed had brought their very souls together in their separate desperation, it compelled them both.

"I was employed as a scullery maid, as I told you. Giles, you would have had to live my life to fully understand what that entails in such a house in my time. Scullions are the lowest form of servant life, and often take cruel abuse from the others. For whatever reason, jealousy surely was part of it, because I was given my own room, the others set out to get shot of me."

"Things are no different in my time, Tessa," Giles said, soothing her with gentle hands as she spoke. "Some things never change."

"I was accused of stealing the mistress's brooch. I did not take it. I had never been above stairs in that house. One of the others stole it and put it in my room so I would be accused. I ran, and the police pursued me. It would have been my day off . . . and this is the part I was afraid to tell you, the bit I feared you wouldn't believe, but it's true. I used to visit the galleries on my days off, one in particular in Cheapside, off Threadneedle Street, where I became fascinated with a particular painting . . . *your* painting, Giles, 'The Bride of Time.'"

Giles stiffened against her and raised himself on one elbow. That had gotten his attention and blunted the edges of the theft. His eyes were riveting now, but not with passion. They were blazing toward her with a look she could not identify.

"*My painting?*" he breathed. "You saw 'The Bride of Time' in a London gallery? How is that possible? How did it get there?"

"I cannot answer that. I do not know. But I went there for many weeks to gaze at it, at the beautiful patchwork hills and the moors. All of your paintings were there, even a portrait you'd done of yourself. I think I fell in love with it before I ever met you."

"That self-portrait is in the collection of the Prince Regent, Tessa. He bought it with several others after I did the miniature for his watchcase, in hopes it would stimulate sales for me. My work impressed him, and he wanted others to flock to my door to buy from an artist who had the favor of England's future king."

"That may be, but I saw it in that gallery with other works of yours. You were wearing a shirt like the one you had on earlier, and buckskin breeches, holding brush and pallet. There was an open window behind you with a view of the hills, and—"

"Zeus! You have it utterly!" he interrupted.

"When I ran that day, I went to the gallery for one last look at your work before I fled Town, only to find that your paintings had been sold to a young couple from Yorkshire. The police followed me there and I ran into the mist. I was thinking of the beautiful patchwork hills in your paintings. I called them that because from a distance they looked like a patchwork quilt I remember from my childhood. I ran, wishing I were there . . . anywhere but running through those London streets with naught but the clothes on my back and the police nipping at my heels. Then the fog thickened and a carriage emerged from it—your carriage! Able was driving. He mistook me for the governess you'd advertised for and, God help me, I climbed inside knowing he would bring me here."

"So that is how you came to be in that carriage."

"I cannot explain it, unless it is as Moraiva told me, that I had stumbled upon one of the lay lines that crosshatch these moors. I didn't believe it then . . . but I do now, Giles. I also believe I was meant to be here with you."

"There are many untoward elements afoot here," Giles observed, grazing her temple with his lips. "I wish you'd told me this before."

"I was afraid you would think I was mad!"

He laughed.

"And . . . after seeing you in a rage over thievery, I was afraid you wouldn't believe I was innocent."

"I paid that bawd handsomely to model for me, nothing more. She abused my generosity and stole from me. That was different. I am a fair man, Tessa, but I do not tolerate persons who take advantage of me."

"I didn't know you well enough to make that distinction," Tessa defended. "You have to realize, I was in a strange place in a strange time. Where would I have gone if you turned me out . . . or worse?"

"Where did you go when you ran from me on the moor—back to London, to your own time?"

Tessa hesitated. Should she tell him the caretaker's tale? Should she divulge how it all would end? The child was gone, but when he returned . . . No! She could not tell him about the fire, not now, not while he was basking in the euphoria of their embrace, and the knowledge that his precious "Bride of Time" had survived him at least until the turn of the twentieth century.

"I don't know," she said at last. "I honestly don't. I was only there for a brief time. A horse-drawn bus driver found me by the side of the lane—"

"A horse-drawn bus?" he cut in. "What sort of conveyance is that?"

"Oh dear," Tessa lamented. "If you think those a funnyosity, whatever would you think of our horseless carriages?"

"Horseless . . . ? How is that possible?"

Tessa giggled in spite of herself and the gravity of the situation. She had completely disarmed the poor man. "Carriages that run on fuel instead of horsepower," she explained. "They are quite elegant, though we still have horse-drawn carriages as well. Some say horseless carriages are just a fad that will pass in time. Of course, they are quite popular amongst the upper classes."

"This bus, where did it take you?" Giles asked.

"I . . . I'm not certain. I was trying to come here. When the driver said I was near, I got out. I didn't dare ask him what year it was; he would have had me straight to Bedlam! I stopped to rest beside the lane. That's when Moraiva found me. . . ." It was as far as she dared go by way of explanation, and she was greatly relieved when he didn't press her further.

Instead, Giles pulled her closer and kissed her gently. "You will never work as a scullion again," he said, "and you will never leave me. Promise me. . . ."

"I promise," she murmured.

"You know what you must do now, don't you?" he said playfully, toying with a lock of her hair.

"What is that?" she asked.

"You must model for me, Tessa. I must finish the painting, now that I know it has a future. Once the boy is found, I shall find another governess."

"You want me to be your model?"

"I want you to be my wife!" he said, as if she should have known. "Though I have no right to ask it as I am. All that aside . . . will you? I know I'm doing this badly, Tessa, and selfishly to boot, but I could never live without you now."

But Tessa's mind was somewhere else, somewhere dark and frightening. "Let the boy go, Giles," she said. "Discontinue the search. He chose to go; let him stay wherever he's gone! If he does return, send him packing off to school—anywhere. I beg you, do not let him back into this house!"

Chapter Fifteen

A sennight passed and the boy did not return. While the search went on, Tessa knew they would not find him. She was certain he had left 1811, found one of the lay lines, and accessed a time corridor. There was no other explanation. They were at his mercy, for as sure as she drew breath, Tessa knew he would return in his own time to seal their destiny—the destiny of all three of them.

Moraiva returned to her encampment, though she remained at the ready. Whatever she knew or didn't know of the Abbey from her time travels through the corridor, she kept to herself, just as Tessa held her peace. For the first time since she'd arrived at Longhollow Abbey, Giles seemed happy. She would not take that from him.

The whole house was buzzing with wedding plans. Though it was a shock happening so quickly, no one seemed surprised. The painting was almost finished. The Prince Regent was still at Carlton House, and Giles sent a missive to him there. The prince responded, asking that the canvas be delivered as soon as possible, as he was leaving shortly for an extended stay at the Royal Pavilion in Brighton. Giles had originally planned to send the painting, wanting to stay close to the Abbey, but there was plenty of time before the next full moon, and in view of the wedding plans, it was decided instead that he and Tessa would deliver the painting in person. Then, while they were in Town, Giles would purchase a special license for their marriage. This was Tessa's idea, and she held out for it on the pretext that she would dearly love to visit London in his time, and Giles finally agreed. In truth, she wanted to range him as far from Longhollow Abbey as possible, as far away as she could coax him from the potential threat of fire looming over the house and her spirits like a pall. Convinced that if she could keep him away from the Abbey, she could change the terrible future she'd seen with her own eyes, she modeled for him gladly, and at the end of the second week, Tessa climbed the attic stairs after dinner for what would be the last time. Only the finishing touches remained to be worked on the painting.

She had no more qualms about appearing nude before Giles now that they shared the same bed, and had done since the night she gave him her virtue. He smiled as she entered. He had been working on the landscape behind the figure, and had just finished when she arrived. Candle branches were set about, flooding the solarium with golden light; and above, the misshapen moon in its second quarter shone brightly down, its silvery glow a stark reminder that soon it would wax full and the beast would rise again. If Giles thought of that, Tessa saw no evidence of it. He had eyes only for her, watching with unabashed libido as she stripped off her azure-blue round gown and removed the tortoiseshell pins from her hair.

"I shall buy you hairpins of gold, and a chinchilla-trimmed pelisse in the Bond Street shops," he said, arranging her on the lounge. "The thin one we bought in Bodmin will not be nearly warm enough for you in Town now. It's much colder there than it is here this time of year."

"I do not need fancy things, Giles," she said, taking the hourglass as he handed it to her. "I have never lusted after such. But you are spoiling me. I was content to order myself with a shard of broken mirror glass at Poole House. Now, I do not know how I could do without the elegant silver mirror in my dressing room. I'm becoming shamelessly extravagant."

Giles laughed outright. How utterly handsome he was when he smiled; it freed his eyes from the deep shadows that clung to the edge of his brow and made them twinkle.

"It will be my pleasure to spoil you. And when we return, I will paint you as you were meant to be painted, in the most exquisite gown in London, with moonbeams in your hair."

He always knew what to say to make her heart swell with love for him, and he meant these things. Tessa had next to no experience with members of the opposite sex. The few times she'd walked out, it was with men of her own class, and never serious. She didn't know what it was to be courted, to be swept off her feet by a man who truly loved her, but she knew Giles did, and it was glorious.

"It ends tonight," he said. "A few more strokes and we will be ready to make the trip to London. A little more sienna to warm your skin tone in shadow . . . a touch of ultramarine to counter it and make the deepest shadows cool and mysterious, and 'The Bride of Time' is finished."

"When do we leave?"

"In the morning," he told her. "There is no reason to wait. Able will drive us. We must return before the moon is full. Better to become . . . what I become here, in the open, with fewer in harm's way than in Town at the height of the Little Season."

Tessa had almost forgotten about that. She was so happy with Giles that thoughts of the wolf which lurked within him had faded into the distance. Only when she consulted the mirror on her vanity did that nagging splinter return to prick her, for the wound was slow to heal, its progress closely resembling the manner in which Giles's wound had healed in color, texture, and stubbornness. Not even Cook's herbal remedies helped much, and Tessa lived in fear of what Giles would do when he discovered that she had been bitten, and that he was the one who had bitten her.

He honestly didn't remember. That was the insidious way of the curse. Only fragments were retained and recalled afterward. Tessa often thought that a blessing. For how could a werewolf bear to remember what he'd done in the night, in the dark, to the innocents in his path?

It wasn't surprising that he hadn't realized he'd bitten her. She knew that in his human incarnation, and in his heart, he would never dream of harming her. Why, then, would he suspect himself? Though she sometimes almost wished he would. Better that than have him discover her secret under the full moon, for she certainly wasn't brave enough to tell him outright. These thoughts she beat back, praying they were foolish. She was about to become Giles Longworth's bride, and she put all her energies into focusing upon that.

"There!" Giles said. "You may relax, my dear. It is finished!"

Tessa leaned her head back on the lounge and set the hourglass aside. The moon was glaring down through the glass ceiling, and she closed her eyes for a moment. When she opened them again, Giles was standing over her, moonlight breaking over his dark hair, his eyes steeped in deep shadow though she read their message clearly. He was aroused, and she was in his arms before she realized she'd left the chaise lounge.

"You are the most exquisite creature I have ever seen," he murmured against her hair. "And you're mine."

Swooping down, he took her lips in a smothering kiss that stole her breath away. With one arm tethering her against his bruising hardness, he tore open his breeches and rushed her against the wall. In an unstoppable frenzy, he freed his member from the buckskins like a man possessed. Then, seizing her buttocks, he lifted her, guiding her legs around his waist, and plunged into her in one shuddering thrust. Tessa clung to him as he moved inside her, plunging deeper than he'd ever taken her before. How he filled her, his hard shaft riding on her wetness, as he buried himself in her warmth. Every beat of his pulse vibrated inside her. Every thrust of his member drove her toward climax—a climax like no other. The shuddering, spiraling thrusts pounded into her as he took her lips in a bruising kiss, his tongue tasting her deeply. Release was inevitable, and she cried out as he found a place inside that saturated her loins with wave upon wave of rippling sensation.

Clinging to him, she matched his ardor thrust for thrust, calling his name as he set her heart racing, crying out as her sex gripped his as she climaxed, her hands laced through his hair. Soon his member was pumped dry, and she was full with the hot rush of his seed.

Enraptured, he stood frozen inside her, his hands splayed over the cheeks of her buttocks crushing her against him, his bowed head resting upon her shoulder, his breath coming short. After a moment, he withdrew himself, gathered her up in his arms and carried her to the bed.

"Sleep with me here tonight," he said. "I want to lie

with you beneath the moon. You are so beautiful by moonlight, my Tessa."

"Whatever will the servants think?" she teased him. "I shall blush at the sight of them."

"They will think what they already think, that I ravish you nightly like a randy beast. What the devil do you or I care what they think?" He gestured toward her lip. "No doubt they think I beat you on a regular basis as well. I must be more careful. That there is slow to heal, and I do believe I've made it worse." He tucked the counterpane around her and kissed her forehead playfully. "So far as I'm concerned, we were one on the night I took your virtue. I need no piece of paper to finalize our marriage. But tomorrow, we embark upon that journey, and you shall see *my* London."

He moved away then, and ordered his shirt and breeches. Striding to the hearth, he stirred the fire to life, then stalked toward the door.

"Where are you going?" she asked.

"We will be leaving very early in the morning, and I must instruct Foster. Stay where you are. I shall have a hip bath brought up for you."

Tessa sat bolt upright. "Giles Longworth, you wouldn't dare!" she cried.

He laughed outright, his handsome head thrust back, a few dark rakish locks of hair decorating his brow. "Very well, I shall have the tub in your chamber filled," he conceded. "But I assure you, after the goings-on in this house before you came, they would rejoice that I have found happiness at last."

"They can rejoice when we return with that 'piece of paper,'" Tessa informed him.

He laughed again. "It's just as well. You will want to pack your portmanteau. Enough clothes for a sennight or so. It will take at least two days to reach London from here, as long as the weather is fine and we don't linger about, and the same to return."

"How long will we be staying in London?"

"No more than a few days. We must return before the moon is full, which is scarcely a fortnight away, and I don't want to cut the time too close. We must allow for weather, detours, and carriage mishaps. Wheels do lose spokes, and leather straps break, as you well know. I want to leave nothing to chance. Besides, we should stay close to home until the child is found."

"We both know where that child has gone, Giles, and good riddance!"

"Moraiva shares your view, that he has crossed over through one of her time corridors, but he *is* still a child, and the authorities will not be so easily convinced of the truth. I've caught the maids nattering about the boy's disappearance on several occasions already. If such *on-dits* circulate outside these walls, there could be trouble. Half the populace of Bodmin Moor already think I'm a drunkard, a blackguard, and as mad as a brush."

Tessa nodded toward the easel. "The paint is still wet on that canvas. Is it safe to transport before it dries?"

"It won't be thoroughly dry for months, and yes, it will be quite safe. I have transported many paintings before the oils dried to the touch. Able is skilled at crating them. The crate has been in readiness since I began the painting. He'll strap it up top on the brougham safe and sound, and all will be well."

"As long as you're sure," she said. "I would hate to see all your hard work laid to waste."

"It shan't be, and besides, that is the last thing you, of all people, should be concerned about, having seen it in that London gallery quite intact in 1903!"

"I suppose you're right," Tessa said.

"Of course I'm right. Now go and pack, while Evers and Rigby fill your tub and Foster fills mine. Then return to me here. That was only a taste before. It's going to be a long night."

Giles sprinted down the stairs to his apartments, rang for Foster, and had him prepare his bath. Sinking into the hot tub, he groaned as the fragrant water scented with crushed rosemary rushed at his tense, sore muscles. The pressure of racing against time, completing the painting in order to reach London and back before the rising of the full moon, had attacked every inch of his body.

"Will I be going with you?" his valet inquired, handing him soap and sponge.

"Not this time, Foster," Giles said, working up a stiff lather. "I need you here, to keep an eye on the staff, and in case the boy returns. Rigby could never deal with the child; neither could Evers."

"Well, I thank you for your confidence in me, sir, but I hope I shan't have to prove my mettle in that regard."

"Agreed. We leave at dawn. Able will drive us in the brougham. The crated painting will fit well on top of it. I shall need you to pack for me; clothes enough for a sennight or so. No longer than ten days. I must be back before the full moon."

"You will be taking your lady?"

"Yes. She is packing now. Have our bags secured in the boot. We will need the top space for the painting alone, and I shall have Able lash down a tarpaulin over it, just in case of rain, though a fine lot that will do if a flaw hits."

"As you wish, sir."

"The main thing I need from you in my absence, Foster, is to try to keep the *on-dits* from spreading. I know that is next to impossible, but if word gets out about the boy, we will have the guards from the watch to contend with, and I will be hard-pressed to prove I haven't done for the little savage. I'm already branded an ogre. I've been careless, and my reputation alone will damn me in a trice if suspicion rises against me. I wouldn't put it past that little blighter for it to be what he wants."

"I shall do my best, sir," said the valet. "I doubt you need fear any such gammon coming from Rigby, and Dorcas is above reproach, but Evers gossips with Cook and the maids, and they visit their families and friends in service elsewhere on their days off. The Lord alone knows what tales they have already spread, sir."

"I will put the fear of God into them before I leave in the morning. Have them assemble in the study at sunrise. Then, while I'm gone, enforce my orders however needs must."

"Yes, sir."

"I'll need you to go round to the Gypsy camp on the south moor and tell Moraiva where I've gone," Giles went on. "She will be a great help to you here if the boy returns, so fetch her straightaway if that should occur. Then stay close to the Abbey. What I'm doing, old boy, is putting you in charge here until I return. It is asking a great deal, but I know you are equal to the task, and you will be duly rewarded."

"I shall do my very best, sir."

"I know you will, Foster," Giles said, soaping himself with the sponge. "And there is just one more thing. If the boy does return, handle him with caution and keep him here. I'm going to make arrangements to have him packed off to either school or sanatorium when I return, whichever suits. Let someone with more expertise than I have sort him out. I will pay to keep him comfortably, just not here. I will not live in fear, or subject others to do so in my own house. I would stake my life on the belief that the little bastard caused my pregnant sister's death. Unfortunately, I cannot prove it, but that does not mean I intend to live with a murderer, no matter his age. Master Monty will not see the sun set over Long-hollow Abbey on the day he sets foot back in here. You can bet your blunt upon that!"

Chapter Sixteen

The sun hadn't cleared the horizon when the Long-worth brougham rolled down the drive, heading east-northeast toward London. Now that Longhollow Abbey was out of sight, Tessa breathed easier. They couldn't be burned alive in the house if they weren't in it.

Though several storms threatened, the weather held, and they reached London in the late afternoon on the third day of their journey. They stopped to spend the last night at the Golden Cross coaching inn on Charing Cross to rest and refresh themselves for their audience with the Prince Regent the following morning. Travel-ing as husband and wife, they shared a light supper of mutton stew and brown ale, and retired to a reasonably well-appointed chamber above the taproom.

Tessa sat brushing her hair without the aid of a mir-ror until Giles took the brush from her hand and began brushing it himself. "They say a woman's hair is her crowning glory," he said. "If that is so, my love, you are queen of all. I have never seen the like. It is an artist's dream to have such as this to work with."

Tessa smiled. "Well, to prevent it from becoming a nightmare, I think I shall style it differently now that we're here in Town. Mr. Gibson's innovative coiffure would be too shocking."

"Clever girl," Giles said. "Though I find your 'Gibson' style quite becoming."

"It's odd," Tessa remarked, "but I was desperately searching for a coaching inn the day I stumbled upon the time corridor and came to you. This could be the very one. It's closest, I believe, to where I was."

Raising her to her feet, Giles took her in his arms. "Will you show me the gallery where you saw the painting tomorrow?" he asked.

"I will show you where it was. Something else exists there now, I'm certain."

"I still want to see," Giles said.

"It was called Tatum's Gallery," Tessa said, "just south of Threadneedle Street."

"That's convenient," Giles said. "I have business at one of the banks on Threadneedle. We shall go there after we deliver the painting."

All at once his lips were upon hers. There was a gentle eagerness about him now, an almost childlike euphoria. How many faces did this enigmatic man have? If she were to pick one word to describe her husband to sum up his many moods, it would have to be "intense." For he loved and raged and rejoiced with the same volatility. She had never met anyone like him. Could it be the wolf that lurked just under the surface of the man that made him so, or was it simply his nature? There was no way to know.

His current mood was the reason she hadn't told him about the fire, or that it was his bite that had pierced her lip, and that it had happened while the wolf possessed him under the full moon. She couldn't spoil his elation. It stemmed from their love, the painting, and his childlike desire to show her his London.

Her heart began to race. He should know these things. She could just imagine his reaction if he found out she knew and hadn't told him. A vision of him running the whore to ground in the driveway on the night they met came without bidding, and she shuddered, despite his warm arms holding her, molding her body to his, his bruising hardness anxious against her.

Giles's posture clenched, and he held her away, looking deep in her eyes. Tessa was afraid to meet them, those deep-set, analytical, all-seeing artist's eyes that saw into her very soul.

"What is it? You're trembling," he murmured.

"I just took a chill of a sudden," she lied. "There must be a draft. I'd forgotten how much cooler it is in London this time of year than it is out on the coast. Another month and there'll be snow."

"I know just the thing to warm you up," he said seductively, leading her toward the bed.

Why did she want to cry when he was so utterly happy? Because he was, and she knew it couldn't last. They weren't two ordinary lovers having a shocking tryst, a delicious adventure that would end in marriage vows being spoken. He was cursed, and she could well be also. Soon the moon would wax full again, and she would know for certain what she already feared to be true. Then the smile would fade from his handsome lips and the dark, brooding shadows would bury his eyes again beneath the ledge of that noble brow. How could she bear it? Somehow, she must. Somehow, she had to give him this brief respite, and give herself this glimmer of happiness, for she knew how it would end. She had seen the evidence herself. She had touched the blackened timbers of Longhollow Abbey and heard the caretaker's speech. Wherever the devil child had gone, he would return to wreak his vengeance upon his guardian; and the insidious thing was that the boy would likely succeed because he was a boy, above reproach in anything so heinous, for who would believe such evil could be wrought by a mere nine-year-old child?

Even Giles himself was loath to treat the boy harshly. Monty wasn't even blood kin, and was suspected of provoking Giles's pregnant sister's death; yet still Giles honored what he saw as his obligation in caring for Monty even after the boy bit him, infected him with the same strange malaise that turned him into a ravaging beast when the moon was full.

Moraiva had said there were many like Monty among her people, and the boy's mother was a pure-blooded Gypsy. What dark curse had been passed on to the child in the womb? What evil had inhabited that small, deceiving body since birth? What power granted such cunning to so small a host? There was no doubt of the havoc the child was capable of wreaking—even now, in his absence, he had made a shambles of her.

All at once, another thought struck Tessa like cannon fire. What if she were to conceive? It could already have happened. Would she give birth to a child such as Master Monty? And if, as she feared, she was infected also, what sort of creature would it be with both parents cursed?

"You really are cold," Giles said, rubbing her upper arms vigorously. "You're trembling all over! Climb into bed while I stoke up the fire; can't have you taking a chill on our little holiday."

He let her go then and strode to the hearth. It was blackened with soot from an improper draft that belched the stuff back onto the brickwork like tongues of dusky fire and hung in the air, stringy black dust raining down. Giles took up a poker and jiggled the little metal door in the back of the fire wall to open the draft, and it began to draw.

"There!" he said, triumphant. Replacing the poker,

he slapped the soot from his hands and swatted the air-borne particles toward the suction the flow had created. "That should do it. Damn hearth is set to fall in on itself from neglect. It could use the services of a good chimneysweep. I shall have a thing or two to say to the innkeeper about that in the morning. I've paid for this room for two more nights, and I'll be damned if I burn in my bed from a faulty flu!"

Tessa's heart slipped its rhythm at those words, and she bit back a moan. Meanwhile, Giles stripped off his clothes, snuffed out the candles with the palm of his hand and climbed into bed beside her, pulling her close in the custody of his strong arm. His body heat warmed her, but nothing could stop her trembling, and he snuggled closer. "Your feet are freezing!" he said.

It wasn't just her feet. Tessa felt as if an icy hand gripped her heart. It was wrong, all wrong, considering what she knew and he did not. She had no doubt that she would pay dearly for her silence. But he was in her arms, his arousal forced against her, his warm mouth, taking care for her wounded lip, sending shock waves of pleasure through her body as their tongues entwined. Reaching between her thighs, he opened her, his fingers riding her wetness. Sliding between her legs, he thrust inside her, lifting her in order to take her deeply. She could feel his hunger, his insatiable need for her as she clung to him. His hands roamed over her body, cupping her breasts, first his deft thumbs and then his lips bringing her nipples to tight, hard buds. It was as if he couldn't get his fill, like a waif turned loose in a bakery, not knowing which delectable treat to taste first. His excitement was palpable, his ardor overwhelming, and everywhere he touched, everything he cherished seemed to burst into flame.

How handsome he was with the firelight playing

upon his moist skin. Tessa couldn't help but touch him, feeling his hard-muscled chest and broad shoulders as he thrust deeper inside her. Every muscle in him flexed at her touch. Every beat of her heart resonated with the pulse of his sex as he hammered into her. There was a shadow of desperation in every shuddering thrust, as if their very lives depended upon the coupling. Did he sense what was to come? Was there some primeval instinct in him that fought to beat back the inevitable? Whatever it was, it had driven him deeper inside her—body and soul—than he had ever reached before, to the very center of her being, drenching her in a firestorm of pulsating heat.

Leaning into his thrusts, Tessa followed the sharp indentation of his spine to his firm buttocks. Giles called out her name as she gripped them. His pelvis jerked forward, and he pulled back and spiraled into her, all the breath escaping his lungs on one long guttural groan that resonated in the very marrow of her bones. There was a feral urgency in his release, in his shuddering climax throbbing inside her that triggered hers as she undulated against the hard, thick rod of his sex and milked him dry.

He rolled on his side still coupled with her, his body heat scorching her skin. She dared not tremble now; she was on fire. Giles pulled the counterpane around them and brushed her hair back from her face where he'd mussed it, looking deep in her eyes. His scent wafted toward her, musky and mysterious, with his own male essence and a touch of the oil medium he used, even though he'd scrubbed himself clean of it. It had to be in his blood.

"Zeus, but you're beautiful!" he panted, grazing her temple with his warm lips. "Tomorrow is our wedding day. I want to make it as wonderful for you as I can,

Tessa, but no matter what, it won't be anything near what you deserve, and I'm sorry for that. But under the circumstances—"

Her finger across his lips silenced him. "Don't reproach yourself, Giles," she murmured. "We're together."

"Till death do us part," he concluded as her voice trailed off into awkward silence, and he sealed his promise with a tender kiss.

Across the way, a burnt log fell in the grate, sending a shower of sparks up the chimney. The flames blazed, crackled and sizzled until the spark shower calmed, and Tessa jumped in his arms in spite of her resolve to relax and beat back the nagging thoughts that would not be stilled.

Giles pulled her tighter in his embrace, folding his strong arms around her as if he feared she'd escape. "Shhh," he crooned. "It's nothing but the logs in the hearth. Sleep, Tessa; there is much to do tomorrow, and you'll want to be well-rested."

"What will we do first?" Tessa asked him.

"We will deliver the painting," Giles said. "We're expected at Carlton House in the forenoon. Remember, he may not take it. It wasn't exactly a paid commission. He expressed an interest and I said I could provide what he was looking for. We may well be returning to the Abbey with that canvas." He seemed to be preparing himself for failure.

"I doubt that," Tessa said, remembering the little gallery. "I'm sure he will be captivated by it."

"At any rate, I shall want to have that settled first."

"And then . . . ?"

"The special license," he quickly said. "We shall get it at Doctor's Commons. It shan't take long. We can obtain it from the Archbishop of Canterbury or any of his representatives authorized to dole them out in his stead."

"Won't a regular license do? Special licenses were . . . I mean *are* frightfully expensive, aren't they?"

Giles laughed. "I'm not a starving artist, Tessa," he chided. "I can well afford four pounds for a special license."

"Four pounds?" Tessa cried. "What is the cost of a regular license?"

"Ten shillings, but it wouldn't matter if it were free. There are too many restrictions. For one thing, we would have to have the ceremony between eight in the morning and noon. Also, the marriage must take place in a church where at least one of us has lived in the parish for a minimum of four weeks, which would mean we would have to return to Cornwall before we could wed. That, my sweet, would have us celebrating the honeymoon, such as it is, before the nuptials, which just won't do. There have been too many sacrifices already. It's bad enough we must forgo the wedding breakfast and a decent wedding trip of at least a fortnight, and all the fripperies you ladies indulge in. With the special license, we may do as we damn well please, no restrictions upon time or place, which suits our needs since we are pressed for time."

"And then what?" Tessa persisted, snuggling closer in a bold attempt to erase the sour note in his voice.

"And then Able will drive us 'round to Bond Street, so that I may outfit you properly for our wedding."

"Oh, that isn't necessary, Giles," she said. "My blue muslin will do quite nicely."

"Indulge me, my sweet," Giles said, giving her a playful squeeze. "Once we've eaten and done the shops, we shall find a likely chapel and have the deed done. St. Magnus, St. Mary le Bow . . . St. Michael Cornhill . . .

Yes, St. Michael would be closest to Threadneedle and
your gallery."

Tessa shuddered in his arms. This time he didn't challenge her on it. Possibly, he made the same connection
she had: *St. Michael's*. So many St. Michael's churches
linking the lay lines. Could this be one of them? Tessa
tried to put the thought out of her mind, but his silence
only corroborated her fears.

"Well! That's settled, then," Giles said buoyantly.
"And now that we have planned our whole itinerary, we
had best sleep, else you risk another ravishing. I am
quite exhausted, and in this state, my . . . er . . . passions
always grow stronger. Now stop wriggling about if you
would have any rest at all this night. I swear you have
bewitched me!"

But Giles couldn't sleep, though Tessa drifted off quite
content to lie cradled against his naked torso. How
beautiful she was with the firelight bringing out the red
in her chestnut hair fanned around them on the pillows.
He inhaled its fragrance and suppressed a moan of delight in her—all of her. And she was his—all his. He
would be a cuckold no longer. This lovely creature from
another time had captured his heart and soul in such a
way that it terrified him.

He had no right to her; no right to take her, much less
marry her. What could he be thinking? That was just
the point: he wasn't thinking. He didn't dare think, for
if he did, he would have to put her from him. When the
moon waxed full in less than a fortnight, he would become the wolf again and she would be in grave danger
from him. It wasn't as if she didn't know, wasn't aware.
He'd finally convinced her, but that did not lessen his
guilt. His unabashed selfishness could well cost her life.
He hated himself then, but not enough to give up the
precious prize sleeping so peacefully in his arms. He

had taken her virtue. He owed her his life and his loyalty. But what of her safety? Didn't he owe her that as well? The answer was a resounding yes, but he would not heed it—*could not* heed it. He wanted this more than he'd ever wanted anything in his life before. She was pure love. Somehow, fate had given him what life had denied him—a soul mate—and he would have her no matter the cost.

He was almost sorry he'd mentioned St. Michael's Church. He hadn't made the connection until it slipped out and he saw the glimmer of recognition darken her eyes, like a storm cloud passes before the moon. Were the St. Michael's churches the links the lay lines threaded through? He was half-hoping the curate there would turn them away, but somehow he knew that wouldn't happen. The lay lines weren't evil, after all, just conduits to other dimensions, strange subterranean corridors, spirit roads that fractured the myth of time; one of the universe's metaphysical mysteries. One day, someone would solve that mystery, but not in his time or hers. It was enough of a mind-bender to know in his heart and beleaguered mind that the phenomenon was real.

Tessa shifted in his arm, uttered a pleasant sound and cuddled closer, calling his attention to her beautiful face nestled against his shoulder. He was as giddy as a schoolboy in her hands, as malleable as putty that she could mold with her will alone. For the first time in as long as his memory served him, he was genuinely happy. It couldn't last, but while it did, he was determined to make the most of it. Heaving a sigh, he grazed her brow with his lips, shut his eyes, and slept.

Chapter Seventeen

"I am not an unreasonable man," Giles barked at the innkeeper the following morning. "The hearth in that room is black with soot. It's coated everything up there. I've paid for two more nights in this establishment, and I do not think it unreasonable to expect a flue to draw without choking a body with soot."

"A sweep's been summoned," the man said. "You've let the fire go out, haven't ya? Can't have the lad burnin' his breeches, now can we?"

"Of course I have, you nodcock! What sort of buffle-head do you take me for?"

"None a'tall, cove, none a'tall," the man said, sketching an awkward bow. "So sorry for the inconvenience. 'Twill all be put right as rain, afore ya come ta supper."

Giles growled. "I'd demand another room, but I expect all the others are the same."

"Pretty much," the man agreed, scratching his bald head. "We haven't gotten 'round ta doin' the chimneys for the winter season yet. It'll all be taken care of over the next few days, ya have my word on it."

"Yes, well, see that ours is done first," Giles said, waving his walking stick toward the sky. "Do you see that fog? It will have turned to rain before the supper hour. This is our wedding trip, and I'll not have it spoilt with soot!"

The man muttered more, but Able had brought the brougham around and set the steps. Considering his dour prediction, Giles was anxious to see the painting delivered safe and sound before the deluge began. Taking Tessa's arm, he led her into the mews and handed her inside the carriage.

"Where to, sir?" Able called, climbing into the box.

"Carlton House, off Pall Mall, in the West End," Giles replied, climbing in next to Tessa. Wisps of the thick black fog filtered in through the open isinglass window like wraiths. Giles quickly shut it as the coach swayed out into the cobblestone street. The conveyance tooled along among the phaetons, high and low-perch carriages of all descriptions, gigs and hackney cabs, even a sedan chair or two, for London was coming to life on this damp fall morning.

Giles squinted through the isinglass. "Not the best morning to show you my London," he said absently. "But we have two more days. I'm hoping the weather will improve by time we must head back."

"Like as not it will worsen first," Tessa observed. "That is, if your Town weather is as perverse as mine."

"Quite," Giles said. "I'm concerned for the painting. It won't stand a drenching." But it wasn't the trip to the prince's residence that worried him. It was the prospect of a two-and-a-half day journey back to Cornwall in dirty weather that creased his brow in a frown.

Carlton House, situated in the posh West End of London, was a rambling structure. Able let Giles and Tessa out in the drive, then drove around to the delivery entrance to unload the painting. A wigged and liveried footman led them to the Blue Velvet Room, the Prince

Regent's audience chamber off the vast and breathtaking main hallway. Along the way they caught a glimpse
of Ionic columns, splashes of brown Siena marble, and
the splendid octagonal double staircase at the far end of
the hall leading to the Prince Regent's private apartments. Ushering them inside the vast audience chamber, the footman bade them wait and disappeared

Time passed too slowly to be borne, and Giles began
to pace the length of a thick Aubusson carpet in the
center of the gleaming polished floor. The room was
painted top to bottom in a soft shade of blue-gray, with
a large three-tiered crystal chandelier fringed in gold
poised overhead and reflecting the misty blue color also.
It was sparely though elegantly furnished, with a long,
intricately carved table with one matching chair, which
obviously served as a desk by the way it was situated.
Several low carved chests were positioned about, upon
which great Sevres vases in colored porcelain were set,
and two gilded armless chairs stood against one wall
hung with a magnificent Gobelins tapestry. This was
clearly a room where visitors were welcomed in style, or
screened before being admitted to the palace proper.
Giles couldn't help but wonder in dark reflection how
Prinny would feel about receiving a werewolf in his
posh lair. It would have been laughable if the situation
wasn't so grave.

Though it wasn't all that long, it seemed like an eternity to Giles before the Prince Regent joined them, accompanied by two footmen gingerly conveying "The
Bride of Time," which they set upon a gilded easel in
the corner after removing a large landscape canvas that
had occupied the space.

"Exquisite, Longworth!" the prince said, strolling
into the room.

Giles executed a flawless bow from the waist, while

Tessa sketched a dutiful curtsy. How lovely she looked in her robin's-egg-blue gown and indigo pelerine with its matching bonnet. *She has taste, by God,* Giles thought, admiring her choices. She was possessed of an elegant bearing and a cultured voice as well, none of which reflected her servant-class status. He must remember to ask her about all that. Whatever the cause, he'd definitely found himself a diamond of the first water in Tessa LaPrelle, scullery maid or no.

The prince was his usual dapper self, decked out in superfine and silk, his ruffled shirt and elaborately tied neckcloth fighting with the brocade waistcoat that barely stretched across his ample paunch. It added pounds to that which already widened his girth. His hair, swept forward and styled *a la Bruitis,* approached his plump cheeks in a rakish manner that suited him, Giles thought, though it wasn't a style he would be comfortable in himself.

"I'm glad you approve, Your Highness," he said humbly, for all that relief flooded his speech.

"And this charming young lady would be the model, I presume?" the prince inquired.

"One of them," Giles said. "There were several. May I introduce Miss Tessa LaPrelle, Your Highness? She was my model for the Bride's hair and hands, and before the day is gone, she will become Mrs. Giles Longworth. We are on our way to obtain a special license." He'd spoken quickly as Tessa sketched another curtsy. Her cheeks were on fire. It was obvious that her embarrassment at having her nakedness flaunted before the Prince Regent was acute. With all the other press, neither of them had considered this aspect until the moment it occurred. The little white lie seemed to put her at ease, and he drew her close with a reassuring caress.

"Congratulations, Longworth!" the prince erupted.

"I'm quite jealous, to be sure. But if my fantasy bride must belong to another, who better than the artist that painted her?"

"You are too kind, Your Highness."

"She shall hang in my private gallery here at Carlton House. I spend more time here than anywhere else these days. You've quite outdone yourself, Longworth. It has far exceeded my expectations, but then all of your work is brilliant. She will steer more commissions your way, never doubt it." He handed Giles a sealed envelope. "For a job well done," he said. "You will let me know if it isn't sufficient."

Giles pocketed the folded parchment without looking inside. "You are most generous as always, I am sure, Your Highness," he said.

"Tell me, Miss LaPrelle, soon to be Mrs. Longworth," said the prince, "are you a professional model?"

"No, Your Highness," Tessa said. "I am governess to Giles's . . . Mr. Longworth's ward."

"I had to sack my last model for stealing," Giles explained, "and Tessa was kind enough to stand in so that I could finish the painting."

"Nicely!" said the prince. "I do so love a romance, don't you know. I'll have it to my framer first thing in the morning, and I'll instruct him to have a care, since the paint hasn't dried. He's a fine chap. Edwin Tatum is his name. He has a little framing establishment off Threadneedle Street. His dream is to open a small gallery there, near the banks, don't you know. Clever fellow, Tatum. I think he means to pick the rich men's pockets coming and going. It's only a dream, of course. The man's on in years, but he has four sons, and mayhap one of them will take up his cudgel. Feel free to recommend him to your patrons, Longworth. His work is above reproach."

Giles watched the color fade from Tessa's cheeks as if

a shade had descended, turning her peaches-and-cream complexion ghost gray before his very eyes. Tatum's Gallery! He felt a pang inside that struck a nerve and triggered a rush of gooseflesh riveting his spine.

"I will make a point of it, Your Highness," he said.

"May I offer you some refreshment . . . tea, wine?"

"Thank you, no, Your Highness," Giles said. "We are anxious to secure the license while it's still early enough for the ceremony."

"Well, of course you are, Longworth, of course you are. Where are you staying?"

"We only have two days, Your Highness. We are stopping at the Golden Cross, at Charing Cross."

"The deuce you are! I'd like you to be my guest right here at Carlton House, Longworth. We shall have an unveiling! I have other houseguests I would like you to meet. The Duke of York is visiting, and the Earl of Rochester. You can't afford to say no." He took Giles arm and strolled toward the door. "You'll stay at least a sennight." When Giles's posture clenched in spite of himself, the prince said, "Tut, tut, I'll brook no argument. Now, go and have your wedding ceremony, then collect your things from that haven for transient cutpurses and thatchgallows before they rob you blind, and return. I will not be gainsaid. We sup at nine. We shall toast your nuptials, and your success before men who can do you some good."

"Giles, how can we . . . ?" Tessa asked, as the brougham tooled through the dreary London streets toward Doctor's Commons.

"We can hardly refuse an invitation from the Prince Regent," he replied. "It just isn't done, Tessa. It would be a cut direct to refuse his hospitality, especially since philanthropy is his avocation these days, and he fancies himself my patron."

"But Giles . . . a *sennight!* The moon will be full. We can't chance it."

"There is nothing for it," Giles said. "We don't have a choice. We shall carry out our plans and return to the inn. There, we will collect our belongings and go back 'round to Carlton House. I will explain to the prince that we can only stay for two days before starting back. Don't worry, I'll think of something. I'll use the boy, if needs must. Prinny has met Master Monty, to my gross embarrassment. He knows the child is difficult."

But Tessa could not shake the tightness in the pit of her stomach, as if an icy fist had gripped it. "I'm frightened, Giles," she murmured.

He pulled her close in the custody of his strong arm and grazed her temple with his lips. They were cold and dry against her flushed face. "Don't let this spoil our day, my love," he murmured, soothing her with gentle hands. He ground out a wry chuckle. "At least the accommodations will be an improvement," he said. "We shan't have to grope about through clouds of soot and sup upon mutton stew and cheap ale. You shall have a wedding feast fit for a queen."

Tessa wanted to say she would settle for gruel and a straw pallet just to be in his arms, but she nodded instead and held her peace. What worried her most was returning to the Abbey now that she knew what would become of it, but didn't know when. It would have to be soon, while Monty was still a child, if the caretaker's tale was true, and the first part of the event had already occurred; the boy was missing. On the other hand, if Giles was right about the curse, she feared a transformation into wolf form occurring at Carlton House, or any setting but the rambling isolated wilds of Cornwall, especially if that curse now affected her as well.

They weren't long at Doctor's Commons. It was really happening! Tessa LaPrelle was about to become

Mrs. Giles Longworth. She could scarcely believe it, examining the piece of embossed parchment as Able drove the brougham toward the shopping district through a raw misty drizzle that wasn't strong enough to chase the fog.

In Bond Street, Giles bought her a beautiful royal-blue hooded pelisse trimmed and lined with chinchilla fur, which she put on in place of the wrapper she'd been wearing. It was warm enough to protect her against the wickedest gale, and the soft gray fur framing her face offset her chestnut hair so strikingly even the shopkeeper was taken aback. Tessa dug in her heels when he wanted to add several extravagant ball gowns to their purchases, citing that if he wasn't careful he'd fritter away the entire sum the Prince Regent had given him. A compromise was made, and one lovely oyster-white muslin gown was allowed, as well as some frivolous trousseau items that Giles insisted she select, a fashionable bonnet and an assortment of gloves among them.

The jeweler's establishment was next, where Giles purchased Tessa's wedding ring, a dainty gold band with a circlet of iolite stones surrounding a diamond in the center that mirrored the violet-blue color of her eyes. Coming out of the little shop, a flower vendor approached them, her basket overflowing with little tussie-mussies of violets wrapped in paper lace. The fragrance drifted toward them and Giles halted in his tracks, took one from the woman and pressed it to his nose, inhaling deeply.

"*Violets!* Of course!" he rejoiced. Pressing a coin in the woman's palm, he handed the nosegay to Tessa. "Your wedding bouquet, m'lady," he said, sketching a bow. "Since the day we met, I have been trying to place your scent, and here it is at last—violets, and in London in September, of all unlikely things. I'd thought only in Cornwall could one find a violet out of season."

"'Tis where they come from, gov'nor," the old woman put in. "We has 'em sent up from Cornwall for the Little Season every year."

"And bless you for it, mother," Giles said, turning Tessa toward the waiting brougham. "Well, that is one mystery solved at least," he said through a chuckle. "See how you have bewitched me?"

Tessa smiled, her nose buried in the violets. "How many Giles Longworths are there?" she couldn't help saying. "You have so many faces, Giles, I hardly know which is the real you."

He laughed. "You haven't seen him yet, my love," he said, hugging her to him. "When all is said and done . . . when the demons are all destroyed and the ghosts driven back to their graves, you will see him, the real Giles Longworth." He smiled sadly, tracing the shape of her face with the tip of his forefinger. "Until then, I'm afraid you will just have to settle for this."

There was no question that Tessa was marrying a man of mystery. Part of that was very exciting, but another part was terrifying. What worried her most was that he seemed to have forgotten what would happen when the moon waxed full and he became a ravaging wolf. Hers was a more practical nature. Tessa wasn't able to call up the climes of euphoria while the tempest of doom still threatened. Someone had to have a level head. But still, how she loved him in this incarnation of the enigmatic Giles Longworth. How she loved that he could pick her violets in the icy rain, albeit from a raggedy flower vendor, and squander his wealth upon fripperies in the Bond Street shops.

There was nothing to be done about it, and worrying would only make matters worse. Besides, a new worry was about to present itself. They were approaching St. Michael's through the eerie, rain-swept fog. While the special license allowed them to waive the banns and lift the restrictions that insisted marriages be performed in the morning hours, the clergy would still frown upon weddings taking place in the late afternoon.

"Steady on," Giles said, handing her down as Able let them out at the rectory. "They shan't bite, though I must admit most of the clergy hereabouts do look as if they might at that."

But that wasn't what was worrying Tessa. It was that it happened to be St. Michael's and not any other saint's namesake looming before them. Could all the St. Michael's churches be linked to the lay lines as Moraiva said? This church was chosen because of its close proximity to the little gallery on Threadneedle Street. Was it here that she'd run blindly in the fog when it all began, setting her on the course to Longhollow Abbey? It certainly could have been. She had been running in this direction when time played its trick upon her. It certainly could have been right here where she stood now that the landscape changed and the very brougham she'd just vacated came tooling along the lane looking for her. It was certainly on the route she'd taken fleeing the city, and she had seen church spires and steeples along the way. A wave of déjà vu at that thought brought crippling chills that rooted her to the spot, the rain notwithstanding.

Giles quickly raised her fur-trimmed hood and took her elbow, snapping her out of her reverie. "Good God, Tessa," he said. "You're getting soaked."

Clutching the little nosegay of violets as if it were a lifeline tethering her to this time and place—*his* time and place—she followed him into the stately building before them to embrace her future as Mrs. Giles Longworth, the wife of an up-and-coming artist prodigy of the Prince Regent himself.

As Giles predicted, the clergy were none too anxious to perform the ceremony. However, after an almost vulgar monetary inducement, the ceremony was performed in an adjoining chapel with all the amenities Giles's could purchase. Then it was on to where Tatum's Gallery stood in her time so she could show her new husband where, for her, it had all begun.

The rain had slackened to a misty drizzle again, and the fog had become so thick Able had to slow the coach for fear of blundering into oncoming traffic they could hear but not see. Then it came into view, Tatum's Gallery; but not. Now, in 1811, the gilded shingle flapping above the door in the wind read:

> *Gallery framing, Edwin Tatum Proprietor, Framer for the Crown*

Giles tapped the carriage roof with his walking stick, and Able pulled the horses to the curb, climbed down and set the steps. Tessa's heart was pounding when her husband handed her down to the wet cobblestones and led her toward the little recessed door of the establishment. Her husband! The last time she'd approached this portal, she was fleeing the police, wanting one more look at "The Bride of Time" before fleeing the city. On that occasion she was hatless, having lost her bonnet in flight, and wearing threadbare black bombazine and a worn pelerine. Now, she was wrapped in a cloud of robin's-egg-blue muslin, with a pelisse of rich royal blue trimmed in sumptuous chinchilla, and a gold, diamond and iolite wedding ring upon her hand.

An elderly gentleman, Edwin Tatum himself, greeted them. His sleeves were rolled back, and his apron was decorated liberally with sawdust. The layout of the shop was nearly the same, though a dimly lit storage area off to the left would become the gallery proper in 1903. Tessa strayed there, while Giles introduced himself as the artist who had painted the Prince Regent's latest acquisition.

How different it smelled. The oil paint smell issuing from canvases waiting to be framed was present under the surface, but a stronger aroma of resin and varnish and seasoned wood permeated the air. Tessa shut her eyes and inhaled deeply.

"We haven't much time," Giles murmured, slipping his arm around her.

Tessa gave a lurch and melted against him. "You startled me!" she gushed.

"Is this where you saw 'the Bride'?" he asked.

Tessa nodded. "Yes," she said, sweeping her arm wide. "There was an alcove right here, where all of your paintings were displayed . . . or perhaps I should say all of your paintings *will be* displayed." She strolled deeper in. "And here there was a loo, a water closet, with a little window that I climbed through to escape the bobbies."

"Bobbies?" Giles queried.

"That's what they call the police who patrol the London streets in 1903," she explained.

The words were scarcely out when loud shouts in the street turned them both around. Able's gravel-voiced bark pierced the quiet amplified by the fog.

"Git back here, ya little blighter! Stop! Git back here, I say!"

Tessa's eyes flashed toward the shop window in time to see a small, lithe shape streak past the window, Able limping after in pursuit. She gasped as recognition struck and her knees suddenly felt as if they'd gone to water.

"Oh, my God, Giles!" she shrilled. "It's Master Monty!"

As if launched from a catapult, Tessa ran from the shop, Giles on her heels. She raced past the slack-jawed proprietor, past the coachman, who had stumbled to a halt soothing his leg, leaning against the horse his bluster had spooked. She was quicker on her feet than either of them. Ignoring their shouts behind, she kept on running, keeping the boy's shape in sight through the thickening fog, which was nearly impenetrable with the eye the farther she ran toward the fringes of Cheapside.

It never occurred to her that she was heading straight for Poole House until it was too late. The lighthearted titter of a child's laughter funneled back at her out of the fog, then the boy disappeared altogether in the milky thick of it.

A familiar spiked iron fence came into view. A whistle sounded, loud and shrill at close range, and she careened headlong into an unsuspecting bobby looming up out of the misty darkness.

Chapter Eighteen

"The little blighter was hidin' in the boot!" Able grumbled, still soothing his leg. "I heard a noise. When I opened the back, the little devil jumped out and landed hard on me foot with both o' his. Then he kicked me a good one in me shinbone—same spot that cob you sold to the Gypsies kicked me last month—and took off like a pistol shot. I'm sorry, sir, I couldn't catch him. He was too quick for me."

Giles dove into the coach. "Get back into that box, man, and drive this thing!" he charged. "We will never catch them afoot now!"

The coachman hopped up top and seized the ribbons, snapping them hard, and the horses pranced off in the direction Tessa had taken. Giles opened the window and poked his head out into the foggy afternoon glare, but there was no sign of either Tessa or Monty. The street was practically deserted, and though he called at the top of his voice, there was no reply.

The carriage struck a rut, and Giles ground out a string of expletives as he hit his head on the window frame. "Watch where you're going, man!" he charged Able, who came back with an inaudible reply, drowned out by the clopping of the horses' hooves and the groaning of the brougham's taxed suspension. Gripping the edge of the seat for support as the carriage listed into another hole in the cobblestone lane, Giles's hand grazed something soft and cool to the touch on the seat beside him. He groaned as his fingers closed around the violet nosegay he'd bought for Tessa. "Faster, man! Faster!" he shouted.

"Make up yer mind!" the coachman barked, snapping the whip over the horse's heads. "I ain't no Corinthian, and this ain't no gig. You've already busted one carriage this month. We can ill afford another gone ta ruin."

"Do you think I give a care about the carriage?" Giles seethed, brandishing his walking stick out the window like a Bedlamite. "I have to find her!"

"How far do ya think she'll git?" Able asked him. "She'll come back when her legs git tired, with or without the boy, and good riddance, if ya ask me, if she comes back alone! We should turn 'round and wait by that framin' shop. That's where she'll be lookin' for us."

Giles threw down his walking stick. Flinging his beaver hat across the carriage, he pounded the seat with white-knuckled fists and raked his hair back ruthlessly with both his hands, as if he meant to keep his brain from bursting through his skull. Able didn't understand. He didn't know. And Giles couldn't even tell him. The poor man would never believe it.

All Giles could think of was that she could have blundered onto one of the lay lines, corridors through time that he had thus far been denied. Moraiva had said once accessed, future admittance to the subterranean passageways became easier. Had she gone somewhere in time where he could not follow? Had he lost her? He was about to run mad at that prospect.

And then there was the church—St. Michael's Church. Why hadn't he taken her to St. Magnus for the ceremony, or St. Mary le Bow, as they were both equidistant to their destination? What had he done? He didn't even know, and Moraiva, the only one he could confide in, the only one who could help him, was keeping vigil back in Cornwall in case the boy returned; they'd believed he'd accessed one of the corridors when all the while the cunning little devil was hiding right under their noses.

Giles let out a deranged laugh and called Tessa's name out the window at the top of his voice again.

"She couldn't have come this far afoot, sir!" Able responded. "We need ta go back, I tell ya. She must have turned off somewhere. She could be back there at the framin' shop waitin' for us right now."

Oh, how Giles prayed Able was right, but he didn't believe it. "Turn 'round then, damn it, man," he shouted, "and let us see."

She wasn't at the frame shop; nor had she been. Giles waited there while Able tooled about the lanes and avenues of Cheapside until dark cancelled the search and the framer turned him out to lock up for the night, but there was no sign of Tessa or the boy.

There was no use going to Bow Street. There was nothing the Runners could do to fetch her back from the year 1903. They would lock him up for a madman. He'd almost forgotten his commitment to the Prince Regent. Praying that if Tessa did find her way back to his time she would go to Carlton House looking for him, he instructed the coachman to take him back to the coaching inn to collect their belongings. He would keep his commitment to the prince, meanwhile sending Able back to cruise the length and breadth of Threadneedle Street. There was nothing else he could do.

"Hold her, I say," a woman's shrill voice cried. "She's the one who stole my brooch!"

Tessa's heart sank. It was Miranda Poole. She had come rushing down the steps and through the ornamental wrought iron gate the minute the bobby's whistle sounded.

"Here now, madam, stand back!" the bobby charged, turning to Tessa. "What's your name, miss?"

"She's Tessa LaPrelle," Miranda Poole put in, "my former scullery maid. She stole my pearl brooch and ran off before we could have her locked up right proper."

"All right, madam, settle down!" the bobby warned her, turning back to Tessa. "Is that your name, miss?"

"Yes, but—"

"Do you see?" Miranda Poole interrupted. "I told you! I demand you arrest her at once!"

"Do you have this woman's brooch?" the bobby asked Tessa.

"No, I do not, and I never did," Tessa defended. "She found it in my room after one of the other servants put it there to implicate me."

"Oh, I see, so ya got your bauble back then," the constable said to Miranda Poole.

"That is of no consequence," she replied. "I want to make an example of her. It's my right!"

"Where do you live, miss?" the bobby asked Tessa.

"She lived here," Miranda Poole spoke up. "But no longer. I'm well shot of her. Look at her! Look at the scandalous clothes on her! She never owned anything but black bombazine when she was in my employ. She's evidently found someone else to steal from, or robbed a brothel. I have never seen the like. Look at the ring on her hand. Where did you get that? Who did you steal *that* from, miss, hmm?"

"Will you let the gel speak?" the bobby said, clearly out of patience.

"This is my wedding ring," Tessa replied, fingering the gold and iolite band. "I have never stolen anything in my life."

"She is lying! She had no suitor. She's a thief, plain and simple, and I want her jailed!"

"Where's your husband, then?" the bobby asked Tessa. "If you're married, like you say, he should be able to speak for you."

"H-he can't," Tessa lamented. "H-he isn't here. He's away . . . on business in Cornwall." What else could she say? She certainly couldn't tell the truth, which only reminded her of what she'd left behind. Her heart sank. Giles must be beside himself with worry, and there was no way she could ease his mind. She couldn't even try to retrace her steps. She was caught, and though Giles would surmise what had happened, there was no way she could tell him where she'd gone.

"A likely tale!" Miranda Poole shrilled. "Do you see? She's a liar! I demand her arrest! I mean to press charges."

A crowd had begun to gather. Jasper Poole had come out of the house, his countenance disapproving. There was no hope; the diabolical child had led her into the corridor that took her back to the very steps of Poole House. The truth would not serve her here, except to see her locked up in Bedlam and forgotten. The clothes, the ring Giles had bought in Bond Street, all damned her. Her only chance lay in the mercy of the magistrates, who she prayed would show leniency since the brooch had been recovered.

The bobby blew a shrill blast on his whistle and seized Tessa's arm. "All right!" he shouted. "She goes to the lockup at Old Bailey till it opens for business in the morning. We'll let the magistrates sort her out. You want to press charges, madam, that's where you'll do it. It needs to be in writing. Come 'round first thing in the morning and see to it, or she goes free, cause she ain't done nothing that I can see to cause me to lock her up. If she stole from you, I can't see why she'd come back 'round here to your very doorstep to risk getting herself nabbed."

Tessa's heart leapt. Was this a ray of hope after all? If the bobby believed her, if he put in a good word for her, might there be a chance?

"I want her jailed!" Miranda Poole carped.

"Now, now, mother, you have your brooch back," her husband said.

"It's the principle, Jasper. She must be made an example of before the others. I want them to see what happens to thieves at Poole House, or that lot below stairs will rob us blind."

"All right, then, off she goes," the bobby said. "'Tis a misdemeanor, so they'll hold her over for the Sessions Court to sort out."

"And how long will that take?" Miranda Poole snapped.

"They only meet eight times a year here in Town. They ain't due again till next month."

"Next month?" Tessa cried out. "I cannot stay locked up until next month."

The bobby laughed. "You should have thought of that before you stole from these nice folks here." He blew his whistle again, attracting the notice of a passing hackney cab tooling out of the fog. "Come on then," he said, propelling her along toward the carriage.

"Where to?" the driver hollered.

"The lockup down 'round Old Bailey," the bobby replied, shoving Tessa into the cab despite her tearful protests. "I just come on duty," he said to the driver, with a wag of his head and a humorless chuckle. "Looks like it's going to be a long night."

A sennight passed, and nearly another, and still there was no sign of Tessa or the boy, though Able and Giles in their turn haunted the highways and byways of

Cheapside. Though the coachman made no protest, nor did he press for an explanation, Giles knew poor Able had to know something untoward was afoot. He would have to be a cretin not to have guessed the hushed tales of lay lines were true, and Able McGowen was far from simple. Still, the stabler cum blacksmith cum coachman was owed an explanation that Giles was loath to give, because to give the truth substance with words would be to make it true, and that he could not—would not—do, else he run mad in the streets.

Brandy blunted the edges of his futility, but no matter how much he consumed, he couldn't manage drunkenness; he didn't dare in any case, if he was to be alert for the miracle he prayed for, the miracle that would give him back his Tessa. There wasn't much time. The moon was waxing full. A few more days and the wolf inside him would surface again. The last place he wanted that to occur was in the middle of London Town at the height of the Little Season, that extra spurt of social whirls for those diehards who refused to abandon Town life before winter cancelled the gaiety again until the spring.

Having excused Tessa by fabricating a family emergency, Giles stayed on as the Prince Regent's guest, until Prinny decamped for Brighton before the winter snows. After bidding his patron good-bye, Giles returned to the coaching inn at Charing Cross, secretly hoping that Tessa would come to him there. But that was a dream dredged from the dregs of the brandy he'd begun to hate, the drink that blunted the edges of his reason yet did nothing to ease his pain.

When time grew short, he sent a special messenger to Foster at Longhollow Abbey, entreating him to seek out Moraiva, the Gypsy. He was desperate for any insight she might impart, for he had exhausted all his options. He dared not return to the framer's establishment.

Edwin Tatum didn't care a whit that Giles was Prinny's protégé. The outraged framer threatened him with the guards from the Watch, or the Bow Street Runners if he didn't take himself off and stay gone, citing that Giles's presence was chasing his customers away. The man was right, of course, but that did not keep Giles from monitoring what went on at the framing shop from a discreet distance. He haunted Threadneedle Street like a wraith in the mist, day in and day out, taking turns with Able.

In between, Giles would drag himself back to the Golden Cross, while Able took his place. Soot still belched into his room just as it had the night he'd first arrived there with Tessa. The innkeeper hadn't bothered to have the chimney swept, since Giles went straightaway to Carlton House, and the malodorous black fog hanging over the room irritated Giles's eyes and clogged his nostrils. He had the man's word that a chimney sweep would be hired, but Giles had given up expecting one.

Four days before the moon would wax full, Giles exchanged places with Able early. It was scarcely dusk when he returned to the coaching inn and collapsed from exhaustion on the bed without undressing. It had been a long day, made longer by a stubborn drizzle that turned bitter cold, threatening hail, and the coachman had brought him back early, fearful that Giles would come down with pneumonia if he stayed out in such dirty weather any longer.

As was always the case when he was exhausted, Giles's passions heightened. Dreams came, soft, radiant dreams of Tessa in his arms, of her supple lips pressed against his own. He could taste her honey sweetness. He could feel the satiny smoothness of her skin, of her gentle fingers wrapped around his sex, bringing it to life, making it hard, making it ready for her silky wetness to envelop it like a sword by its sheath.

He groaned as the bittersweet torture brought him nearer to climax, and yet release would not come, even though he could taste her skin, feel her nipple harden beneath his tongue as he laved it erect. His artist's eye was seeing her now—every contour, every slope, every plane as it was etched in his mind. He cursed the eye that had emblazoned it there, for he had lost her, and the image was sheer torture. It gave him no peace, not even in the sanctity of his dreams. Try as he would, he could not make her materialize before him. He could not give the wraith she had become corporeal substance. He could not breach the time that separated them. He was still denied access to the corridors. Why? What had he done to offend the gatekeepers? Or was it that they just did not see him, would never see him no matter how he tried?

His desire was all-consuming, and he ached for release. Her scent was all around him, in him, ghosting past his nostrils. The violet tussie-mussie he'd bought her on their wedding day had shriveled and died, yet he couldn't bear to part with it. Instead, it lay upon the mantel, where the heat rising from the hearth could spread its scent. It filled his consciousness and his subconscious with Tessa's very essence. It taunted him waking and sleeping, like now, when he reached out with his arms and his very soul to embrace her, but all he clutched to him was empty air.

A knock at the door bled into his dreams. It came again, louder, but it didn't seem real. He heard it as if through an echo chamber, just another torment to keep him from Tessa, to keep him from embracing her, from releasing in her, from bringing her to climax and himself to ecstasy in those exquisite arms. He would ignore it, and did . . . until his name accompanied the infernal hammering. The voice that delivered it was a man's voice, a careless voice. It sat Giles bolt upright, unfulfilled and unrelieved, and his eyes slowly focused upon something being slipped under the door.

Giles rubbed his eyes to clear the cobwebs of sleep; nothing could slow his heartbeat or erase his disappointment that he lay in that bed alone. Swinging his feet over the side of the pallet, he marveled that he was still wearing his turned-down top boots. No matter. He got to his feet, staggered to the door and snatched up the missive. Recognizing his own seal sobered him, and he broke the wax and ripped the parchment open to reveal Foster's flawless hand:

> *Sir,*
>
> *You must return at once! The boy has not been found, and the Watch has been by. Your absence has fed fuel to the fire that you have done for him. They are threatening to send word to Town to run you to ground. You must return, or it will be the worse for you.*
>
> *I have spoken with Moraiva as you wished. She, too, says you must return. She told me to tell you this, though I do not presume to understand it: "Leave her to find her own way. Tax not the gatekeepers. Avoid St. Michael's churches until we speak."*
>
> *Yours faithfully,*
> *Foster*

Chapter Nineteen

Giles had the hostler saddle a horse, and he rode out in search of Able. He would leave the coachman behind to continue the search for Tessa, but he could hardly leave without telling him where he was going and why. It was time to tell Able more than he'd hoped he would have to. Whether the faithful servant believed or not, he would have to know what Giles believed.

Despite an oilskin borrowed from the coaching inn stables, Giles was soaked through when he reached Threadneedle Street. He hadn't eaten, and his stomach roiled for want of food, which did little to resurrect his good humor, something long lost since Tessa disappeared in the fog on their wedding day.

He'd made several passes by the frame shop and cruised Cheapside for a good half-hour before he spotted the brougham. There were several public houses nearby, and Giles directed Able to one he'd often frequented when in Town—The Spotted Falcon, off Cornhill near Lombard Street—that afforded privacy and hearty food for its customers.

It was busier than usual, the rain having driven customers in. The two men settled at a table in a recessed alcove, where Giles could speak to the coachman as confidentially as was possible in such a setting, and ordered tankards of porter and plates of savory rook pie.

"Ya should be abed," the coachman grumbled, taking a swig of the rich, dark brew. "You're courtin' pneumonia or consumption goin' about in such tempests as this."

"It's starting to slack," Giles observed, craning his neck toward the window. "By the time I set out at first light, it'll have stopped altogether."

"Set out, is it? Where are we goin', then?"

"Not 'we,' Able; needs must that I go alone. I want you to remain here and keep searching."

The coachman froze, his fork suspended. "All due respect, sir, but could it be that she don't want ta come back? It appears ta me that—"

Giles waved him off. "Able, things are not what they seem," he said. "You must know by now that something untoward is afoot here. I don't presume to know exactly what that something is, but I do know that . . . I know that Tessa came to us out of the future. Unless I miss my guess, that little demon led her right back to her own time."

The coachman looked surprised. "And where did he go, then?"

"I have no idea, but I don't think he went with her. He's here somewhere; I'd stake my life upon it. He wanted to get shot of her, just as he got shot of all the others. They were easy. They were afraid of him. Tessa was not."

"I heard tell o' lay lines hereabouts. The Gypsies say they exist, but . . ." The coachman shook his head, unconvinced. Yet it wasn't necessary for Able to believe, just to be aware.

"You picked her up that first night," Giles reminded him. "She tried to tell you she wasn't who you thought she was; she tried to tell us both. She was fleeing pursuers in her time when she crossed over, and now she's gone back among those who mean her harm. I am half-mad with this, Able. You don't have to agree with me, just obey. I've had a missive from the Abbey. The Watch thinks I've done for the child and that I've run. I must return to Cornwall at once . . . but I cannot leave Tessa."

"I'll do as ya say—that goes without question—but 'tis more than a man can comprehend, what you're sayin'."

Giles couldn't help but wonder what the coachman would say if he knew the master of Longhollow Abbey would turn into a wolf in but a few short days, too. How would the poor man comprehend *that?*

"Just think on this," Giles said. "Somewhere in time, my bride is walking the same streets we walk. She is here, Able, among us right now, only in a different year, and she's trying to get back to me. If it is at all possible, she will. You brought her to me once. I only pray you can do so again."

It was nearly dawn when Giles reached the coaching inn. He would return to Cornwall by post chaise. Going thus was expensive, but it was the swiftest means and time was of the essence. After making the arrangements, he went straight to his room to collect his belongings. The innkeeper had warned him to let the fire go out, since they'd finally hired a boy to sweep the chimney. But it was too late for such amenities, and Giles was halfway to the stables when the sweep climbed up on the roof with his brushes.

The chaise was waiting, the coachman decked out in his colorful rig, from the crimson traveling shawl beneath his wide-skirted green coat to his wide-brimmed, low-crowned hat of brown felt. Giles had paid for four horses and two postilions for haste. Though there was

room for two inside—not including the dickey at the
back for the groom—he would be the only passenger,
which suited him. It was a long distance to Cornwall,
two days at best, and he was in no humor for idle conversation with strangers.

What made him look back before entering the chaise,
Giles didn't know. He certainly wouldn't miss the inn.
But when his eyes strayed toward it, his heart nearly
stopped beating. There, on the roof, the chimneysweep
had begun to ply his long-handle brushes. And it wasn't
just any sweep. It was Monty.

The boy hadn't noticed him, and Giles crept back
along the building, flattening himself up against the
inn's outer wall until he reached the ladder. Crouching
low, to prevent the boy from seeing him until the very
last, he rushed up the rungs, leaped onto the slippery
tiled roof made slipperier by the rain, danced his way up
the slope and yanked the boy from the chimney by the
scruff of his neck.

"So, this is where you've been hiding, is it?" Giles
seethed, hefting the boy over his shoulder. It would
stand to reason. Chimneysweeps were always in demand, and the position earned him room and board.
"What have you done with her? Speak up! Where is
she?"

"I don't know what you're talking about. Put me
down! Let me go!"

"Ohhh no," Giles said, jerking him back as the boy
tried to bite him. "Go ahead!" he said. "Sink those teeth
into me if you must. You can do no more harm than
you've already done, and you might just cause me to
lose my grip upon you. It's a long way down off this
roof, Master Monty. One slip and I will be well rid of
you. Now, I'll ask you again: where is she? What have
you done with her?"

"I took her home," the boy said, dangling precariously as Giles shimmied down the ladder. "She won't be coming back. Lemme go!"

"Well, you will be coming back," Giles triumphed, "to show the guards from the Watch at home that I haven't killed you. You're a cunning little blighter, Master Monty Montague." He hoisted the boy into the chaise and climbed in beside him. "Let us see what tune you sing by time we reach the coast."

Tessa wiped the damp tendrils of her hair from her face and straightened up, soothing her back. Sessions wouldn't convene for another fortnight, and in the meanwhile she'd been assigned custodial labor at the jail, which freed her from her cell for a time each day. While she was under constant scrutiny, that little bit of freedom gave her hope that somehow she could escape, for she would have a better chance of finding Giles if she were free to seek the corridors that she knew might reunite them. She was also pleased that her jailors hadn't found her coin purse, which she now wore around her neck.

But things were not perfect: the moon was full, and she didn't have to wonder if it would affect her when it rose. She had felt its pull for two days now. The wound upon her lip had healed, though traces still remained. It reminded her of the wound on Giles's wrist in color and condition. There was no question. Next to her coin purse, she still wore the pentacle amulet about her neck beneath her frock. Already, it had begun to irritate and burn. The wolf inside her would rise with the moon. She was terrified that it would occur within the dingy walls of that dank London jail. But on the other hand, she was glad that Giles wasn't there to see what would happen, especially since he was the one who had infected her.

Darkness came quickly. Her good behavior had

gained her favor with the turnkeys. That was her plan: to lull them into a careless mode. There was one called Samuel, however, a leering, foul-smelling individual whose familiar gestures and lewd advances terrified her. It was he who came on for the evening shift.

Tessa had deliberately drawn out scrubbing the lobby floor. It was torture being that close to freedom and not being able to escape. They hadn't given her anything to wear, and her beautiful robin's-egg-blue muslin was hopelessly soiled and tattered. They'd taken her wedding ring, and she knew she would never see her chinchilla-trimmed pelisse again. But none of that mattered as long as she could somehow find Giles.

She had worked herself closer and closer to the door, when something held her back, and she whipped her head around to face Samuel, who had tethered her with the toe of his heavy boot upon the hem of her frock.

"You're done," he said, hauling her to her feet. There was no mistaking what he wanted of her as he none too gently led her along toward her cubicle.

A high-set window at the end of the corridor showed her the moon, full and round and bloodred, as it often was this time of year. It was happening. There was nothing she could do to prevent it. All around her the moans and cries and restless laments of the inmates more mad than sane rose in reply to the commotion she and the turnkey were causing as he tried to force her back into her cell. This she could not allow, for he would have his way with her, lock her in, and all would see her turn into the wolf that even now was swallowing her consciousness. Already it was erasing her memory of the here and now, as it would much of what lay ahead when she transformed into the creature she feared she'd become.

All at once, her screams became guttural snarls. Her vision narrowed, and the periphery appeared through a blurred auburn haze. There was pain—a great deal of pain as bones shifted, as muscle and sinew stretched and flexed, expanding and contracting into the shape of the creature taking control.

Tessa vaguely remembered knocking Samuel down. She had no other recollection of her flight until she plunged headlong through the foyer window. She only remembered that because the jagged shards of broken glass pierced her shoulders as she crashed through, tearing away what remained of her frock that Samuel hadn't torn from her body during their struggle. The very air was rife with shards and specks and splinters of glass illuminated in the gaslight glow of streetlamps that had just been lit, and she hit the cobblestones on all fours, streaking through the moonlight faster than any man could have done on two.

On the vague periphery of her human consciousness, the she-wolf ran through the all but deserted streets, through the misty darkness beneath the risen moon. An echo in her soul directed her then, a fading, distant splinter of recollection nagging at her mortal incarnation. She found herself heading straight for the gallery, just as she had when she ran that first fateful day with the bobbies on her heels. Only, this time she was approaching it from a different direction, from the jail instead of Poole House. The wolf she had become wouldn't know this, but Tessa knew, and not even knowing why, she ran until she feared her heart would burst through her barrel-chested body until she'd reached Threadneedle Street and Tatum's Gallery.

The shop had long since closed for the day, though a light inside illuminated the alcove she had visited so often in the past. But it wasn't empty now. "The Bride of Time" had breached time again. It was standing where it always stood, surrounded by Giles Longworth's other paintings. His self-portrait beckoned. Could she have come back through the corridor to a point in time before the paintings were sold . . . before that awful moment when she reached the little gallery for one last look only to find that they were gone?

She blinked, and the scene before her changed. The light inside the little gallery was snuffed out. Giles's paintings were gone again, and all was in darkness. It had been a fleeting, dreamlike episode that didn't seem real; but then, this was Tessa's first time in the body of a wolf, and nothing did.

Her human periphery was closing in upon her again. She was losing control of her real self and becoming more and more the wolf. She threw her head back and loosed a howl that sounded shrill in echo all around her. She howled again, as if she desperately fought to beat back the inevitable, the mindless possession of the lupine creature in her that would kill her memory. Then, with her last shred of human consciousness, she ran behind the buildings into the alley the way she'd run when she'd escaped from the gallery loo.

Suddenly, the gallery seemed far away. The shrill cries of the lamplighter and two drunken slags calling "Mad dog!" and "Werewolf!" faded into the distance. Her vision was closing in altogether, except for what stretched directly in front of her, and that she saw only through an auburn haze that resembled dried blood. Another howl pierced the awful unfamiliar silence, Tessa only marginally aware that it was coming from her own throat. She could no longer draw the line between human and wolf. The edges were blurred. The light was fading. A ghost-like mist rose up around her like a cottony blanket, choking her lupine whines and turning them into guttural snarls. A hunger like no other overwhelmed her—the hunger of a ravenous beast seeking its prey.

The auburn stain before her eyes had turned bloodred. Through the crimson haze, she saw a tall church belfry streak by; or was she streaking by the church it crowned? She could no longer distinguish motion, only need: an all-consuming passion to ravage and destroy. All trace of her humanity was gone. She was pure wolf now, streaking through the fog, bounding over cobblestones and paving stones, curbstones and milestone markers. On the she-wolf ran, over gravel and bracken-tufted dirt as the lane narrowed, on until her wolf's heart felt as if it were about to burst. She bounded over the patchwork hills, on and on . . . until she ran headlong into another wolf: a wild-eyed, ravaging male.

Chapter Twenty

For a moment, the two wolves stood transfixed, staring at each other in the moonlight. The male was larger, darker. The female almost appeared silver in the haloed glow of first light trickling over the horizon.

The female howled into the mist, head thrust back. The desperation in the sound backed the male wolf up a pace, and Giles's consciousness slowly bled into the madness of the wolf's mind. His vision was widening. He could once again see with human eyes, though he remained trapped in the body of the wolf. It was agony, and he, too, howled at the sky.

Recognition was returning. He looked deep into the eyes of the female wolf—into *Tessa's* eyes, limpid and sad. Rearing back on his hind legs, he sailed through the air, a guttural lupine snarl baring deadly fangs that turned into a human cry as he collided with her naked upon two feet, and fell to his knees, embracing the female wolf.

"Noooooo!" he groaned, fisting his hands in her silvery wolf's coat, burying his face in the thick, lush ruff about her neck, clinging to her with all his strength.

The she-wolf wriggled in his arms, let loose a bestial howl and broke free, bounding away, off and over the moor through the mist shrouding heather and bracken. The brush slowed her pace and she finally sprang, surging to her full human form in a silvery streak of displaced motion, an agonized whine pouring forth as the transformation took place. Sinew and bone reshaped itself, muscle and flesh, and she finally emerged naked and whole, tears streaming down.

But the shape-shift didn't break her stride. On she ran, over clumps of tall swaying grass, bracken and furze wet with the morning dew, her long chestnut hair streaming out behind her like a pennant waving in the dawn breeze.

His long, corded legs pumping furiously, Giles gave chase. He was gaining on her. Why was she running from him? Her sobs were like needles piercing his soul, and he called her name at the top of his voice.

"Tessa, wait!"

But she kept on running, and his heart leapt inside as he recalled another time he'd run after her and lost her to a time corridor. He couldn't let that happen again; not now. That fear gave his feet wings until they collided again, and he spun her around screaming in his arms, and drove her down in the mist-draped heather.

"Why are you . . . running from me, Tessa?" he called out, panting, the debilitating exertion of transformation coupled with the chase having rendered him breathless. "How did this happen? Answer me!" he demanded, shaking her.

Her sobs replied, and he shook her again, none too gently. She was close to hysteria, but he needed answers.

"Don't, Giles," she sobbed. "I didn't want you to find out this way. Let me go!"

"Let you go?" Giles seethed. "You are my wife, Tessa. What is all this? How has this occurred? Was it Master Monty?"

Tessa let out a mournful wail, struggling in his arms,

and he crushed her close, burying his hand in the long silken flow of her hair. Her body, pressed so close against his own, naked but for a small purse around her neck, sent shock waves through him. Shapeshifting always prompted arousal. He was on fire for her.

"No," she murmured. "It wasn't."

"Who, then? My God, Tessa, who? Where were you bitten?" He began searching her body with frantic hands. How warm she was, despite the thin veil of mist that moistened her skin from the morning dew. The tactile experience of caressing her petal-soft skin drenched in dew drove him over the edge. She felt like hot silk in his arms, fluid and malleable, seeking her own level against him the way a silken scarf slides across the flesh of the wearer, sensual and subtle, as if it had a life of its own.

The frantic search for wolf bites became an unstoppable frenzy of palpable lust. She felt it, too; he could tell by the way she opened to him, arching her body against him, twining her legs around his waist as he lifted and filled her in one swift, deep thrust.

How warm she was inside. How warm, and silky smooth inside and out as he rode her, thrusting deeper and deeper, reaching farther than he had ever reached before. Undulating beneath him, Tessa matched his passion thrust for thrust in such wild abandon it took his breath away. The transformation had obviously heightened her sexual awareness just as it had his. They were perfectly matched. How could she have run from him?

All around them the subtle scent of heather rising from the blooms their bodies crushed wreathed them like an aura. The heady fragrance ghosted through his nostrils, mixing with the scent of violets drifting from her hair. The combined scents were like a drug taking him under, devouring his inhibitions, making him ravenous for her. All else was forgotten. Nothing mattered but their coupling. In that one brief and perfect burst of raw desire, there were no werewolves. There was no Monty. Nothing existed except their bodies joined in mindless oblivion. A whole month had passed since he'd left London and abandoned the search, and in truth, he'd feared that he had lost her, never to see or feel her, never to love her again.

Oddly, Giles didn't feel the cool mist rising around him. The climate in Cornwall was fairly in for October, though in London they would soon be feeling snow. Besides, the wolf still lurking deep inside him could stand a colder clime; he'd felt that in his human incarnation since he was bitten. Every sense, every physical experience was heightened come to that, especially his sexual awareness. Now it was magnified a thousand-fold.

First his fingers and then his lips caressed her breasts, laving the nipples into hard, erect buds to feast upon. Tessa arched her back to receive those lips, that tongue. Her very posture was a banquet for his dilated eyes, eyes shared with the feral beast within him.

Her climax riveted him with waves of fiery sensation; her sex gripped his relentlessly as he thrust into her. His release was a volatile surge of unstoppable explosions and she milked him dry in a way he had never experienced before. It left him weak and trembling in her arms as if she'd sucked the very marrow from his bones, as if those bones had melted inside his body and rendered him helpless under her command.

Gathering her, he crushed her close against him, his broad chest heaving; and he devoured her lips, tasting deeply of her sweetness. It was—oh, it *was*—his Tessa in his arms again. It wasn't a dream, some mad hallucination brought on by the transformation and his longing. She was real and soft and warm in his arms, and he hadn't harmed her. He hadn't bitten her, savaged her, ravaged her in his mad, rampaging werewolf incarnation. Still fearful that he might have, he touched her body all over to be sure, to be certain he hadn't harmed her in some way known only to the wolf.

Leaking a lupine whine, he crushed her close, rocking her gently as the mist swirled about them like a living blanket. The clothes he'd cast off when the transformation began were but a few yards away—he'd returned to where he'd begun—but he feared to let her go to fetch them. What if she were to run from him again? It would not be borne. Scooping her up, he staggered to his feet, commanding his melted bones to move him, and carried her to the pile of damp clothes scattered about the heath.

Snatching up his greatcoat, he set her on her feet and wrapped it around her. "You will catch your death," he murmured as she snuggled into it. He eyed his breeches longingly where they lay impaled out of reach upon a clump of bracken and nodded toward them. "May I?" he asked. "Will you allow me the same privilege, or will you run from me again the minute I let you go?"

Tears welled in her eyes, and she nodded. Whether that meant she would or wouldn't flee he wasn't certain, but he had to trust it. After a moment he let her go, snatched his breeches, and tugged them on, his eyes never leaving her face. Ready to run after her again if she were to run, he shrugged his shirt on, left the rest, and took her in his arms again.

"Tessa, why *did* you run from me?" he murmured, searching her eyes deeply. What he saw there terrified him. But it was her tears that troubled him most. He wiped them from her cheeks, from her bruised lip with his thumbs. *Her bruised lip?* There wasn't another blemish on her anywhere. His frazzled mind reeled back to that first time he'd embraced her on the heath, and his thumb froze upon the stubborn bruise that still lingered, just as the wound upon his wrist still lingered, though the broken flesh had healed. Cold chills washed over him from head to toe and he shuddered.

"This has still not faded," he observed.

"Giles . . . don't," she sobbed, trying to twist out of his arms.

He held her fast. "No," he said. "I want to know what's going on here, and you're going to tell me right now! Able and I stayed in London, taking turns prowling the streets looking for you for nearly a month before we abandoned the search altogether." He shook her gently. "I thought you were lost to me forever, Tessa," he gritted out through clenched teeth. "I thought you were trapped in your own time, or somewhere else in time, or dead. Have you no idea what that has done to me? Where have you been? How has this happened to you? Why did you run from me just now? Answer me, Tessa!"

"I . . . I didn't want you to see me this way," she sobbed. "I didn't want you to find out this way. . . ."

"Find out what?" Giles said.

"That I have become . . . what you have become."

"And how should I have found out?"

"I . . . I don't know. Just not like this."

"Who did this to you, Tessa? *Who?*"

He could barely stand to look into her eyes; they were so brimful of tears he winced. She drew a ragged breath. "You really don't know, do you?" she asked.

"How could I know, Tessa? The last time I saw you, you were running into the mist on Threadneedle Street in pursuit of that damnable demon child from hell! We had just come from our wedding ceremony."

"But I already had this," she said, touching the bruise on her lip.

Giles's hands fell away from her arms. His eyes trembled toward her, flashing toward the bruise. His racing mind reeled back in time to the day the straps broke on the little carriage. He saw himself embracing her, saw himself holding her prostrate in the bracken and furze, saw himself kissing her . . . kissing her . . .

"N-no," he breathed, shaking his head in denial. "No! Tell me I didn't . . . I couldn't have! Tessa, *tell* me."

"I didn't know how to tell you, Giles," she wailed. "I didn't know how . . ."

"Well, I know now, don't I?" he snapped, raking his hair back roughly. "Why can't I remember?"

"It was a kiss," she murmured, "and your teeth pierced my lip. You were on the verge of turning into the creature."

"You should have told me," he said in a voice he scarcely recognized. She must have heard that strangeness, too, for she backed away from him then, and he seized her again, crushing her close in his arms. "You know I never would have done this if I were in my right mind," he said. Tears stung behind his eyes, which remained dry to the point of physical pain. He screwed them shut and loosed a bestial howl that rang back in his ears like a thousand echoes. "I cannot live with having done this to you," he cried.

Deranged, he fell to his knees, doubled over in the heather, pounding the ground with white-knuckled fists. Thrice from the corner of his eye he saw Tessa reach out her hand only to retract it again. There was no comfort for this. He was so distraught he didn't hear the wagon approaching, plowing through the heather, or see the driver's hunched figure snapping the whip over the horse's head until the animal lumbered to a halt beside him.

"Daughter, come," Moraiva said.

Giles vaulted to his feet and seized Tessa's arm as she moved toward the barrel-shaped, yellow and turquoise-colored wagon. "Where are you taking her?" he demanded.

"Away from you till you are calmer," the Gypsy said.

"You think I would harm her, Moraiva?" Giles asked. He was incredulous. "You actually think it?"

"Not deliberately, no," said the Gypsy. "But there is still danger for one more night. When the moon wanes she will be returned to you all of a piece. I give her to you now, and she will die at your hands when the moon rises again. I see the pentacle in her here"—she tapped her forehead—"and when you become the wolf again, you will seek her out and ravage her, for she is your next victim."

Cold chills riddled Giles's spine. "I would never harm her!" he insisted.

The old Gypsy smiled her patronizing smile. "You already have, Giles Longworth. It is why we stand here, and you will do so again if you do not let me take her."

"Have I no say in this?" Tessa shrilled.

"No, none," the Gypsy said flatly. "Not if you would live. He has marked you. The wolf inside him has chosen you. It is because you two are soul mates, and because of the madness in the blood that makes the wolf kill that which it loves most."

"I have not had my answers from her, Moraiva," Giles said. "Am I not entitled to those at least?"

"You shall have them when the moon wanes," the Gypsy said. "You have waited this long. One more day and night will not matter, and it could well mean her life. Are you that selfish, Giles Longworth?"

"She will run again."

"She will not."

"If I lose her . . ."

"You will surely lose her if you do not heed me," Moraiva sallied with a wry chuckle. "When have I ever caused either of you harm?"

"I cannot lose her!"

"Why do you speak of me as if I am not here?" Tessa cut in.

"Do you still have the pentacle, daughter?" the Gypsy asked her.

Tessa reached beneath Giles's greatcoat and produced the amulet on a chain about her neck.

The Gypsy nodded. "Good," she said. "It has spared you much, but it will not spare you this. Get into the wagon. You need more than pentacle magic now. You need Moraiva."

Chapter Twenty-one

Moraiva lent one of her costumes, an indigo skirt and embroidered gauze blouse, as well as a paisley pongee shawl, and Tessa changed inside the wagon. The Gypsy didn't return to her people's camp. Instead, she drove the wagon deeply into the woods at the edge of the moor. When the sun finally broke the horizon line it was bloodred, its rays turning the pink streamers bleeding into the bleak gray dawn to crimson.

"Where are you taking me?" Tessa asked. Giles seemed comfortable with the woman, but she herself didn't know her well enough to share his opinion.

"A storm comes," the Gypsy said. "We go where it will be safe."

"Safe from what?" Tessa snapped. "I have weathered many storms without seeking shelter in a forest."

The Gypsy smiled. "But you were not a werewolf then," she said. "And this is no ordinary storm that comes, daughter. It is what the Cornish call a *flaw*. The winds would toss this wagon like a broom straw in the open. We go in among the ancient trees. I will find a likely place where they will protect us."

"Will the winds you speak of not uproot the trees?"

"Not deeply in the wood, where roots entwine and

support one another. Boughs and branches will fall; there is no way to avoid it, but there will be far less damage than there would be in the open. Did you look at this wagon, daughter? Does it appear damaged to you?"

Tessa hadn't taken special notice of the wooden vehicle, except to admire the brightly colored designs painted in yellow on a teal background.

"No," Tessa said. "It seems quite sound."

"Mhmmm," the Gypsy grunted. "It has weathered dozens of flaws." She gestured toward the treetops. "See?" she said. "Already the wind blows, and the sun has scarcely risen above the land. By noon the sky will darken. The sun will try to prevail, but great black clouds will scurry across its face, casting moving shadows on the land that look like living things crawling over the hills. Then the clouds will swallow the sun altogether, the sky will take on a jaundiced hue, and by mid-afternoon the rains will come—stabbing, punishing, horizontal rain driven by the cyclone. You will be glad of this shelter then, daughter, and even at that, protected though we are, the hailstones will pummel this old wagon as if the gods themselves were trying to pelt us to death."

"Perhaps then, in such a storm, if there is no moon—"

The Gypsy's coarse laughter interrupted her. "The moon will rise full whether we can see it or not," she said. "And you will feel its pull regardless."

Tessa didn't want to admit it, but she felt the pull already. "W-will Giles feel it, too?"

The Gypsy nodded. "Aye, daughter, he will feel it and he will come for you, but we will be ready for him, eh?"

"Why will he come for me? How will we be ready? I do not understand any of this."

"Poor child, you are marked. He has marked you, just

as the child has marked him. I told you why. When he bit you, he marked you with the sign of the pentacle. Not everyone can see it in the flesh of the victim, but we Gypsies are endowed with the power of divination, those of us who embrace the gift. What makes it worse is that you are soul mates, and he is the Alpha wolf. He must subdue you—and in your case it would mean death to face him under the full moon."

"Death for me?"

"Poor fledgling she-wolf, yes, for you," the Gypsy said. "He bit you when he was turning. This is why he did not remember it. His human consciousness was fading. His was the mind of the wolf."

"But he would not harm me."

"Not deliberately, no," Moraiva said. "But the wolf inside him is another entity—a cursed being whose mindless instinct is to kill, to ravage, to destroy. None can escape the werewolf's lust for blood, least of all you, who are already joined with it in your soul."

"Wolves mate for life, Moraiva," Tessa said emptily.

The old Gypsy nodded. "So we must cancel the curse so you two may live in peace together."

Tessa lurched on the wagon seat. "Can it be done?" she begged.

"We shall see," said the Gypsy, climbing down. "But first we get through one more full moon to give us time to see, eh?"

They had reached a place in the copse where woodbine creepers, dead vines and fallen branches tethered to two ancient oak trees had formed a snarled bower ahead. The tunnel-like tangle of branch and vine was wide and deep enough to accommodate the wagon easily, but the horse refused to enter, and the Gypsy had to lead the animal. It would make the perfect shelter from the sort of storm Moraiva described, Tessa thought.

The arch of petrified debris seemed impenetrable. Once the wagon was secured, Moraiva unhitched the horse, tethered him instead to one of the oaks, and covered him with what looked to Tessa like leather armor.

"To protect him from the gale," the Gypsy explained.

But Tessa's mind was occupied with far graver and more urgent thoughts. "And . . . if we cannot cancel the curse?" she asked the Gypsy. She was terrified of the answer, but she had to know.

The Gypsy gave a start. "Trust a *Gadje* to ask such a question," she said, wagging her head.

"What is a *Gadje*?"

"One who is not Roma," Moraiva said. "We Gypsies take a positive stand. It helps the magic work. If I were you, daughter, I would not give such thoughts room in that pretty head. Right now, we must be more cunning than the wolf that soon stalks you. Lend your energies to that."

Tessa hesitated. Should she confide what she'd learned, what she'd seen with her own eyes? It seemed only fair to share the knowledge, since the woman was trying to help her.

"He will not kill me tonight," she said. "I saw how it will end."

"Eh?" the Gypsy grunted.

"When you came upon me sitting on the stile by the lane in that other time, and brought me back here . . . surely you saw the Abbey."

The Gypsy nodded. "So?"

"Before you came upon me, I spoke with the caretaker of the place. He said the child set the fire. He said the boy ran away, that Giles was thought to have done him in until he returned. It is shortly after he comes back that the fire is said to have destroyed the Abbey with Giles and myself inside. So, you see, it is not my time. I will be quite safe until the boy returns, and once he does . . . What is it? My God, you look as if you've seen a ghost!"

"Longworth found the boy in London," Moraiva said. "He brought him home a month ago."

Giles paced the length of the Aubusson carpet in his study, brandy snifter in hand. He'd consumed half the bottle but had yet to feel the numbing effects he sought.

Storm clouds robbed the daylight early. Though it was barely mid-afternoon, the sky had darkened so severely that Evers and Rigby had lit the candles in their hall sconces. All other able hands were lending themselves to the chore of fastening shutters and battening down for the flaw. All hands, that is, except Foster's. The task of locking Master Monty in the attic chamber early in view of the storm had been assigned to the valet. Consequently, it was some time and several knocks before anyone was near enough to answer the pounding upon the Abbey doors. That chore fell to Evers, and Giles was lighting the candles on the drum table when the footman announced himself.

"'Tis Mr. Henry Forsythe from the Watch, sir," the footman said, hovering on the threshold.

"What the devil does Forsythe want?" Giles snapped. "I had the boy to him the moment we returned—took him straight to the gudgeon's home to prove I hadn't done for him."

"I'm sure I don't know, sir," Evers said.

"All right, all right, show the nodcock in," Giles grumbled. "I shall receive him here."

The footman scurried off, and Giles refilled his snifter. Whatever the guard wanted, he would have to be rid of him quickly. He could already feel the pull of the wolf inside, and with the clouds obscuring the moon he would not be able to gauge his time before the transformation, which was why he'd had Foster secure the child early.

He heard the echo of the guard's heavy boot heels clacking on the terrazzo floor outside long before the footman announced the man and showed him into the study. The sound held a hint of agitation, and Giles tossed back the contents of his snifter before addressing the man.

"What brings you here on such a day with a flaw looming, Forsythe?" he asked.

The guard forced his breath through flared nostrils and offered a nod. "Longworth," he greeted. "I told ya I'd be comin' back 'round ta check on the lad."

"The lad is fine, Forsythe," Giles told him. "You've wasted the trip."

"Good! Then you won't mind my havin' a look-see for myself," the guard returned.

"Actually, I would mind," Giles snapped. "He's been sent to bed early due to the storm. I see no need to disturb him."

"Well, I do," the guard came back. "Look here, Longworth, I'm no fool. Something untoward is afoot here, and I mean to know what it is. You've got that poor lad locked up in here. I have it on good authority—"

"Whose authority?" Giles interrupted, his eyes flashing.

"I'm not at liberty to say."

It had to be someone in the house, one of the servants trading in *on-dits* again. By God, he would put a stop to that, but first he needed to get rid of the guard before the moon rose, or there would really be something to gossip about.

"That tale had to have come from one of the servants in this house," he said steadily. "They are simple folk, Forsythe, and like as not have half the tale. Master

Monty has a penchant for destroying valuable property. When such moods come upon him, he is confined to quarters as punishment. You saw the boy when I first returned. Was there a mark on him?"

"Oh, now," the guard warbled. "How was I to tell with him so plastered thick with soot? Methinks ya might have brought him to me thus a-purpose. The good Lord knows what I would have seen if you'd have cleaned him up first. He's clean enough now, I'll wager, and I ain't leavin' here till I see for myself."

Giles stomped to the bell rope and gave it a vicious yank to summon Foster. "My valet will bring him," he said. "It may be a while. We are understaffed here, and those few servants we do have are busy battening down for the storm. Even my stabler has been pressed into service at that. This is a large house, Forsythe."

"I can wait."

"You might want to have a seat, then."

"I'll stand, thank you," said the guard.

"Brandy?" Giles offered, exhibiting his snifter. Where was Foster? It was full dark now, he prayed from storm clouds and not the sunset. Inside, the wolf was clawing at his guts, reminding him that it would soon be let free.

"No thank ye," said the guard. "I'm on official business, don't ya know; can't be fogged with spirits."

"Have you no other citizens to harass, then, no other mysteries to solve?" Giles asked, speaking the last with not a little drama.

The guard shrugged. "More sheep were slaughtered over at Jonathan Crabtree's place. Funny how it only seems ta happen at the full moon. Some folks say 'tis a werewolf. Some say 'tis *you*—since others 'round here have died in like manner, your poor wife included. And you do live a . . . peculiar sort of life out here. What do ya have ta say about that, Longworth?"

Giles laughed. "I say you've gone as simpleminded as the rest around here if you mean to hang that upon me."

"Folks say your new lady wife has disappeared, too," said the guard. "They say you never brought her back from London."

"My wife returns tomorrow, Forsythe. Why don't you come back then?"

"Oh, I will. You can bet your blunt upon it."

Giles was just about to evict the guard when Foster appeared in the doorway.

"You rang, sir?" the valet said.

"Yes, Foster. Bring Master Monty, please, so Forsythe here can satisfy himself that I haven't killed the boy."

"Killed the boy, sir?" Foster breathed. "I've never heard anything so preposterous. The boy has retired. Can Mr. Forsythe not return in the morning? It was a difficult task getting young master to bed. He's in another of his moods, sir."

"No, Foster," Giles said. "I'm afraid it must be now. He's coming back tomorrow to see that I haven't murdered my wife. We don't want to overtax the poor man with too many coils to unwind in one day. But I fear we may have done that already. He thinks I'm the werewolf that's been savaging the sheep hereabouts."

"Werewolf?" Foster said. "Surely you jest, sir. There are no such things . . . are there?"

"All right, you two," Forsythe spoke up. "Fetch the boy and have done. I'm not leaving till you do."

"Yes, Foster, do fetch him. It will be night soon, the full moon will rise, and we wouldn't want our esteemed guard from the Watch blundering into a werewolf when he takes his leave."

Giles hoped he had spoken the last with enough emphasis to warn the valet that time was of the essence. The guard would see his werewolf in the flesh if much more time was wasted. Judging from the valet's response in rushing to carry out his orders, Giles drew a ragged breath of relief and sloshed more brandy into his snifter.

"Ya think you're clever," the guard said. "Artist to the Prince Regent himself. Like that gives you license to defy the law."

"No, I don't think I'm clever. I think you're a bufflehead, sniffing around here, when there are sheep being savaged and objects d'art being stolen. I would have pressed charges against the slag who stole my snuff box if I knew you needed something to do."

"Hold on now, Longworth, there's no need to get testy."

"*Testy?* Ohhh, you haven't begun to see 'testy,' my good man. I am this close"—he illustrated with pinched fingers—"to rushing you out of here by the seat of your shiny breeches. Coming in here with trumped-up accusations and nothing to back them up! I would be totally within my rights to—"

"Here we are, then, sir," Foster interrupted him, ushering the boy into the study with a firm hand clamped to the back of his neck. "Master Monty."

The guard bent down, extending his hand. "There now, Master Monty," he said. "A mite cleaner than you were the last time we met, eh?"

The boy dosed the guard with a rage-bitten stare, and Giles let loose a lighthearted drunken laugh.

Foster's fingers tightened against the back of the boy's neck until the flesh beneath turned white around his fingertips; Giles noticed but hoped Forsythe did not. "Take the guard's hand, Master Monty," he charged. "Show him what a little gentleman you are, then. There's a good boy."

"Do you want me to strip him?" Giles asked, earning himself a deadly glower from the child.

"That won't be necessary," Forsythe said. "But you haven't seen the last of me, Longworth. I'll be back tomorrow for a little talk with that wife of yours. You married her in something of a rush, so I'm told."

"Since when is there a law against that?" Giles returned.

"You aren't fooling me, Longworth. Something is not as it seems here, and I mean to get to the bottom of it."

"You do that, Forsythe," Giles shot back. His humor dissolved, he slapped the brandy snifter down on the drum table, squared his posture and advanced upon the guard. "Now get out of here before I forget I am a gentleman and show you out personally."

"I don't want to go back to that room!" the boy whined pitifully.

"Get him *out* of here," Giles seethed through clenched teeth, addressing the valet, who quickly steered the boy into the corridor. Foster's hand remained clamped to the back of the child's neck, keeping him out of biting range.

Transformation was imminent. Foster was in danger, and so was Forsythe, Giles knew, from both the boy and himself. He'd broken out in a cold sweat; his brow was running with it as he continued to back the guard along the corridor.

"Out!" he thundered, driving the guard out with long-legged strides. "Out—out—out!"

The guard fled on spindly legs, leaving the door flung wide to the wind. The rain had started falling, hard, on a horizontal slant out of the southwest. Giles narrowed his eyes to the gusts that ruffled his hair and billowed his poet's blouse. It was going to be a screamer, and he was on the verge of changing. The wolf inside was gnawing at his body and his reason.

Suddenly, Foster's agonized cry rang out in concert with a thud as the valet hit the second-floor landing. He hadn't made it to the upper chamber before the boy shape-shifted into a full-grown wolf and knocked him down, but at least he hadn't attacked him. Instead, he soared through the air and streaked past Giles out into the storm, disappearing in the direction the guard had taken.

There was no time for Giles to see to Foster, else he put him to a far worse hazard than Monty had. The wolf in him would no longer be denied. Tearing at his clothes, flinging them into the wind as he ran, Giles the man gave way to the great black wolf inside him. Human sinew and muscle, flesh and bone became lupine jowl, fur, and fang, and he hit the ground running on all fours, sped off to disappear in the ink-black maelstrom of flesh-flaying wind and horizontal rain.

Chapter Twenty-two

Hail and rain pelted down over the little copse where the Gypsy's wagon stood beneath that tangled bower of vine and branch. Locked inside the wagon, Moraiva sat nursing the wound on her arm with herbs and salves and holy water that she knew would do no good. It was hard to gauge time deep in the copse, unable to see the moonrise for the storm, and she hadn't gotten Tessa tethered in time. She'd completed the task, but not before the wolf had bitten her in the process.

"Aiiieeee!" the Gypsy cried, plastering salve on the jagged wound, which she held in place with a fallen oak leaf secured with a length of honeysuckle vine. "You got me good, daughter," she breathed, addressing the wolf tethered with chains at the back of the wagon. "Now I have become what you are, eh? That is twice this life-time such as this has happened to me, and this was through no fault of your own. I knew the danger."

Across the way, the she-wolf whined as if it understood. Outside the wind howled like a banshee through the tangled snarl of undergrowth, lifting dead leaves and mulch into the air and slamming them into the barrel-shaped wagon with force enough to pierce it through. Low-hanging branches grazed the canopy above, driving vine and bough, nettle and thorn into the wood like nails as the wagon rocked with the gusts. Over it all bled the sound of howling wolves, and the old Gypsy pricked up her ears at the sound.

"Two more come," she said. "Your beloved and the child. They both prowl the moor tonight." Outside, the horse's frantic whinnies caught her attention. "I fear for that poor animal if they do not find other victims to slake their lust for ravaging before they reach us." She shrugged. "It cannot be helped. We shall hope for the best, eh, daughter? Better the horse than us, eh? We shall hope all this rain will dull your brethren's sense of smell. Water will do that."

The she-wolf struggled against the chains that bound it, its frantic whines and plaintive howls filling the little wagon.

"Be still!" the Gypsy commanded. "Do you want to bring them? You understand me, I think. It must be close to dawn. It seems as if it might be. It has been a long night for us both, but now I see where you are in the circle of things, and I know what we must do to put it to rights. So listen, daughter, and remember. This may be the last time I can mentor you." She raised her bitten arm and brandished it. "Your handiwork this night has made that so. My path lies in another direction now, so heed me well. It may be the only hope you have to survive what you have become."

Outside, the howling came closer, and the she-wolf answered the call. Would the dawn never come?

"Silence, little fool!" Moraiva charged. "And pray first light will save us—aye, and them from each other. There are many dangers afoot in these woods tonight. Yes, you understand me, so listen well. You have the favor of the keepers of the lay line gates, those that permit mortals to enter the corridors. Not everyone is privileged with such favor. Your own husband is not, at least not yet. Please the Powers he will be when the time comes, because it is the corridors that will save you. . . ."

Moraiva went to the little window in the curved side of the wagon and cracked the shutter. The sky was lightening, and the wolves' voices were growing distant of a sudden. "Yes, soon it is over . . . for tonight," she observed, fastening the shutter again. "What I tell you now, I tell you while you are on the verge of shifting back to your human self because I want no opposition or interruption." She waited for the she-wolf's whine in response. "Good!" she said. "You know the ways of the lay lines, and you know that to re-access a given time you must stay in the lane you chose while leaving it. You have done this. When the time is right, you must do so again, and I will not be there to help you, which is why you must listen carefully to me now."

Again the wolf responded.

"Good!" said the Gypsy. "You can save yourself and Longworth by going back through the corridor to a time and place other than one in which you were bitten, and there you must remain—*together*—if you are to break the curse. You have just come from that place, daughter. Retrace your steps and you will live the life you were meant to live, and do not regret it or tempt fate—"

Across the way, the she-wolf loosed a howl that turned the Gypsy's blood cold, wriggling out of her fur and into her naked human skin, screaming with the pain of transformation, which clearly taxed her whole body.

Moraiva covered Tessa with a fur rug and loosened her chains. She used her right arm gingerly, the arm that had been bitten, and it drew Tessa's eyes; there were tears in them.

"What have I done?" she sobbed. "I have bitten you."

"Do not trouble over that," Moraiva said. "Did you hear what I just told you?"

Tessa nodded. "I heard," she said. "But what of you and the boy and the fire?"

Moraiva sighed. "We do not know when the fire occurred," she said. "That is the only obstacle now."

"The caretaker said it happened shortly after the boy returned. That could be any time now. He has been back a month. We know the boy sets the fire, but what of him after?"

"Leave the boy to me," Moraiva said. "You must concentrate upon getting your husband into the time corridor that will free you from the curse before more damage is done."

"But I have bitten you!" Tessa cried.

"It is of no consequence," Moraiva replied. "I have been bitten before. We who know the time corridors and how to access them are not doomed by the werewolf's kiss. Neither are you, if you will only heed me. Do not reproach yourself, daughter, just mind what I say. You have until the full moon rises again to settle this, or all is lost to you. All is lost to us all."

First light brought no relief from the storm, and Giles dragged himself back to Longhollow Abbey naked through the teeming rain and merciless winds of the first flaw of the season. Driven by desperation, he scarcely felt the sting of the sharp rain splinters, or the punishing assault of the hail that pelted him relentlessly. He hadn't been of sane mind since he'd found the savaged body of Henry Forsythe, guard of the Watch, in a drainage ditch at the edge of the moor.

Had he himself killed the guard, or had Monty? He had no memory of anything that had occurred since he shed his clothes and sprang out into the storm in pursuit of them both. Had he stalked Tessa? Was she safe? He was on the verge of running mad for want of knowing, meanwhile fearing the knowledge. Moraiva called his situation rightly by the name of curse.

The sky had just begun to lighten as he staggered over the Abbey threshold and dragged himself up to his apartments. The rooms were empty, though a change of clothes had been laid out on the bed. This was a good sign: Foster had been well enough to set them there.

Giles shrugged on his dressing gown, and was just about to go to Tessa's chamber to see if she had returned, when Foster shuffled into the bedchamber from his adjoining quarters, limping severely. Giles's heart sank at sight of the faithful valet so altered.

"Save your steps, sir," Foster said. "She has not returned."

Giles's posture collapsed at that news. "And Master Monty?" he inquired. "Has he returned?"

"He is in his rooms," the valet said. "He arrived just ahead of you, sir, naked and covered with blood just as you are. I've had Evers and Rigby fill your tub. Forgive me, but I wasn't fit enough to fill it myself. I think the little blighter meant to kill me when he pushed me down those steps to the landing. I fear he nearly succeeded."

"Covered with blood, you say?" Giles murmured, examining his hands. They were, indeed, streaked with blood, as was his face. He didn't need a mirror. He could feel it drying upon his skin, and smell its sickening metallic sweetness. "Well, one of us has killed Henry Forsythe. I have no way of knowing which. I have no recollection of anything that occurred after I shapeshifted. I came upon the deuced guard in the drainage ditch returning just now. His throat was torn out, just like all the others."

The valet gasped. "Oh, sir, my God, you couldn't have!" he breathed.

"Well, I was half-castaway, and Forsythe and I did quarrel before I put him out."

"I refuse to believe it!" Foster said. "That has naught to do with anything. 'Twas the beast that killed him. You must disassociate yourself from it or you will go mad, sir."

"God bless you for that, old boy," Giles said sadly. "But I fear it is already too late."

"Is there any news of the mistress? I know how her disappearance must be wearing on you, sir."

"The mistress has returned," Giles said, debating whether or not to go into detail of their meeting on the heath, but under the circumstances, there seemed no alternative. The valet could well be in danger from that quarter also. "She, too, has been infected, and I am the one who did it," he said flatly. "She is with Moraiva, the Gypsy. I expect she will be returning shortly."

Foster swayed at the news. There was no way to soften the blow, which was clearly too much. Giles's quick hand steadied the valet and guided him to the wing chair beside the hearth.

"I didn't mean to be so blunt, but there it is," Giles said. "We are a house at sixes and sevens, I'm afraid, and I don't know what to do. . . ."

He would have continued, but for a loud banging at the doors below echoing up the staircase. Giles held his breath, listening. After a moment the knock came again.

"I'd best go down," Giles said, striding toward the door.

"You cannot, sir!" Foster called after him, struggling out of the chair. "Not like that. The blood, sir! You'll stretch a rope before noon if they see you like that. I shall go down while you order yourself. Whoever it is, I shall put them in the study."

"We both know who it is," Giles said bitterly. "Carry

on, then see the boy stays out of the way while I tend to this."

Giles stripped off his dressing gown, then cleaned himself with hot water stolen from the brimming tub. How inviting that bath looked. His whole body ached from an ordeal he couldn't even remember. He sighed. That pleasure would have to wait. Satisfied that he'd removed all traces of the blood of that ordeal, he dressed hurriedly and met Foster coming up the stairs as he began jogging down.

"It's the Watch, sir," the valet said.

"Yes, well, we knew that, didn't we, old boy? I'll see to it. Just keep the child out of sight. I'll ring if I need you."

Giles continued down the stairs, squared his posture and strode toward the study, where he found two men waiting. One he knew, John Stokes, from the far side of the moor. There was no central office. The Watch was made up of local householders working out of their own homes to keep the peace. The other man was younger, a well-built man close to his own age whom Giles hadn't seen before, though he did look somewhat familiar.

"What can I do for you gentlemen?" he asked. Feigning ignorance was called for here. It wouldn't do to let on that he'd seen the guard's ravaged body in the drainage ditch.

"Henry Forsythe's body has been found out on the moor," Stokes said. "He's been done ta death in an unspeakable way."

"Unspeakable!" the man's companion echoed.

"That is dreadful," Giles said steadily. "But what brings you here?"

"He's on your land, ain't he?" Stokes said.

"I fail to see—"

"Last we heard, he was comin' out here ta check on

the young lad, and he never come back." He turned to his companion. "This here is Royal Forsythe, Henry's oldest son from Bodmin Village. He's just recently joined the Watch."

Giles nodded toward the other. So that's why he'd seemed so familiar. He saw it now. Add a few years and a paunch and he could be looking at the father. "I'm certainly sorry for your loss," Giles said, "but I don't see why—"

"I wanted to come with him yesterday," Royal spoke up, "but he would have none of it. If I had done, he might be alive today."

"What we need to know is if he got here," Stokes said. "It's only fair ta warn ya, we're goin' ta interview the servants, so ya may as well tell us the truth up front."

"Well, yes, he did," Giles responded. "He came and examined the boy just before dark and left before the flaw worsened. Look here, I do not appreciate the insinuation that I would lie to you. Interrogate whomever you will. The man came, and the man left alive. That's the long and the short of it, gentlemen."

"His horse came home without him," Royal put in. "Spooked bad, he was. We thought me dad might have been thrown, or struck by lightning. When the storm slacked enough we set out. That's when we found him."

"I am truly sorry," Giles said. "But if you are trying to hang this foul deed upon me, you are wasting your time."

"He was found on your land," said Stokes.

"So you pointed out earlier."

"And you have to admit there's been some strange goin's on out here," Stokes continued. "Murders, folk with their throats torn out, just like Forsythe, all hereabout 'round Longhollow Abbey.

Giles uttered a strangled sound. "Are you accusing me

of murder now?" he asked. "This is preposterous! My first wife was savaged in just such a way as you describe. No! I'm going to have to ask you to leave, gentlemen."

"Hold on now, we ain't said that," Stokes admitted. "We're just statin' the facts."

"But you insinuated it, and I shan't stand here and be maligned in my own house! When you have proof, accuse me. Until then, I must ask that you leave me in peace."

"Has your wife returned, sir?" Royal Forsythe said. "My father was particularly concerned about her absence."

"No, she has not, but I expect her shortly. What in God's name has my wife to do with anything?"

"Most betrothed couples that go off to Town for a special license to wed usually return together," Stokes put in. "Never seen a bridegroom return alone."

"Yes, well, I am not 'most bridegrooms.' Look here, this is bordering upon the ridiculous. We were invited guests of the Prince Regent in London, and my wife remained behind to settle some of her affairs when an emergency necessitated my return to the coast. It's no secret that my ward had gone missing. I found him in London and brought him home straightaway to silence the sort of gammon that has brought you here this morning at great inconvenience to myself and my bride. All due respect, Mr. Forsythe, but if your father wasn't mixing into affairs that were none of his business, he would indeed be alive today. Now, you really must excuse me, gentlemen. I can bring nothing more to bear in regard to this matter. If you wish, I will be more than glad to offer you the services of my stabler should you need a hand removing the . . . er, body in this storm."

"That would be most kind of you, sir," Stokes said. "Perhaps in the meanwhile, your wife will return and make an end of this unfortunate business."

"There it is again! I really fail to see—"

"Did I hear my name mentioned just now?" a musical voice said from the doorway, and Tessa swept over the threshold in her Gypsy finery, heading straight into Giles's arms.

"A most fortuitous entrance, lady wife," he said. "These gentlemen have all but convicted me of your murder this morning."

"My *murder*?" Tessa warbled. "Surely you jest?"

"No, I am quite serious." He took her measure. "Where did you get that ridiculous rig?" he said.

Tessa swatted her skirt. "This?" she queried. "Moraiva lent me this costume; it's one of her own. Mine became quite soaked coming from the lane in this maelstrom. I'm afraid it's quite beyond repair."

"There now, gentlemen," Giles said buoyantly. "This should satisfy your insatiable lust for my blood. If that will be all, you may go round to the stables and tell Able I said he is to help you." He offered a crisp bow, leading Tessa out into the corridor, stopping at the door. "Again, please accept my sincere condolences on the death of your father, Mr. Forsythe."

"This ain't quite put ta rest, Longworth," Stokes said, stomping out into the hall. "You ain't fooled me. Somethin' untoward is goin' on out here, and you can bet we'll be back. Meanwhile, the men o' the Watch will be patrolin' hereabouts, just so's ya know, and they'll be armed with silver balls in their pistols . . . just in case."

"Far be it for me to dictate how you waste your time," Giles said. "But for now, gentlemen, I have wasted all I care to waste of mine. Good day."

Chapter Twenty-three

Giles was holding Tessa so close in his arms she could scarcely breathe. It didn't matter. Those arms were warm and strong and welcoming, and in that one glorious moment in traitorous, benighted time, nothing else mattered.

He had taken her to her rooms so she could change, but thus far he hadn't let her go long enough to do it. Threading his fingers through her hair, he raised her face to his and covered her mouth in a fiery kiss that stole her breath away, drawing her lips after his as he leaned back and deeply searched her eyes.

"How can I ever forgive myself for what I've done to you?" he murmured, crushing her close again.

"I . . . I've lost my hairpins," she said.

"I shall buy you a cartload of hairpins," Giles said, showering her face with kisses.

"I think it happened when I turned into the wolf in that dreadful jail down 'round Old Bailey."

"*Jail?* What jail? Tessa, what happened to you? Where did you go? Able and I searched everywhere for you for weeks."

"I was there . . . right there where you were, Giles, but in my own time. I saw Master Monty and ran after him, and the next thing I knew I was running down the street straight for Poole House, the home of my former employer. I collided with a bobby in front of the very gate, and Mrs. Poole came running down the steps and had me jailed, to make an example of me before the other servants."

"They jailed you?"

Tessa nodded. "When they saw my fine clothes and the ring, they were convinced I'd stolen those, too. I hadn't anything so fine when I was employed there. They're gone, Giles . . . all the fine things you bought me. The ring, my beautiful fur-trimmed pelisse—everything."

"That doesn't matter. Things can be replaced. You are here in my arms again. That is all that's important now. I never thought I'd see you again. I thought you were lost to me forever in one of those damned time corridors. How were you able to come back?"

"I changed into the wolf when the moon waxed full and broke through the window in the jail. I ran and kept running until I came across your wolf out on the moor. I don't presume to understand it. Moraiva says I have the favor of the keepers of the lay line gates. I have always had that. It is how I came to you in the first place."

"A gift that I unfortunately do not possess," Giles said dejectedly.

"You will—you must! Moraiva says it is the way that we can undo all this here."

"How?"

"I do not know yet, Giles. She means to help us, and I feel so dreadful. I attacked her when she was trying to tether me in the wagon. I became the wolf and *bit* her! There are four of us now. She said there was a way to reverse it for us, but . . ."

"Shhh, there's nothing to be done about that now. Something happened out on the moor since I saw you last that could have repercussions . . ."

Tessa had sensed something untoward from the moment she entered the Abbey, something that sent cold chills racing along her spine. "Who were those men when I came in? What did they want?"

Giles let her go and raked his hair back roughly. "Men from the Watch," he said. "John Stokes and Royal Forsythe. Forsythe's father came 'round here late yesterday demanding to see the child. The servants in this house have been spreading tales, and the Watch seems to think I mean to murder the boy. Forsythe and I had a dustup over it. I all but put him out bodily. The short of it is: he left here at moonrise. Monty and I both shape-shifted as he was leaving, and one of us killed him out there. Of course, they think I did it."

"Oh, Giles, my God. No!"

He took her in his arms. "We are not responsible for what we do when the curse takes over, Tessa, just as you are not responsible for biting Moraiva. We are victims, just as those who suffer us when we become ravaging wolves."

"What are we going to do?" Tessa pleaded.

"We have one more night to get through this cycle," he replied. "The moon won't wane for still another night, and the pull has been growing steadily stronger. It used to be just two days at the moon's height, with an unstable day before and after. Now it's three. It is changing. The periods of transformation are lengthening. The occasions of the wolf surfacing, at least in myself, are becoming more frequent. Who knows where it will end."

"But what can we do?"

"Right now, I'm going to have your tub filled. Foster filled mine before the gudgeons from the Watch arrived. It must be icy cold by now. I need to have a word with him. Arrangements must be made for us all before nightfall, and I need to put the fear of God into the servants in this house. I ought to sack the lot, but then the rumors would really abound. Once I have seen to all that, I will return and we will talk, Tessa. I would like to here more of Moraiva's plan to see us out of this."

Tessa scarcely heard. Her conscience was gnawing at her. It would no longer be denied. He'd warned her of the dangers they were facing. He needed to know about the fire.

"Giles," she said, calling him back from the threshold. "There is something I haven't told you . . . something you need to know . . ."

He strode back into the room and took her in his arms, his hooded gaze lingering on her face, and he kissed her deeply, molding her body to his until the bruising bulk of his arousal leaned heavily against her. Slowly, reluctantly, he leaned back, his hand buried in her hair, his glazed eyes flashing over her from head to toe.

"My God, but you are exquisite," he murmured. "How fetching you look in that costume, with your hair loose and wild like a Gypsy." He let her go reluctantly and made a dash for the door. "Do not tempt me, little vixen," he called from the threshold. "You are a distraction I can ill afford until I settle things in this house. Then you can tell me anything you wish, my love, so hold that thought."

"It's going to happen again tonight, I can feel it," Giles said, stepping out of his bath into the plush towel Foster held at the ready. "How we've managed to keep it from the others is thanks to you, I know. I also know it can't last, old boy. It isn't just Master Monty and myself any longer. I accidentally infected Tessa, and last night, she infected Moraiva. There are four werewolves on the prowl here now that we know of, and there are bound to be more."

"What's to become of us, sir?"

"Moraiva says there is help for it. I do not know the particulars yet."

"I spoke with the guards from the Watch," Foster said. "I told them you were here at the Abbey last night. They will be back to speak with the others. I fended them off, telling them the rest of the staff was too busy preventing storm damage to be assembled, but that won't keep them at bay for long, sir."

"When they come back they'll likely bring a rope, Foster."

"Begging your pardon, sir, but what really happened out on that moor last night? Did you . . . ?"

"I don't know," Giles said. "I never remember what occurs when the wolf takes me. One of us—Monty or myself—tore that poor gudgeon's throat out last night, and we have one more night of this horror before the moon again begins to wane. And of course it will wax full again. Please God an answer is found before that time comes, old boy, because I cannot live like this much longer. Not like this!"

"What would you have me do, sir?"

"Assemble the staff in the salon. Seat them, and wait. I will join you directly. First, we make an end to the gossip going 'round before it gets me hanged. Let us begin with that."

The valet shuffled off, and Giles dressed himself. There was no time to stand on ceremony. He had no idea how severely the curse would take him come moonrise, and much had to be accomplished beforehand if he were to put this month's nightmare behind him.

Lottie and Lettie, Rigby and Evers, Cook, Dorcas, even Effie from the scullery were on hand with Foster when Giles reached the salon. Able and Andy were not among them, having been pressed into service by the guards from the Watch to help remove the body from the drainage ditch. Giles would address them separately once they returned. The real culprits, he was certain judging from the guilty look on some of their faces, were among those seated before him now.

Hands clasped behind his back, Giles strode into the room and began pacing the length of the Aubusson carpet between him and the sea of anxious faces staring up in rapt attention—and not a little apprehension—as he began to speak.

"I should sack the lot of you," he began, enlisting his most formidable scowl. "I have not dismissed the notion. Have I not been good to you over the years?"

A rumble of out-of-rhythm *yes*es responded.

"Do I not pay you handsomely?"

Again the *yes*es rumbled through the salon.

"Then why do you repay me with treachery?"

Silence.

"Which one of you is responsible for the *on-dits* circulating through the parish? Come, come, I haven't got all day here. Speak up, because if you do not, it's going to be the worse for the lot of you."

The rumble grew louder. Now he was getting somewhere. The bristling servants were casting accusing looks amongst themselves. He didn't expect anyone to admit to spreading gossip. He needed to frighten them enough to prevent the tales from continuing.

"All right," Giles said. "I see that this is going to be difficult. It's admirable that you do not wish to implicate your fellow servers. I respect that. But let me tell you what your flapping jaws have done. One or more of you has carried tales of the goings-on in this house. That would not have been so serious if the tales you carried had any basis in truth, but they do not. Your foolish, hurtful imaginings may have just put a noose 'round my neck."

Milling voices crescendoed into a virtual uproar, which Giles allowed to reach fever pitch before ending it with a booming response. "Silence!" he bellowed. "You are guilty, one and all! What? Do you think I'm blind? You should see your faces. Some more so than others, I'll grant, but you may well have ruined me with your gammon. You are entitled to absolutely no explanations, but just to set the record straight: I did not murder my wife and her lover. I do not keep Master Monty in chains. I do not tramp whores in and out of here for the purpose of bed sport—they are my models. Employing them to model for me keeps them *off* their backs for a time, and it puts a decent, honest wage in their pockets. . . ."

A chorus of gasps replied to that. Yes, he was definitely getting somewhere. "I did not rush into marriage with Miss LaPrelle, now Mrs. Longworth, to some evil purpose. I was cuckolded, my generosity and good nature maligned and abused, and I was taken for practically every haypenny I possessed by a designing woman. Having finally met a different woman who could love me as a woman should love her husband, I saw no reason to prolong my agony. I married her. Contrary to your latest *on-dits*, I did *not* do her in, in London. She is upstairs in her apartments as I speak. It was Master Monty running away that separated us.

"I haven't done for him, either," Giles continued. "He is in his rooms until I see fit to have him come amongst us again without destroying valuable objects in this house. The boy has a condition of the blood inherited from his mother that makes him behave in a shocking manner at times. The episodes seem more frequent when the moon is full, as is the way with many mental illnesses, and since there seems to be no cure, confinement—for his own good, as well as the good of all in residence—is necessary in these instances."

Another rumble of discordant sound rippled through the gathering, and Giles stopped and faced his staff, arms akimbo. "Last, but certainly not least," he went on, "you are all aware that Henry Forsythe of the Watch came by yesterday to examine the child that one or all of you has said I've chained in a dungeon here, and God alone knows what else. Forsythe was found dead on the moor this morning. He never reached his household after speaking with me. As result of the tales you've carried, I am suspected, and may well hang for the act of some vicious animal. Have you any idea what it is that you've done?"

"Beggin' your pardon, sir," Cook spoke up, her fat round cheeks turned crimson. "It weren't me!"

"That is commendable, Cook," Giles said above the rumble leaking from the others. "Silence, all!" He waited until the surly monotone died down. "Since it's clear I am about to have a chorus of 'not me's' from you, here is what shall be: If one more word is uttered by any one of you, all will suffer. I will sack the lot. If I am carted off to Tyburn over this, the same holds true. Meanwhile, *none* of you will venture beyond the green baize door in the servants' quarters unless you are summoned by myself or the mistress of this Abbey. Your privileges to roam free in this house are hereby cancelled until further notice. I do not care if the dust collects to the ceilings. Anyone who does not wish to abide by these new conditions may leave forthwith. Have I made myself plain?"

A low rumble of "Yes, sir," replied, and after a painfully long hesitation, Giles said, "Very well, then, carry on. Remember . . . not one word out of any of you, or you condemn the lot! Do not think to put me to the test."

Chapter Twenty-four

Tessa was sound asleep when Giles returned to her apartments. Evidently exhausted after her bath, she had dressed in a yellow muslin frock, wrapped herself in a woolen lap robe, and lay curled on her side atop the counterpane on the bed, awaiting his return.

He didn't have the heart to wake her. It was best that he didn't. There would be plenty of time to take her in his arms and make love to her after all danger was past. Now he needed to instruct Foster in regard to Monty's confinement come nightfall—as well as his own, and Tessa's, come to that. He also needed to seek out Moraiva. He would hear her plan to cancel the nightmare. The pull of the moon was as strong as ever. Only a few more hours and it would happen again. There wasn't a moment to lose.

Deciding to seek out Foster first, he found the valet straightening the dressing room in his suite. "It isn't over," he said. "When the moon rises, the wolf will overtake me again."

"Are you sure, sir?" the valet asked, straightening up from where he'd been stooping over the bathtub, drying it with a towel.

"Very sure, Foster," Giles replied. "The pull is incredible, and it's scarcely midday. I need to find Moraiva. She has knowledge that may help us all."

"She has returned to her camp, sir."

Giles nodded. "I expected as much, but she won't stay there and risk putting her fellow Travelers to the hazard. They may have taken shelter from the storm. In that case, she will either go off somewhere on her own, or access one of the lay lines until dawn. I must find her before that."

"Yes, sir. What must I do here?"

"Master Monty will need to be restrained. Put him in the attic room again. If all goes well and I return before dark, I can be confined in the studio. Have Able affix a bar on the outside like the one on the attic chamber. Have him place it high, out of Monty's reach. If he questions it, tell him I want to keep Master Monty out."

"Yes, sir."

"If I don't return, needs must the mistress will have to be restrained as well. Any suggestions?"

"The root cellar, sir."

"Excellent! There are no windows. Tell her I said to do as you say."

"Begging your pardon, sir. Shouldn't you stay here until after . . . Just in case? I will do as you say, of course, but . . . couldn't you wait to speak with the Gypsy until morning?"

"It might be too late then, Foster. There are armed patrols on the prowl out there. She could be dead by morning if she becomes the wolf on that moor tonight. I need to warn her of the danger. Besides, the guards from the Watch are going to return. It's only a matter of time, and mine is running out. I only pray I have enough left to do what must be done before they return. They see eliminating me as the answer to all their unsolved crimes."

"That is preposterous, sir!"

"Preposterous, but true," Giles said. "If I am not here when they come to arrest me, I have a better chance of surviving this. If they were to incarcerate me now, when the moon rises they will see their werewolf and I will be dead; one of their silver pistol balls will see to that. No, I cannot be here now. My little talk with the others was a moot point, I fear. The Watch has already made up its collective mind that I'm their man. It won't matter what the others in this house say now. The damage is already done."

What would he do without the trusted valet? The man knew when to speak, and when to hold his peace, like now. Giles's instincts were correct. He had to leave Longhollow Abbey now, before the guards returned, and before Tessa woke to persuade him against it. For she alone had the power to do that. He could still see her lying so peacefully on the bed in her chamber, her long chestnut hair fanned out about her on the pillow. He could smell the scent of violets drifting from it. How he longed to scale the stairs two at a stride and live in that exquisite body. He went to the stable instead.

Neither Able nor Andy had returned. It was just as well. He saddled a sorrel gelding and mounted. The horse, usually quite docile, seemed out of sorts, rearing and bucking. For a moment he thought he'd cinched the girth too tight, but no, that wasn't the case. It spooked because of the wolf inside him. His heart sank, and he coaxed the animal out of the stable and onto the lane that led to the Gypsy camp.

The wind was still raw and blustery, but the rain had stopped falling except for a stubborn misty drizzle coming in spurts out of bilious clouds hugging the horizon. He had seen this before. It was nothing more than a brief respite between squalls. One would spawn another until the flaw was spent. This was only the beginning.

The Gypsies had decamped by the time he reached

their site. All that remained of them were the patches of flattened-down grass where their wagon wheels had rested. It was a disappointment, but nothing he hadn't expected. They weren't safe in the open in such a storm. They would have sought shelter elsewhere. The wood that edged the moor was the next likely spot, and Giles coaxed the horse in that direction.

Despite the fact that he was an accomplished horseman, it was all he could do to control his mount. He nearly lost his seat twice on the way to the camp, and the later it grew, the more animated the animal became. Making matters worse, though he combed the woods until late afternoon, he could find no trace of Moraiva or the others.

The sky was beginning to darken. Had he lost track of time, or was the storm worsening? There was no way to tell. The eerie, bilious color of the clouds had changed to boiling slate-gray tumblers rolling low over the moor. Overall, a jaundiced yellow aura prevailed, just as it had when the first flaw began. The rain had stopped, but Giles took no comfort in that. The wind had picked up. Blatant gusts ruffled his hair as if a thousand fingers combed it. Shielding his eyes, he scanned the sky in hopes a break in the cloud cover might help him determine if the pending darkness was storm-related or simply nightfall approaching. He dared not take chances. There was nothing for it; he had to return to the Abbey and restrain himself.

That decided, he drove the horse northeastward over the moor at the fastest pace he could manage given the animal's reluctance to have him on its back. He hadn't seen a soul since he set out. It wasn't until he reached the approach to Longhollow Abbey that he spied two riders coming on at a gallop, pistols drawn. At first, in the gathering dimness summoned by the storm, he thought they might be highwaymen. Cornwall was rife with thatchgallows. Prepared to lose his horse, since he had neither blunt nor a pistol to make a stand, he slowed the animal's pace only to see as they drew nearer that they weren't highwaymen at all. It was John Stokes and Royal Forsythe from the Watch, and their pistols were drawn against him. They were coming from the Abbey.

Giles glanced about. His first instinct was to flee, but that would have been unwise, since he was within pistol range. Besides, it would be a blatant admission of guilt. Suddenly he knew how Tessa must have felt when she ran in innocence from the police pursuing her for the theft of her employer's brooch. He was innocent as well, of all save Forsythe's murder. That was still in question, since he had no recollection of it. It could have been him, or it could have been Monty. He wondered if he would ever know for certain.

"Hold there, Longworth!" Stokes said. "You'll be comin' with us. Come peaceable and you won't be the worse for it."

"By what authority do you arrest me, Stokes?" Giles demanded.

"One o' your own," the guard replied. "Your gentleman's gentleman swore you was at the Abbey after Forsythe left last night."

"That's correct," said Giles. "So . . . ?"

"So, we came back to talk with the rest o' your staff, and one o' them saw you out on the moor without a stitch on ya—nekked as a jackrabbit—comin' home from somewhere at first light this mornin'."

"That's ridiculous. There must be some mistake. Which of my servants said such a thing?"

"Oh now, I don't know as I can say, Longworth, and it don't matter. She's sworn to it, and that puts your valet in the same boat as you. That lie'll cost him."

"I think you're all mad as brushes!" Giles said, struggling to control the anxious horse underneath him. "Put those damn pistols away and let me pass. I'll get to the bottom of this."

"Ohh, no you don't," Royal Forsythe put in. "My father's lyin' dead in our parlor, and you're the one that's put him there."

"That is preposterous. Where is your proof? You're going to need more than one giddy, hysterical servant's supposed sighting to convict me of murder."

"What was you doin' roamin' around nekked in a ragin' flaw?" Stokes demanded.

"I wasn't!" Giles defended. "Whomever she saw, or thought she saw, it wasn't me."

"Well, we'll just have to let the magistrates sort it all out, won't we?" Stokes said. He motioned with his pistol. "You're goin' ta the debtor's jail at Lamorna, till we can send for the prison coach ta take ya in. Move! And don't try anything funny."

There was no doubt about the time now. The light was fading quickly. It would be full dark by the time they reached Lamorna. The pull of the wolf was already gnawing at him from the inside out. Rain was starting to spit down out of the boiling clouds, and the wind gusts had reached cyclonic force again.

"You are making a grave mistake, Stokes," Giles warned him. "I'll see you raking seaweed out at Land's End by time this is done!"

"You can go like a gentleman, or I can take ya in trussed up in irons. What's it goin' ta be?" said Stokes, jangling the shackles dangling from his belt. "Either way, you're goin'."

"Have it your way, Stokes," Giles said, kneeing the horse beneath him. He couldn't let them clap him in irons. If the horse beneath him would behave, he might be able to escape. The animal obviously sensed the wolf, and it was all he could do to keep it on the lane.

The guards rode so close he couldn't even think of breaking away. Suddenly a fresh worry surfaced. Trying not to sound as panicked as he was, he said, "I suppose you've incarcerated my valet as well." If they had, who would confine Monty and Tessa before moonrise?

"Not yet," said Forsythe. "He'll keep till we sort you out."

"He'll break once he finds out we've took you in," Stokes said.

"If you harm one hair on that man's head—"

"Shut your hole and ride, Longworth!" Stokes trumpeted. "You're in no position ta be makin' threats. Ya need ta think about comin' clean and sparin' all concerned."

Giles said no more, and they rode on in silence. They were nearing Lamorna debtor's jail, a one-room unmanned enclosure tended by the Watch, when dry lightning began to spear down over the patchwork hills, spooking Giles's mount even more. It was almost full dark. His breath was coming short. His vision had begun to narrow. The darkening sky had taken on the color of dried blood. An unbearable tingling sensation overspread his whole body as muscle and sinew, flesh and bone struggled to become the wolf. The tingling became pain—deep, searing pain—as the transformation began. It was happening!

It had to be now, while he was still in control, before he lost his human consciousness to that of the predator wolf inside. He began clawing at his shirt and trousers. The jail loomed up before him, and there was no more time. The guards had reined in and were climbing down. Giles started to follow, but the horse had other ideas. It reared as the rain began to pelt down, peppered with hail and lightning—closer now—and then streaked off over the moor.

In the midst of the awkward transformation, Giles

fell out of the saddle, and the animal bolted back the way they'd come. It soon disappeared behind the dense curtain of horizontal rain.

Forsythe was unlocking the jail, while Stokes was struggling with their now-spooked mounts. The second man's gruff voice boomed, "Shoot, damn ya, Forsythe! He's gettin' away!"

His wolfish feet slipped easily out of his top boots, and Giles bounded off through the bracken, furze and black heather carpeting the moor. Another flash of lightning lit the sky, illuminating all as he ran, streaking through the underbrush on all fours, leaving a trail of clothing behind.

"Where'd he go?" Stokes bellowed, snatching Giles's shirt from the wet ground. Giles's heart was reverberating in his ears louder than the thunder as he ran. Had they seen him? He prayed not, but . . . yes. "Shoot that animal!" Stokes commanded. "That wolf! It's *him*. Shoot, damn ya, man. Bloody hell! I'll let the damn beasts go and do it myself!"

Two shots rang out almost simultaneously. Something hot and searing ripped through Giles's shoulder, but he kept on running. The guards' spooked horses passed him by, galloping crazily over the moor. More shots rang out, but he was out of range now, and the guards' angry shouts were growing more distant with every step.

Blood was running down his right foreleg, now, and yet still he ran. On he traveled, on and on until a sprawling shape loomed ahead on the moor, silhouetted black against a blacker sky, miles in the distance. Sudden lightning snaked down, showing it clearly, even to his dazed wolfish eyes: Longhollow Abbey. It was still a long ways off, but it was the last thing he saw before crawling into the barrow and spiraling into unconsciousness.

Chapter Twenty-five

The Abbey was in an uproar. Tessa awoke to the sound of pounding at the doors below funneling up the stairs. This was no ordinary knock, and the blood ran cold in her veins when another knock closer at hand vaulted her off the bed. The fire had died in the hearth. Pulling the lap robe in which she'd wrapped herself closer around her, she padded to the door.

"W-who's there?" she asked. She knew it wasn't Giles. Something was wrong, terribly wrong.

"It is I, madam. Foster," the valet said.

Tessa opened the door. One look at the valet's face set gooseflesh loose over her back, and she misstepped. "What is it, Foster?" she breathed. "What's happened?"

"Forgive me, madam," the valet said. "The master has made me privy to your . . . eh, situation. You must come with me else you be found out. The master was very clear that I was to . . . confine you should he not return before moonrise."

"Where has the master gone?" Tessa asked him.

"He's gone looking for Moraiva the Gypsy. He must have been detained. I do not wish to alarm you, madam, but I still have to confine Master Monty, and I am duty bound to see to your safety first."

"Let me fetch a ribbon and dress my hair," Tessa said, moving back from the door.

"There isn't time, madam. The guards from the Watch are downstairs. They are questioning the others. They will want to question me again after. We must hurry, I'm sorry."

"So that was the pounding that woke me . . . the guards," Tessa said. "I'll just fetch my cloak."

"Please hurry, madam!"

Tessa slid into her slippers, skittered into the dressing room, plucked her cloak from the armoire and swirled it about her shoulders. The strange uneasiness had begun inside her, just as it had in the little jail in London when the wolf first possessed her. It was nearly dark. Soon she would change again. Why had Giles left her? Her mind was reeling as she followed Foster to the staircase.

"Where are you taking me?" she asked as they began to descend toward the second-floor landing.

"Please, madam," he responded. "Trust me to cause you no harm. I would never! I suggested the root cellar as a likable place to keep you, and the master agreed. There are no windows. We were thinking that might . . . minimize the transformation. Of course, it may not." Snatching a candle branch from the hall table, he opened a door hung in the wainscoting and gilded plasterwork that didn't even look like a door, and ushered her inside a service access to another landing and a narrow staircase winding below. "Watch your step," he said, leading her. "The stairs are slippery. Dampness prevails in this part of the house."

They seemed to descend forever before they reached a landing with a door that barred from the outside; it had an iron hasp and heart-shaped padlock. Foster hurried her in. "I don't know that it's safe to leave you the candles," he said. "You would know better than I."

"I'm not afraid of the dark, Foster," Tessa said.

"It just seems such a cold thing to do," said the valet.

Tessa smiled sadly. "It's all right, Foster," she said. "I might set myself afire if you leave them. Just . . . don't forget me down here come daybreak, hmm?"

"Never, madam!"

"See to the boy. I will be fine," Tessa assured him. They were brave words, but then he closed her in and she heard the heavy bar drop outside, and the lock snap shut. Unable to see anything in the deep darkness surrounding her, she slid down the wall to a pile of burlap sacks on the floor and waited for the wolf.

Foster retraced his steps and emerged through the invisible door in the wainscoting to face the guards from the Watch looking up at him from the first-floor landing below. Palpitations gripped his heart. There was no time for this. They had already questioned him. He needed to secure Master Monty before moonrise, which was imminent by the look of the darkening sky through the oriel window at the end of the hall.

"Come down here, Foster," Stokes said. "We'd like a word with ya."

"Can it wait for just a bit, gentlemen?" the valet replied, holding his ground. "Needs must that I see to Master Monty. He becomes . . . agitated during storms. I shan't be long."

"That'll have to wait," Stokes returned. "In the study? Now."

Foster did as they bade him and went below. The study was dark, and the fire had gone out. He set down the candle branch and moved to light another, but Stokes stopped him.

"Leave that," he said. "We've just had a chat with your fellow servants below stairs, and one of 'em says she saw Longworth nekked comin' off the moor at first light."

"Who said such a thing?" Foster asked, giving a start.

" 'Twas one o' the chamber maids. Lettie—or Lottie; can hardly tell 'em apart."

"Given to fantasies, the pair of them," Foster defended. "These are young, impressionable gels, prone to romantic air dreams. It comes from reading too much Byron. Pay her no mind."

"That won't wash, Foster," Stokes said. "She was quite sure o' what she saw, and scared o' sayin' it for fear o' reprisal. What we want ta know is, how come you, his valet, privy to his every move, told us he was in here all night after Forsythe left, when he wasn't; and what kind o' evil was he up to going about nekked out there? That's what witches do. Is that what he's into, the master o' Longhollow Abbey: *witchcraft?* He's into somethin', and there's murder at the bottom o' it. What have ya got ta say ta that?"

"I say, being his valet, sir, that he was in residence all evening after Mr. Forsythe left, and if Lottie or Lettie told you she saw a man going about in the altogether on these grounds, you should be off looking for a prowler or a lunatic, not bothering respectable folk with no powder to back up your musket."

"Oh, we'll get our proof," Royal Forsythe spoke up. "My dad is dead, and he didn't rip his own throat out."

"A rabid animal, more than likely, is responsible for your good father's death, Mr. Forsythe," Foster said. "No mere man—naked or otherwise—could rip out another man's throat. If you weren't so grieved you would realize that."

"Where is Longworth now?" Stokes queried, his eyes narrowed upon Foster. It was clear he hadn't changed his opinion.

"He is out," Foster said succinctly.

"I can see that. Where has he gone, man?"

"I believe he's gone to visit the Gypsies camped on the south moor."

"And that's another thing," Stokes barked. "We don't encourage that lot hereabout. They're nothin' but trouble—thievin' rabble. I'm goin' ta run them off. They're inta all that mumbo jumbo witchery, too."

"This being the master's land, I believe he's entitled to have as his guests any whom he pleases," Foster said loftily.

Stokes *hmm*ed. "We'll see about that. Where is his wife?"

"In her bath, sir," Foster said testily. "She has had a long, difficult journey from London, and I wouldn't dream of disturbing her."

"Mmmm. I s'pose she'll keep," Stokes said. "She's told us no lies. You, on the other hand, had best get your story straight. Lyin' to the law is a grave offense, especially when there's murder involved."

"I haven't lied to you," Foster said. "And you have no proof that murder took place. More than likely an animal killed Forsythe. Whatever the case, the master was at home in this house last night, sir. I have nothing more to add to it."

Stokes studied him for a long moment, gazing down the long, crooked shaft of his nose. "We'll see," he said at last. "Meanwhile, you stay put. Somethin' untoward is goin' on out here, and you're in the middle o' it."

"If there is nothing more, I really must see to Master Monty, Mr. Stokes."

"Mmmm. Carry on, then, but just remember, you aren't in the clear, Foster. We'll be back."

Foster didn't bother to show the guards out. It was almost full dark. The boy had to be confined in the tower room at once, and the valet scaled the staircase like a man half his age and went straight to Monty's third-floor suite. He found it in darkness. Holding the candle branch high, the valet ran through the rooms calling

Monty's name at the top of his voice, but there was no answer. The boy was gone.

Foster stood in the middle of the boy's bedchamber, the candle branch trembling in his hand, murmuring a string of blue expletives he hadn't uttered in forty years. It was only a passing moment, and he was grateful that the master of Longhollow Abbey wasn't present to hear him slip so shockingly out of character. He had failed in his duty, albeit through no fault of his own. Correcting this was paramount now. He had to find the cunning child, who might or might not have become a werewolf, of all unlikely things. It mattered not that he would probably lay his life on the line doing so.

Bursting back into the corridor, he went first to Tessa's chamber. The boy had stolen there before; he may have done so again. It was a desperate fantasy, and Tessa's rooms were vacant also. Was the strange child somewhere watching, gloating over his triumph, or had the wolf taken possession and rendered him mindless, reduced him again to the savage beast that had begun the nightmare? Either way, the boy had to be found and restrained. With that to drive him, Foster went below to the master suite, praying he would find the child there.

As he stepped off the second-floor landing, the plaintive howl of a wolf pierced his heart and paralyzed him where he stood—not with fear, however; he was trying to isolate the sound. Where was it coming from? The echoes in this old Abbey made it next to impossible to pin down. The howl came again. It seemed to be coming from the master suite, and the valet tiptoed along the darkened hallway until he reached it, then hesitated.

The door was ajar. Being the master's personal manservant, and since his own room adjoined, Foster possessed a key, which he kept on a chain attached to his waistcoat pocket. Slipping it out, he seized the door handle, pulled it to, and turned the key in the lock, a flood of relief rushing over him like an ocean wave at the sound of the click as the door locked. But there were three other doors that gave egress into the corridor from the master suite: the bedchamber, dressing room, and his own chamber. The same key fit them all.

Vaulting down the corridor, he quickly locked the bedchamber door, then the door to the dressing room. But when he reached the door to his own apartment and seized the door latch it was jerked out of his hand. The door flew open, and the valet stood, not before the wolf he expected, but before the boy, mimicking the cry of a wolf. He swung a heavy candlestick into the valet's head.

How long he lay there, the valet couldn't tell. When he finally moaned awake it was to total darkness—thick, palpable darkness—malodorous darkness, stifling, smothering. He coughed then choked. *Smoke!* Great, billowing clouds of smoke were funneling through the corridors.

Fire!

Terror gripped the valet's heart like an icy fist. He tried to rise and failed. His gashed head was throbbing, pounding. His pulse echoing in his ears, he raised himself to his knees, then with the help of the door handle, pulled himself to his feet.

Snatching a candlestick from the table inside, he touched it to the wall sconce in the hall to light it. Blood was leaking into his right eye from a deep gash in his forehead, and vertigo starred his vision with tiny pinpoints of blinding light. He'd thought he was confining a wolf. The boy had caught him completely off guard.

That Monty was possessed of such uncanny strength testified to the severity of the curse upon him. But there was no time to analyze it; the Abbey was on fire and his first thought was of Tessa, bolted inside the wine cellar in the bowels of the servants' quarters. He had to free her, else she burn to death or suffocate—if it wasn't already too late.

With that thought to drive him, the valet plowed through the curls of black smoke, his handkerchief over his nose and mouth. Wheezing uncontrollably, he made his way toward what appeared to be a faint ray of light coming in brief glimpses from the oriel at the end of the hallway, since the feeble candle he carried was useless in that pitch-black ink. The oriel glow picked out the door in the wainscoting on the second-floor landing, and he flung it open and reeled inside. Could he have been unconscious the whole night?

The upper regions were engulfed in flames. The solarium studio was full of flammable materials that must surely have exploded. Fiery bits were raining down as the valet shut the little invisible door behind him and hobbled down the narrow stone stairs that led to the wine cellar below, leaning against the wall as he went, for his footing was anything but sure. The dizziness hadn't subsided. Inhaling the smoke had made it worse. A fog of the acrid stuff prevailed there also, and the wall separating him from the rest of the servants' area was hot to the touch the lower he went. Could the child have run through the Abbey igniting it top and bottom? He must have done. Foster could see it in his mind, and groaned aloud at the terrible loss of property—and possibly life. But he dared not think about that now. The rest of the servants were on their own; he had to free the mistress. That was the single thought driving him.

"I'm coming, madam!" he called through a strangled gasp, as he set down the candlestick and fumbled with the key in the heart-shaped padlock. His eyes were smarting from the smoke swirling all around him, as were his lungs, and his hands were shaking. "Please, madam, would you give a holler so I know you're all right?"

But there was no reply, and Foster hurried with the padlock, the rasp of metal against metal grating against his patience as he finally turned the key in the lock and opened the door.

Snatching up the candlestick, he held it high. The sight that met his eyes stopped him cold. Half the wine bottles were broken, their racks turned on end. A sea of wine peppered with broken glass bled over the floor toward the pile of burlap sacks beside the door, where the Tessa lay half-dressed, unconscious under a blanket of smoke.

She had evidently transformed back—dawn had come, or at least enough of it for this purpose—and started to dress when smoke overcame her. She'd gotten into her frock, but her cloak still lay on the floor where she'd cast it down. The valet quickly snatched it up and wrapped it around her shoulders.

"The Abbey is afire, madam!" he choked out. "We must away! I fear I cannot carry you up those stairs as I am. Madam, please!"

But Tessa didn't move, much less reply, instead lying like a rag poppet in her bed of burlap sacks.

Chapter Twenty-six

Giles woke just before first light, naked and cold, hunched in the barrow, which was deep enough for a wolf but hardly adequate to contain a man. Like so many other cairns in the area, time had changed its original proportions.

His first sensation was pain in his right shoulder, then teeth-chattering cold and nausea as recollection returned. The guards had seen him shape-shift. He had left his clothes behind. It was over now. They knew. He could bluff no longer. Whether he was the one who killed Forsythe or the boy had done didn't matter any longer. He would hang for it now regardless. His only hope was to flee.

He had lost much blood, but somehow he had to get back to the Abbey, collect Tessa, and leave the area. There was no other alternative. Crawling out of the barrow, he sniffed the air. One advantage of his condition was that his sense of smell had heightened. He had the feral nose of the wolf in either incarnation. Now it was in tune with the human scent. He sensed none in the immediate area. Even if he had, it wouldn't have mattered. He had to reach Tessa as quickly as possible. His life and hers depended upon it.

The sky to the west along the horizon had turned a fiery shade of gold. An odd sunrise, Giles thought, stumbling off in that direction, but at closer observation, gooseflesh riddled him from head to foot. This was no sunrise. The sun rose in the *east*. This peculiarity was taking place in the west. It almost looked like . . . fire! It was! Longhollow Abbey, which he'd seen last night just before he passed out, was now engulfed in flames. He ran toward it over the dewy bracken, gorse, and heather, blind with pain and weak from blood loss, praying he wasn't too late.

As valiant as his effort was, it wasn't long before he fell facedown on the heath, his breath coming short and his vision blurred, but not so blurred that he couldn't pick out the shape of a familiar wagon lumbering toward him in the darkness.

Moraiva!

All at once he found himself cradled in the crook of the old Gypsy's arm, leaning upon her as she probed the wound in his shoulder. After a moment, she staggered to her feet.

"Get up, Giles Longworth," she commanded in a tone not to be denied. "I cannot lift you, and you must get into the wagon. That pistol ball must come out of there at once. It is silver, and it is draining your strength. You are fortunate that it hasn't struck a vital spot or you would be dead now. Get up, I say!"

"O-old woman, I fear you ask more than I can give," he replied. "My home is in flames. I fear for my wife, my staff. I have lost much blood—"

"You can and you will rise up and get into this wagon!" Moraiva ordered, pointing a rigid arm and wagging finger. "Do it now, before the guards come. There is much to be done before that event, but no time to do it if you linger here. Get up!"

Giles pulled himself to his feet and staggered toward

the wagon, and Moraiva clicked her tongue. "Such a sight to tempt a poor old woman," she said, raking his body familiarly. "If I were thirty years younger, I'd give your lady wife a run for it."

"The . . . Abbey!" Giles panted, hauling himself up into the wagon. "I must reach the Abbey before the guards do, and that fire can be seen for miles!"

"Once I take that bullet out," the Gypsy returned. "The clothes of my dead husband await you. Put on the breeches but not the blouse, and lie down on the bunk."

Giles did as she bade him, and she brought a lantern and knelt beside the bed, which was no more than a straw pallet in a low wooden frame. Handing him a crock, she said, "Drink. It will dull the pain."

Giles tossed down a healthy swallow and fell back panting as she took the crock from him.

"Open," she said, thrusting a folded leather belt toward his mouth. Giles clamped his teeth down hard and screwed his eyes shut tight as she probed the hole in his shoulder with a sharp knife. Beads of cold swear broke out upon his brow and ran down his neck as she dug deeper.

Amid the awful pain, he felt the pressure lighten as the Gypsy's deft fingers removed the ball. He spat free the leather belt, crying out when she poured the rest of the contents of the crock into the wound.

"Your strength will return now," she said, slathering on an ointment from a cobalt-blue glass jar on the boxed-in shelf on the wagon wall. It smelled foul and burned for a bit, especially when she bound the wound with linen strips. Her wagon was an apothecary on wheels, for it was her function to heal among the Gypsies, and her skill was legend.

"We must hurry, Moraiva," Giles said. "That is Longhollow Abbey on fire!"

"I know," Moraiva said, climbing onto the wagon seat.

"I have seen what becomes of it in another time. Lie still! Regain your strength. You will need much for what is to come."

"What is to come?" he spoke up. With the door open as it was, they could easily converse as she drove.

"Your Abbey is no more," she said. "Your life here is no more. You cannot stay, for if you do you will be put to death for that which you did not do."

At last, someone who believed him to be innocent! He had begun to doubt himself, unable to imagine a child capable of such atrocity.

"There is a way to help us all. I know you do not truly believe in the corridors, because you have not yet experienced them, but they are your only hope now."

Giles ground out a bitter laugh. "Then I am doomed, because the corridors want no truck with me. They have barred me at every pass."

"I think because there is only one corridor for you, Giles Longworth, and when you find it, it will be open to you."

"Can this horse move any faster?"

"He will get us there."

"What must I do?" Giles asked through a grimace, wishing she hadn't wasted all the contents of the crock upon the wound. His strength was returning, but the pain was excruciating.

"Trust your lady wife, she knows the way," Moraiva said. "You cannot stay here any longer. Through no fault of your own, your life is over here. The child was tainted when he came here. It may have happened in the womb, or after. You may never know. This is something I alone will know, and once I take you to your Abbey, you shall see me no more. Our paths will not cross again if I am to help us all."

"I do not understand," Giles said flatly. What seemed

to make complete sense to her made no sense at all to him.

"In order to reverse the curse that has come upon you, you must go to another time," Moraiva explained. "But it will not be easy, as not any time will do. Only certain pathways will work. Your lady wife will take you there. She bit me, so now I am as you are, and I must avail myself of a corridor to do this also—"

"But what of the boy?" Giles asked. "I cannot just abandon him. His curse was hardly his fault, either."

The Gypsy smiled. "I mean to take the boy with me," she said. "It is he who set the fire."

"How could you know that?"

"I know, because I have seen it in a different time. Your Abbey becomes quite a curiosity in the future. Your lady wife saw it, too—"

"She said she had something she wanted to tell me, and I put her off. Could this be what she meant?"

"Yes," the Gypsy said. "But do not reproach her for not telling it sooner. She had no idea when in time the fire took place. Had you known, you could have done nothing to prevent it. The tale is well told. None were ever seen again. It is presumed that all perished in the holocaust, though no remains were ever found. They blame that on the flaws, assuming that the Cornish winds blew all the evidence away; but we know differently, don't we, Giles Longworth? You must trust me."

"But how do you know this? How can you be so sure?"

"I know because I have lived it before," the Gypsy said. "I have done what you must do now, and cancelled the curse. When your lady wife bit me, it was not the first time a werewolf sank its fangs into my flesh. I know the corridors well. It worked for me once. It will work again. I will take the boy, and it will work for him also, if it is so ordained. He is Roma. My people will raise and protect him. Either way, he cannot remain to ravage the coast and infect all here, for since he has come many have been tainted. It is the only way."

"Then we must go quickly," Giles said. "The guards are already convinced that I killed Forsythe. If they reach the Abbey before us and take me into custody again, my life is over, especially since they saw me change into the wolf. That blaze will bring them sure as check. The sky is lit up like the dawn. In my confusion while returning to my human form, I thought it was first light, until I realized I was facing west."

"They will come, yes, Giles Longworth, once they find their horses who ran fast and far from you last night. I am hoping they will be a while at that. Rest and save your strength until you reach a place before the wound occurred. Then you will be restored, as if that silver pistol ball never entered your flesh."

Giles said no more. There was no use. It all sounded so odd, and made little sense, yet he was certain the Gypsy would give him no more answers.

Why was the wagon moving so slowly? He slid his feet onto the floorboards and dropped his head into his hands, trying to avoid the sight of the fiery blaze in the sky ahead, but it was no use. His life as he knew it had just gone up in flames and turned the sky to blood.

Tessa was semiconscious when Foster half-dragged, half-carried her up the narrow staircase and through the service door in the wainscoting to the second-floor landing. Coughing uncontrollably, the first word she uttered was Giles's name.

"Oh, madam, thank God!" Foster said, leading her down to the main floor. "I feared for your life. Can you make it below?"

Tessa nodded, leaning on the valet. "Giles?" she begged. "Where is Giles?"

"He is not here, madam. He never returned."

"You are . . . certain, Foster?"

"Yes, madam."

"Where is Master Monty?"

"I do not know, madam. He wasn't in his rooms. He was in yours the last I saw of him. He did this"—he touched his brow gingerly—"before setting the house afire."

"Oh, Foster, that cut is deep. It needs attention!"

"It will mend, madam. Right now we must concentrate upon getting you to safety."

The Great Hall seemed so far away as they struggled down the corridor through the bilious black smoke and fiery bits raining down around them. They hadn't gotten halfway when the third floor collapsed onto the second floor in the east wing, and much of that fell below to the main floor in a crimson rush of shooting flames, high-flying sparks and debris.

They had nearly reached the gaping doors where first light had begun to dilute the darkness with fish-gray streamers when Foster let her go with a gentle shove toward the exit. "Madam, do not stop," he said. "Keep going. You are safe in seconds."

"No! Where are you going?" she cried as he staggered away from her, retracing his steps.

"Keep on as you are!" he called. "I must fetch notes from the valuables chest in the study for the master. It is all the money he has recently made, and with his estate in flames—"

"No!" she cried. "He will not need them, Foster." She took the pocket from the side of her frock and showed it to him. She was grateful she had managed to keep most of her savings since the odyssey began, for it would now be invaluable. "It is my currency he will need now. His will be useless where we are going. Leave it!"

"I must do what I must," he returned. "You are safe now . . . just a few more steps. I shall join you directly."

He disappeared through the study door then, and Tessa pressed on until she staggered through the open doorway on a belching cloud of sooty smoke and collapsed on the courtyard lawn.

All around her, pandemonium had broken loose. Able had herded the servants into the stable as they streamed out of the house when the fire started. Sobs and shrieks, outcries and whimpers rose over the thunder of the holocaust as the flames leaped high into the sky, sending showers of fiery sparks aloft on the blustery wind. Tessa knew the servants were safe: No harm would come to them in the stable; it had been intact in the future when the caretaker told her the tale. He had made it his home.

Her watering eyes trained upon the doorway, she scarcely blinked, sifting through the smoke for some sign of Foster. Floors were collapsing, shooting fresh columns of smoke, fire, and ash into the dawn sky. Falling timbers crosshatched the corridor she had just fled. Could the valet still pass through? And where was Giles? If only he would come.

Then, through the fog of drifting smoke belching through the doorway, she saw motion—a figure; no . . . *two*. She rose to her feet just as Foster came stumbling into the drive with Master Monty in tow. One hand held a satchel she assumed was full of money. The other hand was fisted in the back of the boy's shirt, and the valet propelled him toward her, whilst from behind, the creaking sound of the Gypsy's lumbering wagon bled through the racket of the panicked servants and the crackle and roar of the fire.

What happened next was fast and simultaneous—so fast Tessa scarcely had time to blink. Able came running, Giles half-climbed, half-fell out of the wagon and rushed into Tessa's arms, and Moraiva rose from the wagon seat, her rigid arm pointing.

"Bring the boy to me!" she commanded, addressing Foster.

The valet rushed Monty to the wagon and lifted him up, despite all the protests, pleas, and threats pouring from the boy's throat. Holding the child at a distance, the valet deftly avoided the small though cruel feet kicking with perfect aim at his shin bones and, as he raised Monty higher, his groin.

"Stop that foul mouth!" the Gypsy charged, securing the boy inside the wagon. "We are about to go on a little journey. Be still! You might enjoy it." She turned back to Giles. "Take her and go quickly. The guards are not far behind. We will not meet again, Giles Longworth. At least not soon if all goes well. . . ."

Giles turned to Able. "Saddle three horses—*now*, man. I must away.

"Aye, sir," the stabler said, set in motion.

"What is happening?" Tessa asked, her eyes flashing among them. "Where has Moraiva gone with the boy?" The courtyard was filled with smoke that had enveloped the wagon, and though she strained to penetrate it, nothing met her eyes but that gloomy veil settled over the grounds. Moraiva's wagon was gone.

"I will explain later," Giles said. "We cannot linger. If the guards come, I am a dead man, Tessa. They saw me shape-shift into the wolf."

Fresh blood was seeping through Giles's shirt, and Tessa gasped. "You're hurt!" she cried. "You've been shot?"

Giles nodded. "It's nothing, my love. Moraiva dug the bullet out. It was a silver bullet. The guards were taking me to the jail at Lamorna to hold for the magistrates. They fired on me when I shape-shifted."

"A silver bullet could have killed you!"

"If it had hit a vital organ, yes, but it did not. All it did was drain my strength. If we can manage what Moraiva said we must, it will soon be healed."

"What did she say?" Tessa begged him.

"That the corridors would save us. That needs must we access one that will take us back to a time before we were bitten, and cancel the curse."

"And . . . the boy?"

"She has taken him and done the same," said Giles. "He is Roma, so she will care for him, but we are not out of this until we find our corridor—and we must do that before the guards come or all is for naught."

"This is what she told me also," Tessa admitted. "But the corridors have not opened to you."

"Moraiva said there is one that will. I have only to find it."

Just then, Able came running with the horses.

"Why three?" Tessa queried, mounting.

Giles glanced about. "Foster!" he called, attracting the valet who stood transfixed by the fire that had destroyed his world. "Will you come with us?" He mounted, and so did Tessa.

"With you, sir?" Foster looked lightning-struck.

Giles nodded. "I do not know where the path will lead, but I want you to travel it with us."

Shots rang out.

"Quickly, man, decide!" Giles thundered, trying to control the rambunctious mount beneath him.

Without another word, the valet swung himself up into the saddle of the third horse, and all three rode east, using the smoke as a blind with the Guards in close pursuit.

Chapter Twenty-seven

Pistol balls whizzed past Tessa's ear as they rode hunched low in their saddles. Moraiva had tried to prepare her for this. What troubled Tessa, now that it was upon her, was that Giles had never been able to access the lay lines; they had always rejected him. Now it was vital he escape through the corridors, and she feared she would be accepted while he would not. That would mean sure and sudden death for him, and the thought of being without him . . . And then there was Foster, facing serious reprisal for complicity. Tessa shuddered at what was yet to occur.

"Where are we going, sir?" Foster asked. "Is it far? You look wretched, sir. Your shoulder is bleeding badly."

"You will have to ask my lady wife," Giles called over the wail of the wind that had risen since they set out. "She is going to find us one of the time corridors I told you about."

"Oh, sir, I believe I'd think twice about that if I were you."

Giles laughed. "What? Would you rather stay here and face the magistrates for complicity in the matter of Henry Forsythe's murder?"

"Certainly not!" the valet replied. "It's just that . . . these times suit me just right, you see."

More shots rang out.

"They're re-loading!" Giles cried, his voice raised in competition with the wind. "Or they're toting blunderbusses. Still want to keep to your own time, Foster?"

"Now, I never said that, sir!" the valet replied hoarsely.

"We do not know what lies ahead, 'tis true," Giles hollered, "but we know what we've left behind: sudden death for me and God alone knows what fate for you and Tessa . . . as she is." She caught his sidelong glance. "Do you know how to get us where we're going?" he asked. "The guards are gaining on us. Soon one of those pistol balls will hit its mark. . . ."

Tessa's mind was reeling with questions and fears. Giles was losing too much blood. He was as white as a ghost, and his lips were tinged with blue. He needed help soon, but they dared not stop. They were heading southwest, toward the moor where the little chaise had broken down what seemed a lifetime ago. All at once, it was as if a candle burst into flame in her brain. They were heading the wrong way.

"No!" she cried. "We have to go back! We are going in the wrong direction. We are approaching the place where I ran from you and accessed the corridor, but you could not follow. This isn't the way."

"We cannot go back, Tessa. That fire will have brought half the parish. The estate will be swarming with guards."

"Not back to the Abbey. You must trust me, Giles. I think I know the corridor that will open to you. Follow me!"

She turned due west toward the hills, confusing the guards in pursuit momentarily, but only momentarily.

They soon turned and galloped after them, pistols blazing.

"Tessa, where are you going?" Giles demanded. "The hills are too open. We're going to be sitting targets!"

"I know what I'm doing!" she called out. "We need to go back to the little hill where our wolves first met face to face. I think it's this way."

"Why?"

"Because the corridor there is the one I believe Moraiva wanted you to travel . . . the one that will admit you. Oh, Giles, if she was right, we can *do* this!"

"No!" he cried. "That hill is farther north. I know it well, and I will never forget our meeting there."

"Lead us, then!" she begged. "Giles, you must. Are they still following? They've stopped shooting."

"They are likely reloading, and they are gaining on us. I can hear their voices."

Tessa could not hear them. Could it be his extraordinary hearing, a condition brought to bear by the wolf inside him? It didn't matter. He had taken the lead. Though he still looked ghastly, he seemed charged with new life as he drove the horse beneath him relentlessly.

He seemed to be struggling, suddenly, and Tessa shouted, "Are you all right?"

"Yes," he replied. "It's the horse. It smells the wolf in me. It's been that way each time I've mounted ever since Monty bit me."

Tessa wasn't having any such difficulty. Things of this nature were obviously subjective, and she was grateful for it, since she wasn't a skilled horsewoman. Though she had often been around horses, her skills were sorely lacking. Being servant class in London didn't lend much time for equestrian pursuits.

The hills rose up before them, and cold chills riddled

Tessa's spine as she took the lead from Giles. This had to be done just so, or they would go the wrong way in time, for the corridors worked in both directions. And the timing had to be precise if she was to implement her plan.

The bloodcurdling sound of pistol fire had resumed, and Foster's voice sent fresh shivers over Tessa's body. "Is it much farther?" he cried. "They are almost upon us! I felt the breeze from that last shot. I hope you know what you're about!"

"Just follow me!" Tessa shrilled. "We must turn back toward London . . . *now!*"

All at once, she turned the horse sharply to the right, its heavy hooves flinging clumps of sodden turf into the air as she coaxed it eastward, wishing she had more riding experience, for it was all she could do to stay in the saddle. A silvery streak of what looked like metallic water shimmered in front of her: an avenue, a transparent ribbon stretching as far as the eye could see.

"It is! Oh, *it is!*" Tessa cried, riding right into it, with the others on her heels.

Suddenly, the flaming sky was gone. There was no sign of Longhollow Abbey. The bilious clouds had disappeared, and the wind had ceased to blow; a breathless mist had taken its place. It was no longer day. Stars twinkled in the indigo vault above, and a three-quarter moon shone down upon them.

Tessa's eyes flashed to behind her, and her heart seemed to rise with the lump in her throat, for she did not see Giles straightaway. He was lost in mist, as was Foster.

"Giles!" she called, and held her breath until he emerged from the swirling fog with the valet. "Oh, Giles!" she cried, tears streaming down. "Your wound . . . it's gone."

Dazed, Giles gripped his shoulder, feeling for the wound that wasn't there.

"And Foster!" Tessa cried. "The wound on your brow . . . it is gone as well."

"W-why . . . so it is!" the valet observed, groping his forehead. "Where are we? Where is this place?"

Tessa ranged her mount alongside them. "Nowhere foreign," she chirped, her euphoria spilling over. "We are in London . . . on the outskirts of Cheapside, in the year or Our Lord 1903—*my* year! I mean, the year I came to you from. Oh, Giles," she sobbed. "Moraiva was right . . . this is your corridor. This is where you belong, where *we* belong."

"How on earth can it be?" Foster said.

"Oh, it can—believe me, it can!" Tessa rejoiced. "Come! There is a public house with rooms to let close by."

"What has happened to the guards?" Foster persisted, glancing behind.

"They have remained behind," Tessa told him. "Do you not understand, Foster? We have escaped them. We have come where they cannot follow. The corridor is closed to them. We are free!"

"You knew this?" Giles said to Tessa.

She nodded. "I wanted to tell you," she said. "I knew about the fire, I just didn't know when it would occur. History has it that we died in the blaze. I was desperately trying to cancel that, since no remains were ever found."

"Well, my love, evidently you have done," Giles said, craning his neck for a view of their surroundings, denied them by the fog. "And I suppose I shall have a look at last at one of your horseless carriages?"

"*Horseless* carriages?" Foster echoed. "Impossible!"

Tessa laughed, as she hadn't laughed since she

couldn't remember when. "You may even drive one if you wish," she tittered.

"We need to find lodgings," Giles said.

"And how will we pay for them?" Foster spoke up. "I saved some of your notes, sir, from the valuables chest in the study, but surely they are outdated if this is the year 1903."

Tessa took out her pocket. "I still have some of my money left," she said. "It isn't much, but it will see us clothed, fed and housed until we can convert your notes into modern-day currency."

Foster uttered a strangled sound. "The notes can be converted?" he breathed.

Tessa nodded. "At the banks on Threadneedle Street," she said. "And they may well have appreciated in value. Collectors do it all the time. Giles Longworth, you may well be on the verge of becoming as rich as Croesus!"

Foster gasped. "And you didn't want me to fetch them!" he scolded.

"I didn't want you to burn to death," Tessa replied. She glanced toward Giles, who turned his gaze to the partial moon above. "What is it?" she murmured. Ranging her mount closer, she laid her hand upon his arm, drawing his eyes.

"We won't *really* know if we are free until the moon waxes full," he said.

"Look at your wrist."

He did as she bade and ran his hand thoughtfully over the unblemished flesh where the wound had been.

"And my lip?" Tessa said, calling his attention there.

He studied the place where the bruise had been, his brows knit in a frown. "I want to believe," he said. "You do not know how I want to believe, but suppose the curse is stronger than time? Moraiva says such curses are as old as eons. I will not rest easy until the moon waxes full again."

"For now, my love, let us take this gift and make it our own."

"What shall we do now?" Foster said.

"Come," Tessa replied, leading them along the lane. "We are quite safe at this hour. None but the slags will be abroad now. I need to be certain what I have in mind is a viable plan."

"Where are we going?" Giles asked.

"To the gallery," Tessa responded. "Slowly now . . . I have just come from jail in this city, and I have no desire to return to it. If what I have in mind works, we shan't be long in London."

They passed St. Michael's Church and several public houses. Tessa pointed out the Black Boar Inn as a likely place to seek lodgings. Lemon-colored light still puddled in the street from its windows, and a mews behind gave both access to the rear of the establishment and shelter for the horses.

Coming upon the gallery, Giles gasped. A light inside from a gas lamp on the wall illuminated a little alcove where a painting was highlighted.

"Yes!" Tessa cried, a little too loudly in spite of her resolve to keep silent.

"Sir!" Foster murmured. "It's your painting! How is this possible?"

"It wasn't a dream!" Tessa said. "Now I know what we must do."

"What must we do?" Giles asked.

"Nothing tonight, certainly," Tessa admitted. "We cannot linger here. The bobbies patrol these streets all night. We will take rooms at the public house. Tomorrow is soon enough to do what needs must."

Giles looked confused. "I thought you said a young couple from Yorkshire bought the paintings."

"I did," Tessa replied. "But I have brought you here before that sale took place. Tomorrow, my love, *we* are that couple."

Giles had scarcely gotten Tessa inside their room at the Black Boar Inn when he stripped off her cloak and seized her in his arms like a man possessed, his hands roaming her body as though he were a starving beggar at a feast.

Unbuttoning his breeches, he freed his anxious member, raised her skirt and rushed her against the wall. A husky moan leaked from her throat as he cupped the soft globes of her buttocks in trembling hands. Raising her up, he urged her legs around his waist and took her. Loosing a groan that was more feral than human, he undulated against her, driving his sex deeper with every shuddering thrust.

How warm and welcoming she was. How their bodies fit together as if they were two halves of a whole. Her breasts were a feast for his eyes as he slid her frock down, exposing the creamy white skin and tawny nipples, so hard and tall, begging for his touch. She laced her fingers through his hair as he strummed the turgid buds with his thumbs, and he was undone. Taking her lips in a scorching kiss that drained his senses, he spiraled into the moist heat of her again and again as he tasted her deeply.

Her release was explosive, enveloping his sex, her whole body convulsed in palpating contractions that triggered his own climax. Giles groaned, and groaned again. It was a shuddering, heart-stopping eruption as he filled her with the warm rush of his seed.

Scooping her up in his arms, he staggered to the bed and fell upon her there, inhaling the fragrance of her hot, moist skin, drinking in the scent of violets from her hair that had long since lost its tortoiseshell pins.

"My poor Tessa," he murmured in her ear, gathering her against his hard-muscled chest. "With no pins for her lovely hair. Tomorrow I will buy you hairpins fit for a queen."

She snuggled close in his arms. "You will have to suffer the dreadful clothes I came to you in," she reminded him. "To go about here now as I am would brand me a lightskirt. What's more," she said through a musical giggle, "you will have to accustom yourself to modern togs."

Giles hadn't thought of that, and he frowned, prying an outright laugh from her. But it was a fleeting expression, replaced by a wry smile as he leaned back and stripped off his shirt. "That shan't be a hardship," he said, stripping her frock off over her head. "I won't be wearing clothes often. I expect to spend the rest of my days naked in the arms of my lady fair."

"Ahhh, but you will have to dress sometime," she teased.

"And what shall I wear?"

"For one thing, breeches are something that for the most part only schoolboys wear, unless the man is shooting grouse or otherwise engaged in sports. Men wear trousers and shoes, and their shirts have detachable collars that fasten with brass collar buttons in back. Poet shirts are a thing of the past. They surely took us for Gypsies when we entered below, which was not a bad thing, since I am evidently still a wanted criminal."

All the while they were talking, he had been burrowing under the counterpane with her. Their naked bodies entwined beneath were slippery with the dew of sex, and would be for the better part of the night, if he had his way.

"And what of Foster?" he asked. "The poor man was born a slave to the fashions of his calling. What is he facing in the year 1903?"

"Believe it or not, menservants' attire has not changed overmuch. But for seeming a bit dowdy until we can outfit him properly, he is quite well to pass as he is."

Giles's hands began to roam over her body again, more tenderly now, feeling every curve, every voluptuous swell, and she leaned into his caresses, bringing him once more erect. "I swear you have bewitched me," he murmured. "I cannot get enough of you, Tessa."

"I cannot stay long in London, Giles," she said. "We must do what must be done and leave the city."

He frowned. How could he tell her what was in his heart? What would she do? He was loath to darken so perfect a night of love with mundane things, but there was nothing for it. It was best to have it said and put it behind him.

"Tessa," he began. "I know you feel you have brought us to safety, and you have—all but yourself, that is, and at great risk to life and limb in the bargain. Well . . . I do not care what clothes I wear or what clothes you wear. I shall become accustomed to horseless carriages, and pavement, and gas lamps, and curbstones in the streets, but I do not believe I could abide Yorkshire."

She stiffened in his arms, and he drew her closer, grazing her brow with fever parched lips, for indeed the fever in his blood that brought his sex erect had heightened the fever in his skin.

"I am a Cornishman, Tessa," he went on quickly, while he possessed the courage to say it. "I can bear the shock of coming into your time, my love, but I do not know if I would be able to stand to never see my homeland again."

"What are you asking me, Giles?"

"I know the Abbey is gone," he said, "but nearly a hundred years into the future . . . would it be safe for us to return to Cornwall? Should we not try? I feel this strong pull to visit . . . and to visit soon."

There was silence, the kind that is tasted like death: so long a hesitation that Giles feared she wasn't going to answer. She'd begun to tremble of a sudden, and he drew her closer against his naked body for the benefit of its heat.

"I do not know, Giles," she finally said. "I honestly do not know."

Chapter Twenty-eight

Tessa's savings were depleted by noon the following day, but they had paid for their food and lodging, and set aside funds to purchase clothing for them to wear without turning heads while venturing out in the London streets.

Foster was enlisted to do the shopping, since he was the only one dressed reasonably enough to go abroad as he was. As Giles's dresser, he knew his master's correct size and tastes, though the latter was of no extended consequence. The object was simply to outfit themselves in the fashions of the day in order to visit the banks on Threadneedle Street and convert Giles's 1811 bank notes into turn-of-the-century currency.

As for the exchange, it was decided not to do this all at once, to avoid casting suspicion upon themselves. Converting enormous sums would certainly be suspect. All they needed was enough money to purchase the paintings and hire a coach to leave London—to a destination at this point uncertain. This was the only facet of the thus far flawless adventure that worried Tessa. She'd woken in Giles's arms after a perfect night of excruciating ecstasy with a nagging fear that would not leave her, fear of returning to the place they'd just so successfully fled.

Of course there would be no one there to remember after a hundred years, but that was not what she feared. It was the lay lines. There were so many, and though they seemed to welcome her, they did not welcome Giles. She feared Moraiva was right, that he had found the only corridor open to him. If that were so, returning to Cornwall might be a grave mistake for them all.

Foster returned shortly after noon with his purchases. He laid several parcels wrapped in brown paper on the bed in Giles and Tessa's room, then hesitated, his eyes flashing, before he placed a hatbox on the bedside table and began unwrapping everything.

"Bad luck to place a hat on a bed," he muttered, for Tessa had regarded as odd his previous deliberation.

Her husband laughed. How very handsome Giles was when he laughed! "Spoken like a true Cornishman!" he said. "We can ill afford any more bad luck, eh? Pay us no mind, my love," he said to Tessa. "We are a superstitious lot, I fear."

"I barely had enough blunt to manage," the valet remarked, clearly embarrassed. He unwrapped Giles's garments first, taking out a collarless shirt and separate collar, and a pair of long red-and-brown-check tweed trousers with cuffs.

"What the deuce are those?" Giles said, raking the trousers with a dubious glance.

"I know, sir. I knew you would say that, but I am assured they are the height of fashion."

Tessa laughed, earning herself a scathing glower. "They are," she said, "very smart-looking."

"And the length is such that they will cover nearly all of those dreadful boots the Gypsy supplied," Foster said. "I didn't have enough blunt to purchase shoes."

Giles sighed. "What is that other garment, there?" he said, pointing at a piece of folded cloth the color of mushrooms.

Giles unfurled the suspicious garment with a flourish. "It's called a motoring coat," he explained. "One wears it when driving one of the horseless carriages to keep the road dust off. I saw one—a horseless carriage. Beastly thing it was. Explosions came out of a pipe at the rear, and it had a horn. It frightened the horses in the street . . . I dare say it frightened *me*. Such things will never become popular."

"Well, this redeems the rest," Giles said, "it will cover everything else. A little too narrow for riding, though."

"Oh, you aren't supposed to ride in it, sir."

"Evidently," Giles pronounced. "Carry on, then. What have you found for my lady wife?"

"First, these," Foster said, withdrawing a handful of hairpins from his waistcoat pocket. "They are only whalebone, but that was the best I could afford."

Tessa squealed with delight and snatched them from the valet's hand, proceeding to order her hair with them.

"Yes, well, I shall buy you fine ones once we change the notes," Giles said, still examining his new togs.

The valet unwrapped a long gored skirt of indigo wool, with a matching capelet and a white pin-tucked blouse. "They are called leg-o-mutton sleeves," the valet explained.

"I know, Foster," Tessa said. "But I believe we have gotten you an education in fashion today."

The valet opened the hatbox and lifted out a wide-brimmed indigo velvet hat covered with downward-pointing pearl-gray feathers and a dark net veil.

"What the devil is that?" Giles cried. "It looks like the aftermath of a cockfight, shroud and all. Tessa, surely you do not mean to *wear* that."

Tessa sank down upon the edge of the bed, convulsing in laughter. She had always longed for just such a hat. But Giles's incredulous expression, and the valet's forlorn attitude while sporting the feathered finery in his hand, was more than she could bear. Not without erupting in giggles.

"And here I thought I'd been so clever," Foster said. "I fail to see the humor here. The veil will hide your face, madam, since you must go abroad in daylight. I was only thinking of your safety, since you are still being pursued."

"Just so," Tessa said. "And I am undyingly grateful for your cleverness. With so much on my mind, I would never have thought of it. What did you purchase for yourself? Anything?"

"Oh, I wouldn't presume to outfit myself, madam," Foster said. "A different-shaped collar and waistcoat, a jacket with a bit more or less material in the cut of it doesn't mean much. No one batted an eye when I was abroad. As long as the clothes are black, well-pressed, clean, and unobtrusive, they can be outdated. Besides, from what I've observed, I can't see that serving-class clothes have changed all that much in a hundred years. Well, except for the collar, which I took the liberty of remedying."

"You are certainly welcome," Giles said. "We'll get you sorted out and up-to-date once we exchange the notes."

"Yes, sir," the valet said gratefully.

"We should do that quickly," Tessa said. "There isn't much time before the banks close. I wish we knew what day of the week it is. We can't very well ask. The curator at the museum knows me by sight. He said his partner sold the paintings. That man does *not* know me. He's in on Tuesdays and Thursdays."

"It is Thursday, madam," Foster spoke up, fishing a newspaper from the parcel wrappings.

"Well, well, you've certainly thought of everything, haven't you, Foster?" Giles observed.

"Yes, sir," the valet said. "I hope so, sir. I will leave you to change."

Foster did not accompany them to the bank on Threadneedle Street. Passing themselves off as newly-weds from Yorkshire wanting to convert funds left to them in an inheritance, they had no difficulty at the bank. The gallery was closed when they reached it, however, and it was with gross disappointment that they returned to the Black Boar Inn. This meant that they wouldn't be able to purchase the paintings until Tuesday next week if Tessa was to be present, which she assumed was proper. That was five days away, and none were pleased about that.

Giles and Tessa dined in their room. Tessa had lost her appetite. She wanted to be out of the city straight-away, and it wasn't going to happen. The longer she stayed in London, the more the danger that she would be discovered.

Seated beside the fire, it was Giles who broke the awkward silence that had fallen like a pall of doom around them.

"I know you are disappointed," he said, "but what can a few more days matter? We have the blunt—more than enough—and plenty more to convert once that's gone."

"A young couple from Yorkshire bought those paintings, Giles. I cannot go when the curator is there; he will recognize me, veil or no. I know it. Yet if we wait until Tuesday week, perhaps I'm wrong. Perhaps a *true* couple from Yorkshire—"

"Wait!" he interrupted her. "I can solve that. I'll have Foster go 'round and leave a deposit on our behalf. I shall send a missive with him. You can trust him to know how and what to do, Tessa."

"Could we?" she murmured.

Giles surged to his feet. "I shall go and fetch him

forthwith to prove the point," he said, striding toward the door.

"Wait!" Tessa called after him.

"What is it?" he asked, halfway over the threshold.

Now seemed a good time to get something else off her chest. "Giles . . . I know you do not want to go to Yorkshire," she began awkwardly, nervously. "Well, I can't be sure, but I believe it's a mistake to go back to Cornwall, even now, after almost a hundred years have passed. We can't stay there. I also know that you will not be content if you do not go—"

"Tessa," Giles interrupted, stepping back into the room. He closed the door.

"No, you must hear me out," she said. "We cannot access the corridors. That would be dangerous. We could lose each other. The only one that has ever opened to you brought us here safely, but I do not trust that luck again. I believe this is where we are meant to be. And not because it is my time—I would live with you in any time. It's just something I know deep down inside. I believe Moraiva knew it."

"Then . . . that shall be the end of it."

"That's just it—it won't be the end of it, Giles, not until you see your beloved Cornwall one more time. If your instincts tell you that you must return . . . But not in your time. That would be suicide for us both. And not by the lay lines."

"What then? My gut says that I must go soon, and we can't possibly return to the coast and be back in five days, Tessa. If we are to purchase that—"

"Yes, we can."

"How?" he asked.

"The railway."

"The rail . . . ?"

"Yes, coaches that run on rails in the ground. They

move very swiftly. I will show you. Experiments with steam engines were done in your day, but the railroads didn't come to the fore until about 1840. It will have us there and back with plenty of time to spare."

"But if you do not think it right . . ."

"A thing must be faced to be put right," Tessa said. "You feel a draw to Cornwall, so we must heed it. Unless you go, you will always wish you had. You must learn what has become of your land in the year 1903, and you will not be happy until you put that longing to rest. I only hope we do the right thing."

While Foster set out to secure the sale at Tatum's Gallery, Tessa and Giles boarded a train at Victoria Station bound for Cornwall. The closer they drew to the coast, the more apprehensive Tessa became.

Beside her, Giles, fascinated with the train, sat speechless. If the situation weren't so grave, she would have laughed at his sobriety. How she longed to take him in her arms, but that wouldn't do. Not here, not now and in public.

After a time, his attention returned to her, and he saw what she so desperately tried to hide. "You really fear the time corridors, don't you?" he murmured, inclining his head to speak quietly, for the coach was filled with travelers.

"I do not know why I am so afraid," she said. "It has been thus since this odyssey began. I am just afraid of . . . of accidentally doing what I did that first time and thereby separating us. The trouble lies in that I do not know exactly what I *did* do that first time, except imagine the patchwork hills in your 'Bride of Time.' Then all at once I was there. It was . . . magical."

Giles sighed. "And I nearly frightened you off, getting shot of that whore who stole my snuffbox. I should have let her have it. At least then it might have survived as an antiquity. It would be priceless today."

"It was scandalous!" Tessa corrected him.

"Quite so," he agreed with a laugh, "but so was I in those days. You've tamed me, lady wife. I am scandalous now only in bed with you."

He kissed her with his eyes then, and it was more of a seduction than if he had used his sensuous lips. Tessa blinked away the urge to melt under that gaze, and the Devil take the spectators who were already gawking at them. Thus it went the entire journey, which only took hours instead of the days it would have taken overland by coach.

A horse-drawn bus was waiting at the station to pick up passengers for Bodmin. Tessa took a chill as they boarded it, recalling the night she saw the burned-out shell of the Abbey. She never had found out what year that was, and she wondered if the same caretaker would be there, if he would remember her.

Thus far, the landscape seemed the same as it was in Giles's time, with the exception that some of the trees in the forest that bordered the moor had been cut down, and another copse had risen on the opposite side. When they reached the rise that led up to the Abbey, Giles couldn't vacate the bus quickly enough. They got out at the stile that had become a bus stop over time, and began to climb toward the blackened skeleton of what once had been Longhollow Abbey.

It was just dusk, and already the moon shone brightly down upon their progress, reminding her that it would only be a few more days before it waxed full. Then they would know—really know—if the curse had been cancelled, if they could live a normal life together, or if they would forever dread the rising of the moon.

It was plain that Giles wasn't thinking about that now.

His eyes were riveted to the Abbey, and to a little puddle of golden light spilling from the open stable doors.

"The caretaker lived there when I last saw this," Tessa said. "His name was Ezra Jones, a strange curmudgeon. He held me off with a shotgun. He told me the place had become a curiosity, that folk came from miles around to see what was left of Longhollow Abbey and hear his tale. He said the Prince Regent set up a trust in your name after your . . . death that protected it, and the proceeds go to the Crown. I don't know what year that was. I never found out. I came down the hill and Moraiva collected me in the wagon and brought me back to you."

"Is that the man?" Giles asked, nodding toward a bowlegged, shogun-toting silhouette in tweeds hobbling toward them, a lantern held high.

Tessa grabbed her veil and lowered it. "It is!" she murmured. "He takes his job quite seriously."

"Hold there!" the caretaker bellowed. "We're closed for the day. You'll have to come back tomorrow. Tours begin at one o'clock. We close at five. Now, git!"

"That is ridiculous, sir," Giles said. "How can you 'close' what is open to the elements? We shan't be here tomorrow. We'll gladly pay your admission price."

"Town folk," the caretaker said in disgust. "Ya can spot them a mile off. Well, this ain't London. Ya can't come out here and do like ya please. We've got rules, open to the elements or not, and I'm paid to follow them."

Giles whipped out a note and offered it. "This should cover any inconvenience. We would like to hear your tale, Mister . . . ?"

"Jones," the caretaker said, snatching the note. "Ezra Jones. You'll have ta settle for the abbreviated version. I need my sleep.

"There was a young woman come out here not long

ago in the dead o' night—another Londoner—walked right up in there, bold as brass. *Nobody* gets ta go in there, not even on the tours; too dangerous after all these years." He raised the lantern, coming closer. "She looked a lot like you, missus, only she weren't no lady. Half-dressed in whore's clothes, by the look of her, said she was a relation o' the doxy what burned up with old Longworth in the fire—name o' LaPell, or some such, she said."

"That's nothing to us," Giles said. "We've paid. Now, let us hear your tale before our bus comes back to collect us, hmm?"

"Anyway," Jones went on, "the gel, her ancestor, was governess to the lad what set the fire. Some say the little blighter was cursed. He was a Gypsy, ya know, Longworth's ward, and that Longworth used ta lock him up when the moon was full. He was a bad hat, old Longworth. Never met an artist yet that wasn't an elbowbender, given ta lay about with the bawds. Yes, sirree, bad hats, the lot!"

"All this happened almost a hundred years ago, so I'm told, and folk hereabout still recollect it?" Giles asked, his brows knit in a frown.

Tessa looped her arm through his and gave it a reassuring squeeze, but the muscles beneath her fingers were as hard as steel bands, and they didn't respond. Ezra Jones had his full and fierce attention.

"Folks hereabouts are a superstitious lot," the caretaker said. "It'll be three hundred years afore they forget the tale of old Giles Longworth, and maybe not even then."

"I'm sorry, please continue," Giles said.

The caretaker spat to the side, and went on with a nod. "Everybody said old Longworth was round the bend, if ya take my meaning—crazy as a loon. He shut himself up in there with whores comin' and goin' all hours o' the day and night, passin' them off as his models, but everybody knew they was his whores . . .'scuse me, missus. And all the while, he was supposed ta be carin' for the little boy. One day, the poor lad up and run off, and who could blame him? Folks hereabout was sure old Longworth had done for the poor lad till young Monty—that was his name: Monty—he come back and set the house afire. They was all in there, so the tale goes: the lad, Longworth, and that doxy of a governess. She was a brazen tart, she was, took ta posin' for Longworth *nekked*, mind, after the blighter run all the other whores off the place. He was workin' on a painting called 'The Bride o' Time,' for the Prince Regent. That was George IV."

"And the painting . . . what happened to it?" Giles put in.

"I'm just gettin' ta that," Jones said testily. "I dunno what it is with you Town folk always interruptin'. That gel what was up here a while back scarcely let me get a word in, neither."

"My apologies," Giles said. "Please continue."

Jones nodded. "Anyhow, after the fire, all the servants dispersed without saying a word. It was if a ghost had sworn them all to secrecy. Old Prinny set up a trust for Longworth. Then all the blighter's paintings sold overnight. Everybody wanted to own a piece o' the bloke who painted Prinny's Bride o' Time. Between that and the scandal out here, Longworth became a local legend to this very day."

"He died in the blaze, you say?" Giles probed.

The caretaker nodded. "No trace was ever found o' any o' them. One of our good old Cornish flaws blew the remains clean away. Rumors spread that they was all werewolves. The guards from the Watch swore they actually saw old Longworth turn into a wolf out on the moor just south o' Lamorna jail. They was takin' him in for the murder o' one o' their own, when the moon come full and he changed before their very eyes. To this day, folks say they hear wolves howlin' when the moon comes full. I heard them myself, and there ain't no more wolves in these parts anymore, so you folks go figure that out if ya can."

"Extraordinary," Giles said.

The caretaker nodded. "Some say Longworth's ghost haunts these ruins, and others say he ain't dead at all. I dunno which is what"—he brandished his shotgun, backing Tessa up a pace—"but I'm ready for him, man or wolf. There's silver shot in this here weapon, just in case."

"Be careful how you sling that thing about!" Giles warned him.

"'Scuse me, gov'nor," the caretaker responded. "Ya wanted the tale. Just givin' ya your money's worth."

"Well, we thank you for your time, Mr. Jones," Giles said, turning Tessa away. "We shan't keep you." He cast one last look at the Abbey ruins silhouetted black against the star-studded sky in the moonlight. The look in his misty eyes turned Tessa's away. "Our bus is due by. Good evening, sir."

With a nod and a wave, Giles turned Tessa back toward the lane. Once they were out of earshot, Tessa said, "Well, you got a bit more out of him than I did."

"I paid him more than you did, too, I'll wager," Giles responded.

"Without a doubt." She cast a glance over her shoulder toward the remains of Longhollow Abbey, which stood like a skeleton in the moonlight, and shivered. There was no sign of Ezra Jones now. "What a strange little man," she observed, as if to herself.

"That is why I left him so abruptly," Giles said, helping her over the stile by the lane. "He was making entirely too free with that blunderbuss of his, or whatever it's called." He glanced back toward the misshapen moon poised overhead. "He did say his ammunition was silver, and until the moon waxes full again and we see how it affects us, I do not think it wise that we take chances."

He settled Tessa on the stile, and turned back for what would be a last look at his former life before boarding the bus that was lumbering toward them at a distance from the south. Moonlight danced in his misted eyes, and his handsome mouth almost smiled, but not quite. The sight of him thus brought a lump to Tessa's throat, and she swallowed hard before speaking.

"Will we be returning here, Giles?" she murmured.

His head snapped toward her, but it was a long moment before he spoke. "No," he finally said. "I have done what I needed to. We go now to purchase my paintings. Your 'railroad' has made the world a shockingly small place, my love. We could never lose ourselves here any longer, and we could never bring the paintings here—not after what that man back there just said. Not amongst the superstitious Cornish folk, who still use silver bullets. 'The Bride of Time' notwithstanding, there is my self-portrait. It is a very good likeness, if I do say so myself. An incredible likeness. Can you imagine the brouhaha if I were to bring it home? Besides, any artist settling in these hills, on these moors, could be suspect now."

"I am so sorry," Tessa said.

"Don't be," he replied, raising her up in the custody of his strong arms. How good they felt, how warm and comforting. "I think I always knew I couldn't come back here for good. God bless you for letting me see for myself."

He stooped to kiss her as the bus drew near. All was still around them until the plaintive howl of a wolf pierced the silence and tore their lips apart. For one heart-stopping moment, their gazes locked.

"Oh, Giles!" Tessa cried, her voice quavering.

"Come," he said, rushing her toward the horse-drawn bus lumbering to a stop alongside. "It's time to go."

Chapter Twenty-nine

Passing the time until Tuesday was the most difficult. Foster had given the curator's partner a deposit on Giles's paintings; nevertheless, they passed by the little gallery in a hackney cab each day just to be certain they were still there. They spent time in the Bond Street shops, choosing proper clothes, converted more funds in the Threadneedle Street banks, and strolled in Hyde Park and Vauxhall Gardens: places that were discreet, not Cheapside or anywhere that someone from Tessa's former life might see and recognize her.

While they were at those pursuits, Foster saw to the mundane arrangements for their journey to Yorkshire. They would travel north by train, and take lodgings at a proper inn or hotel while they sought a suitable permanent residence. They would keep their given names, since they were common enough to pass, and choose a different surname for the sake of anonymity. Giles and Tessa Lang was chosen. Who knew but that the Giles Longworth scandal had reached as far as Scotland, which was looking better and better as an option for their permanent residence, come to that. This was something to be worked out once they reached the

North Country, though. The horses would be boarded at the livery and sent on once they had a place to send them. Paramount now was getting out of London without incident.

Tuesday morning dawned white with cottony fog ghosting in off the Thames, much to Giles's relief. Thus far, except for converting notes and the daily, well-concealed reconnaissance from the shadowy confines of a hackney cab, they had avoided Cheapside and surrounding areas completely.

Giles was hopeful that new togs, his slicked-down hair parted in the middle, and the shadow of stubble he'd been nurturing since they returned from Cornwall, much to Tessa's chagrin, would change his appearance enough to prevent the curator's partner from noticing any likeness during the brief visit. Now it was time for the test, and he set out with Tessa, who was wearing the veiled hat that brought a smile to his lips, in a hackney cab to finalize the sale.

"What is it, my love?" he asked, watching her gaze into nothingness.

She squeezed his hand. It felt clammy and cold, even through her gloves. "I think it outrageous that you must pay such a sum for your own paintings," she said.

"Thirteen-thousand pounds is hardly a fortune these days, and the way blunt is gained and multiplied in your twentieth century, I should soon earn it back. Hah! The gudgeon wanted double that. You have Foster to thank for the negotiations. He spied some worn spots on 'The Bride,' and why wouldn't there be in almost a hundred years? It's nothing I cannot fix. He found imperfections on the others as well, and talked the curator down. Foster's a genius. I'd have not done half as well."

Tessa smiled. "You will have to do something about your 1811 expressions," she said.

"You got used to them," Giles pointed out.

"Yes, but I am in love with you," she shot back, giving his hand another squeeze.

"I should certainly hope so," Giles said through a wry chuckle. "As soon as we finalize the sale, I shall take you back to the little jewelers where I bought your wedding ring, and buy you another—and decent hairpins."

"You needn't do that, Giles," Tessa said.

"Oh, yes I shall," he replied. "I saw the dubious look the innkeeper shot you during dinner yesterday. I'm sure they think we are quite the scandal. Your reputation is at stake, and I shall rise to the occasion."

"If you must," Tessa said, "but I am quite content with the lovely whalebone pins Foster found."

"Perhaps something with pearls . . ."

"Oh, no! I want nothing to do with pearl, not after the pearl brooch that started all this."

"Ahhhh, but if it wasn't for that brooch, we never would have met," he reminded her.

"I shall have to think about that," Tessa remarked, and said no more as the cab tooled through the London streets, sidling out of the way of motorcars, which Giles had been taken with from the moment he first set eyes upon one.

"I must have one of those!" he said now, leaning his head over the side of the cab until the car in question rattled on and disappeared in the fog.

"Well, you had best hurry and buy one," Tessa said. "The novelty won't last long. Motor carriages will never replace the horse. Horses have been too reliable for too long to be replaced by such an expensive conveyance."

"You could be wrong, my love," Giles remarked. "You don't have to feed those carriages like you do horses, or muck out stalls. Who knows but that they could be the coming thing. I wonder what Prinny would have thought of them. . . ."

"He would have probably thought them the figment of one of his elbow-bending bouts, and sworn off the stuff he drank," Tessa replied.

"Mayhap, but I guarantee you he would have been the first to own one."

He would have carried the argument farther, but the cab had pulled to the curb before Tatum's Gallery. Bidding the driver wait, Giles took Tessa's arm and stepped inside. His eyes were riveted to the little alcove where his painting stood sporting tags that read SOLD in bold red letters. The familiar smell of linseed oil and paints that hadn't yet dried rushed up his nostrils. He had almost forgotten the way those smells invited him, charging his imagination. He needed to paint again. Oh, how he needed to paint.

"Justin Phillips, Mr. Tatum's partner, at your service, Mr. Lang," the man introduced himself. "I am pleased to make your acquaintance, sir."

"Likewise," Giles said, taking the tall, thin man's measure. Other than the fact that his clothes fit him poorly, Giles found nothing remarkable about him.

"Your man is quite the shrewd negotiator," Phillips said. "Do you mean to sell the paintings . . . at auction possibly?

"No," said Giles. "I am a collector of sorts."

"Well, sir, you've bought a curiosity here," said Phillips.

"How so?" Giles said.

The man took up a pointer and strode to the large easel that held "The Bride of Time." He pointed toward the mansion in the background. "The artist's home was the model for this," he said. "It was consumed by fire shortly after the painting was sold to the Prince Regent in 1811. The fire was set by Longworth's nine-year-old nephew—"

"His ward," Giles corrected him.

"Oh, you know the history, then? You've saved me the trouble of giving a demonstration."

"Yes," Giles said. "We visited the site and spoke with the tour guide there. The boy was no blood relation to Longworth. He was the offspring of his sister's husband."

"Quite so," said Phillips. "Where would you like the paintings sent?"

"Sent?" Giles said, unsure of the procedure. He glanced at Tessa for some help, but she evidently didn't know what was expected, either. Boarding horses was one thing. He certainly wasn't going to let the paintings out of his sight ever again. "Eh, what would you suggest, sir?" he finally said. "What is customary?"

"We will crate the paintings, and deliver them by rail to your Yorkshire home, if you wish."

"I prefer to take them north with me," Giles said. "Could you crate them and deliver them to . . ."

"Crate them, please," Tessa said as his words trailed off. "And have your deliveryman bring them to Victoria Station at two-thirty this afternoon. Northbound trains leave at three. Have him wait with them. We shall pick them up from him there."

"That will be quite impossible, madam," the man said. "My carpenter won't be in until the morning, and there will be an extra fee."

"That is of no consequence," Giles said. He turned to Tessa. "One more night in Town won't matter, will it?"

"No," she replied.

"Done!" he said to Phillips and moved off to pay the man, while Tessa lingered before "The Bride of Time."

Once the transaction had taken place, Giles went to Tessa's side and slipped his arm about her waist—shocking behavior in public. It would have even been worse in his time. *His time.* Could he really belong in her time? The alternative, to live without her, wasn't an option.

"You will have a lifetime to gaze at it," he murmured in her ear. "But now, we have a ring to buy."

"I know," she said. "It's just . . . I wish . . ."

"If wishes were horses, beggars would ride," he said wistfully.

"Are you resigned?" she probed him.

He nodded. "I love you, Tessa," he said. "My home is where you are. Come."

Giles whisked her into the waiting hackney cab and directed the driver to the little jeweler's where he'd long ago purchased Tessa's iolite and diamond wedding ring. It wasn't far from the gallery, and it was still there, and he ushered Tessa inside, where a confrontation was taking place between the clerk and a young woman.

Giles hung back, steering Tessa to a ring display case on the opposite side of the shop, not wanting to be rude and stare. It was a small establishment, however, and they couldn't help but overhear.

"Where did you get this?" the clerk was saying. "According to our records you aren't the woman who—"

"It *was* purchased for me," the woman interrupted, "and I want me money back! It don't suit," she snapped.

"Why doesn't it suit, miss?"

"It don't fit proper, and the iolite stones is all set crooked."

The clerk examined the ring in question through a jeweler's loop placed against his eye. "This piece is not flawed, miss," he said. "Let me see you try it on for fit."

"I will not! If I say it don't fit, it don't fit," the girl insisted. "If I say it ain't comfortable, it ain't comfortable. Look here, I don't want the ring. Are ya goin' ta give me me money back, or not?"

"It is not our policy to refund a customer's purchase price, miss," the clerk said loftily, handing the ring back to her. "All sales are final. I'm sorry. And it's not your money. You did not purchase this ring. It was originally bought . . . Well, besides; even if you had purchased it, without a receipt—"

"Is this your merchandise or not?" the girl persisted.

"It is, yes, but you didn't buy it."

" 'Twas my sister what bought it," the girl shrilled. "How many times do I have ta tell ya that? That's why it don't fit. Her fingers are fatter than mine. She come in here with me intended, Mr. High and Mighty Jewelry Store Clerk. 'Twas supposed ta be a surprise for me, and it sure was, cause it don't fit!"

They argued on, and Tessa gripped Giles's arm. "That voice," she murmured. "I would know it anywhere! It's Bessie, the scullery maid from Poole House. I believe she's the one who planted that pearl brooch in my chamber."

"Did they say it was an iolite ring?" Giles asked her.

"They did. Oh, Giles! How could *she* have gotten hold of it?"

"I'm sure I don't know, unless the jail returned your belongings to Poole House after you disappeared. But you can bet your blunt I'm going to find out."

Giles stalked toward the two still arguing at the other end of the counter. "Excuse me," he said. "I believe I can shed some light upon this coil. May I see that ring, please?"

"Certainly sir," said the clerk. "Although—"

Giles flashed him a quelling glance. "Yes," he interrupted, glancing at the woman. "Where did you come by this ring, miss?" he asked. The girl had suddenly gone white as mist.

"Yes, Bessie," Tessa spoke up, strolling close. She removed her veil. "Where did you get my ring? The Longworth ring," she added, giving a knowing glance at the jeweler.

Bessie gasped. *"You!"*

"Is this your sister, then?" the clerk put in.

"No," Tessa said. "This is Bessie Harper, a scullery maid in a house where I worked before I was married. I thought I'd lost that ring, but now I see something more sinister has occurred."

"Wait!" Bessie cried. "They said you was a . . . they said you . . . !" Spinning on her heels, the maid darted out into the street, screaming, and ran west through the mews into the deserted alley, with Tessa on her heels.

"I shall fetch the bobbies!" the clerk cried, skirting the counter.

"No, don't," Giles said. "Let us handle this. I shall explain later. Hold on to that ring for me. I shall return to collect it straightaway."

Dashing out into the street, he scanned the milling vapors for some sign of Tessa. The fog was drifting past St. Michael's Church. It was heavier there. The bell tower was scarcely visible. All at once he knew what Tessa was doing. She was driving Bessie straight for the corridor that would take the maid back in time—back to *his* time. But it might also take Tessa back, too, and his heart rose in his throat as he sprang after them.

"No, Tessa!" he thundered. "It could take you with her, and I would never see you again! Let her go!"

"No!" Tessa called over her shoulder. "She shan't get away—not again!"

Running upon legs pumping wildly, Giles finally reached her and jerked her to a standstill, taking her in his arms. "Let . . . her . . . go . . . !" he panted.

The fog drifted then, and they both watched as, in a blink, Bessie Harper disappeared in it.

Tessa strained against his grip. "Let me go, Giles!" she cried. "I have to know! I have to be sure she shan't threaten me again!"

"Look around you. I'm new at this, but even *I* can see it. The mist is fading everywhere but that one spot. Go into that fog and you are lost to me. I know it—I *feel* it.

She is gone, Tessa . . . she is gone. It doesn't matter
where. Come . . . before that clerk back there calls your
bobbies. We are not out of this yet."

Tessa lay curled in Giles's arm in their bed at the inn,
her beautiful iolite ring sparkling on her finger. They'd
had no difficulty convincing the shopkeeper that the
ring was theirs.

"Giles, do you think . . . ?"

"I do not want to think, not about anything but you,"
he replied. "Tomorrow we begin our new lives. It will
be easier for you than it will be for me, but in the
north—in the country—given time—"

Her finger across his lips silenced him, and he gathered her close and kissed her deeply. He tasted sweet, of
the wine he'd drunk at supper and traces of mellow tobacco from one of the cheroots he'd purchased at the
tobacconist's shop before they left the shopping district.
How handsome he was, all dreamy-eyed, gazing toward
her now, that look alone a seduction.

This was yet another facet of the inimitable Giles
Longworth, the fiery passion that gripped him now. It
was a dangerous passion, as yet untapped, she sensed,
for there was a feral gleam in those bottomless, fathom-
less eyes that devoured her so shamelessly that she lowered her own. Knowing her bridegroom was like
peeling away the many layers of a tasty onion, bittersweet and mildly salty, one by one, only to find another
more mysterious layer beneath. Would she ever discover them all? Whether yes or no, she was prepared for
an exciting future of attempting to explore each and
every one as it surfaced. The Giles Longworth with her
now, lying naked with her, skin to skin, took her breath
away.

"What?" he said through a throaty chuckle.

"I do not think I yet know you, sir," she managed, for

his closeness had tied her tongue. "You are so many men all rolled into one, I hardly know which one is holding me now."

He laughed. "The one who loves you," he murmured.

"And the others do not?" she teased playfully.

"We all worship you, my love, but tonight . . . oh, *to-night* . . ." He silenced her with another kiss and spread her legs, climbing between.

Just the sinuous motion was a seduction. The touch of his hands upon her body, revering every inch of her, was more than she could bear. She reached for him, tracing the knife-straight indentation of his spine to the firm, taut buttocks beneath, wrenching a guttural groan from so deep within him she scarcely recognized it as his voice.

His aroused sex leapt against her thigh, and she could not resist touching it, to close her fingers around it and feel the shudder of its response. How warm it was in her cool hand, how hard and silky-smooth to the touch, its pulse beating just for her, as if it had a will of its own.

He groaned again as her hand spiraled down along his shaft. Gripping her buttocks, he coaxed her legs around his waist and plunged into her deeply, filling her in one pulsating thrust that sent ripples of drenching fire coursing through her loins.

He took her slowly at first, then faster, deeper, and she matched his rhythm thrust for thrust, soft moans ringing in her ears that she scarcely realized came from her own throat. Bewitched by his passion, she clung to him, lost in the excruciating ecstasy of her release.

Cradled in his arms, she breathed a deep, contented sigh. How he had loved her. How he pleasured her in ways she never knew existed. How very much she loved this enigmatic man she'd crossed the threshold of time to surrender her heart to what seemed like a lifetime ago.

They would love again before dawn, and again, and

again. The night was young, so young. The moon had just risen, silvery-white beaming down round and full . . .

Full?

Tessa vaulted erect, leapt out of the bed and padded to the window. A shaft of moonlight spangled with dust motes fell at her feet, bathing her naked skin, her hair, her face, and she uttered a squeal of delight.

"What is it?" Giles asked, stretching in the bed behind.

"Giles, oh, Giles . . . come quickly! Oh do!" she cried.

Climbing out of the bed, he did as she bade him. "What is it, my love?" he drawled.

"Don't you see?" she cried, jogging in place. "The moon, Giles . . . it's full, and we are still . . . *us!*"

"Lud, so we are!" he murmured. Lifting her off the floor, he spun her in circles, convulsed in deep, riveting laughter.

After a moment, he let her slide the length of his hard-muscled body. He was aroused again, and he scooped her up in strong arms and carried her back to the bed.

"There's been so much happening, I'd totally forgotten the moon was waxing full," he said, gathering her against him. "I'd become accustomed to sensing its change and dreading . . . See how you've bewitched me?" he asked.

Smothering her with kisses, he loved her again and again, while the moon passed through the indigo vault among the stars, and finally faded from view. They scarcely saw. Enraptured, they clung to each other in total abandon. They scarcely heard the twitter of the lapwings and skylarks, starlings and morning doves that came to life in the misty darkness before dawn . . . or the distant mournful echo of a wolf's plaintive howl riding the cool dawn breeze.

JADE LEE

A new, stand-alone novel from the *USA Today*
bestselling author of *Dragonborn* and *Seduced by Crimson*

THE DRAGON EARL

Revenge. It poisoned everything he'd learned, everything he'd done, and yet every fiber of Jacob Cato burned for it—just as he burned for the beautiful but very English Evelyn Stanton. Long ago, the conspiracy to kill his family had stranded Jacob in the exotic East and made him unrecognizable to his countrymen...and women. In far-off China, Jacob had found sanctuary. In a Xi Lin temple he learned to be strong, but now he had a grander goal: to reclaim his English heritage as the Earl of Warhaven and the woman he'd left behind.

AVAILABLE SEPTEMBER 2008!

ISBN 13: 978-0-8439-6046-4

Kathryne Kennedy

Author of *Enchanting the Lady*

Lady Jasmina was in a world of trouble. A simple spell had gone disastrously haywire and now there was a woman running around London who looked exactly like her—a woman with no sense of propriety whatsoever. All Society was whispering, and a baronet she'd never met was suddenly acting like he knew her…in a most intimate way. To find her double and set things right, they'd have to work together—braving the fog-shrouded streets, a mysterious group called the Brotherhood, and a passion stronger than any magic.

Double Enchantment

ISBN 13: 978-0-505-52763-9

THE HUNGER IS BOUNDLESS...
AND IT CANNOT BE DENIED

THE RAVENING

The stunning conclusion to the Blood Moon trilogy
by award-winning author **DAWN THOMPSON**

ISBN 13: 978-0-505-52727-1

Buy *The Ravening* and the rest of the Blood Moon
series wherever books are sold.

Book One
ISBN 13: 978-0-505-52680-9

Book Two
ISBN 13: 978-0-505-52726-4

DAWN MACTAVISH

Lark at first hoped it was a simple nightmare: If she closed her eyes, she would be back in the mahogany bed of her spacious boudoir at Eddington Hall, and all would be well. Her father, the earl of Roxburgh, would not be dead by his own hand, and she would not be in Marshalsea Debtor's Prison.

Such was not to be. Ere the Marshalsea could do its worst, the earl of Grayshire intervened. But while his touch was electric and his gaze piercing, for what purpose had he bought her freedom? No, this was not a dream. As Lark would soon learn, her dreams had never ended so well.

The Privateer

ISBN 13: 978-0-8439-5981-9

The Druid
Made Me Do It

NATALE STENZEL

For centuries he's worked his magic, seducing and pleasuring women as befits his puca nature. But Kane made one big mistake—punishing his brother for a crime he did not commit.

Oh yeah, he also left Dr. Janelle Corrington after the most amazing night of her life.

She thought she'd made a once-in-a-lifetime soul connection, but he was simply having sex. Why else would he have disappeared without a word?

That's why the Druid Council's punishment for Kane's other crime is so delicious: for him to be Janelle's ward, to make amends to all he harmed, to take responsibility for his actions. Finally, Kane would have to take things seriously. And only true love would be rewarded.

Sometimes, it's good to be guilty.

ISBN 13: 978-0-505-52777-6

Phantom

Every night at midnight Dax could start to feel the change. The curse that made him less human as the Phantom inside struggled to take over, reminding him that he was never safe. Nor were the ones he loved.

As a girl, Robyn had pledged herself to him. But that was a lifetime ago. Now she was a woman. Beautiful. Pure. Every time she was near—her soft skin, her delicate scent—the Phantom wanted to claim her, to bring her body to the greatest heights of pleasure. Then steal her soul. Dax couldn't allow that to happen. Deep down, he knew her love could save him. If the Phantom didn't get her first.

Lindsay Randall

AVAILABLE JUNE 2008

ISBN 13: 978-0-505-52765-3

☐ **YES!**

Sign me up for the Love Spell Book Club and send my
FREE BOOKS! If I choose to stay in the club, I will pay only
$8.50* each month, a savings of $6.48!

NAME: _____

ADDRESS: _____

TELEPHONE: _____

EMAIL: _____

☐ I want to pay by credit card.

☐ **VISA**   ☐ **MasterCard**   ☐ **DISCOVER**

ACCOUNT #: _____

EXPIRATION DATE: _____

SIGNATURE: _____

Mail this page along with $2.00 shipping and handling to:
**Love Spell Book Club
PO Box 6640
Wayne, PA 19087**
Or fax (must include credit card information) to:
610-995-9274
You can also sign up online at **www.dorchesterpub.com**.
*Plus $2.00 for shipping. Offer open to residents of the U.S. and Canada only. Canadian
residents please call 1-800-481-9191 for pricing information.
If under 18, a parent or guardian must sign. Terms, prices and conditions subject to
change. Subscription subject to acceptance. Dorchester Publishing reserves the right to
reject any order or cancel any subscription.